Other books by Kirt Hickman

Worlds Asunder

Worlds Asunder
Venus Rain
Mercury Sun
Methane Moon

Age of Prophecy

Fabler's Legend
Assassins' Prey
Host of Evil

Nonfiction

Revising Fiction: Making Sense of the Madness

For Children

Purple
I Will Eat Anything

HOST OF EVIL

AGE OF PROPHECY: BOOK III

The ultimate betrayal

Kirt Hickman

Published in the U.S.A. by
Quillrunner Publishing LLC
Albuquerque, NM

Printed in the U.S.A.

Cover art by Elizabeth Leggett

Book design by Susan Schwartz-Christian
Typeset in: Iowan Old Style 11/14.5, American Frights, Valhalla

This book is a work of fiction. All plots, themes, dates, events, persons, characters, and character descriptions contained in this material are completely fictional. Any resemblance to any events, persons, or characters, real or fictional, living or deceased, is entirely coincidental and unintentional. All locations and organizations are products of the author's imagination or are used fictionally. Kirt Hickman and Quillrunner Publishing LLC are not responsible for any use of these character names or any resemblance of these character names to actual persons, living or deceased.

Copyright© 2025 by Kirt Hickman. All rights reserved. No part of this publication may be reproduced, stored in a retrieval system or transmitted in any form or by any means, electronic, mechanical, photocopying, recording, or otherwise without the prior written permission of the copyright holder, except brief quotations used in a review.

Cataloging-in-Publications Data is on file with the Library of Congress.
Library of Congress Control Number: 2024912450

ISBN 978-0-9851157-5-3

*For Ben, Larry, Gerry, Alex, Erle, and Rick,
the real heroes of the story.*

Acknowledgments

A book like this can't be created by one person alone. It took the tireless effort of many people to make *Host of Evil* a reality. My thanks go out to all of you.

To Ben Valerine, Larry Koch, Gerry Raban, Alex Raguini, Erle Guillermo, and Rick McLaughlin for your help in developing such a dynamic plot.

To my network of critiquers and test readers: D. E. Williams, Larry Koch, and Bryan Weaver. Special thanks to David Corwell for catching the things the rest of us didn't.

To my editor, Susan M. Grossman, for ensuring that *Host of Evil* is the best that it can be.

To all my peers at SouthWest Writers, for your constant moral and technical support. I've learned so much.

To Elizabeth Leggett for the spectacular cover illustration.

To Susan Schwartz-Christian, for exceeding all my expectations for book and cover design.

To my wife, Terri, for giving me the time and encouragement to begin, to endure, and to finally complete *Host of Evil*. I couldn't have done it without you.

And most of all, to God for blessing me with the necessary time and talents.

The Story So Far

After enjoying a day at the Cedar Falls weekend market, Nick Mirrin and his ice-mage friend, Zen, were ambushed by a group of Black Hand bandits, who interrogated Nick about a journal his grandfather had supposedly written. Nick knew nothing about this journal.

When Nick arrived at his home, he found that his house had been burned to the ground—with his mother inside—by the Black Hand bandits and a sentient air apparition. Nick learned from his father that his grandfather had spent his life seeking a way to prevent the fulfillment of a prediction known as Mortaan's Last Prophecy, and the journal contained his grandfather's notes. The pair surmised that the bandits, unable to locate the journal, had burned the house in an attempt to destroy the information so it couldn't be used to stop the Prophecy' fulfillment.

Nick and his father recovered the journal, which had been hidden behind a loose stone in the hearth. The fire had damaged the pages, but some of the information remained. Nick and Zen took the scraps to Zen's home to study the pages. Beltrann, a servant who had grown up in a nearby monastery, suggested that the monks' library might have a copy of the Prophecy. The three decided to find out.

On the way to the monastery, they met Rancid Sevendeath, a rogue who had been engaged in a years-long blood feud against the Black Hand bandits who menaced the area near his childhood home in Palidor. Rancid joined Nick and the others in hopes of gaining their support in his fight against the bandits.

Nick and his friends studied the monastery's copy of the Codex of Mortaan, a tome that contained all of Mortaan's prophecies—including his Last Prophecy, the only one that hadn't yet come to pass. The Prophecy had three preconditions of fulfillment: slave riots in Palidor, civil war in Trondor, and the return of dragons to the Civilized Lands. The Prophecy said the evil god Vexetan would raise up a human High Priest called "the Master." The Master would choose twelve lieutenants, his Chosen, and use twelve enchanted medallions to communicate with them and control them. Three armies would mobilize to conquer the Civilized Lands.

A band of heroes, the Prophecy foretold, would face the Master, but the heroes would fail because no weapon "forged of this world" could harm him. The Master would ultimately enslave the goodly races, bringing about an Age of Darkness. This ending matched the dark tales of the Last Prophecy told in taverns, but the text was confusing and Nick had heard renditions with more optimistic outcomes.

The Prophecy sometimes referred to this Master as "the Master of Air," so Nick wondered if the air apparition who had helped burn his home was one of the Chosen. If so, he concluded, the fulfillment of the Prophecy might be imminent.

Both the Prophecy and the journal scraps referred to a blessing by Alamain, High Priestess of the elves' god Aeron, so Nick decided to go to Lorentil, the elven capital, and seek Alamain's advice.

The monks lent Nick their copy of the Codex and assigned Jasmine, a young demon-kin acolyte, to join Nick's party and safeguard the copy. Jasmine had been left at the monastery as a newborn and the monks believed her to be the product of a failed experiment by her father to magically combine a human with a demon. Her father's home, nearby Pruitt Keep, had been abandoned ever since.

The air apparition and the accompanying Black Hand bandits tracked Nick to the monastery, so Nick and his party snuck out through a secret tunnel. When the apparition caught up, it attacked the party and stole the journal scraps. Nick retained his notes, however, and Jasmine still had the monks' copy of the Codex.

On the way to Lorentil, the companions hired a guide, Dara, to lead them through the elven forest. They met Vinra, a priest of Robala who had attempted to traverse the kingdom without a guide and had become lost. Vinra joined the party for the rest of the journey to the capital city.

Once they were there, High Priestess Alamain advised Nick and his friends to find the original Codex of Mortaan and determine the true ending of the Prophecy. The original Codex had last been seen in the library in Eckland, in the kingdom of Palidor. She warned them that if they were to face the Master, she must first bless them and the weapon they planned to use against him.

Alamain sent Beltrann on a separate quest to contact the fairies, who had exiled themselves on the Mist Isles, to warn them of recent developments that pertained to the Prophecy.

Zen, always hungry for power and finding himself in the magic capital of the Civilized Lands, asked around for clandestine ways to acquire enchanted items. He met an information dealer named Gwyndarren. Gwyndarren learned that Zen was more loyal to his quest for power than to his friends and would be willing to sell out his friends if doing so would gain him enough power to make it worth his while.

Gwyndarren traded a few minor enchanted items for information about Nick's quest and the news that the Prophecy's fulfillment might be drawing near. Gwyndarren believed that the Master—surely a man of means with a lot at stake—would pay handsomely for information about Nick's goals and Zen's loyalties. Assuming that the air apparition was a Chosen and knowing that it was working with the Black Hand, Gwyndarren set out to Palidor to find the bandits, hoping to get a lead on the Master.

Dara guided Nick and his party to the border of Palidor and parted ways with them there. Having finished his business in Lorentil and needing to go next to the capital city of Palidor, Vinra joined them.

Once in Palidor, near Rancid's home, Rancid offered to lead the party to Eckland. Instead of taking them there, however, he diverted them into Black Hand territory, attempting to lure them into a battle that would decimate the bandit gang. At the request of Gwyndarren, who had made contact with the Black Hand, Zen turned the party away from the area and back toward Eckland.

On the way, they found the whole of Palidor plagued by goblin slaves who had attacked and escaped their masters. Nick recognized this as the slave riots foretold by the Prophecy.

Nick and his friends didn't find the original Codex of Mortaan in Eckland. It had been returned to the king of Trondor and likely resided in the library in the king's palace there—all the way across the Civilized Lands. To save time, they boarded a ship and sailed to North Reach. Vinra, who had bought into the importance of Nick's quest, joined them. Before they left, Gwyndarren warned Zen to avoid fighting any of the Chosen in Trondor. Rancid, preferring to continue his feud with the Black Hand, remained in Palidor. Dara and Beltrann rejoined Nick's party in North Reach.

The kingdom of Trondor was mired in civil war—another precondition of the Prophecy. In order to gain access to the library, Nick and his friends agreed to help the rebel leader, Balor Culhaven—by all accounts a goodly man with a legitimate claim to the throne—win the war. They used their status as foreigners to gain an audience with the current king, Gremauld Santari—by all accounts a brutal tyrant who had weaseled his way onto the throne after having assassinated his predecessor. Once inside Gremauld's command tent, Nick and his friends killed the king, thereby ending the war and handing the kingdom to Balor Culhaven.

Nick and his friends located the original Codex of Mortaan in Balor's library and compared Jasmine's copy to Mortaan's original. Jasmine's copy of Mortaan's Last Prophecy matched the original exactly, but it was the only prophecy in Jasmine's copy that did so. In the original, every other prophecy exhibited weird spacing anomalies in the text and demonstrated numerous differences between the original and the copy. Nick didn't know what this meant, but it gave him hope.

At this point, Vinra revealed himself to be one of the Chosen: not a priest of Robala, but an assassin named Vinsous Drakemoor. He murdered Beltrann and declared his intention to confiscate both the original Codex and Jasmine's copy. Zen, having agreed not to engage in battle with any of the Chosen in Trondor, faked a magical paralysis and stayed out of the fight against Drakemoor. By the time the battle ended, Drakemoor and Dara both lay dead.

Balor Culhaven, his top general, and a scout in his Home Guard burst into the library, all three displaying Medallions of Vexetan, identifying them as Chosen of the Master. Backed by a multitude of Trondorian soldiers, the scout pointed to Nick's party and said, "That's them! They murdered the King!"

In the kingdom of Palidor, Rancid managed to locate and sneak into the Black Hand hideout. The leader of the Black Hand reported to an ogre named Groot, who wore a Medallion of Vexetan. Groot mentioned that Nick and his friends had found the original Codex of Mortaan. The Chosen in Trondor had confiscated it and imprisoned Nick's party. Balor would execute them as soon as he was crowned king, which would happen when the mandatory waiting period of forty days had passed—a period designed to allow any legitimate challengers to the throne to come forward and make their case.

Rancid realized then that the Prophecy was real and much more important than his vendetta against the Black Hand. He stole a horse and raced across the Civilized Lands to help his friends before Balor's forty-day waiting period expired.

Once there, Rancid dressed as a Trondorian guard and bluffed his way into the dungeons. He killed the guards and released his friends, who then freed two additional prisoners: a former constable named Otto and an old stargazer, a Sorcerer of Tradestar named Xanth. Nick convinced Otto and Xanth of the truth of the Prophecy, and both men joined his quest.

During their escape through the catacombs under the city, Zen became separated from the others. Gwyndarren helped him find his friends. In return, Zen agreed to use an enchanted scroll to keep Gwyndarren informed of Nick's plans.

Xanth led Nick's party to an old observatory, the abandoned guild house of the Sorcerers of Tradestar. The guild had often tracked rocks that fell from the sky—pieces of other worlds, bits from the tiny lights that filled the night sky. The Sorcerers had recovered small samples of these rocks, enough to learn that they were made mostly of metal. They had tracked one such rock that might contain enough metal to forge a weapon Nick could use against the Master.

Xanth provided a map to the approximate location in the Wild Lands where the rock had landed. He also gave Nick the Seeking Stone, an item of earth magic that glowed in proximity to the other-worldly metal, and glowed more brightly as it drew closer to the metal. With this, the party set out to find this rock from the sky. Xanth, too old for such a quest, remained at the guild house.

Zen notified Gwyndarren that they were going into the Wild Lands, and why. He added that they would return to Lorentil to have High Priestess Alamain bless whatever weapon they had forged.

In the meantime, Balor and the rest of the Chosen launched an all-out effort to recapture Nick and his friends. They hung Wanted posters all over the kingdom. Balor offered a huge reward, which attracted many bands of mercenaries seeking bounty. The air apparition mobilized the remainder of the Black Hand to search for the fugitives. The Master recruited L'Nordian, a dragon from the depths of Spitfire Mountain, as one of his Chosen. He sent L'Nordian with

Ryanna, his demon-summoning mage, to Trondor. Once there, Ryanna called five Assassin demons to track and kill the five fugitives.

One of the mercenary bands, under the leadership of the elf Sierra Glenwood, ambushed Nick's party. Nick and his friends decimated Sierra's band and escaped into the Black Forest, but Zen and Jasmine sustained critical wounds in the battle. A tribe of centaurs took the companions in and escorted them through the forest. Jasmine used her healing meditation, and her condition improved. Zen's wounds turned foul, and he slipped closer to death.

The elf Ellessar, a demon hunter and priest of the elves' god Aeron, spotted L'Nordian flying overhead, the first dragon anyone had seen in the Civilized Lands in over four thousand years. He recognized the dragon and the recent civil war as portents of Mortaan's Last Prophecy.

Ellessar tracked one of Ryanna's Assassin demons into the Black Forest and caught up to it just as it attacked Nick. Ellessar helped the fugitives chase off the Assassin and used his healing magic to save Zen's life. Because Assassin demons could translocate at will, Ellessar knew it would be futile for him to try to hunt the thing. His best chance to kill it was to stay by Nick's side and wait for it to attack again.

The companions escaped Trondor and arrived at Spitfire in time for the harvest festival. They stayed in the local temple of Aeron, where the Shield of Faith resided. Rumors said the Shield, made from the scales of a dragon, could withstand a direct blast of a dragon's fiery breath. Ellessar convinced the priests to lend him the Shield, but only after each member of Nick's party took the Oath of Aeron, a promise to act with honor, defend the weak, and seek justice.

Sierra tracked the party to Spitfire. Though she didn't find the fugitives there, she did recruit a new band of mercenaries and continued the hunt.

South of town, Nick and his friends lured the Assassin demon into a trap and killed it, learning that the secretions from its skin quickly corroded metal weapons. Ellessar discovered that additional

Assassin demons were tracking the party, so the companions cut the two-foot-long claws off the dead demon and used them to make rudimentary swords. They hoped the claws would hold up against the Assassins' corrosive skin secretions.

In the town of Dragon Tears, Zen tried to hire a man to steal something for him, which violated the Oath of Aeron. Aeron punished Zen by making him too sick to eat or drink until he confessed and repented. Once he did, the party continued south to Roybal Keep, a fort that guarded the only known pass through the Great Divide into the Wild Lands.

Nick found the Roybal Keep armory filled with dwarven-made weapons that, according to the markings on the handles, had belonged to his merchant uncle, Harimon. The armory was selling the weapons for far less than Harimon would have charged for them. This didn't seem right, so Nick confronted the armorer about it. He confessed that the weapons had been found strewn across a mile-long stretch of road near South Bend. A huge beast had attacked a merchant's caravan. Though the caravan's guards had severed a black, crab-like claw from the monster, the monster had killed the entire merchant party and escaped. It hadn't shown any interest in the merchandise.

The companions went over the pass into the Wild Lands. A fairy living at the summit sensed Jasmine's demon blood and attacked the party. Zen managed to run her off, but only after the fairy had struck Jasmine with a blindness that lasted several days.

The remaining Assassin demons followed the party over the pass, as did the remnants of the Black Hand bandits, driven by the air apparition. The dragon rider, Ryanna, also followed the fugitives into the Wild Lands, but the Master called her back to complete an urgent task that required her unique talents.

The companions followed the Seeking Stone's signal into a huge swamp, which was infested with lizard-kin. The lizards attacked, but Nick's party proved too large and well-armed for them to fight. The lizards then settled for keeping an eye on the party from a safe distance. They did the same with the Black Hand, who followed Nick into the swamp.

After having lost one of their own to Nick's party, the remaining Assassin demons also bided their time, waiting for an opportune moment to assassinate their respective targets.

The leader of the Black Hand remnant grew tired of his band being driven—usually to their deaths—by the air apparition. He decided to recruit the fugitives, especially Zen, to help kill the apparition. One of the bandits snuck into Nick's camp with a letter outlining their proposal to join forces against the apparition.

The Seeking Stone led Nick to a perfectly round lake in a clearing devoid of trees. A large animal with a deadly mace-like tail lived in the water. Nick was forced to kill the behemoth to access the lake and search for the other-worldly stone.

As soon as Nick had the stone in hand, the air apparition ordered the Black Hand to take it. Per the bandits' plan, the Black Hand advanced but then turned on the air apparition. The Assassins choose that moment to attack. In the middle of it all, the mother of the behemoth from the lake, much larger and deadlier than the pup Nick had killed, showed up and began smashing anyone within reach of her tail.

By the time Zen killed the air apparition, the Assassin demons had either departed or been dispatched. Zen translocated to their previous night's campsite with the other-worldly rock, the prize they had come for.

Everybody else scattered into the swamp.

CHAPTER 1

Nicklan Mirrin staggered into the trees, and the darkness of the swamp swallowed him whole. Only the dim glow of the moonlit lake in the clearing behind him provided any reference at all. He was on the east side of the lake...probably...and the nearest edge of the swamp lay somewhere to the south, so he put the clearing to his right and stumbled on.

People crashed through the brush and trees on all sides. Many of those were Black Hand bandits who'd fled the clearing to escape the massive, mace-like tail of the behemoth of the lake, the wailing mother whose pup lay dead on the shore, killed by Nick's own sword. Any one of the bandits might run him through if they came upon him in this darkness, either to steal any provisions and coin he might have or to gain favor with the Master of the Prophecy. Lizard-kin too prowled the darkness, riding their huge crocodile mounts, lurking in the brush or climbing through the canopy of trees that shut out the moonlight.

Nick's friends were out there too, those who were still alive. They would likely head south or west. He'd win clear of the swamp and see who he could find.

Tangles of undergrowth grabbed at Nick's feet. Pain screamed and blood ran from every wound. Sweat stung his eyes.

Bellows of grief poured forth from the behemoth mother.

At least Whisper, the air apparition who had driven the Black Hand in their pursuit of Nick and his friends, was dead, dissipated into the fetid swamp air.

Something approached, or someone—the footsteps sounded like those of a human or elf.

"Who's there?" Nick hissed into the darkness.

"It's Jasmine." The monk's taloned fingers wrapped around his arm.

"Oh, thank Aeron. Are you well?"

Her grip was firm, her breathing measured and easy. "No, but I'll manage. This way." She drew him into the night with awkward movements, as though she shouldered a load heavier than that of her usual travelling bundle.

Noises surrounded them. How Jasmine could pick out one from another in the darkness, Nick didn't know. Her instincts were born either of her training in the monastery where she'd grown up or of the non-human half of her demon-kin heritage. Either way, Nick knew her well enough to trust her judgment.

Behind them, the behemoth roared again. Nick glanced back. Even the moonlit clearing had become lost beyond a screen of trees.

A soft whinny led them to a horse. The bog sucked at its hooves with a wet slurp as it tried to shy away. Nick felt his way around the animal. Its reins had become tangled in thick-branched vines and roots greasy with slime.

Before he could make any headway on the knot, something heavy struck the ground nearby with a thud. The hisses and clicks of a lizard-kin, suddenly beside them, sounded angry.

"I'll get him." Jasmine laid her burden across the saddle. "Free the horse."

Nick shook his head at her confidence. He sighed heavily. This swamp had shown them nothing but death. The slaps and muffled thumps of a fistfight drowned out the other noises of the night—all except the roar of the behemoth.

Nick didn't have time to work the horse's leads loose. Having lost his sword during the battle by the lake, he cut the reins free with his knife. "Got it."

A smack. A grunt. A rustle of the ferns. Then the sounds of the night returned.

"Jasmine?" Nick ventured.

"Nick!" A bright blaze appeared, pure and white. The light filtered through the trees from the direction of Ellessar's call. The elf's two-tone demon-skin hat and coat were recognizable even through the screen of foliage and a thick layer of caked-on mud, as was the massive Shield of Faith from which the blaze emanated. "Jasmine!"

"This way." Jasmine waved her arms for the demon hunter.

Ellessar waded toward them. Rays of light fell across the horse Nick led—Rancid's, from their trip into the swamp. Jasmine had lain Otto over its saddle. The constable's clothes had been melted or burned away. The skin on his back looked charred.

Nick's stomach soured. "Is Otto..." He couldn't finish the question.

"I don't know." Jasmine ran toward Ellessar, the light, and more sounds of combat. This night, it seemed, was far from over.

Nick slogged the few steps back to the saddle and checked Otto's neck for a pulse. None. A knot formed in the back of his throat. One more of his friends had died for his cause.

When he could bring himself to move once more—to go on because there was nothing else to do—he followed Jasmine, leading the horse and its grim burden. He caught up to Ellessar and Spirit. A short spear protruded vertically from Spirit's rump, as though the spear had been thrown from the tree canopy. Rancid lay broken and awkward over Spirit's saddle. Nick's legs went weak and his throat tightened—another friend dead. That accounted for Nick's whole party except Zen, who had probably translocated far from the swamp.

Two dead lizard-kin lay at Ellessar's feet. A third leapt from the trees and charged. Before it closed the distance, four Black Hand bandits emerged from the darkness. One, a slim man covered in blood, ran at Ellessar with his axe drawn.

The demon hunter, bleeding like the rest of them, swept the lizard-kin's club aside and slew the scaly creature with a single sword stroke. He turned to face the rushing bandit.

By then Nick had grabbed the crossbow from Otto's belt and loaded it. He stepped into the light and leveled it at the rushing Black Hand. "Stop!"

The bandit slid to a halt in the wet loam and threw both hands in the air, still holding his axe. "Don't shoot! I was after the lizard."

A spear flew from the canopy and struck Nick's horse in the shoulder. The mount stumbled, then righted itself, holding its left front hoof off the ground. Another lizard-kin dropped from the trees.

Two of the Black Hand, a dwarf and a female in black monk's robes, struck the lizard-kin down with a pair of crossbow bolts.

The fourth bandit, a young man with tousled hair, stood back from the rest, unwilling to engage. He was the only bandit not covered in blood.

The bandit with the axe backed away from Nick and Ellessar, his gaze settling on Rancid's body. The Black Hand had finally resolved their vendetta against Sevendeath. With Whisper dead as well, both reasons for which the Black Hand had pursued Nick's party were gone. Nick still couldn't trust the bandits, but he had to acknowledge the value in numbers against the lizard-kin who surrounded them.

He kept the crossbow pointed at the bandit with the axe. "No trouble."

"None. We just want out of the swamp."

The other bandits nodded their agreement.

"Fine." Ellessar led Spirit forward. "Nick, get your horse."

Nick, who had lost all bearing beyond the globe of light, grabbed his mount's truncated reins and hurried after.

Hurled spears and frantic clicks from the lizard-kin followed.

Minshara backed farther into the trees without taking her eyes off the ice mage until he vanished from the lakeshore through one of his magical portals.

The swamp around her was alive with the sounds of brush and footsteps. Horses and men, elves and their kin, bandits, and more swarmed through the thick growth. Scraping claws and moving branches betrayed lizard-kin climbing and leaping in the canopy overhead. The shouts of Sevendeath's friends reached Minshara as they tried to find one another in the dark. And the behemoth mother, loudest of all, cried into the night.

Minshara ignored them all. Her role in this night's treachery was not yet finished. She wove a night-vision enchantment for herself, hiked her long red robes up to her knees, and ran for the small clearing she and Halidreth had selected before sunset. Once there, she paused for a moment to catch her breath before chanting into the weave, her voice no more than a murmur even to her own ears. The energies remained less chaotic here than those surrounding the lake, less disturbed by the manipulations of mages at war.

She drew the strands together and built them up, one by one, until a mud hut took shape, rising from the floor of the clearing—just ten feet on its longest side and six feet high, with but one doorway and no windows. Within minutes, it stood complete. She struck a lantern, set it on a corner of the roof as a signal to the other Black Hand, and ducked inside.

The interior, hot and humid, looked much like the outside, with walls of black-gray mud and a dirt floor. It had no furnishing, no lighting, no hearth, and no way to escape in the event that a flood of lizard-kin rushed the doorway. But this hut held the strength of the weave. As long as it stood, no enemy would breach it.

Halidreth arrived first, bleeding dark blood from a deep stab wound in his belly, assisted by Quartin Finnlin, one of the Black Hand healers. The portly man puffed out labored breaths from beneath a stout mop of black hair as he helped Halidreth inside and laid him down on the dirt floor. Quartin lit a second lantern and prayed for Vexetan to mend their leader.

Only three others showed up, all Black Hand. None of Sevendeath's friends came looking for aid, which was just as well. The bandits had broken off their attack as soon as the air apparition had perished, but that was the extent of the deal, and bandits offered no charity. Among Sevendeath's band, Minshara might have helped Zen. He had served as a useful ally in the past and might one day do so again. But based on his mode of departure, Zen was probably far from the swamp.

The six Black Hand hunkered down in Minshara's shelter. The longer they stayed, the more lizard-kin would gather around them, but the bandits had no choice. They couldn't hope to navigate the bog at night, and some—Halidreth chief among them—were too wounded to travel.

Minshara's weave would hold together until sunup. That would give the healer time to do what he could for the wounded, and for Minshara to rest and regain some of her own strength. In the morning, they would fight their way clear of the bog.

Zen sensed no enchantments about the stone he'd pulled from the behemoth's lake—no magic, as he understood it, at all—yet warmth emanated from within the stone. "A rock from the stars," the old sorcerer from Tradestar had called it. Maybe it had some form of earth magic, like that practiced by the dwarves. He had no way to know.

He packed the stone away and kicked out the campfire. Unlike the canopy in the swamp just to the east, the trees of the forest didn't completely blot out the moonlight. The chirp of crickets had replaced the burp and gurgle of the bog. Squirrels and the occasional owl replaced lizard-kin in the trees.

Yet he hadn't left the Wild Lands. He needed a safe place to sleep without having anyone to keep watch. It might take him days to locate his friends. If he didn't find them, he would do as Nick had asked. He would take the stone to the best smith in the dwarven kingdom, to forge a weapon they hoped could harm Vexetan's High Priest, the Master of Mortaan's Prophecy, before he and his Chosen could bring an age of darkness to all of the Civilized Lands.

The ground seemed altogether too accessible to many kinds of creatures, so Zen turned to the trees. The battle at the lake against the air apparition, its Black Hand minions, the behemoth mother, her pup, and the Assassin demons sent by the Master of the Prophecy had drained him. Nevertheless, the jeweled silver band on his forehead kept his thoughts clear enough for one more transformation. Zen pulled a length of rope from his pack and set it on the ground. He gathered up the threads of the weave and used them, along with material from the pseudo-plane of ice, to reshape his body into an eagle of ice. An owl's eyes would have helped him find his way in the moonlight, but Zen needed a larger bird to carry the branches and other materials required to build a nest big enough for Zen to sleep in. Besides, an eagle offered broader utility, along with grace and majesty.

He leapt from the forest floor and worked quickly, configuring a few large branches into a rough triangle, with each branch wedged against the others and the pair of tree limbs beneath them. Using his beak as a third hand, he tied the whole structure together with the length of rope. As soon as the frame was secure, he gathered the rest of the materials he needed. Fatigue quickly forced him to release the eagle's form, but by then he had enough branches, vines, and leaves piled up to fashion a cozy bed. Zen threw down his blanket in the bottom, wrapped his cloak around himself to ward off the night's chill, and curled up to sleep.

Tomorrow, he would search for Nick and his friends.

The absolute dark of the swamp beyond the blaze of white light from the Shield of Faith offered nothing by which Nick could take a bearing. The trees and the stagnant bodies of water all looked the same. He walked behind the Black Hand, only one of whom appeared to be seriously wounded, and kept a close eye on them as they slogged through the thick, wet air.

The group hiked for a couple of hours, avoiding as well as they could any water crossings more than waist deep. When exhaustion forced them to stop, Ellessar picked a dry patch of ground and dropped his pack. "I think we've left the lizards behind us. We should be safe here for a time." He beckoned Jasmine over and examined her wounds.

"Save your gifts for the others." Her soft voice betrayed little of the pain and fatigue she must have felt. "I need only to meditate, and my body will heal."

Ellessar gave her a long, evaluating look, which Jasmine met evenly until he moved on to Nick.

Jasmine had more cuts and bruises, but Nick's were deeper. Only his complete focus on the Black Hand threat had kept him moving. "I welcome anything you can offer. I've lost a lot of blood. And the pain..."

"You've made it this far. Take off what's left of your shirt and pants." Ellessar examined the cuts on Nick's chest, arms, legs, and back with an emotionless facade that would have served him well at the dice table. "I suspect you'll live if you survive the rest of the night. Lie down."

He gave Jasmine a meaningful glance and she placed herself between her friends and the bandits, three of whom were scouting the perimeter of the campsite. The fourth, the wounded man, sat on a cypress log, leaning on his axe, the handle of which had sunk several inches into the soft swampy ground.

Ellessar raised his head to the black sky and prayed to Aeron in the lilting tones of his elven tongue. Waves of warmth thrummed through Nick's body. The pain receded gradually with each wave. Though Nick had managed to keep the Black Hand blades at bay, at least to the extent that none had pierced his vital organs, the combined blood loss had mounted. Most of the pain came from his ribs, several of which must have cracked or broken under the pummeling he'd received from the air apparition.

Moment by moment, his breathing eased. A bit of his strength returned and his dizziness waned. By the time Ellessar finished, the worst of Nick's pain was gone as well. His wounds remained, but they no longer bled. "Thank you."

"You're welcome, my friend. Rest." Ellessar rose.

"I can't."

Ellessar had started to turn away, but his attention returned.

Nick's voice dropped to a whisper. "You'll need sleep to be of any help to us tomorrow, and I fear we'll need your gifts. Someone must watch the bandits while you sleep. Jasmine and I will split the watch."

Ellessar's mouth formed a thin line. Finally, he gave a curt nod. "I must tend the horses as well, or neither will make it until morning." He went to the mounts and gently lowered the bodies of Rancid and Otto to the soft ground.

Spirit welcomed him with a nudge of her nose as he walked past her head toward her flank.

"This is going to hurt," he said, as if she understood more than his comforting tone. He braced one hand on her rump and yanked the short spear out in a single swift motion.

Spirit whinnied and pranced to the side on three legs. Blood oozed from the wound.

Ellessar placed his hand over the puncture and spoke a prayer to Aeron. When the hole closed, it left a fresh patch of new, pink skin, bare of her snow-white coat. "That muscle's going to be sore for a while, girl, but it's the best I can do for now."

He repeated the process for Rancid's horse, and then finally turned his attention to the wounded Black Hand bandit. "What's your name?"

The man looked up, his movements weary. "Nendrick."

"If you'll allow me, I'll see to your wounds."

Nendrick's head drooped and bobbed slightly as though he could no longer hold it up. The motion resembled a nod.

"Ellessar..." Nick started, but the bandit clearly needed help. Even if Nendrick had personally committed some of the crimes Rancid accused the Black Hand of—and Nick wasn't sure that he had—the bandit still deserved to live. Nick climbed to his feet and helped Ellessar lay the man on the ground.

The other bandits returned from their patrol and approached with their weapons lowered. Their faces held only concern for their friend.

"Back off." Nick's palm rested on the hilt of his sheathed knife. "He's a healer. If Aeron is willing to help your kind, you should let him."

Slowly, the bandits complied.

By the time Ellessar finished with Nendrick, the bandit slept peacefully. The worst of his wounds had seen days of healing in a matter of minutes. Nick voiced his permission for one of the bandits to approach close enough to confirm Nendrick's condition.

The female monk, an elf-kin from the sharpness of her features, stepped forward. Her black robes were far from the earth tones preferred in Jasmine's order, but the cut of them, and the elf-kin's posture, were unmistakably monastic, probably from some order that worshipped Vexetan. She checked on Nendrick, then approached Nick. "I'm Noma. This is Lammeer and Cairn." She gestured to the young man and the dwarf in turn. "We'd like to share the watch."

Nick gave each of them a long, hard look. "Fine. You'll do it from the far side of the camp. I want only one of you up at a time. The rest, sleep where we can see you."

"We mean you no more harm," Noma said.

"Forgive me if I don't trust you."

The monk nodded without further comment and the three bandits retreated to the far edge of the light.

Ellessar stepped away from the others and said a prayer for himself that he might heal and continue his work for Aeron. After building a small fire, he extinguished the blazing light from the Shield of Faith and lay down to sleep.

"You too," Nick told Jasmine. "Meditate and rest. I'll wake you in a few hours." He built up the fire as high as he could with the damp fuel available. In one sense it served as a beacon for all the denizens of the swamp, but the animals would likely avoid people in any case. All, that is, but the lizard-kin, and they would come anyway. At least this way, Nick and his friends could see them coming.

When the sky began to lighten with the new day, Nick woke Jasmine, trusted his life into her care—there was no one he could count on more—and took his turn to sleep.

As soon as Nick closed his eyes, it seemed, Jasmine shook him awake. "Time to move."

By the position of the sun and what little of its light filtered through the dense canopy, Nick had slept until noon. He rolled to his feet. Ellessar, Nendrick, and the rest of the Black Hand were already up. The bodies of Otto and Rancid once again lay over the horses' backs. The camp was ready to go.

"Ellessar woke about thirty minutes ago," Jasmine told him. "We let you sleep as long as we could, but the lizard-kin grow thick around us."

Nick stretched. His wounds had stiffened, and the movement pulled at the tender new flesh. Around him, the swamp was alive with familiar sounds: the rustling of leaves in the canopy, the clicks and hisses of the lizard-kin, and even the deep groan of their giant crocodile mounts.

"We're deeper in the swamp than we were at the lake," Ellessar was saying. "If we head south, I think we can win clear by midnight. I'm anxious to perform rites for the dead, but not here. The ground is too soft and the scavengers too vile."

Nick grabbed his gear, already packed for travel, and hefted the load onto his sore shoulders. As he'd done the previous night, he let the Black Hand precede him and then took up station where he could keep an eye on them. Ellessar and Jasmine led the horses at the rear of the party.

The sounds of the lizard-kin remained with them throughout the day, sometimes behind, sometimes ahead, but the primitive, warlike creatures kept their distance. Apparently they had decided, as they'd done before, that several warriors armed with weapons fashioned by means beyond their understanding were too many to challenge.

The company cleared the swamp just as the sun began to set and walked several hundred yards out onto the southern plain before Nick called for the bandits to stop. He held out his hand to keep them from backtracking and closing the distance Nick had allowed to accumulate between them. He whispered to Jasmine, "Has anyone checked the Seeking Stone?"

"I peeked at it during your watch last night. Zen hasn't gone far. A few days travel, at the most."

"That's comforting. Any guess which direction?"

"I'll check it again after full dark. Maybe we'll know more."

"Until then," Ellessar said, "we must use the remaining daylight to cleanse ourselves of the swamp. Leaches carry disease. Then I'll see to our horses and food."

The three dropped their packs and gear on the ground.

Ellessar unstrapped his leather breastplate. "Arrrghhh!" He fell to his knees, clutching his head between his palms. His face twisted in agony, and his eyes rolled up so far that only white showed in his wide sockets. His head snapped back with another blood-chilling cry. Then he collapsed forward onto the ground.

"Stay there," Nick told the bandits, who had started to approach.

He and Jasmine rolled Ellessar over. The elf was conscious, but his breathing came in ragged, shallow gasps.

Nick scanned the tall grasses around them and the edge of the swamp for signs of an attacker while Jasmine did what she could for Ellessar.

"What is it?" Jasmine asked. "What happened?"

"The Portal," Ellessar managed between gulps of air. "The Portal of the Damned…it's open."

CHAPTER 2

When the sun came up, the six remaining Black Hand bandits prepared to leave Minshara's enchanted hut. The healer had spent the night tending to Halidreth's gut wound, and by morning their leader seemed well enough to walk. Quartin looked spent. Be that as it may, the time to leave had come.

The bandits gathered what meager gear they'd managed to retain and took their weapons in hand. Halidreth gave Minshara a look of grim determination. With the heat of the swamp and the stifling air in the hut, a generous sheen of sweat had already formed on his bald forehead. The six formed a tight circle, facing outward. Minshara released her weaving, and the hut crumbled back into dust.

The startled lizard-kin, several riding their large crocodile mounts, drew either short bone spears or long-handled dart throwers. Beyond that, however, they just clicked in their odd language and looked back and forth from one to another, as if for moral support or community courage.

Already weaving, Minshara ignored them. She called a dragon-kin from the nether plane, roughly the size and shape of a horse with a dragon-like snout, wings, and tail. It flitted through a rip in the veil between its dimension and the world of men, materializing in the air above the Black Hand. All of the lizard-kins' eyes locked onto the hellish creature.

The bandits tensed, ready to attack, but Minshara had other plans. "Wait!"

The dragon-kin swooped toward the largest lizard, who sat on a crocodile mount, wearing an ornate breastplate made of animal-rib bones sewn together with a beaded sinew cord. He launched a long dart at the dragon-kin.

The dart stuck in the creature's chest near the left shoulder and slowed it not at all.

A second dragon-kin appeared, and Minshara kept weaving. When the third of the beasts arrived, she had called as many as she dared, unwilling to tax herself further this early in the day, since they still had a whole swamp to traverse. The dragon-kin scattered the lizards, and all of the slimy little creatures disappeared into the trees.

"Now we can go." Minshara glanced up at what she could see of the light on the tops of the trees. She determined which direction the morning sun was shining from and led the others north, toward the Great Divide. Though she could sustain the dragon-kin in this world for only a few minutes, that had proven sufficient to give the lizard-kin a healthy respect for the Black Hands' abilities. As they had during the bandits' trek southward, the lizards kept their distance.

The mid-morning sun was beating down on Zen by the time he awoke. Exhaustion from his exertions with the weave the previous evening had caused him to oversleep. But his friends couldn't have gone far in those few hours.

Zen stretched, feeling suddenly years older than he had when this business with the Prophecy began. The mud on his shimmering blue-gray robe had dried, making the garment as stiff as his joints. He wrung it in his hands and the dirt flaked off in clods. That alone did much to clean it. The robe was disheveled and torn, but all in all, he'd fared pretty well.

He peered out over the edge of his makeshift nest at the forest floor, at least forty feet below him. If his friends guessed where he'd gone and came straight to him, they'd probably arrive before dark. If not, they could rely on the imprecise illumination of the Seeking Stone to hone in on the otherworldly rock Zen had pulled from the behemoth's lake. In that case, it would take days for Nick and the others to reach him.

On the other hand, Nick had told Zen to take the rock to the dwarves' best weapon smith. That was before they'd killed Whisper and before the Black Hand had broken off their attack, but Nick might assume Zen had already left for Glintbroc. If so, Nick would likely lead the party back to the Civilized Lands without consulting the Seeking Stone.

Zen tried to piece together the path they'd taken to get from Roybal Keep to the lake. It had taken them weeks—two at least—to find the rock, but they'd been lost in the swamp for most of that time, wandering aimlessly at the bidding of Xanth's primitive earth magic. By a direct route, the trip to Roybal Keep would take only a few days. Four, Zen decided, was the shortest time he could count on before his friends might arrive there.

Three days, then, Zen could spend at his forest campsite, holding the object of the Seeking Stone's sensitivity, waiting in one spot to avoid confusing the Seeking Stone's signal, for his friends to arrive.

But he could do more than just sit and wait. His friends would most likely consult the Stone at night, when its signal was most visible. Zen morphed into an ice eagle, further mending the residual wounds from the previous evening. During the day, he would search for his friends from the sky, provided the dragon didn't return.

"The Portal of the Damned is open?" Nick asked.

Ellessar nodded, still gasping for breath.

"How do you know?"

Ellessar combed the long curls of his black hair out of his face with his slender fingers, and his breathing finally settled. He recovered his two-tone demon-skin hat and climbed to his feet in the knee-high grass. "Every member of my order possesses a spiritual link to the Portal. Right now, my brothers are mobilizing for the defense of the Civilized Lands. The head of our order rides to the royal palace in Brinheim to claim his right as the queen's champion to wield the Demonbane sword against the hordes of demons pouring, at this moment, from the Abyss."

"And you?" Nick asked.

"My place is with you."

"Not with your order?"

"I understand now why Aeron has placed me by your side, and it has nothing to do with the Assassin demons we vanquished last night. The open Portal will unleash tens of thousands of demons, perhaps hundreds of thousands. We can never hope to defeat them, only to delay them long enough for the kingdoms to mobilize.

"My order includes hundreds of the most skilled fighters in the Civilized Lands. If I were there—" sadness filled Ellessar's eyes— "I could lend my sword, but it wouldn't change the outcome. Aeron has blessed me with a higher purpose. We must find Zen, take the rock he pulled from the lake to the dwarves, and have them forge your weapon from another world. Only by killing the Master can the demons truly be defeated. He'll have demons by his side, perhaps even among the Chosen. I must clear them from your path so you may face him."

Sierra Glenwood searched for Nicklan Mirrin and his band of fugitives for weeks before she finally picked up the trail she'd lost at the Trondor-Faldor border. After replenishing her supplies and recruiting a whole new team of mercenaries, she stayed in the kingdom of Faldor until she became convinced that the fugitives hadn't been seen in any of the cities there. Then she worked her way south, stopping at every city, town, and village across central and southern Meuribar.

She'd considered giving up several times, but these fugitives had killed the king of Trondor, and the Ruling Council had offered a reward far too large to walk away from.

After visiting South Bend, she'd gone just about as far south as she could without leaving the Civilized Lands altogether. It was time to head east.

She almost skipped Roybal Keep. If the fugitives had fled into the Wild Lands to escape justice, they'd likely meet the fate they deserved there. Sierra, however, hadn't succeeded as a mercenary by not being thorough, so she took the day-long side trip to the keep before extending her search into the kingdom of Brinheim.

From the north side, the keep itself seemed little more than a twelve-foot-high stone wall that ran the width of the narrow canyon to abut sheer cliffs on either side. The gate stood open, but an iron portcullis barred their way.

Sierra presented her writs of arrest for Nicklan Mirrin, Zenobrian Zersaash, Otto Lassel, Rancid Sevendeath, and Jasmine of the Order of the Sage to the guard at the gate. Each writ contained a detailed description of one of the fugitives she sought.

A guard raised the portcullis at once, and the captain approached. "You're a little late for that particular quarry. They went over the pass a couple of weeks ago."

"They were here, then? You're sure it was them?"

"Oh, yes. Hard to mistake that bunch. Another band of mercenaries followed about half a day behind them." The captain gave Sierra's team a cursory once-over. "A band about twice the size of yours, I'd say. Neither group has returned."

Sierra glanced back at her weary crew. Besides the five mercenaries she'd recruited in Spitfire, she'd also picked up a knight of Aeron—if the man was what he claimed to be when she'd met him in the capital city of Meuribar. The knight, Kelton, had pledged his allegiance to the church and to his god rather than to any human king or kingdom. So why he had any interest in Sierra's quest to capture a band of fugitives was beyond her. He must have fallen out of favor with his church. Yet he still wore his medallion of allegiance.

Kelton had said Aeron had bidden him to join Sierra's quest. It was conceivable. The fugitives were genuine outlaws. Sierra's cause was just. And she could certainly use another skilled sword against these particular fugitives.

"Any other passes out of the Wild Lands?" Sierra asked the captain.

"None that I know of. Heard rumors of one or two near the far east end of the Wild Lands, but that's got to be at least a thousand miles from here." He thought for a moment, then shook his head. "If they're coming back, they'll have to come through here."

"That's good news," she said. "You have quarters, I assume."

"Of course."

All of Sierra's mercenaries were smiling.

"Then we'll wait."

CHAPTER 3

The watches went more smoothly that night. Nick and his friends had left the stench and cloying wetness of the swamp, along with all its inherent dangers, behind them. They had a full night to sleep on the firm ground of the Wild Land plains, and the Black Hand had camped a short distance away, providing a buffer between the two parties.

The night was not altogether pleasant, however. The duty of burying their friends hung over the companions like a pall. If they'd had a choice, Nick would have hauled both bodies all the way back to the Civilized Lands before interring them, but heat and decay made that choice impractical, even if they could go straight back to Roybal Keep. They couldn't. They had to find Zen. He had the stone they'd come all this way to find, and for which Rancid and Otto had given their lives.

In the early hours of the morning, Nick and Jasmine dug the

graves while Ellessar cleansed himself spiritually for the ceremony. The burial took place at dawn, with the rising of Aeron's light over the spirits of the dead, so that he might guide them on their final journey.

Nick felt like he had a rock in the back of his throat and another in his stomach as they covered the graves with patches of grass they'd carefully set aside. How many more of his friends would die for his quest? How many more could he stand to lose? He took a deep breath and shoved the questions down deep inside. There were no answers. Only time would tell. They left the site unmarked, unsure of how the indigenous wolf-kin would treat the remains of outsiders.

Nick replaced the severed reins on Rancid's horse with short lengths of rope while Ellessar packed up the camp. Then the demon hunter caught Nick's attention. He nudged his chin toward Jasmine, who was approaching the Black Hand.

Nick hustled after her to keep her from offering the bandits four-to-one odds that they might take advantage of. He caught up just as she came to a stop before them.

"I hold no ill will toward you personally," Jasmine told the bandits. "I cannot speak for my friends, but only for myself, when I say that I understand the compulsion you must have been under from the Master's Chosen."

Nendrick chewed his lower lip and said nothing. The remaining bandits stared at the ground.

"We ourselves have served his purposes," Jasmine said, "though at the time, we didn't know that we did so. That, perhaps, is the difference between us."

Nendrick's back stiffened and his eyes flared with defiance.

"As for your vendetta against Rancid Sevendeath, I trust you consider the matter resolved."

Nendrick nodded.

"I suspect he provoked much of it. Take this." Jasmine handed him a bundle of rations and a water skin. The bandits had no supplies of their own besides their weapons. Apparently they'd left their packs somewhere in the swamp. Even the black, fingerless gloves of their order were gone from their hands. "I suggest you lose yourselves somewhere. The Master will not take kindly to—"

"You can't be serious," Nick said. "After what they've done—"

"What they've done," Jasmine stated flatly, without taking her eyes off Nendrick, "is to rid us of Whisper, who has hunted us since we left the Order of the Sage. They have bought us time, helped us to kill the Assassin demons, and restored the secrecy of our purpose. Despite what they may have done in the past—"

Nick's fist clenched. He yearned to feel the weight of his missing sword. "The Black Hand burned my home and murdered my mother."

Jasmine met Nick's gaze squarely. "These four were not among those involved. Whisper, Jade, and Sledge were the only survivors of our battle with that group of Black Hand. They're all dead now. Will you hold their crime against these four, who helped to destroy the very Chosen who did murder your mother?"

Nick took a long moment to answer. Whisper, for sure, had been party to the attack on his home those many, many months before. Nick's father had described how the flames inside the house had "whipped around something fierce, as if caught in a whirlwind, blowing first one way, then another." He'd described the movement as "unnatural." When his father had tried to get into the house to save Nick's mother, he'd been struck back by a blast of air so strong it had nearly knocked him out...exactly as Whisper had slammed Nick, over and over again, every time they'd fought. But Jasmine was right. As far as Nick knew, these four bandits hadn't been there.

"No," he said finally. "I can't."

"I'm glad to hear that," Nendrick said. "We believe there's safety in numbers, especially if we have to pass through the swamp again, with all those lizard-kin lurking about. We'd like to accompany you until we reach the Civilized Lands."

Jasmine started to reply, but Nick's knife cleared its sheath before the first word passed Jasmine's mouth.

He laid the blade with the tip at Nendrick's throat. "Know this, outlaw. Just because you weren't there when my mother was killed doesn't mean we trust you. You give us one reason to and we'll take back the food Jasmine gave you and leave you to fend for yourselves."

Nendrick swallowed hard and nodded carefully.

For the next two days, the seven of them worked their way west around the southern lobe of the swamp, the same area Nick and his friends had skirted just a few days earlier while searching for the rock from the sky.

They traveled west in hopes of discovering a route through the Great Divide into Gildstone, despite the fact that the soldiers at Roybal Keep had known of no passes in that direction.

They couldn't circumvent the swamp to the east because the northeast corner of it abutted the Great Divide. By exploring to the west, even if they didn't find a way directly into Gildstone, they might come across a route to Roybal Pass without having to reenter the swamp.

On the morning of the third day, after Ellessar had completed his communion with Aeron, he reported the presence of a demon in the Wild Lands. "It's a day's travel to the north."

"In the swamp," Jasmine said.

"Maybe not." The perimeter of the bog curved northward toward the point where the swamp transitioned into a forest, a site where Nick and his friends had made camp a few days before. "If the demon is in the swamp, it's near the edge."

"Another Assassin, you think?" Nick asked. For months, Assassin demons had hunted the party—one Assassin each for Zen, Rancid, Otto, Jasmine, and Nick. Two of the demons had succeeded. The party had killed the rest. "One hasn't come for you yet."

Ellessar shook his head. "If there was one coming for me, it would have done so at the behemoth's lake."

"Could something from the Portal have traveled this far south already?" Jasmine asked.

Ellessar shrugged. "There's no way to know until we find it. Aeron provides me with only a direction and an approximate distance to those demons he wants me to hunt."

"Nothing about what kind of demon it is?" Nick asked.

"No."

"Don't you find that disconcerting?"

"I trust that he'll help me defeat any demon he calls me to hunt."

"Then you're going after it," Nick said.

"That's why Aeron reveals them to me. We're planning to go that way anyway. Are we not?"

Jasmine nodded. "It will help to know if the Master has called more Assassins to stalk us."

"Indeed," Ellessar said. "And whether the demons have encroached this far since the opening of the Portal. If so, our passage to Gildstone may cause us more trouble than we thought."

"Not to mention," Nick added, "our passage from there to Lorentil."

Jasmine glanced meaningfully at the Black Hand bandits, still walking out in front where they could be watched. "No need to advertise our travel plans beyond Gildstone."

Nick nodded and said nothing more.

Throughout that day, Ellessar took Spirit to venture ahead of the group and scout for tracks of the demon or signs of other dangers. Having seen nothing, the party approached the forest boundary late that afternoon.

Just before they entered the woods, an eagle the color of fresh snow screeched overhead. It glided downward in a wide circle, alighted on the ground nearby, and morphed into Zen.

The elf-kin mage pushed his hood back to reveal disheveled hair and a beard more ragged than usual. The pale skin of his face appeared splotchy, mottled with patches of pink. Dark circles drooped beneath his haggard eyes. His magical exertions over the past few days must have been extraordinary.

Nevertheless, his gait remained steady as he approached. "I have something for you," he told Nick, noting warily the presence of the bandits. Zen set his pack down. He untied a long bundle from it and unwrapped Nick's great sword.

Nick wanted to hug the mage. "You salvaged it from the lakeshore!" He gave the weapon a cursory once-over and slid it into its sheath, still strapped to his own pack.

"There's more." Zen glanced again at the bandits. "Perhaps now is not the time."

"Agreed." Nick took Zen's hand. "It's good to see you. You don't look well."

"I may have overextended myself, but there was need. The forest and the swamp are hard to search. If I hadn't spotted you before you entered the woods, I might have missed you altogether."

"You've been searching the woods?" Ellessar asked.

"And the swamp, for a day's travel in every direction."

"Have you seen anything that looked like a demon? I've been tracking one since dawn, near here or a little farther north."

"Something strange came into my camp early this morning."

"An Assassin?" Nick asked.

"No. This creature was smaller. A bulbous body with spiny tentacles dangling beneath it. It didn't seem to touch the ground."

"That explains the lack of tracks," Ellessar said. "Did it have wings?"

Zen shook his head. "It just hovered there. It didn't move very fast, so I turned into an eagle and flew away. The moment I did, it went straight for my nest."

Nest? Nick didn't interrupt to ask.

"I wasn't planning to return," Zen continued. "If I hadn't found you today, I was going to translocate to Roybal Keep and wait for you there."

"Sounds like a Devourer," Ellessar said. "A lesser demon. They consume the residual energy left by the manipulation of the weave.

They detect and slip through holes in the structure that seals away the Abyss. It probably didn't come from the Portal. Show me this nest."

Ellessar approached Zen's nest without much caution. He'd slain Devourers before. This one should be no different, except for the fact that this time Ellessar had several capable warriors at his back, along with a powerful mage.

"That it?" Nick pointed to the creature, a mottled pink orb floating atop a dozen tentacles in a nest forty feet off the ground.

The demon hovered over the branches of Zen's makeshift structure, silently consuming the residual energies of the weavings Zen had performed there over the past few days. Ellessar nodded as he strung his bow.

Nick pulled Otto's crossbow from his belt and loaded it. The Black Hand dwarf, Cairn, did the same with a crossbow of his own. Jasmine readied a sharpened steel star about the size of her palm. Zen formed a handful of ice shards in his palm, shrouded in a frosty mist to keep them from melting.

The Devourer seemed to respond to Zen's weaving. It levitated over the top of the nest and descended until it hovered amid the undergrowth and the old trunks of a pair of fallen elm trees.

They all waited to follow Ellessar's lead. As soon as the demon hunter released his arrow, Nick and the dwarf impaled the Devourer with a pair of crossbow bolts, Jasmine struck it with her throwing star, and Zen launched his ice shards.

With a squeak and a sigh, the demon plopped to the ground.

"Should we search the area for more?" Nick asked.

"No." Ellessar checked the demon's body to confirm its death. "They're loners." He recovered the crossbow bolts and returned them to their owners, then cleaned his own arrow and placed it back in its quiver.

Jasmine retrieved her throwing star from the demon's flesh and checked it carefully for corrosion before returning it to her belt. "Then we head west, to the mountains of Gildstone."

Nendrick spoke up for the Black Hand. "I think we should go back to Roybal Pass. At least there we know we can get across the Great Divide."

"He's got a point," Nick said.

"I'm sure I can get over the mountains, no matter how rugged they are." Zen gestured specifically to Spirit and the horse that had been Rancid's. "What about the rest of you?"

"I think we should try," Jasmine said. "It'll save us days if we can find a way directly into Gildstone."

"I agree." Ellessar mounted Spirit and turned her west.

"All right." Nick mounted the spare horse. To the Black Hand, he said, "You're welcome to do whatever you like. We're going west."

Ellessar nudged his horse forward and prayed that they wouldn't have to double back later. With the demons loose, the Civilized Lands couldn't afford any delay.

Ellessar scouted the forest for a campsite. The sun had dropped below the horizon and they hadn't passed a suitable location for at least an hour. As he approached a glade that held promise, Spirit began to fidget. Ellessar stopped. Heavy, shuffling footsteps moved through the thick wooded growth beyond the clearing. Ellessar thought he might have stumbled across some game as well as a campsite, so he loaded his bow and nudged Spirit to the edge of the trees.

There, across the glade, maybe a hundred feet distant, stood a ten-foot-tall creature with the build of a gorilla. Splotches of black fur protruded between plates of bone that seemed to have grown randomly about its body.

The animal looked up as Spirit stepped into view. Another ape-kin emerged at the side of the clearing to Ellessar's left. Both trumpeted a clear note through long, tusk-like snouts. Nearby, another answered. Then another.

As one, the creatures charged with the speed and grace of battering rams. Ellessar loosed his arrow at the first one. The missile bounced off a breastplate of bone, and the thing came on.

The forest erupted with sound as all of Ellessar's friends, and more of the ape-kin, raced forward. Ellessar fired again. This time the arrow struck between bone plates and lodged there. The ape-kin didn't slow.

As the creature reached Ellessar, Jasmine appeared at his side, emerging from the trees with a graceful, flying kick. Her foot snapped out and struck the ape-kin, knocking its head back with a mighty thump. The ape-kin stumbled back a step on its short, hairy legs as Jasmine dropped into a crouched fighting stance. She held her *sai* in one hand, its central shaft as long as her forearm and honed to a sharp point.

Nendrick, armed with his battle axe, rushed to intercept the ape-kin barreling in from the left.

Two more of the beasts crashed through the trees and into view to Ellessar's right, shuffling forward on their short legs, long bony arms raised like barbed cudgels.

Zen chanted, tapping the weave to access the plane of ice, from which all of the material for his magic originated. The air grew cold as he threw a swelling ball of ice and slush past Ellessar. It reached the two newcomers, hovered for a moment, and then exploded. A wave of freezing air, slush, and splinters of ice ripped into the ape-kin pair. Each blew a fierce note full of pain and reeled away from the blast.

Zen launched a gust of freezing wind as well, which slammed into the same two ape-kin. The weavings left both creatures crusted with frost and stained red with their own blood. Still they came on.

Ellessar slipped his arm through the straps of the Shield of Faith and drew his sword.

Beside him, Jasmine's *sai* jabbed the soft tissues between the bone-like plates of the first ape-kin, and it stumbled back. It recovered quickly and lumbered forward. The creature brushed away her block, and its arm crashed into her body with a bone-jarring crunch.

A fifth ape-kin, this one more brown than black, charged into the far side of the clearing. Ellessar pressed Spirit ahead to intercept this latest beast before it could join the first. The skinless, hairless bone of its forearm brushed Ellessar's sword aside and smashed into him, nearly knocking him from Spirit's back.

Spirit shifted underneath him to compensate, but the blow threw Ellessar's balance too far off center to counter. As a second monstrous arm descended toward his head, the Shield of Faith came up to deflect the blow. Ellessar sucked air into his strained lungs. He praised Aeron and pulled himself upright in the saddle.

Zen surveyed the battlefield. Nick, on foot, skirted a pair of stout maple trees and charged the frost-covered pair advancing from the right. One, limping, had fallen behind.

Nick swung his sword at the leading ape-kin. The beast blocked the blow with its long, bony, club-like arm and raced past him. Nick let it go. He set his stance to meet the other.

Zen waited for an opening.

Nendrick intercepted the beast charging from the left. The first swing of his axe glanced off the creature's chest. With brutal efficiency, the ape-kin clubbed him with one bony arm, then the other, and the axe dropped from Nendrick's hand. The beast wrapped its arms around the bandit, locked the barb of one arm around the barb on the other, and squeezed. Its teeth, sharp as a tiger's, tore a chunk from Nendrick's shoulder.

The ape-kin that had passed Nick ran straight for Zen.

Lammeer stood a short distance to Zen's right, chanting a minor weaving. Noma, the elf-kin monk, snatched the reins of Nick's horse and swung herself into the saddle. She charged into the clearing. Cairn loaded his crossbow and stomped off to get an angle on the ape-kin mauling Nendrick.

That left Zen to stand alone—he dismissed the Black Hand mage as inconsequential. He raced to complete a weaving as the ape-kin closed the distance with its bony arms raised to strike. The creature reeled back and blared a truncated wail as Zen froze its brain from the inside out.

Zen stepped aside, and the ape-kin's momentum carried it past. With a final snarl, it collapsed, lifeless, to the ground.

Noma raced on Nick's horse to Nendrick's aid with the steel-pointed end of her quarterstaff stretched like a lance before her. With the arm not holding Nendrick, the ape-kin blocked Noma's lance. The beast lashed out as she raced past, spooking the horse enough to prevent it from coming close enough for a second pass.

Nendrick's captor trumpeted into the deepening twilight. The clear note sounded like the signal horns once used by the Black Hand. Others echoed its call. Then the ape-kin flung its arms wide, each taking a share of Nendrick's body. The grisly pieces splattered to the ground.

In the meantime, Ellessar, Nick, and Jasmine each faced one of the ape-kin. Nick stood toe-to-toe against one of them, his great sword a match for the ape-kin's giant cudgels. Nick blocked one, and then the other. Within a few strokes, his sword slipped past the monster's defenses and carved deeply into its unprotected shoulder.

Nick ducked an ape-kin arm and swung his sword low. He took off one of the creature's stubby legs at the knee, and it went down. His next swing removed the beast's head.

Ellessar remained mounted as he fought the brown ape-kin. At that distance, without a clear opening, Zen had only one weaving that could help the demon hunter. He wove a few ice shards into his hand and cast them at Ellessar's opponent. They sped effortlessly past the last row of trees and into the ape-kin's neck. The distraction allowed Ellessar to slip his sword past the beast's cudgels and down into its chest. The ape-kin sank to its knees, leaning on one bony arm, coughing blood with every labored breath.

Jasmine stood over the lifeless corpse of her own opponent, her bloody *sai* in her hand.

That left only one, but the calls of additional ape-kin in the woods seemed to be growing louder.

CHAPTER 4

Nick retreated with the others to Zen's position within the trees as the sounds of additional ape-kin grew closer. "We're not safe here."

"We'll have to backtrack," Jasmine said. "The whole forest might be dangerous."

"What about Nendrick?" Nick asked, directing the question more to the Black Hand than to his friends.

"Leave him." Noma boosted Cairn onto Nick's horse so the dwarf wouldn't slow them down. "He knew the risks when we crossed the Divide."

"That's a bit cold." Nick turned to Jasmine for support.

The clear note of a nearby ape-kin split the air. The one that had killed Nendrick sat down to devour a large chunk of the bandit's torso.

"If we try to chase off that beast to collect and bury the pieces,"

Lammeer said, "we may all end up like him."

"Even a Black Hand deserves better than that." Ellessar gestured toward the darkening glade. "But Lammeer's right. We have to move."

They retraced their path until well after midnight before the sounds of the ape-kin faded behind them, and then for another hour before they finally stopped for the night.

In the morning, Zen scouted their surroundings from the air. When he returned, he cleared a thick blanket of pine needles and rotting leaves from a flat patch of ground and sketched a crude map with the butt of his staff. The northern half, he labeled swamp; the southern half, forest. "The forest stretches as far to the west as I can see. Several days at least."

"Did you see any mountains?" Jasmine asked.

"Here." He drew a jagged line along the northern edge of the map. "It can't be far from the pass, but we'll have to cross the swamp to get there."

"Any in the west?" Jasmine pressed.

Zen shook his head.

"There must be mountains that way," Ellessar said.

"I'm sure there are, but I can't see them, which means they're farther away than we'd hoped." Zen scanned the demon hunter's cuts and bruises from the previous night. "You want to go back through those ape things to find them?"

Jasmine studied the map for a long moment before addressing Zen. "Yesterday you wanted to try the mountains. It sounds like you've changed your mind."

"I still think I can make it across. I'm just not sure it'll be any faster." Zen poked his staff at the drawing. "The swamp narrows here. I think we can cross it in a few days. Then we can follow the base of the mountains east to get to Roybal Pass."

Nick looked up from the map, toward the bandits. "What do you think?"

Only Noma seemed willing to speak. "We'll go with you whatever you decide, as long as it leads toward the Civilized Lands. We're safer together, and we'll not try to tell you your course."

"Ellessar?"

"If we knew we could cross the Divide, I'd say west. But if we get there and can't cross, we'll have wasted a lot of time."

"Jasmine?" Nick asked.

"We've come farther north than I thought. I think it's wise to take the sure course."

"Then Roybal Pass it is," Nick said. "We'll cross the swamp as quickly as we can."

The group trudged through the filth of the bog. Each day they traveled until the light failed them. Then they struck sputtering torches made of damp wood wrapped with oil-and-mud-soaked cloths, and pressed into the night until exhaustion won out or their direction became unclear. Every morning Zen pointed the group once more toward a familiar cut in the mountains. By the evening of the third day, they had won clear of the swamp.

Fear, largely foreign to Jasmine, welled up inside her as she stared at the mouth of Roybal Pass.

When the party had first traversed it on the way into the Wild Lands, the fairy who kept watch at the summit had detected Jasmine's demon blood and struck her blind. The result had left her feeling more helpless—no, not just feeling, actually *being* more helpless—than she'd ever been in her life. The monks at the Order of the Sage had taught her self-sufficiency and molded her into an able fighter. Yet the fairy had stripped all that from her in mere moments. It had taken days for Jasmine to recover her sight. She loathed the idea of meeting the fairy again.

"You all right?" Nick asked her. "You've been quiet for the last few days."

Jasmine nodded without comment.

"The fairy may be gone by now," Nick said. "The Assassin demons came through the pass right after she attacked us. If she set upon them as well, they will have killed her."

Jasmine met his gaze. "Is that supposed to comfort me? If she opposes the demons, she's on our side. An ally strong enough to stand against us is one whose well-being I welcome."

Ellessar strode up beside them, walking Spirit. "A good point. I don't know how the fairy determined your heritage. Maybe she can sense a demon presence in the pass as I sense them through my communion with Aeron. If so, it was the Assassins she sensed. She'll have figured that out by now. Or she might have guessed based on your appearance. Either way, she stopped before she killed you. I would never give such quarter to a demon. That tells me she had doubts. Besides, I gave her something to think about last time. She may let you pass."

The Black Hand observed the exchange in silence.

"Did you see her?" Ellessar asked them. "The fairy in the pass?"

Noma shook her head.

"Just the same," Jasmine said. "I will travel in front. Give me at least a fifty-foot berth. If lightning bolts start dropping from the sky, I don't want anybody else hit."

"Another thing," Nick told Zen. "The fairy's on our side, whether she knows it or not. If she attacks, we'll run the gauntlet. If you can hinder her efforts, fine, but don't hurt her."

Zen shrugged. "Whatever you say. Worse comes to worst, I can skip out. I'll be safe in a cot at Roybal Keep before any of you can say 'hailstorm.'"

The fairy had lost track of how many millennia she had guarded the pass. She no longer even remembered why she was there, nor did she care. She stayed because her life force was bound to the summit. So she watched and waited. Whenever demons tried to traverse the pass, she killed them if she could. Aeron had created her race for that very purpose, and she knew no other life.

But she'd seen none for decades…until about three weeks ago. A demon had come through the pass then. Its visceral presence had twisted the fairy's gut, so she'd readied herself and her enchantments.

The demon wasn't alone, however. It traveled among men-folk and with an elf, a divine brother of Aeron. One such as he would never knowingly befriend a demon. Therefore, he'd been deceived. He knew not what traveled with him.

So the fairy tried to free him. Ultimately, she'd managed only to blind the fiend and escape with her life. "Take your blind demon and go," she'd yelled, to warn the elf of the thing that walked beside him.

What the elf said next had saddened her: "You should look into your heart before you attack those you don't know, or you'll find your efforts misplaced as they were today." After all the fairy had done, the elf refused to see the truth about his travelling companion.

Later that evening, though, more demons came through the pass. Assassins. The fairy had never seen so many at one time. She remembered then what true demons felt like—what they smelled like. To her senses, a dark cloud of hate fouled the ether around them. The stink of the dark god suffused the air, the rock. Even the meager foliage in the pass screamed for relief from the demons' presence. The fairy could not have killed all of the Assassins, but had she been healthy, she would have tried. Weakened as she was from her battle with the men-folk that day, she could merely endure the pain of their presence.

She knew then that her senses had deceived her.

Now, that same demon-kin female from weeks before was back. Members of her group were missing. Instead she kept company with people from a group that had followed the Assassin demons through the pass. This time the fairy could see that the brother of Aeron bore a talisman. To her eye, the Shield glowed with a holy light. Aeron had blessed the elf and therefore favored him. These men-folk, and the demon-kin with them, apparently had a higher purpose.

The fairy let them pass.

"Any progress?" Ember asked across the scarred wooden table in the taproom at Roybal Keep.

"What do you think?" her brother grumbled. "Impossible task, if you ask me." Borim ShatterStone emptied his honey drops onto the table. He popped one into his mouth and crushed it between his rotting teeth. The dwarf had brought a pound of the candies with him from their home in Gildstone, but he'd nearly finished them in just two days of bargaining with the keep's supply master. And the more frustrated he became, the faster he consumed those he had left.

Ember winced at the crunching sound. If Nick Mirrin and his band of fugitives from Trondor didn't return soon, Borim would run out of the sweets. Then he'd become intolerable.

"When the Forgers' Guild sent me out here," Borim said, "I didn't expect to find the swords. Figured that thief Harimon had defaulted on his payment and—"

"Harimon Mirrin was an honest merchant," Ember said.

Borim met his elven sister's gaze. "A shipment that size could make even an honest *dwarf* go into early retirement, let alone a human. The guild musta been daft to extend so much credit." Borim pushed the crumbs from his candy around on the table with his stubby finger. "You don't suppose they sell sweets at the provisioner's shop?"

Ember shrugged. She had come here for a much larger purpose than the business of the Forgers' Guild. For that matter, so had Borim, though he didn't actually know it. It mattered only that he didn't come to some accommodation to buy back the salvaged weapons from Harimon's doomed shipment before the fugitives returned from the Wild Lands. If he did, Ember would have to find some other pretense to remain at the keep without blowing her own cover.

She'd had trouble enough convincing the guard captain that she really was Borim's adopted elven sister, true though it was. It would have been easier if she could have lied about it, but that would have tipped off Borim that she was up to something.

At least Sierra Glenwood, the mercenary from Trondor, was still there. With all her contacts, she apparently believed the fugitives not only remained alive, but that they would pass through this very keep on their return from the Wild Lands. It was a small comfort, but it did corroborate Ember's information from the Dwarven Intelligence Guild...and the DIG had the most expansive information network in all the Civilized Lands.

Nonetheless, stories from the keep's guards, about a lightning storm that had erupted from the clear blue sky near the summit of the pass on the day the fugitives had traversed it, didn't bode well for their return. Neither did the reports that a large band of mercenaries had pursued them through the pass a day later.

Ember glanced at Sierra over Borim's left shoulder. The fact that a knight of Aeron kept company with the mercenary had already been catalogued in Ember's mind and would appear at the forefront of her report to the DIG. It bore heavily upon Ember's own mission and was bound to make it either easier or infinitely harder, depending on the fugitives' reasons for venturing into the Wild Lands.

For the moment, Ember had to trust her superiors, who had assured her that the fugitives would survive and return through Roybal Keep.

A young man who'd arrived with Sierra and had played a lyre in the tavern for coins the past couple of evenings—and who'd been stationed at the southern watchtower during the day at the behest of the mercenary—burst through the front door, tore across the taproom, and skidded to a stop before Sierra's table. "They're here," he panted between breaths. "The watch captain stalls them even now at the south gate."

Sierra split the air with a shrill whistle. "Form up," she shouted to her mercenaries, all of whom were sitting somewhere in the bar. "It's time to earn our pay."

CHAPTER 5

Guards rushed into position on the battlements of Roybal Keep as Jasmine and the others approached the gate. Apparently people returning from the Wild Lands was indeed rare. When the captain of the guard appeared on the wall, Jasmine addressed him. "Permission to enter the keep?"

"And who might wish entry?" It was an odd question. The man could see very well that they were all from the Civilized Lands, being humans or their kin—except perhaps Jasmine, with her triangular face, flat nose, bald pate, and the three-clawed talons that served as her hands and feet, but surely the guards remembered her from their passage south.

Nick stepped forward. "Name's Nicklan Mirrin. My friends and I passed through about three weeks ago from the Civilized Lands."

The captain conferred with one of his men, who glanced down into the keep's yard before answering. "I remember. How about your prospector? Did you find the gold you sought?"

Jasmine had almost forgotten about the cover story they'd concocted when they had passed through the keep on their way south. So much had happened.

"Alas, no," Zen called back. "I can still sense it, but as your men tried to tell us, the land is too dangerous. We lost friends, I'm sad to say."

The captain seemed distracted, discussing something with the man beside him. "I'm sorry," he said finally.

"I'm sure some bets need to be reconciled in the taproom because of our return," Jasmine said. "Perhaps you'll let us in, so the rightful owners of those tankards of ale may claim them."

The captain hesitated. He glanced twice into the yard and then laughed. "Indeed. And I'm one of those to collect." He finally nodded to someone at the base of the tower inside the keep. "Raise the gate."

The weary group trudged under a wall ten feet thick and thirty feet high, and into the courtyard beyond. Jasmine focused on putting one weary foot before the other until she could get a hot bath and a full night's sleep in a sturdy cot. As soon as the last of them entered, the portcullis slammed closed behind them.

"That's far enough." The voice sent ice down Jasmine's spine.

Sierra Glenwood stood in the middle of the yard. Around her, arrayed in a half circle against Jasmine and her friends, were half a dozen hired mercenaries. On one side stood a knight—a disenfranchised one, if he was hanging out with this crowd—a lad maybe a few years younger than Nick and a lot leaner, and a dwarf swinging a spiked ball on the end of a short chain. On Sierra's other side stood a man of Nick's large build with a great sword and full chainmail, backed by an elven mage with a wand in her left hand, and a woman in studded leather armor with a drawn long sword. Sierra had apparently lured them all to the hunt with the bounty offered by the kingdom of Trondor.

Sierra's brow furrowed as she scanned her quarry. Otto and Rancid were missing, fugitives for whom she also had warrants.

More than a month had passed since the company had last seen Sierra, and that had been hundreds of miles to the northwest. The elf was tenacious, Jasmine had to give her that.

She took a single step forward. "What is the meaning of th—"

A dozen crossbows clicked into place, nearly in unison, on the wall behind her, and several guards took up station around the perimeter of the courtyard. The guards all wore the uniforms of the defenders of the keep, lawmen in their own right, ready to support Sierra in the issuance of her warrants.

"I'm here to bring you to justice." Sierra's manner was confident, her tone condescending. "You yourselves called these the 'Civilized Lands.' How civilized would they be if we let killers of kings roam free?"

The dwarf, Cairn, leapt from Nick's horse, falling in his haste to separate himself from the party. "We ain't with them." He scrambled to his feet. "We only met them a few days ago."

Lammeer sought the guard captain. "We came through in a larger party a day behind the fugitives."

The captain's eyes never left Jasmine. "I remember. You and your friends may go. Sierra's warrants don't include you."

The three Black Hand bandits who had arrived with the companions scurried to the side.

"So, Sierra," Ellessar said from behind Jasmine. "Still serving the Chosen, are you? Sent to the very edge of the Civilized Lands to do the Master's bidding?"

"I serve justice. Today I do so on behalf of Trondor, with a writ that authorizes me to kill you, if necessary, to return these fugitives to that kingdom."

Jasmine hadn't seen the warrants herself, but Nick had. They were guilty of the crime for which King Balor Culhaven had sentenced them all to death, though the circumstances of that event had been grossly misrepresented to Trondor's Ruling Council in order to secure such a penalty.

But all of that was irrelevant. Zen, Nick, and Jasmine were trying to stop the prophecy that foretold the conquest of Balor's Master, the High Priest of the evil god Vexetan, and the enslavement of the civilized races. They couldn't afford to give themselves up to Sierra and her mercenaries.

Beyond Sierra's formation stood Minshara, the Black Hand mage, in her flowing blood-red robes, somehow cleansed of the swamp's filth. With her stood another Black Hand, the bald man in the white linen tunic whom Nick had gutted. He must have received magical healing to have survived such a wound. Behind them stood another Black Hand mage, one Jasmine hadn't seen before—an old man, stooped with age, with combed white hair and a forest-colored cloak. The opportunistic bandits would probably help Sierra, then claim the right to a share of the reward. If they did, Noma, Lammeer, and Cairn would follow suit.

"You've been given a new lease on life," Jasmine said to the latter three, in an effort to keep them out of the imminent fight. "Use it well."

Everyone else—the squires, pages, tavern girls, and stable boys—had cleared the courtyard. All except for a pair of visitors: a raspberry-haired elf girl and a brown-bearded dwarf with a green knit skullcap stretched over his broad head. The two were engaged in a heated discussion beneath the taproom's sign.

"There're a couple of ways we can do this," Sierra continued. "Personally, I'm hoping you'll force me to kill you here and now. That would make getting you back to Trondor much easier."

Jasmine strode toward Sierra. "We've walked the length and breadth of the Lands to fight the demons that pour forth from the Devil's Cauldron at this very moment. We'll not sacrifice the future of the Civilized Lands for the sake of your evil king."

With a snarl, Sierra pulled out her swords and launched into a charge.

Today, though, Jasmine was ready. She stood stock still and unarmed, in as casual a stance as she could muster with her mind screaming to her limbs in deadly alarm. Sierra had nearly killed Jasmine the last time they'd met. *In all circumstances, be at peace.* She recited the tenet to herself to bolster her calm façade. Sierra had left her cowl off her head, and the magic of her concealing cloak lay dormant, a sign of overconfidence on a battlefield she had selected to give her every advantage. *Fool.* Overconfidence was a trait Jasmine had learned to foster and exploit.

Sierra's swords whipped back in unison, one poised to strike high, the other low.

Jasmine's foot shot up and smashed Sierra in the chin with an audible crunch. The elf's head snapped back. Her swords flew from her hands as she fell backward. With a groan, she rolled over onto her stomach, relying on her band to keep Jasmine at bay. A trickle of blood and two of her teeth dribbled from her mouth as she struggled to stand.

Three mercenaries rushed in.

Ellessar had never seen Sierra, but he recognized her name as that of the mercenary who'd been searching for Jasmine, Zen, Nick, and the others when they passed through Spitfire. The fugitives, as Sierra called them, had confessed their deed to him, and through him to Aeron. They had pure intentions. And when Ellessar accepted possession of the Shield of Faith, they all took the Oath of Aeron to prove it.

Mercenaries, by and large, had soiled hearts and served nothing but their own greed. Maybe Sierra had the documents she said she had, and maybe she didn't. She could have simply bribed the guard captain, or seduced him, to gain his assistance. Either way…

Ellessar drew his rune-inscribed longsword.

Nick held his hand out at hip height, his palm toward Ellessar. "This isn't your fight."

"Our quest is greater than the King of Trondor. You don't fight alone." Ellessar took a closer look at the faded crest on the shield of Sierra's knight, the morning sun shining past a mountain peak onto an elf-like image of Aeron. If the crest was to be believed, the man was a knight of the church, not of the crown.

Ellessar handed Nick the Shield of Faith. "Go with the grace of Aeron."

Nick slid the Shield onto his arm just as Sierra charged Jasmine. Then he rushed to aid his friend.

"You're confused, brother of the star," Sierra's knight yelled to Ellessar. "You fight among outlaws."

"No," Ellessar replied. "Sierra Glenwood serves a Chosen of the Dark Master of legend."

The knight seemed to hesitate as he stepped forward to block Nick's path to Sierra. Ellessar watched him closely. If the knight failed to recognize the Shield of Faith, or if he attacked its bearer, he would prove himself to be an imposter.

Ember and her dwarven brother moved to the door of the taproom as the gates opened. Sierra was facing off against the fugitives, whom she and her allies outnumbered at least two to one. The guards on the wall backed the mercenaries.

"They are so thrashed," Borim said with a grin. He nudged Ember in the hip with his elbow. "Care to wager against the mercenaries?"

"That would be unfair." Ember had information her brother didn't. "These mercenaries are the ones who are 'thrashed,' as you put it."

Borim glanced up at her. "How do you figure that?"

"Think about it. The outlaws survived in the Wild Lands for weeks. You've heard the stories...sixty-foot monsters and—"

"Bah." He flapped his hand at Ember. "Old brides' tales."

She gestured to the walls behind the fugitives. "No one builds a keep to protect themselves from brides' tales."

An odd-looking female—the demon-kin monk, if the DIG's reports were accurate—advanced on the mercenary.

Borim rubbed his palms together. "Looks like it's startin'. It's been a while since I've gotten to bust some heads."

"I don't think that's a good idea."

"Aren't you the one who likes to stir up trouble?"

"I've matured in the years I've been away. The diplomatic service has taught me to think things through."

"Brimstone! You just can't fight." Borim looked from one group to the other. "Which side should I choose?"

Ember planted one hand on the hilt of her dwarven-made short sword and the other on her hip. "I can fight, and better than you."

"Well then." He looked her skinny, elven body up and down critically. "Let's see what you got."

Ember had gotten so used to distracting her brother from trouble that she almost did it out of habit. But she needed him to fight today. "Hey!" She pointed at Nick Mirrin. "Doesn't that man have one of the swords you're looking for?"

"He does." Borim's eyes widened. "And he's got the Shield of Faith!"

Yes! Borim might not believe in the human gods, but he knew the Shield of Faith belonged to the church that represented good. That would be enough to put her brother on the right side in the battle. He wouldn't oppose the wielder of the Shield.

"We fight against these mercenaries, then." Borim swept the mace from his belt. "It's going to be glorious."

"If you must." Ember's seriousness returned. "But don't attack the keep's guards."

"Whatever." Borim started forward. "Let's bust some heads."

"If you assault a guard," she hollered after him, "you'll spend a month in the hold."

Borim flipped a gesture of dismissal over his shoulder. He bellowed his battle cry, "ShatterBrand!" as he charged into the fray.

CHAPTER 6

A knight in full plate armor, his drawn sword every bit as large as Nick's, intercepted him from the right.

Beyond the knight, Minshara's hands and mouth moved in some weaving. Nick raised the Shield of Faith in case the Black Hand mage released some explosive magic into the fray, but she finished by simply pointing at the captain of the guard and shaking her head.

The knight placed himself between Nick and Sierra, his sword poised. "What say you, Shield bearer? Shall we *hold* as your priest suggests?"

Nick eyed the knight with suspicion. "All right. Follow me and we'll discuss it." He tried to draw the knight away from Jasmine.

The man held his ground, as did the lad behind him, who twirled his long sword in a circle about his wrist twice with a cocky showman's grin on his baby face.

By that time, three of Sierra's mercenaries surrounded Jasmine, but the dwarf from the taproom doorway rushed the chainmail-clad warrior and forced him away from her.

The Black Hand remained on the periphery of the yard. The guards on the wall held their fire. Those on the ground maintained their positions, waiting for orders, like those on the wall. Zen had disappeared entirely. They could have used the help of the ice mage right about then.

Sierra came unsteadily to her feet and faced Jasmine.

The raspberry-haired elven girl from the taproom doorway, a beauty like Nick had never seen, casually approached the knot of fighters. She didn't reach for her sword. Instead, she pushed up the flowing sleeves of her loose white blouse. She held one hand out before her and threw a stream of fire into the back of the reeling mercenary.

Sierra's enchanted cloak burst into flames. With the cry of the damned, she staggered away from the battle and toppled to the packed dirt of the courtyard floor. She writhed for a moment, unable to smother the flames, and then finally lay still.

Jasmine dropped into a defensive stance, ready to hold off the two mercenaries who still faced her: the dwarf with the morning star on her right, and the woman in black leather armor on her left. The woman seemed wary, remaining outside Jasmine's immediate reach with her long sword held ready. Jasmine yelled over the clash of weapons between the dwarf from the taproom and Sierra's warrior. "I withdraw! I have no quarrel with any of you. Only with she who attacked me."

Flames continued to consume Sierra's body.

"Call them off, brother," Ellessar said. "What kind of justice is this? Jasmine has withdrawn."

The knight gave the Shield of Faith a hard look of consideration, as though coming to grips with an uncomfortable truth. "Stand down!" he yelled to the remaining mercenaries. "Stand down! This is not the way!"

The mercenaries stopped their advance but remained gathered around Nick and Jasmine with no apparent intent of letting them escape their circle.

The elf and dwarf from the taproom doorway stood near Sierra's smoldering body, the crossbows of the keep's guards now trained exclusively on them. Flames licked the fingers of the elven beauty, ready to leap forth once more, as she stepped around the body to stand with the dwarf.

The Oath of Aeron ran through Nick's mind. *Act with honor. Defend the weak. Seek justice.* If the knight truly served the church, then he lived by the Oath. He wasn't just another mercenary hoping to collect bounty. He sought justice. The promise of coin that had brought the others would not sway him.

Ellessar led Spirit forward until he stood before the knight of Aeron. "I propose a Zone of Truth. It's—"

"Yes." The knight sheathed his great sword. "I'm familiar with it."

"Aeron has granted me this gift. If the fugitives agree, you may question them within the Zone, so we might all know the truth."

The Shield on Nick's arm grew heavy. The Oath he'd taken to carry it wasn't a burden, but he and his friends had indeed killed the former king of Trondor, a fact they couldn't lie about within the Zone of Truth. How, then, would this knight interpret justice? In Rancid's words, whose justice would he seek? Maybe Ellessar planned to just feign the enchantment. That might give them all a chance.

"I will submit to the Zone, of course," the knight said. "Gather the fugitives."

"We haven't agreed." Nick turned to the battlement above the southern gate. "Captain of the watch, what's your position on this?"

"I will uphold the law."

"Whose law?" Ellessar called up to him. "Trondor's or Aeron's?"

Such a challenge wouldn't be helpful, but Ellessar had already spoken.

"I've sworn to uphold the laws of men," the captain replied.

Nick raised his hand to silence the demon hunter, but Ellessar ignored him. "You would uphold the laws of an evil king?"

"That has yet to be proven, brother," the knight said.

"How do you know Sierra served the law?" Jasmine yelled from within the ring of mercenaries. "If she has documents, let us see them."

Clever. If Sierra had the warrants on her person, her smoking remains left no doubt that they'd been destroyed.

"Her warrants are valid," the captain said. "Obviously she can no longer produce them, but I've seen them, and I'll back them."

"And what if this Zone of Truth reveals our innocence?" Nick asked him.

"Parlor tricks," the captain said. "It's up to the courts in Trondor to decide your guilt or innocence."

Minshara, her attention still focused on the guard captain, shook her head at him again.

The captain glanced over at her, and then he gave them an opening they just might slip through. "Unless these mercenaries withdraw their legal claim upon you."

Besides the knight, five mercenaries stood against Jasmine, Nick, and the unlikely pair from the taproom doorway.

"In that case," Nick said, "though I can't speak for my friends, I'll submit to the Zone of Truth…if you all agree to withdraw your claim of bounty in the event that we're found innocent of the crimes that were listed on Sierra's warrants."

"No," shouted the mail-clad warrior on the far side of Jasmine. "This is your deal, knight, and we have nothing to gain from it. We'll not withdraw our right to bounty."

"What's the matter?" Ellessar asked him. "Afraid of the truth?"

The man turned a nasty look upon him, which Ellessar met evenly.

"If you insist on fighting," the raspberry-haired elf girl said, too quietly for the guards on the battlement to hear, flames still licking her fingers, "the five of you will be dead before the guards on the wall can intervene."

The man looked uneasily at his own elf-kin mage, at the woman in black leather armor near Jasmine, and then finally at the dwarven mercenary. He didn't even acknowledge the young lad, who still twirled his sword. Sierra's remains smoldered on the ground not ten feet from him. Of the lot of them, the warrior stood closest to the elf girl's flaming fingers. Even if she couldn't burn them all before the guards struck her down, she could certainly kill him.

Nick scanned the courtyard. Zen remained unaccounted for, but he likely wasn't gone. If Nick had to place a wager, he'd bet that Zen had moved to the battlement, maybe in the form of a small animal made of ice, ready to revert to elf-kin form and strike all of the guards at once. The mage would have no qualms about making such an attack, and doing so might even the odds quickly. If they were all lucky, it wouldn't come to that.

"Would you really do this, knight?" the mercenary asked finally.

"I'll yield no quarter where justice is due. But if these people are innocent, I'll not let you take them."

"Nobody's innocent," the mercenary grumbled, his position weakening by the moment. He asked the others, "What do you think?"

The young man at the knight's shoulder stopped twirling his sword and shifted uneasily. "I'm not willing to die for this if they're not guilty."

Begrudgingly, the woman in black leather armor agreed.

"Very well." The mercenaries' elf-kin mage lowered her wand. "We'll not claim the innocent."

"And you?" Nick pointed his sword at the last mercenary, the dwarf swaying his morning star on the end of its chain. If he stood, he stood alone.

The dwarf nodded once, the gesture almost hidden behind his broad helmet and bushy black beard.

"Then it's decided, brother," the knight said. "Gather the accused and bring forth Aeron's Zone of Truth."

The mercenaries parted to allow Jasmine and Ellessar to join Nick and the knight. All of the Black Hand and the remaining mercenaries backed away. Perhaps *they* feared the truth.

The raspberry-haired beauty and her dwarven companion returned to their place beneath the taproom sign.

Nick held his ground until the Zone descended and the very fist of Aeron gripped his heart. The constriction in his chest wasn't quite painful, and it didn't affect his ability to breathe, but it seemed clear that if he chose to speak a lie, the fist would close and his heart would beat no more. So much for Ellessar's faking the Zone to allow Nick to honey-coat the truth.

The faces of those around him remained calm.

Ellessar looked at each in turn. "Let's begin with an introduction. I am Brother Ellessar Miriel, Order of the Shining Star, defender of the mortal plane, speaker of the word of Aeron."

The knight removed his helmet and tucked it under his arm. "I am Brother Kelton Kramer, Order of the Rising Sun, seeker of justice, defender of the weak."

There it was. Kelton was no pretender. He truly was a knight of Aeron. Nick and his friends might yet survive the day.

"I am Jasmine, Order of the Sage, seeker of knowledge and balance in all things."

Suddenly it seemed that everyone belonged to one order or another. Nick shrugged. "I'm Nick."

"Nicklan Mirrin?" Kelton asked. "The Nicklan Mirrin sought by the kingdom of Trondor for the 'assassination of King Gremauld Santari'?" He quoted the charge exactly as it had been stated on Sierra's warrant, which Nick himself had seen in the Black Forest. Kelton knew exactly whom he sought. Or at least he thought he did.

"I am wanted in Trondor," Nick said.

"And what of you?" Kelton asked Jasmine. "Are you wanted for the murder of Gremauld Santari, late King of Trondor?"

"I am *wanted* for that crime, yes."

"Did you commit it?"

Jasmine stood at ease, hands clasped behind her, staring straight ahead with the air of a pupil addressing her instructor. "That is a complicated matter, which we must discuss at length to ensure that there is no misunderstanding, as definitions of the term 'murder' may vary and circumstance weighs heavily upon that definition."

The knight's voice took on an edge as hard and sharp as steel. "Answer the question, fugitive, if you wish us to dismiss our claim."

Jasmine didn't so much as blink. "I'll answer your questions if you will allow me to explain completely before you pass judgment."

The knight snorted and cast a glance at Ellessar. "It sounds to me like you keep company with deceit, brother."

"She has spoken the truth to me and has done no wrong. Hear her words."

"Where are Otto Lassel, former constable of Twin Peaks; Zenobrian Zersaash, the one they call the ice mage; and the elf-kin who goes by the name Rancid Sevendeath?" Kelton asked.

Nick answered. "Rancid and Otto died in the Wild Lands, killed by Assassin demons. We buried them there."

"And Zenobrian Zersaash?"

"He's a mage. He entered the keep with us, as you probably saw, but he has the ability to translocate. I don't know if he's still in the keep, or if he has fled elsewhere." Nick took a deep breath, relieved to have been able to say that last bit honestly.

"Very well," the knight said. "I'll question Jasmine before we return to the matter of Zenobrian Zersaash. Speak your truth, sister of the sage. Did you kill the late King of Trondor?"

"I did not kill King Gremauld, though I was there when it happened, and I played a role."

"What role?"

"The kingdom was in civil war at the time. Gremauld Santari sat on the throne, but his claim to it was said to be invalid."

"How do you know this?"

Nick stepped forward. "According to Balor Culhaven, the current King of Trondor, Gremauld Santari was not in the line of succession. He was an in-law to the royal bloodline. He came to the throne through treachery and deceit." The fist around Nick's heart tightened until he qualified his statement. "Or so we were told."

"Nevertheless," the knight said. "A role in murder is no less egregious when committed upon a peasant or on an in-law, as upon a king. By your own tongue, you are guilty."

CHAPTER 7

Jasmine didn't move. "I haven't finished."

Kelton's silence gave her leave to continue.

"The entire kingdom had taken sides in the war. Everyone was killing for the sake of one king's claim or the other's. You may label them all murderers, but they all fought for what they believed was right."

"To rebel against any king is unlawful," Kelton said. "You could have taken your grievance to the Ruling Council."

"I must be honest." Jasmine's words would have been exactly the same even if she wasn't under the Zone of Truth. "We did not know of the Ruling Council, nor did we have time to issue a grievance. Balor Culhaven promised us access to the royal library, which we needed, in exchange for our help on his side of the war."

The knight stiffened. His hand moved to the hilt of his sword.

"But we could have made such a deal with Gremauld Santari as easily as we did with Balor. We chose our side based on what we had heard of the two men. Balor had a reputation for compassion, Gremauld for brutality. We fought in a war. We did not commit murder."

"Civil wars are always a tricky business," the knight said. "The winning side is always right. The losers, criminals. Nevertheless, the circumstances of your crime do not absolve you of responsibility for your actions. For this reason, we cannot release our claim over you. There is something I don't understand, however. If you killed Gremauld Santari for the benefit of King Balor, why did Balor label you criminals and place a bounty upon your heads?"

"Because we know that he is a Chosen of the Dark Master of the Last Prophecy of Mortaan," Nick said. "And because we now oppose him."

Kelton's eyes shot open wide. He glanced at Ellessar as if to confirm that the Zone of Truth remained in place, though he could surely feel its compulsion upon his own heart as the rest of them felt it on theirs. "Why then did you help place him on the throne?"

"We found out after Gremauld was dead," Nick said. "We've seen the Medallion of Vexetan around his neck, and one each around the necks of his general, Pandalo Gundahar, and Dalen Frost, a captain in his Home Guard."

"If you take them back to Trondor," Ellessar said, "they'll receive death, not justice, and the Master will fulfill the Final Prophecy of Mortaan."

Kelton remained silent for a long time, either weighing Jasmine's tale or waiting to make sure she had finished. When he spoke, he raised his voice to carry all the way to the battlement. "We release our claim on the fugitives."

"Then they're free to go," shouted the captain of the guard.

The soldiers on the keep wall shifted their aim to the remaining mercenaries as if they feared the group might dispute Kelton's verdict, given the size of the bounty they'd just lost.

The captain yelled, "Seize the elf and dwarf." He pointed toward the two who had intervened against Sierra on Jasmine's behalf. The raspberry-haired elf girl had, in fact, killed a representative of the king of Trondor during the conduct of her official business.

Minshara made a gesture that once again captured the captain's attention. She shook her head in disapproval.

"On the other hand," he shouted, "the writ Sierra used to establish her authority was apparently issued under false pretenses. They, too, may go."

With a deep breath that did much to relieve the tension that had built up in Jasmine's spine and shoulders, she strode toward the bath house. Nick followed. Their path took them past Minshara. As they approached, the old mage behind her stood up straight. His white hair and eyebrows literally melted away to reveal Zen's face. The dark cloak he wore didn't just resemble Rancid's. It was Rancid's, which they'd stowed in a pack on the spare horse.

Zen hadn't been the one to influence the watch captain, though. Minshara had. Jasmine walked up to the Black Hand mage. "I trust our business is through."

"What business?" Minshara replied with a smirk. She winked over Jasmine's shoulder at Nick and turned to walk away.

Nick caught Minshara's arm and whispered, "What was that you did?"

She stared at Nick's hand until he removed it. "Just a little trick of the weave I've used against merchant caravans. If you can sway the leader, the guards will hesitate." She glanced at Zen as he reached inside the doorway for his staff and the rest of his gear. "You have nothing more to fear from us." She strode into the women's barracks and was gone.

Ember extinguished the flames in her palm and walked from the courtyard, her brother beside her muttering something about not having gotten to bust any heads. Her superiors had been right, not only about the fugitives surviving the Wild Lands and returning through Roybal Keep, but about something else as well. Wherever the fugitives went, they stirred up trouble, and they seemed to have the skills, devices, guile, or allies to come through every scrape alive.

The DIG had known from the beginning that the fugitives had committed the crimes of which the king of Trondor had accused them—their sources in King Balor's court had confirmed this information the day the Ruling Council had locked Nick and his friends in the palace dungeon—but that didn't make the fugitives evil. And it didn't make them wrong. Gremauld had indeed been a brutal tyrant who'd weaseled his way onto the throne.

But what was the fugitives' purpose? That's what the DIG had sent Ember to find out, so they might advise the dwarven leaders on the building crisis. Omens from the Prophecy were sprouting up all across the Civilized Lands, from the war in Trondor to the slave riots in Palidor. A dragon had even been seen in the sky for the first time in nearly four thousand years, right here over Roybal Keep, on the same day the fugitives had passed through on their way into the Wild Lands. Somehow these people were connected to every vein of information about the Prophecy that was available to the DIG.

Now Ember had uncovered, for the first time, the specific circumstances of Gremauld's assassination. And the convenience of the demon hunter's having used the Zone of Truth meant she didn't have to find a way to corroborate Jasmine's account.

With that realization, a sinking feeling crept into Ember's stomach. Never before had an assignment gone so smoothly. The DIG had a saying: Beware the mission that begins well, for it will end badly.

Still, Ember had much work to do. The fugitives hadn't crossed the Civilized Lands at a gallop and braved the dangers of the Wild Lands just to sit on their hands in Roybal Keep. They would depart in the morning, and if Ember hoped to learn the details of their plans, she and her brother would need to leave with them.

After Jasmine had cleaned the filth of the Wild Lands bog from her body, she went looking for a decent meal. She walked into the taproom and surveyed the tables. The place should have been nearly deserted this early in the evening, but today wagers were being paid. The room wasn't full, but it was loud and the patrons raucous.

The elven girl who had killed Sierra sat at a table near the dagger targets along the northern wall. She didn't appear any older than fifteen harvests, which for an elf meant she was probably at least thirty or forty.

Jasmine approached her. "I have a debt of gratitude to pay. May I join you?"

"Of course."

A serving maid delivered a tankard of ale to Jasmine that she hadn't ordered.

"What is this?" she asked.

"It's from a man at the bar."

One of the keep's many guards raised a mug in salute as Jasmine looked his way.

The serving maid continued, "He won more than a tankard today because of your return and that of your friends."

Jasmine waved to the man and took a seat across from the elf girl. "I am curious," she said. "Why did you help us today? It was not your fight, and it could have gone very badly. Even if it didn't, the guards could have detained you, or worse, for killing a licensed mercenary in pursuit of her contract."

Ember's smirk seemed to barely contain her mirth.

"What?" Jasmine scanned the room while they talked. None of her friends had arrived. The mercenaries and the Black Hand seemed to have made themselves scarce, or had left the keep altogether. Some of the patrons gave Jasmine curious glances or the hateful glares she'd learned to accept on account of her unusual features.

"I know I look young," the elf girl was saying, "and I've been told I'm pretty."

"You are at that."

"It makes most people underestimate me. I'm not so helpless as I may seem."

Jasmine gestured toward the elf's hand. "Your fire made that clear. Still, you could have been arrested."

"Not likely. I have the means to translocate my brother and I—"

"Your brother?"

"Borim. The dwarf I was with. He's my brother." She shrugged. "I was adopted."

Jasmine took a sip of her ale and grimaced at the bitter taste. She set the mug aside. "I'm sorry. I didn't mean to interrupt."

"It's quite all right. Most people don't believe it." The girl extended her hand. "I'm Ember, and you're Jasmine."

Jasmine gripped Ember's palm briefly in the three digits of her own talon-like grip. "How do you know my name?"

"It's a small keep. Apparently, all the bets about your party's return increased tenfold when Sierra showed up with her warrants. Most assumed you had no intention of coming back."

"That still doesn't explain why you helped us."

Ember shrugged. "Borim's a bit of a brute. He likes to 'bust heads,' as he puts it. If there's a fight, he'll be in the middle of it."

"But why our side? Surely you must have thought we were in the wrong."

"We did, until we saw the Shield of Faith." Ember sipped a mug of hard dwarven spirits, the smell of which turned Jasmine's stomach from clear across the table. "That's why *I* stepped in. Borim can take care of himself, but I couldn't sit back and let some mercenary play her game against the oppressed righteous." She raised her hand to forestall any objection. "Not that I thought you were oppressed. You handled yourselves well, but the game against you wasn't being played fairly."

Nick and Zen came into the bar and Jasmine motioned them toward the table.

She choked down a swallow of her own cheap ale and wondered at an elf who could stomach even stronger dwarven spirits. "Indeed it wasn't, and we are grateful. Perhaps we might impose upon you for one more favor."

Ember raised her mug in a noncommittal gesture.

"My friends and I have business in Gildstone. I wonder if you might recommend a route."

"Of course. Head out the north gate." She pointed. "Turn west at the fork, just before you reach the ferry crossing, and then south at Silversmith. The only entrance to the kingdom is fortified and heavily guarded. Unless you have an invitation, you'll need to convince the authorities that you have legitimate business there. And by 'legitimate,' I mean, 'lucrative for the dwarves.'"

An hour later, Ember slipped into the armory.

The armorer beamed when she crossed the threshold. "What might I do with such a fine lass as you?"

"What might you do *for* me," Ember corrected.

"Of course."

Ember slipped a small sack of platinum coins from a pouch on her belt. "My brother has made you an offer to purchase your entire stock of dwarven-made weapons."

The armorer grunted. "Not a very attractive offer. Did he think your fair looks would soften my resolve? Because if he did—"

Ember dropped the sack onto the man's workbench. "Take my brother's offer, and I'll give you that."

The man pried the bag open with soot-blackened fingernails. "Holy Aeron. Where did—"

"Do we have a deal?"

The man couldn't seem to catch his breath. "Yes. Yes, of course."

"Good. Contact him this evening. Tell him you've changed your mind. And not a word about this conversation or that bag of coin. He gets insufferable if he thinks he's lost at anything."

CHAPTER 8

Wearing a new suit of plate armor for which he'd traded Rancid's horse, Nick approached Ember in the courtyard, near Roybal Keep's northern gate. She and Borim were readying a wagon laden with the bulk of the keep's inventory of dwarven-made weapons.

"You two were sent here by the Forgers' Guild in Gildstone?" Nick asked her.

Borim continued to secure a team of mules to the wagon. He began to grumble loudly in his own tongue.

Ember glanced back at him. "Patience, brother." To Nick she said, "We were. The armorer told us the weapons had belonged to your uncle."

"That's true."

"He never paid the balance he owed for them. Ownership has reverted to the Forgers' Guild."

That stung. Some monster—perhaps something that had wandered down out of the Great Divide—had attacked his uncle's caravan before he could reach the rich markets of Palidor. He never got a chance to sell the weapons and make the balance payment. Instead, someone had salvaged the weapons and sold them to Roybal Keep for a fraction of their market value.

"I'm sorry," Ember continued. "I understand that your uncle was killed."

Nick nodded. It took a moment for him to find his voice. "By all accounts, he was. I haven't been able to confirm it. He was an honest man, though. If he was alive, he would have returned to settle his debt."

Ember put a gentle, slender hand on his arm. "I believe he would have, at that."

Nick took a deep breath and let it out slowly. "Look, I came by because I have a business proposal for you."

Ember studied his face. "I'm listening."

"You're taking this wagon back to Gildstone?"

She paused. "Yes."

"If you'll allow us, we can accompany you and serve as guards for your merchandise."

"And in return?"

"Speak on our behalf at the Glintbroc gate. It would smooth our admittance into the dwarven kingdom." Not to mention that joining a dwarf and an elf with a wagonload of wares would make Nick's party far less recognizable to their enemies.

"We'll speak *honestly* at the Glintbroc gate. Don't give us reason to speak ill of you, and we won't do so."

"Fair enough. Are we agreed?"

"We are." Ember glanced back at Borim, who had finished with the mules.

He leaned against the wagon, glowering impatiently at Ember, grinding sweets between his teeth.

She inclined her head toward Ellessar, who stood on the far side of the courtyard, conversing with the knight of Aeron who had come into the keep with Sierra and her mercenary band. "Whenever you and your friends are ready."

"Will you come with us, brother?" Ellessar asked Kelton. "We have much to do for the good of the Lands, and the obstacles we face are truly daunting. We would welcome your help."

"Alas, I cannot." Dark circles clouded the skin around the knight's eyes. "Aeron bade me join Sierra for a reason. At the time, I thought it was to bring your friends to justice. I know now that it was to prevent the mercenaries from impeding your quest. I prayed the night through that he might reveal what he would have me do next."

"He has. I see it in your eyes."

"I must warn the people of the Civilized Lands that the Portal of the Damned is open, that the demons have returned."

"The brotherhood of the Shining Star will do that."

"Perhaps, but they'll all be engaged with the demon armies. If word spreads only through them, it will travel no faster than the battle itself. The kingdoms will have little warning. I can reach Meuribar in a few days and encourage them to be ready if the brotherhood fails."

Ellessar clasped the knight's shoulder and spoke with the certainty he felt in his heart. "*When* the brotherhood fails. Not *if*. They can't hope to stand for long against the hoards that must be pouring from the Abyss at this very moment. They can only buy the people time. That's why I can't join them. I must complete my own charge, to help Nick Mirrin and his friends defeat the Master himself within the time my brothers purchase, even now, with their lives."

"It must trouble you that you can't be there to die with them."

"More than you know. But we must all bear the burden of Aeron's will."

Kelton thrust his chin in the direction of the gate. "Your friends are waiting. With your permission, I'll travel with you as far as the South Bend ferry. Then I must head north to the city of Meuribar."

"Of course."

The sun lightened the eastern sky as the party passed through the gates of Roybal Keep, but it didn't illuminate the ground for another hour. Four times that day, Zen changed form to that of an eagle and scouted the land ahead, searching for the remnants of Sierra's mercenary band. He didn't find them. Too few of the mercenaries remained to oppose the companions without Kelton's skill and Sierra's leadership. No, they had gone to South Bend or were themselves on their way to Meuribar, or to Silversmith or Loran. Nevertheless, the Master had other agents. Even if Sierra's mercenaries weren't among them, the remaining Chosen would find either them or the Black Hand and purchase the knowledge that Nick and his friends had survived and still fought to prevent the fulfillment of Mortaan's Last Prophecy.

That afternoon, the group reached the river and bade Kelton farewell. With no need for the others to cross the ferry into South Bend, they turned west and pushed on until sunset.

At that point, Borim's mules gave up and refused to pull the wagon another step. Ultimately, he left the stubborn animals in the road, beside which the party set up camp. Once the things they needed were unpacked, Borim released the mules from their yoke to enjoy the lush grasses in the river valley.

In the meantime, Jasmine built a small cooking fire. She grabbed two of the four live chickens she'd purchased at Roybal Keep from a wooden crate she'd secured to the back of the wagon.

Borim climbed to the top of a twelve-foot boulder, where he could see the road for at least a mile in each direction and much of the landscape around them. He plopped onto his bottom, pulled his cap down snugly on his head, settled a new bag of maple chews in his lap, and scanned the horizon.

Ellessar approached Nick, whose skin appeared pallid. Dark bags hung under his red-rimmed eyes. "You don't look well. Are you ill?"

"My stomach has been upset for the past few days, and it's hard to find a comfortable position to sleep in. I'm not sure what's wrong. It doesn't feel the same as a seasonal fever."

"Chills?"

"Not really."

Jasmine and Ember began to pluck and prepare the chickens.

"It's not often we have a fresh meal on the road," Ellessar said. "It looks like the ladies will be a little while preparing it. Spread your blanket and lie down. Maybe your illness is nothing. Maybe not. I'll say a prayer of healing over you."

Grumbling drifted their way from Borim's position.

"What was that?" Ellessar asked the dwarf. "See something?"

"A fool," Borim said.

Nick unpacked his blanket and spread it on the ground amid inviting clusters of raspberry bushes, small pinion pine trees, and sage. Ellessar scanned the road in the direction Borim had been watching.

"Not out there," Borim said.

Ellessar regarded the surly dwarf. "Where, then?"

"Right here, in our own camp, relying on an elven god. My sister tells me you've got a healer right there." He swung one stubby arm in Jasmine's direction. "Herbs'll do yer friend more good than prayers will."

Jasmine looked up from her work. A sly amusement shown in the smirk beneath her pink, almond-shaped eyes and flat nose. "I've seen Aeron perform greater feats of healing through Ellessar than I'll ever accomplish with herbs and salves."

"Bah." Borim stuffed his mouth so full of molasses chews he couldn't possibly speak. He crossed his arms over his chest and again fixed his gaze on the road.

Jasmine shrugged and resumed her work on the chickens. Ellessar chuckled softly. He shook his head and motioned for Nick to lie down. Nick removed his armor and shirt, then settled himself on his back.

Ellessar tugged on the skin around Nick's eyes to examine the whites. They weren't bloodshot. He shaded the eyes and the pupils responded normally. It didn't appear to be any form of intoxicant. Nick's forehead didn't feel warm. "No fever, as far as I can tell."

Nick nodded.

Ellessar gripped his holy symbol, a medallion with an image of Aeron and a bright star near the upper left corner. "Blessed Aeron, this man, who does your work tirelessly, needs your help. If it is your will, keep him strong for the journey."

Nothing discernible happened, but then Aeron often chose to work in subtle ways.

"Well?" Nick asked.

Ellessar shrugged.

Zen had approached by then. "Maybe it's some disease of the swamp. I felt something similar in the Wild Lands. I'm feeling better now. He'll probably get over it in a few days."

CHAPTER 9

Ellessar woke to find Jasmine stripping the last of the raspberries and pinion nuts from the nearby bushes and trees. As soon as she packed them away, their trek began anew.

An hour later, the companions topped a low rise, revealing several miles of their trail ahead, a shallow valley cut through the middle by a dry wash and dotted with a scattering of trees. On the road, a band of a dozen or so riders came their way, too distant to yet make out any details. They seemed in no hurry, but neither did they have any laden wagons as a merchant caravan would.

Ellessar didn't like the look of them. "Mercenaries."

Jasmine came to a stop beside him. "On what errand, I wonder."

"Possibly searching for us," Nick said. "Another band sent by King Culhaven."

Zen nodded. "Or another of the Master's Chosen."

"Bah!" Borim unhitched the mace from his belt. "No point in

guessin'. Let's go find out."

Ellessar turned to Nick. "Ember, Borim, and I will go. We won't be recognized. If there's danger, we'll find out."

"We'll watch the mules and wagon," Nick offered.

Jasmine pulled up the cowl on her robes and tucked each of her clawed hands into the opposite sleeve.

Ellessar started forward, with Borim and Ember on either side of Spirit. Ember walked tall, serene and composed. Borim swung his mace and hummed a cheerful tune whose only actual lyrics seemed to be "bust some heads," which he sang softly.

About the time they had closed half the distance, a snow-white eagle soared past them. As the two groups grew closer, it became evident that Ellessar had overestimated their number. Eight men, all human—large warriors, by the look of them—rode in two neat ranks of four, all armed and armored.

The eagle alighted on a branch, high in a tree behind the mercenaries and within shouting distance. If trouble arose, Ellessar would appreciate having the ice mage nearby.

"Hail!" Ellessar shouted.

Six of the men stopped just after they crossed the wash. The front two continued forward.

"You two wait here," Ellessar told the siblings.

"There are two of them," Ember observed. "I'll go with you."

"Brimstone," Borim said. "You ain't goin' without me."

"I can handle myself."

"Not by my reckonin'. I'm to keep you safe."

A smile passed over Ember's lips. "Did you see nothing at Roybal Keep?"

"Bah. I'm goin'."

"Then at least put your mace away," Ellessar said, "until we know if you'll need it."

Ellessar, Ember, and Borim advanced, weapons sheathed, three to meet the approaching two.

"Well met," Ellessar said as the riders drew up before them. "Any news from the west?"

"None worth telling. Where you headed?"

Ellessar gestured to Borim. "Escorting the dwarf and his merchandise to Glintbroc." There seemed no reason to hide their destination. This was, in fact, the cover they'd chosen when they joined the siblings at Roybal Keep. And it was true. "We want no trouble."

The men appeared clean and their gear well cared for. They bore no emblems or markings of any order or association with any municipality or kingdom. "Neither do we."

"What's your business then?" Ember asked.

"Truth is, we're seeking work."

"I suggest you go to the capital city of Meuribar," Ellessar said.

"That's where we're headed. What have you heard?"

"The demons have been freed from the Abyss."

Borim's head spun toward Ellessar. "What?"

Ember didn't seem surprised by the news.

Ellessar continued, "As we speak, they flow like a river from the Portal of the Damned in the heart of the Great Sand."

"Well, then, let's go bust some heads." Borim turned to his sister. "Do they have heads?"

Both strangers laughed. One said, "We'd be fools to believe such news. Where did you hear it, my gullible friend?"

Ellessar produced his medallion, with the symbol of his order. "I'm a brother of the Shining Star. It's our business to know. Our god, Aeron himself, gave me the news."

One of the men frowned. "I've heard of your order. Demon hunters."

"That's right."

The other man chuckled again. "Then I'd say you're heading in the wrong direction. Your prey lies that way." He pointed over Ellessar's shoulder, back the way Ellessar had come, toward the Great Sand.

"Indeed it does," Ellessar said, disgusted that Aeron had sent him away from the battle for which he'd trained his entire adult life.

When Ellessar declared that the demons had been released, it was all Ember could do to keep from staring, open-mouthed, at him. Only her training in the diplomatic service kept her face straight while her mind ran rampant. The demon hunter must have been testing the mercenaries or running some sort of con. If he was, though, she had thoroughly misread the elf. Ellessar didn't seem the type to joke or to rely on deception to gain his ends. He was too earnest for the former, and his god wouldn't approve of the latter.

As soon as the mercenary band had passed without incident, Ember approached Ellessar. "Why did you tell them the demons have been freed?"

Ellessar met her gaze. "Because it's true."

It took Ember a moment to recover from the statement. Finally she said, "What makes you think so?"

"Aeron wouldn't lie."

"Your god told you?"

Ellessar returned his attention to the road. "A little over a week ago. I'm trying to gauge how far the news has spread."

"*Aeron* told you?" The fact wasn't registering. Did the DIG know? Were they keeping this from her? From the dwarven people? From the civilized races?

"He's not often specific. I get impressions mostly. But my order was created to be the first line of defense for the Civilized Lands in just such an eventuality. We all received visions when the Portal of the Damned opened. Make no mistake. The demons are in this world. All of them. Or coming through as quickly as the size of the opening will allow."

"And nobody has heard?"

"That's good news and bad," Ellessar said. "It means the demons haven't advanced beyond the Great Sand. But it also means the humans, elves, and dwarves are unprepared. We must raise the alarm as we go."

"Even if everybody thinks you're crazy?"

"Includin' me," Borim muttered from behind them.

Ellessar ignored him. "Especially then. The less they're inclined to believe it, the more important it is for them to understand the truth."

"You mentioned at the keep that you lost friends in the Wild Lands," Ember said as they sat around the cooking fire that night.

"Yes." Nick swallowed hard. "Otto and Rancid."

"I'm sorry," Ember said. "What happened? If you don't mind my asking."

Jasmine had prepared the remaining two chickens from the keep, this time seasoned with sage and served with a pan-roasted mix of pinion nuts and raspberries. Exquisite. Maybe the best Ember had ever tasted on the road.

Jasmine squatted beside Ember with her own plate in her hands. "That's a long story."

Borim spoke around a mouthful of chicken thigh. "What else we gonna do 'til mornin'?"

"All right." Nick set down his plate before he began. "They caught us at the edge of a lake. The Black Hand, led by one of the Master's Chosen and...what was it? Five Assassin demons?"

"Four," Ellessar said. "One each for Jasmine, Zen, Rancid, and Otto."

"The latter two succeeded," Jasmine added.

Ellessar's expression soured.

"Well," Borim prompted after a moment. "Tell it."

Ember could always count on Borim to spur on the storytelling, which Nick and his friends seemed to take as idle conversation. Borim went on to ask for details about the battle, the swamp, the lizard-kin, the behemoth, and the Assassin demons that the Master had sent against the party—anything Nick and his friends were willing to say.

Ellessar sat quietly, carving something that looked like a piece of bone, until Borim asked about the Assassins. The demon hunter described them with scholarly precision. "Two-foot horns and claws, crimson skin coated with corrosive secretions." He drew an odd-looking sword from one of the sheaths at his hip. "We had a few of these made from the claws of an Assassin that came after Nick, so we could fight them without ruining our metal blades."

Ember held out her hand. "May I?"

Ellessar handed it to her. The blade was indeed about two feet long, slightly curved, and without an edge to speak of, but the tip came to a sharp point. Ember scratched at it with her fingernail. The material seemed harder than wood but softer than ivory.

Ellessar drew his other weapon, a white-handled sword with prayers to Aeron beautifully etched in elven runes down the length of its dwarven-made blade. "As it was, I lost the companion to this blade to the secretions of one of the Assassins." He returned it to its sheath and displayed the bone he'd been carving. "I'm whittling a handle to affix to a new blade when we get to Gildstone."

"Best forgers in the Lands," Borim stated.

"And you?" Ember asked Jasmine. "You fought them bare-handed?"

"I'm part demon. My skin might have held up against the secretions, but I didn't take that chance." She pulled from her robes a handful of leather scraps. "Ellessar gave me some strips of demon hide to wrap my hands in."

Ember tried to extract as many details as she could for the DIG without being obvious about it. The conversation was illuminating, to be sure, and the companions made clear that they'd gone into the Wild Lands on an errand related to their efforts to oppose the Prophecy, but all four of those who had returned to Roybal Keep alive remained tight-lipped about specifically what they'd gone into the Wild Lands for. They'd needed something from there—a talisman maybe, some ancient magic, or perhaps only information—but they never said what it was.

After the others had gone to bed, Zen and Ember stood watch together—a situation Zen had orchestrated by suggesting the two mages would need uninterrupted sleep to retain their magical endurance and therefore should both take the first watch.

Once the others had gone to sleep, Zen approached the elf girl. "Is all your magic based on fire?" he asked, as casually as he could manage.

She looked into his ice-blue eyes. "No. I understand yours is based on ice?"

"How do you know that?"

"Your reputation precedes you." Ember shrugged. "Or maybe follows you. I'm not sure which."

"Where did you hear about my magic?"

"Roybal Keep."

"Really? We told the soldiers I was a gold prospector and that the weave had led me to believe there was gold in the Wild Lands."

"They only believed that until the Black Hand bandits came through behind you and told them you were fugitives wanted in Trondor—a story Sierra corroborated when she arrived."

"So you heard it from Sierra." It was a statement, not a question.

"We talked extensively before you and the others returned. She said you gave her quite a beating in your first encounter."

Zen chuckled. "I got her pretty good with a hailstorm."

"Sierra also said the beating was mutual. Said you took an arrow in the gut. You were almost dead when she last saw you. She was surprised to hear that you'd survived."

"I wouldn't have if Ellessar hadn't come along. He's a healer, that one."

Ember nodded, then waited for Zen to continue.

"Anyway." Zen shifted. "I wanted to ask you about your magic."

Ember met his gaze, her brow furrowed, for a long moment. "What about it?"

"You didn't seem to make any gestures or speak an incantation to invoke the fire you used on Sierra. Impressive, by the way." He settled in next to her. "I've learned a lot about the weave over the years, mostly from other mages, by trading services for knowledge. I've never seen a mage who could manipulate the weave without gestures and incantations. Are you a priestess of some sort? Is your magic divine in nature?"

"No." Ember thought for a moment, deciding how much to share or how to put it into words. "Not a priestess, or a follower of any deity for that matter, but I'm not exactly a mage either."

"Not a charlatan," Zen said, again not a question. "Unless you're really good. An enchanted object?"

"No. I produce the magic myself."

"Now I'm intrigued. I've never heard of such a thing. I've heard of earth magic, the magic of the dwarves, but I don't know anything about it. Is it some ability of theirs?"

"Earth magic is based on a knowledge of the magical properties of certain materials. Some crystals, for example, if shaped properly, can focus light or energy, transform sunlight into a rainbow of colors, or take something small and make it look large." She pointed. "That crystal in the headband you wear. It helps you focus the energy of the weave."

"Yes."

"That's an earth magic, a property of the crystal, combined with your learned manipulation of the weave."

"Is that what you use? Earth magic?"

"No. Well, yes, partly. The dwarves call me a witch—which is derogatory, by the way—because I use an innate magic, a weak form of that possessed by the earliest elves. The ability has been handed down through the centuries, but it gets weaker and rarer with each generation. I have a little bit of it. I use focusing crystals, charms, and other catalysts—like you have in your staff—to augment and magnify my innate abilities. I don't always use gestures and incantations, but I'm dependent upon my charms and catalysts to give sufficient power to the things I can do." She opened a pouch on her belt and poured a little of the contents—a mixture of powders—into her small hand. "This is an earth magic. It gives strength to my fire. I can produce a small flame from the weave. The energy in this powder does the rest. It's the fuel."

"Does it drain you?"

"Some of my abilities do. Not my fire, though, as long as I have the catalyst."

"I envy you that. I find my magic draining."

"Not all my materials are easy to come by, or cheap. And those I use as fuel are consumed by the magic."

"Anything about it that you can teach a willing and talented student?"

"What are you offering in trade?" Ember asked.

"I was hoping to teach you mine in return, but the more you talk about it, the more it sounds like our magics are incompatible. Is there anything you can tell me about your charms?"

"Later, perhaps, when you have something to trade or we share a common objective beyond our destination at the Glintbroc city gate."

CHAPTER 10

Silversmith teemed like any port town. What set it apart was the majestic backdrop of the dwarven mountains just to the south, the stone construction of the vast majority of the buildings, and the profusion of dwarves—it boasted the highest percentage of dwarven residents of any city outside Gildstone.

The companions stayed only for the night, and for Borim to buy more sweets by the pound, or tens of pounds, after which his disposition markedly improved. At first light, the companions set out again.

The narrow and winding road to Gildstone climbed for hours into the hill country that skirted the dwarven mountains. When they drew within a few miles of the nearest peaks, Zen said to Nick, "I'll see you at the gate."

"Where are you—"

Zen transformed into a snow-white eagle of pure ice and soared toward the dwarves' border fortress of Glintbroc. When the companions had returned to Roybal Keep from the Wild Lands, Zen had assumed it would be safe—they all had—because it had been safe when they'd left it. He wouldn't make such a mistake again. Before they entered the city of the dwarves, Zen would ensure that they weren't walking into an ambush.

He soared over the final ridge and the battlement came into view—a wall of exquisite stonework that towered at least two hundred feet above the valley floor and spanned from mountain to mountain. Even with an eagle's keen eyes, Zen couldn't make out the mortarless seams between the massive blocks. The edifice so dwarfed the door at its base that the entry seemed fit only for a mouse. Dwarven knights crawled atop the battlement like fruit flies on a slice of melon.

As Zen flew over the wall, the truth of the city's construction alarmed him more than he cared to admit. The wall itself was the only visible structure. Behind it lay a narrow cleft between the mountains' breasts, its depth half the height of the wall, with nothing in it but loose shale, scrub growth of the hardiest sage, and a few stunted elm trees. The entire city lay underground.

Zen perched on a branch halfway up the hillside and observed the two dozen stout dwarven knights armed with short swords and crossbows. From their height, they'd be hard pressed to hit a target on the road below. But fighting was obviously not the knights' purpose. A wall as high and as thick as the mountain itself needed no defending. These were sentries, there to raise an alarm. Nothing more.

A small steel door at each end of the battlement provided the only access from the wall into the city. Without resuming his elf-kin form, Zen would have no way to open either of them. The doors were probably locked, in any case.

Zen watched the sentries until his companions rounded the corner, and then he flew back down to the trail, let the weave collapse, and resumed his true form. By then, the sunlight had begun to fade.

The trail ended at the door, twenty feet high and ten across.

Borim marched up to it without hesitation, grabbed a heavy steel mallet that hung from a chain beside it, and pounded three times. The deep, metallic booms echoed off the canyon walls.

A small panel slid to the side, and a face as hard and rutted as stone appeared in the opening. The gatekeeper muttered a dwarven phrase that sounded like a curse. Borim yanked off his knit skullcap, crumpled it in his fist, and responded in the trade tongue favored by the humans, an obvious courtesy to his non-dwarven guests. "Borim ShatterStone. On business for the Forgers' Guild."

The dwarf beyond the door surveyed the motley band behind Borim. He paused at the sight of Jasmine, as if trying to discern exactly what she was. Finally, he shifted his gaze to the mule train and wagon laden with crates, the emblem of the Forgers' Guild branded on the front. The dwarf grunted noncommittally before his face disappeared and the panel slid shut.

A moment later, the heavy door lifted silently into an unseen recess in the rock. From beneath, it looked like a solid block of steel, as thick as it was wide. Some hidden space inside the block held the gatekeeper Borim had just spoken with.

"Very impressive," Ellessar remarked.

Jasmine just raised one hairless eyebrow.

Beyond the gate stretched a cavernous plaza, lit by hundreds of blazing lanterns that trickled white smoke into unseen vent holes in the dark ceiling high above. Stone buildings made up an entire bustling city within the huge cave.

"You can put your horse up there." Borim pointed to a stable marked with a picture of a mule. "I have to deliver the guild's wares. I'll meet you in the Stone Tankard in an hour, make sure you get settled here, and help you find whatever it is you're lookin' for." He jerked his thumb over his shoulder toward a sign that sported a picture of the inn's namesake over bold dwarven text.

"I, too, will return shortly," Ember said. "I have to pay a brief visit to our Auntie Vane. She worries so whenever we travel. Watch yourselves in the bar. Some of the locals can get a little rough with outsiders. Don't take any of their spit, though, or they'll just get worse."

"We can take care of ourselves," Ellessar assured her.

"I don't doubt it. Nevertheless..." Ember gave him a reassuring nod, and then trotted off into the shadows.

Nick pushed open the double doors of the Stone Tankard's taproom with Jasmine at his side, Ellessar and Zen a step behind. The place bristled with early evening activity that filled half the tables, many of those with non-dwarven merchants, traders, and mercenaries—all of them unwashed, by the smell of the place. A murmur of hushed discussions clouded the air. Bitter looks crossed from table to table, as though some unpleasantness had just taken place and the companions had stepped into the middle of it.

A stout oak chair scraped the stone floor at a nearby table. The drunkard there, no more than chest high to Nick and nearly twice Nick's width, tottered up to him with one fat hand wrapped around his mug. The other clenched the handle of a heavy miner's pick. The dwarf thrust his knotted, gray beard at Jasmine. "No pets. The stable's across the plaza."

Ellessar drew his rune-inscribed sword, and several dwarves from the drunkard's table climbed to their feet.

Zen clamped his hand on Ellessar's arm. He spoke softly. "We can't afford trouble here."

Jasmine stepped between Nick and the drunkard. "I am no one's pet."

"Whatever you are, you're not welcome here."

Several of the non-dwarven patrons watched with interest. Which side they would take was anybody's guess.

"This woman has earned my respect." Nick chuckled at the gathering dwarves. "I suggest you control your tongue, or she'll likely earn yours as well." Without touching his sword, he strode past them all to the bar. "A pint," he said to the barkeep, "of whatever you do best." He surveyed the room as he waited for his drink, pretending not to care about what was happening at the entrance.

Ellessar resheathed his sword. He sidled past Jasmine and the drunk dwarf.

"Whatever she may look like," Zen said to the dwarf, "she's as human as I am. And as deadly." With that, he gestured in the air and translocated himself to the bar.

Jasmine stood, seemingly alone, against the host of bigoted locals. Her serene posture and unreadable features left the lot of them fumbling for the courage to refuse her entry. None of them had ever seen the likes of her, and they had no way to judge what she might be capable of. After a tense moment, she strode forward, and the locals stepped aside.

"Well played," Ellessar acknowledged when he caught up to Nick. "It's going to get worse, you know, as news of the Portal's opening spreads."

Nick sipped the harsh brew that the barkeep sat before him, then grimaced at the burn in his throat. "Somehow, everything always does."

Nick and the others settled into a table along the left-hand wall of the taproom, not private by a long shot, but as far from unfriendly ears as they could get in the place. If they spoke carefully, they should be able to converse without giving up any secrets.

A young dwarf approached the table. "What'll you have?" He was well on his way to the stout build typical of his race, and a thick mat of stubble promised to grow into a beard the lad could be proud of.

Everybody stuck to dwarven ale, the darkest and stoutest Nick had ever seen. It burned going down—a pleasant warmth—and carried a strong aftertaste of cloves, a rich flavor Nick had missed since his days of traveling with his uncle's trading caravan.

About half an hour later, Borim showed up. He alone proved brave enough to drink hard dwarven spirits, the smell of which made Nick's head spin from across the stone table. At least it overpowered the more-unpleasant smell of the three or so dozen sweat-laden dwarves in the place.

Borim dropped a handful of honey drops into his quart-sized tankard and let them dissolve before taking his first long pull. He sighed heavily. "Now there's a drink I can wrap my gullet around."

Nick waved away the alcohol-laden miasma that wafted across the table from Borim's exhalation. "You're a member of the Forgers' Guild. Who would you say is the best smith in Gildstone?"

"My great uncle," Borim said without a moment's hesitation. "Azurite StoneFist."

"*Your* uncle is the best forger in the whole of the dwarven kingdom?" Jasmine asked.

"Yep," Borim said, as though that should settle the matter.

"It just so happens?" Nick asked.

"Yep." Borim downed the rest of his spirits and nearly knocked Nick out of his seat with another hearty sigh.

"All right," Nick said. "Let's suppose he is. How do we find him?"

"Far side of Glintbroc. I'll take you there on the morrow."

"Good." It was a place to start, at least. "We'll put ourselves up here." The Stone Tankard boasted the best rooms and lowest prices—contradictory claims to be sure—on this end of the city. But he'd stayed here before, when he'd worked for his uncle. The rooms weren't fancy, but they were temperate and secure, if not exactly comfortable for someone of Nick's stature.

Ember strode past her aunt's dwelling and went straight to the entrance of the Dwarven Intelligence Guild, a nondescript timber door banded with steel, locked to all but those with a key. Even lock picks were said to be ineffective on this particular mechanism, a rumor Ember was ill-equipped to test, never having been trained by the guild to serve as a thief.

No, she'd always been a diplomat, having spent her first ten years in the guild as an adjunct ambassador to the elves, keeping her eyes and ears open for any events, or even gossip, that the DIG might want to look into.

The Nicklan Mirrin assignment had just fallen into place for her. The Forgers' Guild had planned to send a representative to Roybal Keep, where weapons purchased by Nicklan Mirrin's uncle had shown up in South Bend and Roybal Keep for prices that could undercut the value of dwarven-made merchandise for a year or more. The Forgers' Guild was determined to recover the weapons at all costs.

That same Nicklan Mirrin, in whom the DIG had an intense interest, had last been seen at Roybal Keep, heading into the Wild Lands. The DIG, convinced that the fulfillment of Mortaan's Last Prophecy was imminent and that Nicklan Mirrin was working to forestall it, was equally determined to know how Nick intended to do that. Because of Ember's relationship with Borim, the DIG had arranged with the Forgers' Guild to send Borim to Roybal Keep, and then they assigned Ember to accompany him.

Ember settled herself on one of the massive benches that lined the corridor outside the audience chamber. She smiled inwardly despite the fluttering in her stomach at the prospect of facing the DIG elders. She'd not only managed to recover the missing weapons but had ingratiated herself to Nicklan Mirrin and secured his protection for the weapons' return to Gildstone.

The only lingering problem was Nick's hesitance to share with Ember his reasons for coming to the dwarven kingdom.

The double doors into the DIG's audience chamber opened, and one of the guild secretaries announced, "The elders are ready for you."

Ember's face felt warm as she entered the marble-floored hall, surrounded by block walls hung with rich tapestries. The DIG elders never considered answers satisfactory, no matter how deep or detailed the information provided.

"What have you learned?" Master RumbleDown asked from the far side of a massive polished-stone table, flanked on each side by three guild elders.

"Much." Ember tried to sound confident. "Nick Mirrin's party is down to four: himself; Jasmine, the demon-kin monk; Ellessar, a brother of the Shining Star; and the ice mage, Zenobrian Zersaash. Otto Lassel and Rancid Sevendeath were killed by Assassin demons, deep in the Wild Lands."

"Have you confirmed this information?"

"Yes. The testimony was given under the compulsion of a Zone of Truth."

RumbleDown leaned over and whispered to the dwarf on his left. The sound was like marble against a grindstone. "Continue," he said finally.

"They did commit the crime for which they're wanted in Trondor, but they did so within the context of the civil war. They're combatants, not criminals."

"Yes. Yes. What is their *current* purpose, aside from forestalling the Prophecy? How do they plan to do it?"

Ember swallowed hard. "I don't yet know. I need more time."

"Time is a resource we don't have. The Portal of the Damned has opened. Did you know that?"

"Y—yes." Ember knew it, but how could the DIG? Even with the resources of the guild, news could only travel so fast. She'd heard no talk of it on the way over, save that spoken by Ellessar, and everyone he had told thought him daft for believing it. She shouldn't have been surprised, though. Dwarves tended to distrust the magic of the weave, but the DIG wasn't above using enchantments to convey information quickly.

"You're keeping it from the people," Ember said.

RumbleDown shot to his feet. "Of course we're keeping it from the people! We can't have a panic, now, can we?" He paused, then settled back into his seat.

The elder on his immediate right continued. "There's more. Two days ago, an armada arrived on the coast of Palidor. Hundreds of ships. Goblins, orcs, trolls, and ogres. The Palidoran army met the invasion at the beaches, but then a hoard of freed slaves, along with orcs from Kraggan-knows-where, attacked the human defenses from behind. They're sorely pressed. We don't expect them to hold the coastline. It's bad, Agent ShatterStone. Very bad."

"News will get here soon enough in any case." RumbleDown rolled up the parchment scroll on which he'd taken a few notes and set it to one side. "We were hoping your information would be more complete."

"I know only that their purpose has brought them here, to Gildstone. I'll stay with them and learn what that purpose is."

RumbleDown sat forward, his eyes as hard as the granite table he leaned on. "Be sure that you do. You must find out before news of the Portal arrives. We want to have our course of action determined by the time it does."

Ember bowed to the elders. "I'll not disappoint you."

"You already have."

CHAPTER 11

Ember went straight from DIG headquarters to Quality Thyme, a small herb, alloy, and gem dealer just off the main plaza. If she planned to continue travelling with Nick Mirrin and his friends, she would need to make charms for each of them—a small physical object that she could associate with each person, something upon which she could focus her thoughts and thereby affect the members of Nick's party with her magic.

Elsee BroadStock, the dwarven matron behind the counter, gave Ember a wide, crinkled smile. "Ember ShatterStone, I ain't seen you here in fortnights. What can I do for you?"

Ember took three long strides to the counter, ignoring the bits of ore, herbs, and shiny rocks that sat in glass jars on the simple pine shelves that lined the wall of the quaint stone shop. "I need to make a few more charms."

"Charms it is. Charms as always. Will these represent people or effects?"

"People this time. Some very unusual people."

The dwarf's bushy eyebrows came together over her large nose. "That sounds ominous. What do you need? I'll see if I have it."

Ember had pondered that question ever since she'd left Roybal Keep. She needed something that uniquely represented each person. For some, that meant finding rare elements—specifically demon parts for Jasmine and Ellessar. For Nick, a pellet of polished steel, representing the strength not only in the man's sword and armor, but also in his body. She walked over to a shelf with a variety of small pieces of pure metal—both precious and ordinary—and some alloyed materials. She selected a teardrop-shaped piece a little smaller than her thumb. For Zen, she chose a glass crystal roughly the same shape as the crystal in the tip of his staff, though less than a tenth its size. Ember already had a charm for her brother, a small piece of a shattered stone she'd picked up once upon a time from a granite quarry they used to play in as kids.

She handed the piece of steel to Elsee. "Can you put a small hole in the narrow end of this?" Ember also handed her the glass crystal. "And wrap this in silver wire, with a loop for a chain on one end."

"Of course. I can do both while you wait."

"No need. I'll drop by in the morning. I also need a piece of human sinew, about as long as my hand, if you have it. And a piece of elven bone, preferably male, also with a hole through one end."

The dwarf's brow furrowed. "Interesting selection. Shall I ask—"

"Do you have anything that comes from any kind of demon? A small bone, perhaps?"

The dwarf's scowl harbored both suspicion and concern. "No. I don't keep nothin' like that. Unusual people indeed!"

"You know I'm not up to mischief," Ember said. "One of my travelling companions is an elf, a demon hunter from the Order of the Shining Star. It's an order of the elf god Aeron. His profession and his god define him." She knew better than to mention Jasmine's peculiar heritage to anyone other than the DIG. Nick's party would have trouble enough without Ember needlessly alienating them from the people whose help they might need.

The dwarf became pensive and nodded. "Yep. Still ain't got nothin' like that."

"How about the elven bone?"

"Sure." Elsee reached beneath the marred wooden counter. After a soft clinking of glass jars, she held up a pale bit of bone. "Small finger bone work for you?"

"Perfect. I'll also need refills for all three ingredients of my catalyst powder." Ember dug three silver vials from the depths of her pack and handed them to Elsee.

"Of course, dear."

"Great." Ember paid for the items. "See you in the morning."

"They'll be ready."

That left Ember with the problem of coming up with some small bits of demon. She thought she might have to wait until they encountered one to acquire what she needed. Then she got an idea.

Zen woke to rapping on his door. When he and Nick weren't quick enough answering it, Borim hollered from out in the hall, "Ah, get yerselves out of bed. My uncle's waitin'." The pounding that followed would have split the wood on any door elsewhere in the Civilized Lands.

"Are you decent?" Ember asked, also from out in the hall.

"Sort of." Zen rolled out of his cot in his undergarments and pulled on his mage's robe. He'd need another one before they left Glintbroc. Though he'd washed his at Roybal Keep, wear from the Wild Lands had left it in need of replacement.

Nick had folded his blankets beneath him and slept on the stone floor. He dressed quickly and opened the door. By then, Ellessar and Jasmine had heard the ruckus and emerged from their rooms into the hall.

"Do you know a forger named Azurite StoneFist?" Nick asked Ember.

"Sure. He's our uncle."

"Is he the best?" Nick asked.

Borim puffed out his gut. "Of course he's the best."

Nick waited for Ember to reply.

"He is really good," she said. "He's renowned for his work, at least in Glintbroc."

"But not the best in the kingdom," Ellessar clarified.

Nick stepped away from the doorway and motioned them all inside. This wasn't exactly the kind of discussion to have in the hallway.

Ember stepped in last and closed the door behind her. "There are better forgers. But we'll have to go deeper into Gildstone to find them."

"Bah!" Borim waved his fat hand in dismissal. "What does an elf know about forgin'?"

"Time is of the essence," Jasmine reminded.

"It's the metal that's important. Not the skill of the smith." Zen glanced at Borim and Ember, realizing he might have said more than Nick had intended to reveal. "If Borim's uncle can forge a weapon for us, I don't see any reason to spend time we can't afford."

"I'm inclined to agree," Ellessar said.

"It's settled then." Nick grabbed his pack and slung it over his shoulders. "Everybody ready to go?"

Jasmine hesitated. "I was thinking. Given the welcome I received in the taproom downstairs, I should probably stay here."

"Nonsense," Nick said. "You're a part of this. You have been since the beginning."

"I don't want to be the cause of any trouble."

"Dwarves are a boisterous lot, it's true," Ember said, "especially when they're drunk. And any one alone is a force to be reckoned with. But inside the city, they're more bluster than anything else. Azurite's place is on the far side of Glintbroc, the side we call the 'in-kingdom' side. It's a more mellow part of town. You should be okay."

Borim hefted his mace and brandished the business end in the air. "Anyone says anything, they'll have to answer to ShatterBrand."

Nick and his friends followed Borim and Ember into the bowels of the mountain, Ellessar walking Spirit. The bustle of Glintbroc's commercial sector gave way to the slums of the inner mountain, too far from either side to benefit from the mineral trade. Only a few mule-driven carts, which squealed on metal rails that ran the length of the tunnel, broke the monotonous shadows of the lamp-lit ghetto.

Dark tunnels, carved from rock, opened into the rough stone walls of the dwarven road like sirens promising passage to the heart of the Abyss itself.

At one point, a handful of dwarven children, wearing nothing but rags, ran from one of the dark alleys. They darted across the main passage without a word. One of the younger kids led something—a ferret maybe—on a string, the animal hopping to keep up. The lot of them disappeared down another alley. By the time Nick and the others reached the passage, the children had disappeared into the darkness. Up to no good, Nick decided.

The smell of the whole warren was gut-wrenching. Still, Borim pressed on.

"Nice place," Zen commented. "No wonder you don't let outsiders past the city proper."

"This is the city proper," Borim grumbled. "The life and health of Gildstone breathes from the people who live right here, and in places like it."

Zen curled his nose at the stench of sewage that fouled the air. "Health? From a place like this?"

Borim spun and shoved the mage into the wall. The dwarf slipped his mace from his belt.

"Easy, brother," Ember warned.

Borim reached up and pressed his thick, callused hand against Zen's chest. "You may not fancy the way they live, but these people—" He waved his mace at the nearby passages— "are the most important people in Gildstone."

Zen's face held more amusement than alarm. "So you said."

"More important than the traders," Borim continued. "Or the shepherds, miners, or forgers. More important than the Knights of SteelStone. More important than the scholars. Even more important than the governing council."

"Why do they live here?" Ellessar asked.

"These are the builders. They carved this whole city, and every city like it, from the heart of the earth. Without them, we'd have no place to live. And the work of the builders reveals the veins of precious metals and stones upon which we build our economy."

"Why do they live here?" Ellessar repeated.

"It takes thousands to build even a small neighborhood," Ember said. "The builders represent the bulk of the dwarven people. And their work is unskilled. Most of them just dig—"

Borim rounded on Ellessar. "Their work is *unappreciated*. That's what it is."

"Not many generations ago," Ember continued, "Borim's family was among the builders of Devil's Forge, a city along the southern coast." She shrugged. "As a people, dwarves remember their roots and honor their ancestors. Don't cross them on that score."

A scream split the air from one of the many connecting passages, a hoarse female cry too deep to be human, too shrill to have come from a mature dwarven matron. Another followed, an echo or a second victim—it was impossible to tell which.

Nick drew his great sword. "Where did that come from?"

The companions glanced at several of the openings and then at one another.

"We don't have time for side treks," Jasmine said.

Borim bolted down the main corridor.

"She's right," Ellessar called after him. "Already the demon's mass—"

"Piss on the demons. Something's killin' my people." Borim vanished down one of the dark, nameless tunnels.

Ember cocked an eyebrow and followed.

"How does he—" Ellessar began.

"He knows." Ember spoke an elven word and ran after Borim. Before she took three steps, her body became translucent, and she faded from sight.

"Neat trick." Nick hurried after, before he lost track of which passage had swallowed their guides. Without Borim or Ember, they had no means but the two pairs of odd metal rails that ran along the main corridor to find their way out of the tunnels. And the rails might lead them into some dead-end mine.

Another scream, ending with a strangled croak.

Jasmine lit a torch and sprinted past Nick. Just as Nick rounded the corner, Jasmine and Borim reached the next intersection—a dark juncture of two back alleys, the cross-passage cut down the middle by a river of dwarven waste.

Jasmine's gaze swept the connecting passage. "Spider!" She tossed her torch to the floor next to the sewage ditch and launched herself down the alley.

"Mimic spider," Borim echoed beside her in his disdainful rumble. "They use dwarf-like screams to lure the likes of you and me into ambush."

Nick rounded the second corner to face the crimson beast, its abdomen as large as the dwarf's. The spider spanned the corridor, including the waste ditch. It grabbed at Jasmine with its two front legs. She fended them off.

Nick leapt to the far side of the ditch to peer beyond the others. The screams of the dying sounded no more. If there were bodies, he couldn't see them.

From above, cold arms as hard as stone clamped around him. The claws of this second spider enfolded Nick's arms and legs, pinned his sword to his side, and tried to drag him to the ground.

Borim too leapt the ditch. "ShatterBrand!" His mace struck with a sickening crack. The spider shuddered as it cried a nearly human wail—the sound they'd thought was a dwarven scream.

Claws tightened around the armor on Nick's legs. He threw his weight back and slammed the spider into the wall.

Borim disappeared beneath a third spider. His mace thumped to the stone. Ellessar charged the creature. His sword severed one of its arms as it held the dwarf down. Zen hung back, pausing halfway down the alley from which they'd come.

Nick grabbed the arms of his own spider, now weakened from its wound, and heaved it over his shoulder to the floor. It hopped to its legs and skittered halfway up Nick's body, fang-like jaws gnashing at the air before his face.

Beside him, Jasmine gripped the jagged mouth of the first spider and fought to pin the beast. Her knee whipped up and shattered its jaw, and it slumped to the ground. Knocked away by the scuffle, the torch rolled toward the ditch, threatening to douse their single, flickering light.

The spiders were too fast, and too many. Three more, larger than the others, dropped from the shadowed ceiling. The newcomers, white as bone, ripped into their smaller kin. Screams like those that had lured Borim into the darkness poured from the dying mouths of the mimic spiders.

Only when the frozen arm of a newcomer brushed Nick's hand did he realize they were made of ice, creatures formed by Zen. Within moments, the mimic spiders sprawled lifeless on the stone floor. The ice spiders swept the adjoining passages for more of the foul vermin.

Borim kicked one of the spider carcasses into the waste ditch, and it floated away. "That be right timin', mage."

Zen returned a wide grin. "Never fight a battle yourself when you can call others to fight it for you."

"True." Ember appeared suddenly beside Borim. "You okay, brother?"

Borim swept up his mace and grumbled all the way back to the main passage.

Ellessar sheathed his sword and smoothed his demon-skin coat. "Everybody okay?" He waited for a nod from both Nick and Jasmine before adding, "Then I guess we're on our way."

"Shouldn't we search for the nest?" Nick asked.

Ember shook her head. "You won't find it. Mimic spiders never hunt in the tunnels where they live. It makes them harder to exterminate." She collected the torch and raised it toward the ceiling. Not a thread of web could be seen. "But these will hunt our people no more. Come. We're hours yet from the southern square."

The south end of Glintbroc didn't resemble the northern trade district at all. The dwarves had built this side solely for themselves. It wasn't dark and dingy like the cavern on the north side. Here the main trading market, the town square, filled a deep alcove cut into the mountain. The entire southwestern end remained open to the afternoon sun, which at that moment lit the sky with the amber glow of sunset. This truly was Glintbroc, the dwarven City of Gold.

"We need to stay someplace cheap," Nick told the others. Having spent most of their remaining coin to resupply at Roybal Keep, they had little left to spend on accommodations. He looked pointedly at Zen. "Unless one of you has some coin I don't know about."

Zen held up both hands defensively. "Not me."

Jasmine shook her head.

"I have some," Ellessar said, "if we need it. But I'm hoping to replace my second sword at our earliest opportunity."

"No problem," Ember said. "This one's on me."

Borim frowned but said nothing.

"This way." She led them to an inn called The Hog's Leg. "Like everything else on this end of the city, the rooms are sized for a dwarf, but it's clean and not too expensive." She booked three rooms for the six of them while Borim arranged lodging for Spirit.

"Nick and I, then," Zen announced.

"This should be interesting," Borim muttered, when he returned and learned that he would be sharing a room with Ellessar.

The room did prove to be clean. The nearly square cots were just long enough for Zen to sleep diagonally but too short for Nick's tall frame. He tried to get comfortable with his calves and feet hanging off the end. Finally, with a sigh, he upended his cot against the wall and spread his blanket on the stone floor.

The next morning, after a quick, uneventful breakfast of scrambled eggs and a strip of fried pork fat, the companions headed out to visit Borim's uncle. Their short walk was well lit by a series of evenly spaced, clean-burning lanterns built into the walls of the tunnel. Each lamp appeared to have a large reservoir of oil drilled into the rock beneath it. They found the forger's workshop amid a row of tradesmen that ran the gamut from leatherworking to weaving, stone tile work, barrel making, and a brewery. All the while, Borim went on and on about the skill of his uncle, with whom he had apparently apprenticed for a couple of decades.

Nothing more than a low iron rail, waist high to a dwarf, with a matching iron gate at one end, separated the forge from the foyer. Azurite sat at a stout wooden desk, which seemed to serve as his business office, in the back corner of the combined space. One young apprentice swept the floor while another polished a rackful of tools.

As Nick and the others rounded the corner into the alcove, Azurite rose and marched forward. His beard hung down to his belly in two black braids, each tied off with a leather band ornamented with a large blue stone. He swung the gate wide and approached Borim with his calloused hand extended. "How are ya, boy?"

Borim took his uncle's hand and muttered, "Not so much a boy anymore."

"Good to see you, uncle." Ember gave the big dwarf a hug. "I'm afraid this isn't a social call." She gestured to Nick. "We have a job for you."

"Well, that's good news if I ever heard it." Azurite hiked up his belt and puffed out his stomach like a man might his chest. "What can I do for ya?"

Nick set down his pack and dug out the stone they'd exhumed from the behemoth's lake. He freed it from the cloth sack he'd wrapped it in and handed it to Azurite.

"Great vein of lead, it's heavy." The dwarf frowned as he ran his hands over the stone's surface. "And warm. Where did you get it?"

"In the Wild Lands," Nick said.

Azurite humphed and returned his attention to the stone. "It has an earth magic in it. I'll give you that."

"Can you work it?" Ellessar asked.

Azurite considered the stone for a long moment, turning it over in his hands. "Sure, but first I must separate the metal from the stone. In the meantime—" he addressed Borim once more— "take your friend here to the Healers' Guild. He looks unwell, even for a human."

Nick accepted the racial jab with nothing more than a slight twist of one corner of his mouth. Azurite was right about one thing: Nick was certainly unwell. Despite Zen's earlier assurances that the illness would pass, Nick's skin seemed an odd color in the light of the forger's lamps. He'd apparently picked up something from the Wild Lands that even Ellessar had been unable to cure.

CHAPTER 12

An hour later, a dwarven healer shoved a polished steel mirror into Nick's hand and thrust a stubby finger toward his face. "How long has that been going on?"

Nick's reflection showed mottled pink lesions on his neck, as though he'd peered too closely into the coals of a fire and the heat had chapped his flesh. "I have no idea." Nick turned his head from side to side. The rash extended down beneath his shirt collar.

"Any other symptoms?" the dwarf asked.

"Did you get bit by that mimic spider?" Zen said.

Nick shook his head. "I haven't felt well since we left the Wild Lands."

"You've been in the Wild Lands?" The healer's eyes shone with both respect and concern. "There's ailments there I ain't never seen, to be sure."

Ellessar stepped in for a closer look. "That wasn't there a few days ago. Your condition is getting worse."

"Could you have been cursed by the fairy guarding the summit of Roybal Pass?" Zen asked.

Nick scratched under his chin absently. Now that he was aware of it, the rash itched. "If she was going to do something like this, she'd have targeted Jasmine."

"What about the woman at the keep?" Ember said.

"Sierra?" Nick considered that a distinct possibility: either Sierra or the mage among her mercenaries.

Zen gestured in the air and then scrutinized Nick's skin. "I detect no enchantments."

"Hey!" The dwarf thrust his beard at the lot of them. "Who's the healer here?" He spoke to Nick at a more civil volume. "You said you ain't felt well. What have you felt?"

"Ill." Nick thought about the odd, subtle sensations he'd experienced since Roybal Keep and how he might describe them. "Queasy, maybe. Warm and cold flashes. Weaker than usual, but only sometimes, like reduced stamina. I thought it was just fatigue."

The dwarf climbed a stool to feel Nick's forehead, then frowned.

"What?"

"Bah! Who knows? Never can tell with humans. No constitution. Bodies always changin'." He climbed down, rummaged through a heavy oak bureau, and pulled out a small earthenware jar. "If it's a seasonal fever, it'll pass. In the meantime, this will help with the itchin'."

"It didn't itch until I got here." Nick took the jar and dug out the hardened wax stopper. The stench of the salve burned the hairs in his nostrils. "By the Goblin Isle, what is it?"

"A mix of hemp, talc, and aloe."

Nick dipped a finger into the goop and dabbed a bit on his neck, as far from his nose as possible. "There's something else in this. Something that stinks."

Borim leaned forward, took a deep whiff of the stuff, and grunted. "I don't smell nothin'." He winked at the healer.

"Five silver coins for the salve," the healer said. "The examination is free."

Nick and the others returned to Azurite's forge the next day, and the day that followed.

It took the forger the better part of both days just to separate the metal from the stone. "That metal, whatever it is, melts at too high a temperature." Azurite handed the irregular lump of separated metal to Nick. It had grown even warmer to the touch than the raw ore had been.

"Did you do something to heat it?" Nick asked.

"Nope. That's a new metal, to my knowin'. Warm all by itself. Never seen the likes of it."

"That's encouraging," Jasmine said.

"Problem is," Azurite continued, "it'll take the fire of the earth to work it. You'll have to go to Brimstone. It's the only place you'll find a forge hot enough. Even then..." He shrugged. "Wish I could do more."

"Great." Nick turned to Borim. "How long will that take?"

"Patience, Nick," Ellessar said. "It's the will of Aeron."

"Delay is the will of Aeron?" Nick asked.

"Apparently."

Borim grunted. "Your gods never did make no sense."

"Delay is the refuge of the undecided," Jasmine said. "It's not delay that's been set before us, but a path forward."

Nick humphed. He stuffed the smelted slug into the bottom of his backpack and followed Ember out.

As they reached the main square, a mule train emerged from a large, smoothed-stone tunnel that penetrated deeper into the mountain, pulling a steel cart filled with rich copper ore. The wheels squealed past on the metal rails that crisscrossed the floor of the market. Ellessar collected Spirit from the livery, and Borim led them out the yawning maw of Glintbroc's southern plaza.

The rest of the day, they picked their way down the steep, zigzagging trail to rugged hill country dotted with stone hovels and herds of stout mountain goats. In a small grassy glade near the base of the Glintbroc cliffs, they set out their blankets and made camp.

***

The watch was diligent but outward-facing. Once the fire burned down to nothing more than a few dim coals and the moon was yet but a sliver, the camp grew dark. Ember whispered an elfish command word to invoke her invisibility. She slipped from her blankets and padded in her soft boots to Ellessar. His sword belt lay beside him, easily accessible.

She listened to the elf's breathing for several seconds. It was deep, slow, and rhythmic. Carefully, Ember lifted Ellessar's demon-claw rapier and tugged it from its scabbard. The sheath wasn't made for this particular blade, which was shorter and thicker than a standard sword and slightly curved. The claw fit snugly, but it lacked the ringing sound a metal blade might make when drawn. She examined the end with her keen elven sight. With her knife, she trimmed a piece about three-quarters of an inch long off the end and whittled the tip to a point similar to that of the original claw before returning it to its scabbard.

Next, she needed a piece of scrap demon hide. She eyed Ellessar's pack, where he supposedly kept his supply of leftover demon skins. The scraps were likely at the bottom, difficult to access without making enough noise to wake the elf, if not the entire camp.

Instead, she crept to Jasmine's bundle. The monk had shown Ember a couple of strips, each a few feet in length, that she kept in a pouch, easy to retrieve if another Assassin demon invaded their camp. The pouch sat next to the few items from Jasmine's travelling bundle, now lying loose without the blanket in which she wrapped everything during the day.

Ember sliced a two-inch length from the end of the longer strip and returned to her bed. There, she used the scant moonlight to wrap the piece of demon claw in a cord of human sinew, completely concealing the original piece of claw. The resulting object was half human and half demon, a perfect charm to represent Jasmine.

Ellessar's was simpler. Ember wrapped the demon hide around the elven finger bone Elsee BroadStock had sold her, and secured it with simple string—an elf in a demon-hide coat.

Satisfied with her new charms, she added them to the tear-shaped steel pellet that represented Nick, Zen's ice-like crystal charm, and the chunk of shattered granite she used for Borim. When they all hung from the silver chain she wore around her neck, she tucked them beneath her white blouse, dropped her invisibility, and went to sleep.

Nick didn't let the party sleep for long. The threat of demons unleashed into the Civilized Lands drove him to wake the party when the sky began to lighten.

As the others packed up the meager camp, Borim scanned the cliffs behind them. Nick followed his gaze. The recess of Glintbroc formed an open maw in the side of the mountain. Around it, dotting the cliff face like freckles, sat hundreds of dwellings with spacious balconies, homes of the rich mining barons, the guild masters, and the most successful of the merchant class, their homes built to take advantage of the mountain view. Borim didn't seem to notice the city at all, however. His gaze swept the lofty peaks above and in the nearby mountains.

Nick tightened the waist strap of his backpack and strode up beside the dwarf. "What are you looking for?" He saw nothing in those heights but snowcaps a thousand feet above timberline.

Borim nodded, apparently satisfied with the results of his search.

Jasmine joined them. "Something wrong?"

Borim didn't answer. Instead, he grumbled a dwarven oath and started down the trail. Nick turned to Ember for an answer, but she just shrugged. Whatever Borim had been looking for, apparently it wasn't of great concern at the moment.

By midmorning, they dropped out of the hills onto the Sunburst Plain, a vast prairie of the greenest grass and an abundance of wildflowers, as far as the eye could see. "The beauty of your kingdom rivals that of Lorentil," Ellessar noted.

Borim grunted and said nothing.

"In its way," Ember conceded. "Lorentil has much to offer as well."

"It's not as open." Nick scratched at an itch on his wrist where the cuff of his armor chafed. "I thought the dwarves lived in mountains."

"Most do. But we have a thriving livestock trade, too. All of our food, plant or animal, is grown or raised in this valley. It spans for more than a week to the southwest. We'll cross to Tinderstone. Until then our journey should be safe and peaceful."

"What do you mean, 'until then'?" Nick's itch began to burn as he scratched, so he stopped.

Again, Borim and Ember chose not to answer.

The road was wide and flat, with two pairs of metal rails frequented by mule-drawn mining carts heaped with stone, ore, feed, or handcrafted wares. It cut through the plains with arrow-straight precision. Herds of an odd form of dwarven cattle, each the size of a sheep with the stocky legs of a pig, horns of a bull, and snout of an aardvark, ambled in the meadows. "Bullhogs," Borim called them.

Ranch homes made from stone, like those in the hill country, dotted the fields. Everywhere, the dwarves they encountered greeted them in friendly tones. Peace seemed to emanate from the very landscape.

After three days, the companions crossed a stone bridge that spanned a sluggish, mile-wide river into the port community of Salt Rock, which boasted one of only two genuine forests in Gildstone. The woods cut a dark-green swath out of the grassland for tens of miles, maybe hundreds of miles, along the river.

Three more days passed. The countryside became a balm for their spirits. The group crossed a second bridge over a narrower river in a similar forest. Beyond this second bridge, the road climbed gradually into the hills that skirted yet another mountain range.

Before long, Borim became agitated. He constantly scanned the sky. At one point he stopped, without seeming to be aware that he'd done so, and fixed his gaze on a dark form soaring near the clouds.

"What is it?" Nick asked.

Borim startled. "What?"

"That." Nick pointed. "In the sky."

"It's not a bird like any I ever saw." Ellessar said. "It looks more like a griffin or hippogriff."

"Ain't none of those in Gildstone," Borim muttered.

"What then?" Nick said.

"Couldn't tell you."

"Couldn't, or won't?" Ellessar pressed.

Jasmine stepped up beside Ember. "Travel seems to be safer here than in Lorentil. You've been there, have you not? You've seen the magical creatures that infest their woods and threaten the unwary?"

"Yes, of course. I spent years in the diplomatic service there. The dwarves thought my unusual combination of elven ancestry and dwarven upbringing might help them make inroads in diplomacy that have remained unsought for centuries."

"I understand that the elves tolerate the creatures in their woods to provide protection for their cities. I guess with your mountain borders, you have no need for such measures here." The wave of Jasmine's hand spanned the countryside. "It's all so peaceful."

"Oh, Gildstone has its share of nasty beasts." Ember inclined her chin toward the creature in the sky. "But they're not tolerated here.

They survive because they live so deep or so high into the mountains that even the dwarves can't reach them."

Zen let out a slow whistle. "I didn't know there were places a dwarf couldn't go."

"In these mountains, there are many."

For the next day, Borim watched the sky with diligence. Then he turned the party south and the road began to wind its way up the steep slopes of a mountain.

The creatures continued to circle in the air.

By late afternoon, Nick could take no more. He stopped in front of Borim. "Tell me what's happening."

The others gathered around.

Borim worked his mouthful of molasses chews for a long time before he finally swallowed. "Okay, human. You see those birds flying overhead."

"They're not birds." Nick didn't need to look. There were four of them, and they'd been up there, off and on, for the better part of the day.

"Darned straight they're not. And they ain't friendly neither."

"What are they?" Ellessar asked.

"Trouble." Borim thrust his beard at the mountain range before them. "They usually stay in the mountains. I seen 'em fly over the plains before, but never in force. And they don't stick around unless they see somethin' they want. They've been followin' our movements."

Ellessar watched them circle for a moment before turning again to the dwarf. "What will they do?"

"Nothin'. We're too close to Tinderstone. They won't bother us here. But I doubt we can slip out of the city and make it all the way to Brimstone. The road is more treacherous there. There'll be trouble then. Mark my words."

With Tinderstone still about three hours away, one of the creatures alighted on a hilltop near the road about a hundred feet in front of the party. Zen could see it clearly, its leonine body as large as a horse. As it landed, it tucked its giant wings next to its sides. Two short horns on its forehead had been scraped to a fine point.

Borim stopped next to Ellessar. "Guess I was wrong."

Zen came alongside them. "You planning to tell us what they are, now?"

Another of the creatures crested the rise at the top of a short ridge to the party's left. Three more circled a hundred yards above the road.

"Mountain sphinx," Borim said. "They're not evil, but they're intelligent, opportunistic, uncompromising, and territorial."

Nick, Jasmine, and Ember formed up so they all stood in a line across the broad dwarven road.

"Are we on their land?" Ellessar asked.

"Not here. They must want somethin'. Few non-dwarven folk travel this road. Maybe they suspect riches in your packs."

Zen almost laughed out loud. A shortage of coin had been one of their primary problems ever since they'd left Cedar Falls those many months before.

"I'll give up my few coins for safe passage," Ellessar said.

"A few coins ain't gonna do it." Borim nudged Zen with the butt of his mace. "You're a mage. They might respect that. Why don't you negotiate?"

Negotiate? Zen knew only one kind of negotiation. He stepped forward a few feet and shouted in the trade tongue, "Let us pass in peace! We're not on your land and we have business in Tinderstone."

The first sphinx to land, apparently their leader, spoke. "You have business with us first."

"Very well." It was time to negotiate. "Here's my proposal: stand aside or die."

Borim's gaze snapped to Zen. "I said negotiate, not threaten. You know why they call a group of sphinx a 'pride,' don't ya? They're not gonna let that one go."

Zen ignored him. He couldn't back down now. "You have ten seconds to decide."

Another sphinx topped a grass-covered rise to the left, next to the other standing there. Zen counted six total. The odds, at least, were even. One of the three in the air swooped down onto a rock outcropping to the right. The other two sphinxes glided lower.

That's it. Zen's hands flashed in the air. *Come closer. Watch your leader die.* Zen wove an enchantment that should have frozen the lead sphinx's skull from the inside out.

The sphinx shook its head as though dusting snow from its mane. "You'll need better tricks than that, mageling."

"What did you just do?" Borim muttered through his clenched teeth. "You call this negotiating?"

Two more sphinxes flew in from a perch high on a cliff behind their leader—now eight total. One landed next to the leader. She didn't have a mane. Probably the leader's mate. The other swept toward the party. The two that circled in the air banked into a dive toward the row of companions.

Ellessar yanked his blanket off the Shield of Faith and threaded his left arm through the Shield's straps. "Here we go." His rune-inscribed sword cleared its sheath.

Zen ripped strands of weave from the ether and formed a ball of ice and slush in his hands, the largest and most powerful such construction he'd ever made, and launched it at the leader and the sphinx beside him.

It exploded into a wave of ice and frozen air many times colder than the worst Trondorian blizzard. None should have survived the blast. Yet when it cleared, the sphinxes stood, crusted in frost, bleeding from the impact of myriad splinters of ice but alive. The tree beside them had been stripped bare of its leaves, half of its bark, and a good portion of its smaller branches.

The two diving sphinxes slammed into the companions.

CHAPTER 13

Although threats and violence sometimes solve problems, they never serve as an effective means of negotiation.

With the threat made, however, the companions' position would only be weakened if Jasmine suggested another course, so she plucked her *sai* from her belt and counted off the seconds in her mind.

Zen waited almost eight of the ten seconds he'd promised the sphinxes before he began weaving. At that point, it came down to who would survive. There must have been a better way, if only she'd had time to think of it.

Nick drew his great sword and stepped forward to challenge the two sphinxes who were diving at the party. Zen squared himself to face the one flying at them over the head of the sphinx leader. Borim stood near his sister, who had her eyes closed, one hand on her brother's shoulder. By degrees, Borim's skin took on the hue and roughness of stone until he seemed to be made of granite.

"Now—" Borim glanced at Zen— "since you've seen fit to start it, let's bust some heads."

Both sphinxes on the ridge to their left launched themselves, wings spread in a graceful, lofting lunge, toward Zen and Ellessar. Ellessar, mounted on Spirit, whispered a prayer to Aeron.

Ember motioned Jasmine toward her. These creatures were beyond Jasmine's strength, and she had but one *sai* to fight with. If Ember wanted to give her a coating of the mystical armor she'd given Borim, Jasmine wouldn't turn it down. Two steps brought her to Ember's side.

With one hand still on her brother, the elf girl reached out to Jasmine. "Give me your hand." She neither waited for an answer nor provided Jasmine with armor. As soon as Ember touched her, Jasmine's world vanished in a brilliant flash of black, darker than the catacombs beneath the city of Trondor. For a moment, it seemed the magic must have gone afoul, but then she appeared with the dwarf and elf on the hill, right behind the sphinx leader.

The sphinx beside the leader spun on Ember, who ducked the horns of the beast. Its claws ripped her back and shoulder, soaking her torn blouse with blood and throwing her to the ground. The sphinx gathered its legs to pounce.

"ShatterBrand!" Borim screamed. The arc of his mace swung wide.

A sphinx from the sky veered away from a dive toward Nick and plummeted at the dwarf. It slammed into him with the force of a battering ram. Borim's stone-like skin shattered the sphinx's horns, but the impact left him flat on his back and out of breath.

The lead sphinx advanced on Jasmine, his hide lacerated and his fur encrusted with frost. His tail flicked in the air.

"Wait!" Ember held up a blood-slicked hand. "I have coin. Three hundred gold for safe passage."

The three sphinxes on the hill hesitated.

The leader turned to Ember. "Not enough. Give us everything

you have, and we'll let you live."

"Deal." Ember struggled out from under the sphinx. She worked her pack off her shoulders and dropped it, along with her dwarven-made sword.

"What of you?" the leader asked Borim. "Will you sell your belongings for your life?"

"Do it," Ember told him. "They're too strong and too many."

Grumbling, Borim dropped his burden of supplies and, reluctantly, his mace.

"You two may go." The leader licked his bleeding chops and stalked toward Jasmine.

"I have nothing," she said. "A few changes of clothes. That's all."

"Too bad for you. We'll take your life then."

Before Jasmine could reply, Ember touched her arm and the world went black once more.

Zen had crammed every thread of power he could harness into the ball of ice and slush he'd hurled at the sphinx leader and his mate. Even that wasn't enough. And of the sphinxes present, only those two were wounded.

Zen went again into the weave as a sphinx plunged toward him. He didn't raise his staff to attack, or even look up at the creature, focusing instead on his own magic. His only concession was to duck his head just as the sphinx slammed into him.

Claws ripped his shoulder and chest. The weight of the beast shoved him to the ground. Zen completed the weave just as he hit. A portal opened beneath them, and he alone was small enough to fall through the opening. A chute bore him through the pseudo-plane of ice to a small, gnarled tree that gripped the side of a scree-covered slope a quarter mile back along the trail.

Ignoring the searing pain of his wounds, Zen levered himself to his knees and threw himself back into the weave.

The surprise Ember had hoped to gain by appearing suddenly behind the sphinx leader with Borim and Jasmine had turned upon her with a swiftness she could never have imagined. She grabbed Jasmine and Borim by their arms and whisked them to a small depression about eighty yards to their left. But if it wasn't too late to save their friends, the cost she'd paid was worth it; it was only gear.

She considered the battlefield. Zen had disappeared—translocated somewhere. Nick and Ellessar were in trouble. If they'd been close enough to one another, she could have just popped in, invisible, and yanked them both out. As it was, she'd have to translocate them one at a time.

"I can get them out," Ember told Jasmine, inclining her head toward their embattled companions, "if you watch my back."

"Of course."

"I'm going with you," Borim insisted.

Ember dismissed him. She couldn't take them both and still translocate the others. She didn't even want to take Jasmine, but any attempt to enter the fray alone and unarmed would constitute suicide.

"I need you to protect the wounded when I get them back here." She turned herself invisible with a single spoken word, then placed her hands on Jasmine's shoulders.

Two sphinxes came down on Ellessar from the left. The first slammed against the Shield of Faith, landing so heavily that

Spirit lost her footing. She skittered to the side while the Shield deflected the sphinx's teeth and claws. The second sphinx alighted on the ground near them. Zen's enraged attacker, no more than thirty feet away, also spun on Ellessar.

Three sphinxes were too many. They were too fast for Ellessar to try to flee, and they had Spirit surrounded. But Ellessar had something they didn't: his god.

Almost of its own volition, the Shield of Faith kept one of the sphinxes at bay. Ellessar did his best to engage the others with his sword, but their claws, teeth, and horns took their toll. Even his demon-skin coat and the leather armor beneath it provided only meager protection.

The sphinx leader called for parlay.

Spirit was soaked with elven blood and Ellessar could barely sit in his saddle. He'd lost track of all of his friends. His sword hung so heavily on the end of his tattered arm that he could scarcely hold it. His face felt sticky with the spray from rent after rent in his enemies' hides, but the wounds he'd inflicted didn't seem nearly enough.

The sphinxes paused, and the leader asked, "Ready to bargain for your life, elf?"

Ellessar nodded weakly. He could no longer hold his head up. The Shield strapped to his arm protected his side only by divine providence. He couldn't afford to move it. He needed his shield hand to hold his stomach together. *My Lord Aeron, is this your will for me? Am I to die here, this day, on this road, with my errand unfinished? If you would have me continue, tell me what I must do.*

As one, the three sphinxes around him looked toward the sky. Five ice hippogriffs were flying in from the north. One of the sphinxes took wing to intercept, joined by the sphinx leader, his mate, and one other.

Thank you, Aeron.

Jasmine appeared from the ether, uninjured. The demon-kin seemed an unlikely beacon of Aeron's guidance. Nevertheless, she beckoned Ellessar.

With a nudge of his knees, he backed Spirit though the opening left by the departed sphinx. While the other two remained distracted by the sudden appearance of the hippogriffs, Spirit spun on her hindquarters and sprinted to Jasmine's side.

Ember is here too," she said. "We're going to get you out."

"In a minute." Ellessar's voice was almost inaudible, even to himself. He slid off Spirit and dropped to his knees. *Aeron, forgive my interruption. I know that with the opening of the Portal you have urgencies that far surpass my own...* "Arrggh!"

His prayer remained unfinished but not unanswered. The flesh of his stomach knitted itself together with pain worse than that of the original wounds.

Ellessar never questioned the price he paid for Aeron's gifts.

The sky darkened above him and the world filled with a rush of roars, shrieks, and a flutter like a thousand battle flags flapping in the wind. Hail and blood rained down as the sphinxes flew through one of Zen's hailstorms to engage the hippogriffs.

When Ellessar's pain passed, he climbed to his feet. Above him, four of the sphinxes now battled six of the hippogriffs. More of the ice creatures continued to appear. Wings beat air down upon Ellessar like a spring gale drawn straight from the heavens. A pair of the hippogriffs took down the wounded enemy leader, but the sphinxes were larger and stronger. Zen's hippogriffs began to falter. Two plummeted from the sky.

Nick was fully engaged with the sphinx from the rock outcropping. Three long, deep cuts bled along its chest and shoulder, and it favored one of its front legs. It looked like Nick might take the sphinx down until the one with shattered horns rushed him. Nick staggered backward, covered in blood, much of it his own.

Beside him, Jasmine's skin darkened. A scabrous growth coated her and hardened—not into rock as Borim's skin had, but into a carapace. It was armor that seemed to come from within, from the essence of the wearer. By the time Ember finished, Jasmine's skin had become a hard, rusty-hued shell.

"Go." Ember's spoke, unseen, beside her.

Jasmine launched herself between Nick and the rushing enemy.

Three more hippogriffs fell from the sky. And another sphinx.

Ellessar, Jasmine—and, Nick assumed, Ember—rallied around him, forming a defensive knot against the three sphinxes that yet surrounded them. The sphinx Nick had wounded hung back. Two more hippogriffs went down.

An ice griffin, twice the size of the hippogriffs, soared into the battle.

Ellessar laid his hands on Nick and spoke a healing prayer. Aeron responded immediately.

The sphinx leader's mate freed herself from the battle above them. She swooped down to attack the cluster of companions. Jasmine spun to engage.

Another bloody sphinx dove at them. Yards above the ground, Zen's ice griffin slammed into it with a wild screech. Its weight bore the sphinx to the ground. Bone crunched on impact. The griffin's sharp beak ripped into the leonine neck of the already dead sphinx.

Nick and Ellessar cut down another.

Two sphinxes leapt from the ground and converged on the griffin.

As Ember moved to extract Ellessar, a sphinx landed between her and the demon hunter. She was still invisible and it didn't seem to realize she was there, but with no weapon to attack it, she could only stand back and let Ellessar engage.

A smile crept onto Ember's face as her brother barreled down the hill, roaring a stream of dwarven profanities that would have made even their grandmother blush.

By then the battle seemed to have turned. A few of the ice hippogriffs remained in the sky. The sheer quantity that Zen had called surpassed the DIG's understanding of his power. Ember would have to report it at her earliest opportunity.

The ice griffin launched itself at the sphinx leader's mate, who already bled from several puncture wounds inflicted by Jasmine's *sai*. The sphinx went down under the griffin's weight, never to rise again.

The remaining sphinxes leapt into the air and fled. After a moment, the griffin wavered, and then transformed into Zen himself. Ember dropped her invisibility.

Borim marched up to Zen, still puffing from his run. "What in the lava-veined depths of Mount Stonehaven do you call that? 'Negotiating'?"

Zen met his glare evenly. "We couldn't afford to negotiate."

Borim sputtered for a moment, apparently unable to find a reply that would satisfy his rage. Finally, he spat a dwarven oath.

"If they had been stronger than us," Zen continued, "they wouldn't have settled for anything less than everything we owned, and we have things we can't afford to give up."

"They weren't stronger," Borim said.

Zen shrugged. "Then there was no need to negotiate."

CHAPTER 14

Nick shook his head at the senseless death that surrounded him. The sphinxes may have had animal bodies, but they were sentient, intelligent beings. "Greed motivates so much evil."

"I fear that none of us have yet seen true evil," Ellessar said.

"We gotta hurry. The ones that fled may bring reinforcements." Borim lopped the tuft off the end of one of the sphinxes' tails with a knife he kept at his belt, and which he used for everything from digging a fire pit to picking his rotten teeth. "Take the tail tufts from the dead. They're worth bounty."

Nick and Borim made quick work of collecting the tufts. Ellessar spoke a healing prayer over Ember's wounds, which produced a fortnight's worth of healing in a matter of minutes. Jasmine and Zen retrieved Borim's and Ember's packs and weapons from the hill where the sphinx leader had left them. By the time they were ready to move out, Borim's and Jasmine's magically armored skin had returned to normal and the ice hippogriffs had vanished.

It took them only three hours to reach the gates of Tinderstone. Even with all of the healing that Ellessar could administer, the group limped into the tunnels of the city as a battered assortment of shredded armor and beaten bodies. Leaking wounds, not nearly half healed, marked everyone except Jasmine and Borim. Blood dotted or soaked all of their skin, clothing, and equipment.

Just inside the gate, they split up. Borim sought the barracks of the Knights of SteelStone to collect the bounty on the sphinxes and to find a stable for Spirit.

Everyone else went to the healer, who dispensed a variety of herbs and more foul-smelling paste into the cuts of the wounded. "To kill the rot before it turns your blood bad," the healer said.

Nick had no doubt that the stuff would kill anything in the wound; the smell alone was enough to stagger a dwarf.

"Make you right in no time," the healer insisted.

Four days later, the companions walked through the gates of Brimstone. Inside, the stifling air of the cavern provided a stark contrast to the cool depths of Glintbroc and Tinderstone.

With the help of Ellessar's prayers, Jasmine's herbs, and the dwarven salve, the party's wounds had largely healed. Nick's rash had neither improved nor gotten worse. Nonetheless, his overall health had declined. He suffered from aches and exhaustion well beyond those caused by the battle with the sphinxes.

Ember booked rooms for them at the Toasted Critter.

"Is that the inn's name," Nick asked, "or the menu?"

"It'll do," Ellessar assured her.

He and Jasmine took Nick into a room for prayer and rest. Borim put Spirit up at the livery and then wasted no time in tracking down the city's master forger, by all accounts an eccentric old coot named Brewster AxSwipe. Borim scheduled a meeting for the following morning.

"The question is," Jasmine asked when they had all gathered back at the inn later that evening, "what exactly do we want this forger to make?"

"Good question." Nick tugged the slug from his backpack and handed it to Borim. "You apprenticed with Azurite. Based on the size of the ingot, can you tell us what our options are?"

Borim hefted it experimentally, then examined it from all sides. "Not enough to make a great sword or battle axe. Maybe a scimitar, or a little more."

"Quarterstaff?" Zen asked with a smirk, earning scowls from the others.

"I think your talents are best used elsewhere," Nick told him.

"We could make several weapons," Jasmine suggested. "A short sword for the dwarf, throwing stars for me, and a host of arrowheads and crossbow tips. I'd hate for one of us to have to face the Master alone."

"I ain't never fought with a sword in my life." Borim patted his mace with a callused hand. "And I ain't about to start now."

"For Ember, then," Nick said. "If you two are planning to go with us."

Borim grunted noncommittally.

"What does the Prophecy say about this weapon?" Ember asked.

"That's the problem." Jasmine dug a thick stack of folded parchment, her notes on the Prophecy, from her travelling bundle and laid it out on the table. "It doesn't. It just says that no weapon forged of this world will harm him."

"Worse than that—" Nick leafed through his own notes— "it says right here, 'Heroes of the land will bring the fight to the Master, but they will fail.'"

"So how does this metal help us?" Ember asked.

Nick glanced at the raspberry-haired beauty. "You plan to join us on this fool's errand?"

"I wouldn't miss it."

Nick gave Ember and Borim a hard, appraising look. He met each of their gazes straight on. The pair had been both honest and helpful. If they were willing to join him, he would welcome their help. "All right." He took the ingot back from Borim and held it up. "This metal's not from this world. It fell from the sky. It belongs to one of the points of light we can see up there at night."

Borim let out a low whistle.

"We're making this up as we go." Jasmine gestured toward the slug. "It's up to us to decide what to make."

"What of Alamain?" Zen asked. "She said something about a weapon, didn't she?"

"Not really." Nick slipped the ingot back into his pack. "She just said not to face the Master without first bringing it to Lorentil for her blessing."

"Great." Borim tossed a honey drop into his mouth and spoke around it. "We gotta go clear across the Civilized Lands for some elven blessing, with that cauldron of demons between here and there?"

"It's more than an elven blessing," Jasmine said. "It's the blessing of the High Priestess of Aeron."

"Indeed." Ellessar nodded solemnly. "Her blessing is akin to that of Aeron himself."

"Humph," Borim snorted. "No offense," he muttered in Ellessar's general direction without meeting the demon hunter's gaze.

Ellessar watched Borim for a long moment. "None taken. I'm used to the dwarves underestimating Aeron."

Ember stepped between them. "Be that as it may, there are potentially two armies between us and Lorentil, not just the demons. Rumors say Palidor is under siege from the Goblin Isle, and from the former slave population within its borders. It'll be some time, I'm sure, before the goblins make their way into Meuribar, but Palidor isn't expected to hold."

"The Prophecy says the Master will lead three armies," Nick said.

"Who's the third?" Ember asked him.

"Probably King Balor of Trondor. He's one of the Chosen, and the Master went through a lot of trouble to put him on the throne. If he hasn't moved into Faldor yet, he will soon."

Borim emitted another long whistle. "This is bad, I tell ya."

Ember nodded. "We'd better hurry."

"We still haven't answered the original question." Zen waved his hand toward the dwarf. "What are we going to have this forger of yours, this AxSwipe, make?"

Borim scowled. "I'd pronounce that carefully if you want him to make anything at all."

"A long sword," Nick said. "Personally I'd prefer a great sword, but apparently we don't have enough metal for that. Besides, with a long sword, either Ellessar or I can wield it. Just in case something happens to one of us. If there's anything left over, we can talk about arrowheads and throwing stars."

North Reach, the second largest city in Faldor, was nothing more than a trading outpost close to where the fields of rural Faldor met the rugged mountains of Trondor to the west and the lush forest of Lorentil to the east. In Trondor it would have been considered a small town. As such, it wouldn't take the whole of Balor's army to capture it. He sent Captain Dalen Frost of the Home Guard, all of Trondor's cavalry, and as many other troops as Balor could provide horses for, around to the south side of the city during the night.

The next morning, when Balor and his foot soldiers crossed the border and caught North Reach unaware, they walked in without so much as a fight.

Refugees swarmed out the southern gate, but none made it past the cavalry blockade. Dalen Frost either turned them back to the city or cut them down for refusing to comply. Balor then put the entire city under martial law. He would spare the citizens who remained docile. The Master would need subjects to rule, after all. The few who resisted died in the streets.

By the end of the day, Balor set his sights on Faldor's capital city.

CHAPTER 15

The next morning, the companions worked their way through the broad, low-ceilinged tunnels of Brimstone to the workshop of the great master forger. Nick stooped to keep from bumping his head on the ceiling. Even Zen and Ellessar couldn't quite stand up straight. Apparently people of the taller races seldom ventured this far into the dwarven kingdom.

Nick's thighs burned. "I'll be glad when we get back to the Civilized Lands."

"Gildstone *is* one of the Civilized Lands," Borim grumbled.

"Then they ought to build civilized passages," Ellessar said.

They ducked through a doorway with an even lower clearance into the antechamber of AxSwipe's forge. Inside, the ceiling soared to a ten-foot height. Nick set his pack on the floor and stood up straight. He stretched a kink that had formed in his lower back.

"What's this?" the apprentice in the antechamber asked.

"We're here to see Brewster AxSwipe," Borim told him.

"Don't mispronounce it!" The bellow from the back room shook dust from the stone ceiling. A forger, wider than he was tall, rounded the corner, his feet so far apart that they seemed to walk separate, albeit parallel, paths across the room. "Who's askin'?"

Borim bowed at the waist, if that was possible for a dwarf. In any case, his head came forward until his brown beard brushed the floor, a gesture of great respect among his kind. "I came yesterday and arranged to meet with you today, great forger."

Brewster waved a hand absently in the air. When his volume dropped, his voice became a soft rasp, like flint scraping on steel. "Don't flatter me. It doesn't become you." He sounded frail for a dwarf. His ashen eyebrows were so long and full that they hid the creases around his eyes. He must have been very old. "What of this meetin'?" Brewster asked the lad who had greeted the companions.

"I'm sorry, sir. I don't know. I was ill yesterday. Mum fixed some sour ram's horn. Don't you remember?"

Brewster glared at Borim through the veil of his gray eyebrows, squinting, though the room was bright with lamplight.

Nick glanced at the others. Surely this wasn't the great forger to whom they would entrust the fate of the Civilized Lands.

Jasmine stood near the stone doorframe, which emitted heat like a furnace. All of the walls did. Heat from the floor seeped through Nick's boots. Ellessar shifted his feet as though he sought a cool patch of stone to stand on. Zen sweated openly. Ember, as always, looked as though she didn't have a care in the world.

"I have a letter from my uncle, Azurite StoneFist," Borim began. "He—"

"You're Azurite's boy?"

Borim growled, nearly inaudibly. "I said he's my uncle."

Brewster thrust a fat finger toward Borim's face. "Don't disrespect me, boy. I'll pitch you out on your arse."

"No, sir. Of course not, sir." Borim glanced at Ember for support. "I meant no disrespect, sir. We have a job for which no other forger is able, let alone worthy."

"So does everybody else." Brewster wobbled like an egg until he managed to get his body pointed back toward the door though which he'd entered.

"Not like this." Nick drew the metal slug from his pack and stepped forward. "Master Brewster—"

"AxSwipe!" The forger waddled back around, his admonishing finger now pointed at Nick. "And don't mispronounce it."

"We have a metal like none other in this world." Nick held out the slug. "Azurite couldn't work it. We're told yours is the only forge hot enough."

Brewster raised one of his bushy brows. "Is that right?" His voice was a mere rasp once more. "It does look peculiar." He strode forward and snatched the ingot from Nick's hands. His brows shot up to reveal eyes as dark as charcoal. "There's magic here." He thrust his chin at Zen, a gesture hardly able to shift his voluminous gray beard. "Earth magic. None of that conjurin' your kind practice."

Zen opened his mouth, but Jasmine silenced him with a gesture.

The forger hefted the metal twice. "It's heavy for its size. What would you have me make?"

"A long sword." Borim gestured at Nick. "To be wielded by the elf or my big human friend here."

"Well, which is it, boy? I can't make a proper sword until I know who's going to swing the thing."

"I'll wield the sword," Nick said. "Unless something happens to me."

"Good." Brewster's eyes measured Ellessar, took in his height, his build, and the swords that already hung at his sides. "A metal this dense wouldn't make a sword light enough for the elf to swing properly anyway."

"As you can imagine..." Zen pushed his way to the front of the room.

Borim glowered at him as though he feared the mage was about to negotiate.

Zen continued, "...That metal was rather difficult to come by and it can't be replaced. Some of us must accompany you to the forge. We'll stay out of the way and—"

"And keep silent," Borim said.

Brewster squinted at the group again. "That'll cost extra." He thrust a finger at Zen. "And no magic."

They hadn't even discussed price, let alone what Brewster meant by "extra." Nick chose not to bring it up. It really didn't matter. They needed the sword. Besides, whatever the price, it would be much, much more than they could collectively pay.

Borim, along with Zen and Ellessar, followed Brewster down several hundred shallow stone steps into a forge.

"You!" Brewster stabbed his finger at one of his apprentices.

Tall for a dwarf, almost five feet in height, with a meager gut that suggested he didn't get enough to eat, the apprentice had a black beard of respectable length and thickness. "Sir?" His voice boomed from the rock walls. In the dim light, he looked older than Borim. Maybe it was the heat and the dry air of the forge, despite the constant evaporation of water from the quenching barrel. Then again, maybe at more than fifty harvests, he really was still an apprentice.

Brewster's five apprentices—apparently all older than Borim himself, the dwarf surmised once he got a clear look at them—came to attention, whiskers jutting stiffly from their set faces.

"These visitors may watch." Brewster grabbed a poker from the rack, jabbed it into a pile of discarded charcoal, and used it to draw a black ring around the chamber, an even two feet from the wall. "Nobody crosses this line. Nobody makes a sound." He thrust the poker toward Zen. "If that one moves a hand to conjure any sorcery, cut it off and throw it into the fire. The same goes for the lot of them."

Borim swallowed hard, glowered for a moment, and then settled back against the wall to watch, eager to see what he could learn from the dwarven master.

Brewster placed the slug on a balance and weighed it against his standards. "Hmmm," the forger mumbled to himself. "That's curious."

His apprentices knew enough not to interrupt.

Brewster lifted the slug from the balance and lowered it in a metered barrel of water to determine its volume. "Curious indeed."

For the remainder of the morning, the master forger labored to work the metal. Sweat that probably had nothing to do with the heat of the forge soaked his gray locks—he'd have been used to the heat from the ages he'd spent working there, day in and day out. He scratched his head, tried tool after tool, implement after implement, stoked the fire as hot as he could get it, and spewed bouts of dwarven profanity.

All the while, Ellessar kept his head bowed in a posture Borim had come to recognize from the elf's morning routine as a constant, silent prayer to Aeron.

Finally Brewster set his hammer down with a solid clunk and wiped his brow with a soot-blackened rag. "Azurite was correct. I'll have to take this to my magic forge."

Zen brightened at the dwarf's statement, perking up even in the blistering heat of the chamber.

"Earth magic," Brewster added. "None of that stuff you conjure."

Zen's smile broadened.

Mages. They were all alike, and Zen worse than most. Magic was power. Power was good.

"Bah! You're staying here," Brewster told him. "You and the elf would wither away down there. Even I can't stay for long, and I'm accustomed."

Borim raised one fat finger. "Um, Brewster?"

"Master AxSwipe to you. And don't mispronounce it."

"Yes, sir. May I be coming with you, sir?"

"Of course. That was the deal. What do you take me for? A goblin?"

"N— no. No, sir. Of course not, sir."

"Well then, don't dawdle." Brewster pushed his way through a heavy iron door, wearing woven hot-mitts on his hands.

They descended deep into the bowels of the mountain, accompanied by two of the apprentices. Borim had to pull his green skullcap back on to keep his head cool. By the time they reached the bottom, the walls were glowing a faint orange.

The forge was laid out in exactly the same way as the one in the room above, but the machines were different. There were no embers, no spent charcoal, no wood, and no flint to light a fire. A pool of molten rock bubbled in a huge ceramic crucible. The quenching barrel required a constant feed of piped-in water to keep pace with evaporation. An opening in the ceiling swept away the smoke, steam, and the worst of the ambient heat. An air vent in the far wall fed in a constant supply of cool air—cooler, at least, than the air in the sweltering forge—from somewhere far above them.

Borim couldn't wrench his gaze from the crucible. What wonders the master forger must have crafted there.

Brewster gripped the rough rod into which he'd managed to beat the slug in the forge above. With a pair of tongs, he plunged it into the molten rock, waited a moment, and then pulled it out, white hot, and began to work it.

Immediately his manner changed. He nodded as he worked, smiled often, and his eyes sparkled. His hammer clanged on the metal with an increasing pitch, until it rang like a clear bell sounding from the Stoneborough Amphitheater.

He grumbled when the temperature forced them to retreat upstairs for a time every hour to take a break from the heat.

"It'll take two more days," Brewster told everyone when they had assembled once again in the antechamber at the end of the workday. "I guarantee my work; the craftsmanship, that is…"

"Of course," Nick said.

"…But I've never forged such a metal. I can't promise anything about the strength of the material. It may break at the first stroke, or the blade may dull in a day. If you'd let me add—"

"No," Nick said. "Just what we brought in."

"It'd bring the weight down some."

"Sorry," Ellessar said.

Brewster straightened. "Bring me steel. That I'll guarantee. This is something else altogether."

CHAPTER 16

The next morning, Nick poked at his food, feeling no better than he had the past few days. When Borim caught him scratching, he suggested Nick see a dwarven priest.

Ellessar looked up from the bullhog steak the waiter had served him. "*Dwarven priest?* The dwarves have a god?"

"Yep," Borim said. "Kraggan."

Ellessar grunted. "I didn't think the dwarves believed in gods."

"We believe in ours."

"Is this priest different from the healer I saw in Glintbroc?" Nick asked.

"Priests use earth magic to do their healin'. More than just herbs and salves." Borim glanced at Jasmine. "No offense."

"None taken. I have come to appreciate the effectiveness of priestly magic to heal."

"This is different from the magic of that elf god," Borim said.

"All right." By that point, Nick was ready to try anything to get rid of the horrible rash that continued to enflame his skin. If that was all it was, he could have tolerated it, perhaps. But his strength and stamina continued to wane. If it kept up, weakness alone would prevent him from finishing his quest. He'd lost weight, too, several pounds at least. He felt nauseated most of the time, and he found it harder and harder to bring himself to eat. "Where do we find this priest?"

"I'll take them," Ember told her brother. "You go on to AxSwipe's. Keep an eye on that metal."

Borim's face lit up, as if he'd just remembered the magic forge. He knocked his chair over getting up, and hurried from the taproom.

"We'll see you back here tonight," Ember yelled after him.

"Well—" Ellessar glanced around the table— "Aeron wouldn't be happy with me if I turned to the priest of another god for any kind of help." He pulled from his coat pocket the demon bone he'd carved to match the handle of his rune-inscribed sword. "I'm going to find another forger." He met Jasmine's gaze. "Would you like to come with me? We both lost a blade to the Assassin demons. I think I have enough coin to replace your weapon as well as mine."

"What about Master Brewster?" Nick asked. "We don't know what he's going to charge us for the sword *he's* making."

Ellessar's smile seemed a little forced. "Aeron will provide."

"You two go ahead," Jasmine told Nick and Ember. "I expect I'll need both my *sais* before this is over."

Nick didn't have the energy to argue.

Ellessar handed the demon bone to the forger Jakin CrumbWell. "I'd like you to make a sword blade to fit to this."

CrumbWell brushed back the ginger whiskers of his unruly mustache and examined the piece of bone.

Ellessar drew his prayer-etched sword with the matching handle. "Dwarven steel, of course. I'm hoping to match this blade exactly, complete with the engraved elven runes."

The dwarf took the sword and tilted it to reflect the lamplight. "Intricate. Give me a minute." He laid the sword on a workbench that ran the length of one wall, and then he produced a sheet of the finest vellum and a smoothed block of charcoal from the drawer of a nearby cabinet.

CrumbWell made a rubbing of both sides of the entire blade and returned the sword to Ellessar. "That's a pretty weapon ya got there."

"No finer than the one you'll make to accompany it, I'm sure." Ellessar gestured toward Jasmine.

"And this." She pulled out her *sai*, which consisted of a central shaft about the length of her forearm with two smaller spikes on either side, each as long as the width of her hand and parallel to the central shaft. All three had sharp points. "Can you make me a duplicate for this?" She handed it to the dwarf.

CrumbWell rolled it over in his hands. "Trickier, without a blade and all, but yes. I've made such weapons before. You want me to match these dimensions exactly?"

"If you can."

"Not a problem."

"I can leave it with you," she offered.

"No need." The dwarf set the *sai* on the wooden counter. He went to a rack of shelves in the back of his shop and retrieved a hinged cherrywood box, long and deep enough to hold a long sword—pommel, cross guard, and all. He carried the box to the workbench and opened it. The top half lay flat next to the bottom half, each the same depth and both filled with a fine, soft clay.

CrumbWell pressed Jasmine's *sai* halfway into the clay in the bottom half of the box. He closed the lid, then leaned on the top with nearly his whole weight.

The forger opened the box. He pulled a utility knife from the belt that held his leather apron closed, and used the tip of the blade to carefully pry the *sai* out of the bottom half of the clay. The impression it had made there looked impeccable. He wiped a sheen of oil that the clay had left on the *sai* and handed the weapon back to Jasmine. "There, you see? Now I've got a shape to match."

"Very impressive. I guess my order has been making them the hard way."

"Nothin' to it. Come back tomorrow." He glanced at Ellessar. "Yours'll take an extra day, for the engravin'."

"That will do," the elf said. "Thank you."

Nick tried to sit still as Alamar ReedBlower, the fidgety dwarven priest, examined his face.

Alamar scratched his cheek as though empathy had transferred the rash's itch to him. "Hmmm. I don't know nothin' of human anatomy, but this ain't no magic I ever heard of."

He rummaged through a variety of stone and steel instruments, some of which appeared disturbingly like weapons fit for a pixie. Others were just strange. The dwarf produced a round piece of clear, polished crystal and some miniature pointed tongs.

He peered through the crystal, making his eye look as large as his face. The weird illusion made Nick's skin crawl. He had the sudden sensation that Alamar had woven some enchantment to make his large eye see more detail.

The priest picked at Nick's raw and irritated face, peeling off flakes of skin with the miniature tongs and laying them carefully on a small, silver plate. "Hmmm." He moved closer, the crystal nearly touching at once Nick's cheek and the healer's face. "Hmmm."

"Would you quit saying that?" Nick said.

"There's no foreign substance here that could account for the inflammation."

"Figures."

Ember remained silent in the corner but watched the priest carefully.

"I'd like to look through your things," Alamar said, "if you'll permit it."

"Of course." The connection between his belongings and the dwarf's healing was lost to Nick, but if the dwarf thought it might lead him to some diagnosis, Nick had no cause to object.

Alamar emptied Nick's entire backpack. Then, with Ember's permission, he emptied hers as well. Then he picked up her pouch of catalyst.

"Careful with that," she said. "It's an earth magic. It'll catch fire. Rather violently."

Alamar frowned. "What's in it?"

"A mix of these." She dug three metal flasks from the bottom of her backpack. "Sulfur, charcoal, and niter."

The dwarf unscrewed the top of each, careful not to lose the leather gaskets that prevented the powders from seeping out through the threads. He confirmed each of the ingredients by appearance, texture, and smell. "'Catch fire,' I'll say. That's some powerful magic."

Ember smiled hugely. "Don't I know it."

Satisfied, Alamar returned her gear and went back to the skin sample. He carried the sliver dish across the room to a metal apparatus—a framework of sorts that held several polished clear crystals like the one he'd used to examine Nick's face—and fitted the dish onto a strut that was obviously designed for the purpose. Then he adjusted another of the crystals to position it between the lamp and the dish. The crystal intensified the light into a small oval, which he centered on the skin sample.

He peered through the stack of suspended crystals. "Hmmm."

"Now what?" Nick asked.

"See for yerself." Alamar stepped away from the apparatus.

Nick peered down through the stacked crystals. What he saw looked like a piece of intricately stamped leather. "Is that my skin?"

"Yep."

Nick stood. He had no idea what the appearance of the sample meant, but it didn't look good. His gaze met Ember's. "Earth magic indeed."

"What can you tell us?" Ember asked Alamar.

"About what's causing it?" The dwarf continued to address Nick. "Nothin'. But one thing's for sure. You're dyin'."

Nick's world stopped. Every muscle tensed. "Dying?" He'd felt sick, sure. But dying? "What makes you say that?"

"Even though the rash is persistent, I should see some sign of regeneration, some new skin formed by your body. There's none. Your body seems to be devouring itself. This rash is only the exterior sign. Your loss of strength, stamina, and appetite tell me your insides are doing the same thing."

"You got all that from your crystals?" Ember asked.

"Yep. I just wish I knew how to cure it. How long has it been going on?"

Nick unclenched his teeth and forced himself to take a deep breath. "A couple of weeks."

"If it don't stop, you'll be dead in a month. Maybe two."

Time enough to stop the prophecy, maybe, if his condition didn't worsen too quickly. But *dying*? Nick merely felt sick. Yet despite Ellessar's prayers, Jasmine's herbs, dwarven salves, and just plain time, he still carried bruises and cuts from the battle with the sphinxes—wounds that should have gotten better. If Nick's body was losing the ability to heal, maybe he really was dying.

CHAPTER 17

That night Ember considered everything she'd learned. With omens of the Prophecy's fulfillment sprouting across the Civilized Lands like grass in the elven woods, this was perhaps the most important mission she'd ever been assigned—that anyone had ever been assigned. She wouldn't shirk her duty to the DIG any more than this determined group of friends would shirk their self-assigned duty to oppose the Master.

The companions didn't see that it wasn't just *their* duty to oppose the Master. It was everybody's duty. And to leave the salvation of the civilized races solely in the hands of these fugitives would be tantamount to negligence.

Ember waited until Jasmine's breathing slowed to the deep cadence of one asleep, and then she slipped down to the taproom with her quill and ink. After purchasing a few sheets of parchment from the innkeeper, she settled into a corner table and wrote:

Honored Elders of the Dwarven Intelligence Guild
Regarding the fugitives from the kingdom of Trondor:

I have discovered the group's purpose and intent. They've hired master forger Brewster AxSwipe to forge some otherworldly metal into a sword to kill the Master of Mortaan's Last Prophecy. According to Nick Mirrin's notes regarding the Prophecy, anyone attempting to attack the Master will fail unless they use a weapon forged of a metal that is "not of this world." They have acquired such a metal. Therefore, their quest has merit.

From here, Nick and his friends plan to take the sword to Lorentil. Apparently, it must be blessed by Alamain, the High Priestess of the elf god Aeron.

In securing the otherworldly ore, the fugitives lost two strong members of their party in the Wild Lands. They would likely have lost at least one more at Roybal Keep and been either captured or scattered if not for my intervention there. They were attacked again on their way to Brimstone. Without the help of myself and my brother, the group would have suffered additional losses. These people have done much, but once they've forged a sword that's dangerous to the Master, they'll become an even greater target.

I see two options: We can send a well-armed force to escort this group to Lorentil by either land or sea, or we can seize the sword and protect it here in Gildstone until our armies are ready to join forces with those of the humans and elves. Either way, to let this group wander around without dwarven support invites ultimate failure.

I recommend escorting the group to Lorentil, but if you choose to seize the sword, I can spirit it away so we may hold it in the possession of the DIG, the dwarven army, or our governing council, as the elders of the DIG deem best.

I await orders.
Agent Ember ShatterStone

Ember stoppered the ink bottle and blotted the letter with a piece of cloth. She sat back and read the text to make sure she hadn't left out any important details. The lights were dim, but her keen elven eyes had no trouble making out the writing. There was indeed much more to say, so she added an addendum describing the members of Nick's party. She mentioned that Jasmine was a genuine demon-kin; that Nick was suffering from some sort of disease or curse for which they hadn't found a remedy; and that Ellessar was a true priest of Aeron in possession of the Shield of Faith. Zen, the ice mage, she wrote, favored area-affect weavings, could morph into animal forms—including those that flew—and could translocate significant distances. Nick would likely have Zen translocate away with the sword if anyone tried to take it by force. The dwarves would need to incapacitate the mage immediately if they did intend to do so.

Ember reread the entire packet one final time, sealed it with wax, and left the inn.

Minutes later, she woke the DIG operative in Brimstone, a leather wholesaler named Angor BronzeHammer. The tanned hides of bullhogs hung on racks along one wall. Against the other, wooden pallets kept stacks of hides off the floor while they awaited shipment to armorers, tent makers, and producers of parchment and vellum throughout the Civilized Lands. The smell of leather and oil was a pleasant respite from the odors of soot and sweat in the forges, of ale and vomit in the taverns, and of Nick's dwarven salve.

"This must travel by the fastest means to DIG headquarters." Ember handed Angor the sealed message. "The fate of the Civilized Lands depends on it."

To his credit, Angor kept any sign of skepticism from his expression. "There's news. I received it by Guild dispatch, but it's not a secret. Rumors will arrive from Glintbroc soon enough."

Ember waited without comment.

"Trondor has invaded Faldor. North Reach has already fallen. They're moving against the capital as we speak. It, too, may have fallen by now."

Ember would like to have been surprised by the news. "Then time is shorter than I'd hoped." She inclined her head toward the rolled parchment in Angor's hand. "Best speed." She spun on her heel and hurried back to the inn.

Nick and his companions were gathered in Brewster AxSwipe's antechamber when the master forger emerged with the new sword. Borim and the apprentices followed.

Brewster carried the blade, wrapped in an oiled cloth, and set the bundle on the marble table with a dull thump. He unwrapped it in the amber light of a dozen clean-burning lamps. It was made of a single piece, with a dark, purple-black hue and a sheen that made the blade look wet.

"It's beautiful." Nick wanted to see how his friends, particularly Ellessar, reacted to the blade's appearance, but his gaze wouldn't leave the talisman. "M— may I?"

Brewster opened his hand toward the sword.

Reverently, Nick took hold of the hilt. The metal was warm, the hilt sized for a two-handed grip and engraved with a rough pattern of intricate shapes to provide a firm grasp. Nick lifted it. "Uugh." He swung it to test its weight, forcing everyone in the room to scramble toward the walls. Though only the size of a long sword, it must have weighted as much as his great sword. "It's almost unwieldy."

"Bah!" Brewster stomped forward and snatched the sword from Nick. He set it sideways, just above the hilt, on a single outthrust forefinger. The sword sat motionless, with not a wobble toward one side or the other. "See there. Perfect balance. It's just too blasted heavy. If you'd let me use proper steel, you'd have a sword you could handle.

"I'll show you something else." Brewster gripped the handle in his fat hands and swung the sword at the marble table.

Nick gasped and lunged to stop him.

The sword cut through the stone as if it was a loaf of bread. A thousand pounds of marble rumbled to the floor.

"I tested yer blade. It's easily twice as strong as any I ever made. Took a diamond grinder to sharpen it. We'll be well into the next age before it begins to go dull."

"I certainly hope so," Jasmine said. "Unfortunately, that won't be long in coming."

Brewster's lips tightened. "What makes you say that?"

"Mortaan's Prophecy ends with the beginning of the Age of Darkness," Nick said. "We're hoping this sword will prevent it. But because this is the last of Mortaan's prophecies, I suspect a new age is coming even if we're successful."

Nick relinquished the center of the room. "Give it a try, Ellessar. Just in case."

The demon hunter took his turn with the blade. By the third swing, his strokes were sagging. He handed the blade back to the forger. "It'll take a blessing from Aeron for me to carry that into battle. But if I'm meant to wield it, he'll grant me the strength."

"I think I'll be able to manage it," Nick said. "This sword's smaller than the one I'm used to, but it's not beyond the weight of my great sword."

"Yours it is then, until Aeron presents another solution."

"Ain't nobody's but Master Brewster's yet," Borim said. "We haven't discussed payment."

"I'm afraid to ask," Jasmine said. "Perhaps we should have brought it up earlier. We don't have much coin."

Brewster's features softened. He showed a hint of a smile. "I've been forging for more years than most dwarves can count. I've got enough coin. Now I'm more worried about my legacy. As I said before, there's a magic in that blade the likes of which I've never seen. It's sharper and stronger than any I ever made. If you can head off this Prophecy that folks been fretting about for the past umpteen centuries, then strike a blow for Brewster AxSwipe."

Borim bowed until the better part of his beard collected in a pile at his feet. For a long moment, he seemed stuck. Finally, he rose. "We'll never be able to thank ya proper."

Nick gathered up the blade's wrappings and handed them to the forger. He did have enough coin to purchase a suitable sheath for the talisman, and he did so. Brewster's generosity buoyed Nick's spirit higher than the snowcapped peaks of the Sharktooth Mountains as the companions filed solemnly out of the antechamber.

"Just don't mispronounce it!" Brewster hollered after them.

When Ember left Angor BronzeHammer for the second time in as many days, her orders from the DIG were clear: find out how the companions were planning to get from Brimstone to the elven capital, and then sell them out. From there, the Council of Elders would decide how to best use the talisman sword against the Master.

"How do you want to get to Lorentil?" Ember asked once they had all gathered in Nick's room.

"We should go by sea," Jasmine said. "It'll be faster than trying to walk all the way across the Civilized Lands, especially with the Master's armies between here and there."

"Perhaps, but we'd have to sail around Trondor," Nick said. "Balor has the royal navy at his command. It would only take a couple of ships to send our precious sword to the bottom of the North Sea."

"If we get into trouble, we can give the sword to Zen," Jasmine said. "He can translocate to the mainland and try to get it to Alamain from there. She can assign others to complete our quest."

"I might be able to save one or two of you as well," Zen said, "but we'd have to stay within sight of the shore."

"How far can you translocate?" Ember asked. "Can you get to the elven capital directly from here or from Glintbroc?"

Zen eyed her for a moment before answering. It was a bold but fair question. If Zen could get to Lorentil directly from the dwarven kingdom, it would save the party a great deal of risk, not to mention time. Either way, Ember needed to know exactly what Zen could do, for the sake of the DIG.

When Zen finally answered, he was less clear than Ember had hoped. "I can translocate to any place I can see. Or to any place I've been, if it's near enough. I haven't tested my range limit, but I found it taxing to go a few miles from the lake to our campsite in the Wild Lands."

"Sailing within sight of the shore will definitely attract Balor's attention," Nick said. "We'll be intercepted."

Ellessar nodded. "I'll feel better going by land anyway. My brothers fight the demons between here and Lorentil. I may be able to help them."

"You have a higher calling." Nick held up the sheathed sword. "*This* is your quest now. Whether you wield it or not, Aeron has placed you with us for a reason."

"I know." Ellessar sank into silence.

"That does beg another question, though," Ember said. "What route to travel? I heard a rumor yesterday that Balor's armies are marching across Faldor, and the demons may already have Meuribar under siege."

"Meuribar," Ellessar said. "It's a more direct route."

Nick nodded. "Whatever we decide, Zen, stay close to me. If I hand you the sword, take it and leave."

The debate continued into the night and ultimately died away undecided.

Late though it was, Ember slipped out with another dispatch for Angor BronzeHammer. She smiled past her sadness. In just a short time, she'd come to respect Nick and his friends, but her people came before any other loyalty.

The importance of the Prophecy and the weight of her duty to the DIG left no room for new friendships. She would do what she must.

And despite the group's indecision, she had learned what she needed to know. Regardless of what land route the companions chose, they would have to depart Gildstone via Glintbroc, for there was only one road north out of the kingdom. Whatever her government decided to do, they would do it between here and there.

CHAPTER 18

The next morning, as Nick and the others waited for Borim to collect Spirit from the stable master and for Ellessar to pick up his new sword and Jasmine's *sai* from the second forger, a contingent of the dwarven military, the Knights of Steel-Stone, lined up inside the Brimstone city gate, every dwarf arrayed with freshly oiled plate armor that sparkled as if it had come straight from Master Brewster's forge.

Spaced every dozen dwarves was a mining cart made of wood, banded in steel, covered with oiled canvas, and harnessed to two teams of mules. The carts and dwarves lined up along the pairs of steel tracks that ran straight out the city's main entrance. Those tracks ran all the way to Glintbroc, and probably to every other city in the dwarven kingdom. Nick and his friends had paralleled them all the way across the Sunburst Plain.

"Form up!" The dwarf in charge stabbed a thick finger at one of the carts. "Tie that corner down. I won't have the cargo gettin' wet if it rains."

When he reached the front of the column, he spotted Nick's company—the only non-dwarves in the cavern. He finished the inspection of his troops and marched up to Nick. His demeanor became suddenly casual. "Headed out, are ya?"

"Yeah." Nick scratched absently at his neck, where the rash persisted despite any amount of Jasmine's ointments or the dwarven salve.

"Back to Glintbroc, I assume." It didn't sound like a question. Where else were a bunch of non-dwarves likely to go in Gildstone? The dwarf didn't wait for an answer. "I'm Captain Sterling Iron-Forge." He gestured to the knights. "Those're me troops."

Nick nodded. He was sure this all had a purpose, but at the moment, he couldn't grasp it. What was he supposed to say? "Impressive."

"You're Nick Mirrin."

Nick narrowed his eyes. He didn't remember having told anyone his last name since he'd entered the dwarven kingdom.

"Your group brought down that pride of sphinxes a few days back," the dwarf continued.

"Yeah..." Nick hesitated. "What about them?"

"Pride that size ain't been seen in a generation, especially out on the Sunburst Plain." Captain IronForge leaned closer. "I heard more have been spotted between here and Tinderstone, keeping an eye on the trail, like they're watching for somethin'."

Behind him, Sterling's contingent of dwarves lined up their mules with dwarven precision. From Nick's higher vantage point, they looked like the first two rows of a block wall. "What's that got to do with me?" He gestured to Zen, Jasmine, and Ember. "With us?"

"Nothin'. Just thought you oughta know." When Nick didn't respond, Sterling continued. "Those sphinxes are trouble. My men and I have been reassigned to Glintbroc. Got orders to deliver supplies and weapons. Seems Trondorian troops are marching through Faldor.

Guess the council wants us to be ready." He shrugged. "Anyway, your group's pretty tough. So's mine. We travel together, those sphinxes'll leave us alone."

"Strength in numbers? How fast are your knights? We're in a hurry."

"They won't slow you down, if that's what's got you worried. Dwarves ain't so slow as people think."

Ember was the first one to leave the tunnels, having preceded the party by a good half hour. She stood on a rock outcropping and drank in the fresh morning air and the warm sunlight, which were a balm for her elven soul after having spent several days underground. When the dwarves did finally emerge, the caravan slogged out of Brimstone at a despairing pace, with heavy cartloads of weapons and provisions pulled uphill by trains of mules in front and eased downhill by trains of mules behind.

"This is ridiculous," Jasmine said finally. "We'll take forever at this rate."

Borim scanned the sky. "If those sphinxes have come back, they'll have brought greater numbers than they had last time. We'll do well to keep the knights' company at least until we get through Tinderstone and out of the mountains. It's just a few days. Then we can take off across the plains and make up the time."

"Besides," Ember added, "these dwarves might surprise you before the day is over." She was counting on that very fact. Sterling's presence was no coincidence. Her superiors, however, had shown enough wisdom—and enough confidence in her—not to take immediate possession of the talisman sword. Ember's role, apparently, was to keep Jasmine, Nick, and the others from refusing Sterling's help.

Sunset came and went. The dwarves lit lanterns and hung them from every cart. A pair of knights scouted ahead for hazards on the rails. Duty officers rode the length of the caravan with rations of jerky, bread, water, and a brew made from a brown bean that seemed to rejuvenate the troops like an elixir of vitality.

By midnight the men and elves were exhausted, and the dwarves had covered more ground than the companions would have in a single day on their own. Still, they didn't stop until sometime in the dark hours of the morning, when Sterling finally called a halt. The dwarves set out buckets of meal and water for the mules, who slept standing up, strung to their loads for the night, and then slept on the trail alongside the loaded carts. By sunup, the troop was moving again.

Sterling had been right when he told Nick not to worry about the dwarves slowing them down. The dwarves were anything but slow. They'd made Glintbroc a full day faster than the time in which the companions had completed the opposite trip a week before. He was right about something else, too: nobody bothered them.

Nick, however, fared the worse for it. He rarely ate, he wrapped his raw hands in strips of cloth, he complained that his skin felt like it was being licked by flames, and his strength waned until he was forced to ride Spirit to keep up.

When they entered the huge central cavern in the northern trade district, the plaza, the streets and alleyways, and apparently the buildings as well were filled with dwarven knights. Ember's heart sank. Her government didn't trust the companions after all. The knights would have gathered in these numbers only to ensure the capture of the sword. And with Zen's translocation ability, this was probably the only way to do it. He could go only so far, and in a city this size he wouldn't be able to make it out of the city proper. No matter where he went, the dwarves would have him trapped.

Nick stopped short in the mouth of the cavern that housed Glintbroc's northern plaza.

"Oh, from the depths of Mount Hellfire, what's goin' on here?" Sterling marched past Nick and up to a dwarven knight who was inspecting a pike brigade. "Are the demons here already then?"

"No, sir," the knight said. "Seems the council's changed its mind."

"'Bout what?"

"About the defense. We got orders to march to Meuribar, to help the humans defend their capital there."

"Nonsense! Who ever heard of such a thing?"

"Who ever heard of demons pouring forth from the Great Sand?" Ellessar spoke quietly enough so Sterling wouldn't hear over the clatter and clamor of the dwarven preparations.

Beyond the two, another knight argued with a group of dwarven miners who were apparently trying to move a train of ore carts through the crowded plaza.

"We can hold the demons against the walls of Glintbroc," Sterling continued, "but we'll never keep them out of a human city, with what serves as battlements in their kingdoms. Who's in charge here?"

"General CragTower."

"Where is he?" The sharpness of Sterling's voice made the pike commander jump.

"Outside the Stone Tankard, sir. Register your cargo there. All incoming supplies must be transferred to him for allocation."

"We'll see about that. Wait here," Sterling told Lieutenant PickRock, his own second in command. He pointed to Nick and his companions. "And don't let them out of your sight." He stormed away, grumbling. "This is madness. You fight demons underground, not out in the open where..." Sterling's voice faded in the tumult as he disappeared into the crowd.

"This could be a problem," Nick said. "Sterling's troops might move quickly by themselves, but if this whole army gets between us and Silversmith, they'll clog the road for days."

"Come on." Jasmine slipped past Nick. "We've got some daylight left—we can re-provision in Silversmith."

Lieutenant PickRock moved to block her path. "You'll wait here like the captain said, until he gets back."

"He has no authority over us," Jasmine replied calmly. "He can't keep us here."

"Look around you." Ember gestured at the cavern. There must have been ten thousand dwarven knights in the plaza alone. "I think he can."

Zen smirked. "Speak for yourself."

Nick shook his head at the mage. There might come a time for Zen to escape alone with the sword, but that time hadn't come yet.

After several minutes, Ellessar approached the dwarven knight who'd spoken with Sterling. "What news is there from the Great Sand?"

The dwarf shrugged, a gesture nearly lost in the bulk of his steel plate armor. "Not much. The queen's champion from Brinheim and some religious brotherhood have gone to Meuribar to intercept the demon hoards."

"Brother Peldair, and the Order of the Shining Star."

The dwarf's eyes lit with excitement. "You know the queen's champion?"

Ellessar thumbed the medallion he wore around his neck and displayed the emblem of his brotherhood of demon fighters. "By tradition, the head of my order is the queen's champion. The demons were sentenced to banishment from the lands of men in the king's hall in Brinheim. It has always been assumed that the demons would attack there first if they ever escaped the Abyss."

"Maybe they did," the dwarf ventured.

"No. Brother Peldair wouldn't have taken the Demonbane sword to Meuribar if the demons were attacking Brinheim. What news of the battle?"

Nick scanned the crowd for Sterling. Nothing.

"Blast it," Borim said. "Where is he?"

"Last I heard," the knight continued, "your friends had taken up defense at the edge of the Great Sand to await the hoard's arrival.

But the news must be at least a week old."

"Indeed." That very morning, after Ellessar's communion with Aeron, he'd reported demons to be closer than they'd been throughout the trek to Brimstone. They were on the move. With only three hundred men, Ellessar's order wouldn't hold them for long.

Nick began to pace. "Suggestions?" he finally asked Jasmine.

Just then Sterling returned. He marched right up to Nick. "I have a confession to make."

Ellessar excused himself from the dwarven knight and moved back to the party.

"We didn't happen upon you by chance in Brimstone," Sterling said. "I was ordered to provide protection for you and your party."

"We appreciate it," Nick replied. "Why didn't you just say so?"

"If I'd put it that way, would you have accepted my protection?"

Nick thought about it. "Probably, but we would have been suspicious—"

"I had to build your trust."

"By lying? Why?"

Sterling frowned. He lowered his voice almost to a mumble. "Didn't lie exactly. Just didn't tell the whole of it. Besides—" he spoke up again— "my orders don't end here. I've been charged to provide escort and see to the success of your mission."

Nick stiffened. His jaw set and his heart rate increased. "What mission?"

"Now that would be a fine thing to know," Sterling admitted. "The truth is, I've been ordered not to ask. But I understand you're to be crossing the human lands." He raised his eyebrows. "The besieged human lands. My orders are to place myself and my knights between you and the demon hoards, if necessary, to see that you get through to wherever it is you're goin'."

Nick turned a questioning eye on Borim.

The dwarf removed his knit skullcap and twisted it in his hands. "The forger musta said somethin'."

Sterling continued. "I needed to demonstrate that we wouldn't slow you down before I proposed accompanying you beyond the walls of Glintbroc. I hoped to impress you." He paused. "The choice is yours, of course, but I can't take no for an answer."

"Then I guess we'd better accept," Ember said. "What about the army?"

Sterling snorted. "I guess they're going to Meuribar, and the elders have all gone batty."

"Time is our enemy," Nick said. "What do we need to do before you're ready to leave?"

"We're ready now, and at *your* disposal."

"Then we leave immediately for Silversmith."

Nick, Zen, Jasmine, Ellessar, Ember, Borim, Sterling, and twenty mounted Knights of SteelStone traveled hard until nightfall, without stopping to trade their mules for horses. They'd have to hope Silversmith's equine supply hadn't already been appropriated for the defense of Faldor and Meuribar. The travel speed of the knights had increased substantially since Sterling had left the loaded supply cars with the dwarven army, along with all of his unmounted soldiers. Once the sun went down, they stopped for the night.

"Tell me, Nick," Zen asked across the blaze of the cooking fire. "What did you do in the Wild Lands that you aren't proud of?"

Nick spent a few moments trying to process the question. "What do you mean?"

"You served as a guard for your uncle's caravan, once upon a time, didn't you?"

"Yeah. For a couple of years. Why?"

Ember and Jasmine listened. Borim and Ellessar were sharing the watch at opposite ends of the campsite. Sterling and his men were off tending to their mules and gear.

"You ever kill anybody you shouldn't have?"

"Not that I know of. Why?" He paused. "What's that got to do with the Wild Lands?"

Zen didn't answer.

Nick set down his bowl of stewed tomatoes, parsley, and bullhog tips. Jasmine had outdone herself on their dinner again, but Nick couldn't bring himself to eat it. "Are you accusing me of something?"

"Nothing specific." The corners of Zen's mouth twisted up as though he enjoyed Nick's discomfort. "Let me tell you a story. I've done some things in my life that some would consider unscrupulous—most of them in my past, before we got wrapped up in this prophecy." Zen's expression lost its momentary humor. "My greed for power sometimes gets me into trouble."

The fact itself didn't surprise Nick, but the admission seemed uncharacteristically honest of Zen. "Go on."

"Most recently, I tried to steal something when we passed through Dragon Tears. Or more accurately, I tried to hire somebody to steal something for me, something I thought might help us in our quest." He settled himself against his backpack. "The problem was, by then I'd spoken the Oath of Aeron, and we had taken collective possession of the Shield of Faith."

Nick shifted uncomfortably. The dull ache that had settled into his skull a week ago had become so much a part of him that he barely registered its presence anymore. He felt it now. This was the time of night he usually took up the talisman sword to practice, but he didn't have the energy. For the last several days, his stomach had become so queasy most of the time that he could hardly eat. Day by day, his strength was waning.

"Not only was I unsuccessful in finding a proper thief," Zen continued, "but Aeron punished me for trying. For two days, I couldn't eat or drink."

"I remember that," Jasmine interjected.

Zen gestured at Nick's full bowl. "You haven't been eating."

Nick shook his head. "I've been too nauseated."

"So, what did you do in the Wild Lands that might have violated the oath you took to Aeron?"

Nick's initial thought was, *Nothing*. But was that true? So much had happened. Even a thought that went against the Oath might count against him. But would that really be enough to cause this slow, wasting sickness?

"Think about it." Zen stood and brushed the loose dirt from the hem of his robe. "We've tried everything else. Your life may depend on it."

For a long time, Nick thought through every event that had taken place in the Wild Lands. His symptoms began about the same time he had taken brief possession of the Shield of Faith at Roybal Keep. That seemed to support Zen's theory, but nothing came to mind that might have brought a curse upon him. Hadn't he upheld the law with his every action? Perhaps, but the laws of the Lands weren't the same as the law of Aeron.

Maintain justice, Nick had promised in reciting the Oath. His idea of justice, as far as he knew, aligned well with the ideals of the church.

Defend the weak. That's what this quest was all about. Defend the masses who didn't have the means to fight the Master themselves, or who were too ignorant to know they should.

But *Act with honor*? When it came down to it, what was honor? The concept was too personal and abstract to define, and Nick didn't know enough about the teachings of Aeron to understand how the god might interpret the word.

He had drawn his sword, and even wielded the Shield of Faith, against Lord Kelton, Aeron's own knight. But that was just a misunderstanding, and Nick had backed down before he'd done any harm to the man. No, it must be something else, something more substantial. Was Nick being punished for skirting the consequences of killing King Gremauld? Should he have surrendered to Sierra?

Nick skipped his practice session completely that evening to reconsider his entire life since he'd taken the Oath. He even stayed up late to speak with Ellessar when the demon hunter came off his watch.

"Whether you know it or not," Ellessar assured him, "you're actually a knight of Aeron."

"I've never studied his ways."

"You've taken the Oath, have you not? And you fight for his cause?"

Nick nodded.

"Brother Kelton spoke with Aeron before we left Roybal Keep. If you weren't meant to be free, Kelton would have taken you. The soldiers of the keep would have supported him. I would have, too."

That ruled out Zen's theory of an Oath violation, but there was another matter that he'd meant to discuss with Ellessar. "Aeron hasn't blessed you with the strength to wield the talisman sword. Normally, I would be able to, but..." He held out his arms to display his body, which seemed to have begun to decay. The skin on his arms was discolored and peeling. He reached up and lifted a pinch of hair easily from his scalp.

"I've been thinking a lot about that," Ellessar said. "Perhaps Vexetan himself is playing a hand in this game. There may be attacks that even Aeron can't completely prevent."

The thought was less than comforting.

CHAPTER 19

Silversmith was a very different town than it had been when the companions had come through just a few weeks before. Nick expected it to be deserted, its men and supplies requisitioned for the war effort against Balor in the northern half of the kingdom. Instead, it had become a refugee camp.

Families from the north and east flooded in with everything they could carry, and they brought their horses with them. But Silversmith was as far south as they could get without going to Glintbroc, and few humans had the courage to approach that imposing bastion of the enigmatic dwarves. At least some of the refugees would be willing, if not eager, to barter or sell.

Nick and Ellessar had a working knowledge of horses and Ember said she had coin, though she didn't say how much. Sterling had been given funds to provide for his knights. So the four of them bought the mounts while the others topped off their food and other supplies.

When Jasmine, Zen, and Borim returned to the group, Ember was paying for the last half dozen horses. She shelled out more coin in that one transaction than the rest of the party had combined.

Borim marched up to his sister. "Where did you get that?"

Ember shrugged, a smirk on her lips and a gleam in her eye. "It seems Auntie trusts me with our well-being more than she does you. Did she not give you coin?"

Borim muttered something under his breath, and then said nothing more.

"We have to go by way of Meuribar," Jasmine told Nick and Ellessar. "The elves have come to the aid of Faldor at North Reach, but they're too late. Balor has already taken the capital city. He holds the whole northern half of the kingdom."

"And that gives him full access to the southern half," Nick finished. Nobody lived there but farmers and sheepherders. The Faldor army wouldn't have given up the palace unless they were utterly defeated. That meant nobody remained to defend the farms. Balor could hole up in the palace while his troops raided the south for food. "We have to hurry. I suggest we bypass the trade route for as long as possible. It may be patrolled. We can follow the Tumbledown River until it turns south, then cut across country to Meuribar."

Within an hour, the whole company was mounted—not a simple proposition for the contingent of dwarven knights who'd never ridden mounts as tall as horses. But at the rate Nick intended to travel, mules, or even ponies, would never keep up.

Throughout the day, Nick practiced in the saddle with the talisman sword. At first his mount spooked frequently. Then, little by little, the horse became accustomed to the whirling movement. Nick could practice only for a few minutes at a time because he tired quickly, but determination kept him trying. By nightfall, he could barely climb down from his saddle without falling.

"Sleep," Ellessar told him each night. "We'll cover the watches."

Two days out of Silversmith, they veered north and eventually merged onto the trade route.

Refugees were streaming out of Meuribar. "You're fools," one man said as Nick's company turned onto the road toward the capital city, which was no more than a few hours distant. "The demons have breached the border defenses. They're advancing toward the city as we speak."

"What news of the brotherhood of the Shining Star?" Ellessar asked.

"Their defense has crumbled. A runner came into town this morning. The survivors are falling back to the city." The man, his family huddled in a cart with about a room's worth of furniture, whipped his oxen to get them moving again.

"How many demons?" Ellessar yelled back to him.

"Enough to fill the Great Sand!"

By the time they approached the city of Meuribar, Nick's illness seemed to have settled in. He could no longer carry the talisman sword. Weakness had forced him to tie it, in its sheath, to the back of his saddle. Jasmine gave him herbal remedies every few hours to keep his fever down.

Ellessar, now riding in front, noted activity atop the thirty-foot-high granite-block walls. Archers manned every crenellation in the parapets. Lookouts stood watch atop every tower.

The guards at the southern gate to the city proper raised the portcullis and swung the doors wide without challenge as the party approached—they could see well enough that Nick's party consisted of humans, elves, and dwarves, not demons.

Jasmine kept her cowl pulled low and her arms tucked into the voluminous sleeves of her monk's robe as they crossed under the wall into the courtyard beyond. As soon as the last dwarf in the line entered, the portcullis slammed down, and the gate swung closed behind them.

"Hold there!" the watch commander shouted. The entire contingent of dwarves, along with Jasmine, Zen, Ember, and Borim, came to a halt. Only Nick, Ellessar, and Sterling rode ahead to meet with the commander. Borim tried to follow, muttering curses past a mouthful of honey drops, but Ember grabbed the reins of his horse and held him back.

"Is this it?" the commander asked. "Is this all the dwarves have to offer?"

Sterling nudged his horse toward the man. "No, sir. The army was making ready to depart as we left. Tens of thousands of dwarves, probably no more than two days behind us."

"You're the vanguard then. Get to the walls. We need everyone there."

"No, sir," Sterling said. "I'm sorry to say we're not."

"We're on an errand of much greater importance," Ellessar said.

"More important than the salvation of the kingdom?"

"If we're successful," Nick said, "we'll put an end to all three of the Master's armies."

"Now what kind of errand could accomplish that? And with what? The commander scanned the party. "Two dozen of you? You yourself can barely sit your horse."

Ellessar lowered his voice. "We're going to take the battle to the Master."

If that was news to Sterling, the dwarf hid his surprise well.

The commander eyed them skeptically. "You're here for supplies, then. We haven't got much we can spare, given what's coming."

"No," Nick said. "We don't even need that. We're here to determine if the road north is still open to Lorentil."

"It was at last report, but that could change. And it's more likely to by the hour. If you're not staying, I suggest you leave the city immediately, before it's too late."

Ellessar gestured toward the city's interior. "If we may?"

"Don't worry, lad," Sterling told the watch commander. "The dwarves won't let you down."

The man grunted and moved aside.

Ellessar didn't lead them through the dense inner city. Instead, he stayed near the outer wall until they approached the eastern gate.

Everywhere around them, people rushed to make preparations for battle. Workmen hoisted large, square-cut, granite rocks to the battlement, either to shore up any sections of the wall that became damaged, or to drop on the hordes of demons when they tried to scale the walls. Extra ladders leaned against the inside of the wall to facilitate the reinforcement and resupply of the archers and swordsman stationed at the top. Civilians moved cots and litters into ground-floor shops along the side of the courtyard farthest from the city wall, and cleared combustible materials—wood, hay, straw, fabric awnings, and the like—from the area.

As the company passed the deserted market plaza, a large contingent of horsemen—Meuribar soldiers, from the soaring-griffin emblem embroidered on the breasts of their blue-and-white uniforms—rode in the east gate from the direction of the Great Sand, their clothes and gear caked with dust. Ellessar spurred Spirit forward and flagged down the lead rider.

The soldier waved his men past.

"What news from the front?" Ellessar asked the man.

"Not good," the rider said. "The city will be under siege by nightfall."

Ellessar's heart seemed to skip a beat. He squeezed his eyes shut and swallowed hard. "Then the Order of the Shining Star has fallen."

"Most of them have. A handful, including the queen's champion from Brinheim, are falling back with the army, buying us time to shore up the city's defenses."

"That would be Brother Peldair. I have a message for him." Ellessar pulled out a parchment on which he'd detailed everything he knew about the Master and the demons he'd seen so far, especially the Assassins. He included the Hunter demon he believed to have destroyed Harimon Mirrin's shipment of dwarven swords en route to Palidor many months before. He also warned of the dragon and rider that they hadn't seen since they'd entered the Wild Lands. Doubtless the Master had deployed them where they would do the most damage.

"I'll see that he gets it."

"We have to go." Nick spurred his horse toward the northern gate. Ellessar reluctantly nudged Spirit to follow.

The companions and their dwarven escort passed through the northern gate of Meuribar city and rode until an hour past dark before Nick's exhaustion forced them to stop for the night. They slept in a ravine to hide themselves from demon patrols.

In the morning, Ellessar walked a short distance away to commune with Aeron. When he returned, his face looked ashen.

"What is it?" Jasmine asked.

"Demons all around us. South and east." He paused. "And north."

"Between us and Lorentil," Zen observed.

Ellessar nodded. "And all within a day's ride."

Nick stuffed his bedding into his pack. "That doesn't change our destination. We'll have to go through them if they get in our way."

Ellessar smiled grimly. "Spoken like a man after my own heart."

"Well then." Captain IronForge turned to his knights. "Let's ride."

The group passed through the lush green grasses and orange sandstone bluffs of northern Meuribar and came to the banks of the River Grand shortly before noon.

"The other side of this river," Nick said, "is the panhandle of Faldor. We don't know if Trondor's army has made it this far east. If they haven't, they're likely on their way."

"I'll scout ahead and to the west." Zen morphed into his eagle form and soared out across the Faldor plains.

It took the rest of them nearly an hour to secure their gear and cross the river. The dwarves, for the most part, couldn't swim. Their horses could, however, and Stirling's knights made it to the other side without incident. Nick was too weak to make the attempt, so Ember translocated him to the other side and returned for his horse. Ellessar and Ember, riding their own horses, led Zen's and Nick's across on tethers.

By the time they were ready to move out, Zen had returned. "Two columns of Trondorian troops headed this way, about twenty miles to the west. They're going from farmhouse to farmhouse commandeering food, livestock, and supplies. And confiscating any weapons larger than a cooking knife. They're moving slowly, but we shouldn't dawdle."

A few hours later, the party entered the deserted village of Dead Man. It looked worse than Tawneydale had after King Gremauld razed it during Trondor's civil war. Not a soul lived there. The bodies—all women, children, and the elderly—lay in pieces, reeking of fresh slaughter. The men had probably gone south to defend the capital.

"This village is aptly named," Ellessar said sourly.

Nick and the others said nothing, but they kept a watchful eye out for demons who might still linger in the area.

North of the village, Ellessar bent to examine some tracks in the churned-up ground of a damp wash. "This set of tracks has eight cloven hooves, heavy in the front, like a centaur's. I'd say half a dozen Scout demons, headed west, possibly looking for us."

"These people probably would have fared better if Balor's army had gotten here first," Nick mused.

"Can we take out the Scouts?" Zen asked.

"With the dwarves, perhaps. But they're fast and have several hours' head start."

"We can't afford the time to chase them down," Jasmine said.

Reluctantly, Ellessar agreed. "We must be cautious."

As the western sky turned crimson at dusk the following day, the failing of the sunlight revealed a pale-emerald glow that spanned the entire northern horizon. Nick glanced at Zen, who just shrugged.

"Come on," Nick said. "Let's try to make the elven lands before we stop for the night."

As the party continued in uneasy silence and the glow intensified, the dwarves muttered to themselves and to each other. They shifted nervously in their saddles, though not one took his weapon in hand. If this was of the Master, it wasn't something weapons could fight.

By midnight, they reached the border. The green glow emanated from an energy field of some kind that seemed to run along the length of the boundary between Faldor and Lorentil, a dome that looked like it might cover the whole elven kingdom. It barred their way forward.

CHAPTER 20

As the party approached the barrier, Zen pointed out another prominent set of tracks along the base of it.

Ellessar dismounted from Spirit to inspect them. "Another patrol of Scout demons." He gestured toward the west. "Headed that way. Not long ago."

The energy field glowed a faint green, a shade somewhere between the color of grass and that of ripe green grapes. Ellessar touched it with his palm. The glow brightened where his skin met it, but the barrier didn't stop him from pressing his hand through it. After a moment, he stepped through and coaxed Spirit through behind him. He turned back toward the party and shrugged.

Zen nudged his horse forward. The animal shied away, so he dismounted and pulled it ahead. As he stepped through, the barrier burned along his skin. He gritted his teeth to keep from crying out in pain, but it permitted him passage. The horse crossed without apparent discomfort.

Nick dismounted next. When he touched the barrier, runes shot from the point of contact and radiated outward like sparks popping from the hot coals of a campfire. To him, the barrier was solid.

Ember stepped through without difficulty.

The barrier glowed an angry green even as Jasmine reached out. When she touched the barrier, she cried out, and it threw her violently backwards. Smoke wafted from her singed palm.

"I guess we need somebody's permission," Borim grumbled.

"Or elven blood," Ellessar said.

Zen glanced up at the bright waxing moon, clearly visible from this edge of the elven forest. "Camp here. I'll go see if I can find somebody to let you in."

"Keep an eye out for those demons," Ellessar added. "They may be scouting for a weakness in the barrier, but if they're searching for us, they might double back."

"You wait with them," Zen told Ember and the demon hunter. "I won't be gone long, and you'll slow me down." With that, he gestured into the ether, chanted a few elven phrases, and morphed into an ice hippogriff.

He stretched out his wings and took to the air. A magical barrier of this magnitude, if it spanned the length of the elven border, must be the work of a legion of mages all working in concert. It would require constant maintenance. It probably didn't matter which direction Zen flew along the barrier. Sooner or later, he would find the elves. He chose west because that was the direction the demon scouts had gone. If they were near, he could return and warn his friends.

Within a few miles' travel, a contingent of sixteen elven warriors, all mounted on hippogriffs, flew toward him, headed back the way from which Zen had come. He banked high, staying in plain view of the riders, who watched him warily. He was no ordinary hippogriff; they would recognize that from his snow-white coloring, and they would perceive an aura of enchantment if they thought to check for it.

The question was whether or not they saw him as a threat.

He swooped around and fell in alongside one of the riders. Several others fanned out behind him, lances drawn and ready.

Zen acknowledged his escort with a nod and continued to pace the patrol all the way back to his companions' camp, where the riders landed and arrayed themselves around Ember and Ellessar, the only two on the elven side of the barrier. Neither made any movement toward their weapons. Both placed their right hand over their heart and bowed their heads in a nod toward the riders.

The leader of the patrol had neither the time nor patience for pleasantries. He drew his sword and dismounted. "Why have you come to Lorentil?"

Zen resumed his elf-kin form, still surrounded by the elven guards. Ellessar presented the amulet of his order, and Ember her diplomatic documents.

"We come on a mission for Alamain," Ellessar said, "the High Priestess of Aeron—"

"We know who she is. Where were you sent from?" The leader seemed to be the eldest among those in the patrol, his face weathered and his hair beginning to gray. He must have been hundreds of years old, not quite middle age for an elf. His question was a test. Alamain lived in the capital city of Lorentil; it was the only place from which she could have sent them.

Because neither Ellessar nor Ember had been with them when they'd first visited the High Priestess, Zen answered for them. "She sent us from the high temple in your own capital city many months ago and bade us to return."

"For what purpose?"

"For her blessing. We have forged a weapon with which to fight the Dark Master of Mortaan's Last Prophecy, the man who released the demons into the Civilized Lands. When we came last, we sought her guidance. She foresaw that we would one day face the Master and warned us not to do so without returning for her blessing."

"An extraordinary tale. You?" He took a quick count of the

dwarven knights and the rest of the company. "The twenty-seven of you intend to take the fight to the Master?"

Zen nodded solemnly.

"Then you come not for her blessing, but for last rites."

"Call it what you will." Ellessar stepped toward the elf. "We will do what we must to stem the tide of demons."

"What of the dwarven knights?" the elf leader continued. "Did she summon them as well?"

"No," Ember said. "The weapon was forged in Gildstone. The dwarven elders charged these knights to see that we, and it, reach the high temple safely."

"Then you may enter, but the knights may not. No offense," he added to Captain IronForge, who was listening from beyond the barrier. "Dwarves don't properly respect the elven forest, and your protection won't be necessary within the confines of the barrier."

"Except for that one." Ember gestured at Borim, the only dwarf without the uniform and armor of the dwarven knights. "He's with us." Borim had not been with them when they last visited Alamain, but including a dwarf in the party would help assuage the inflated dwarven pride of the Knights of SteelStone.

Borim stepped forward. He removed his cap and displayed his most innocent-looking grin. It didn't suit him.

Ember presented her documents once again, drawing attention to the official diplomatic seal of the dwarven elders. "I'm an ambassador. He and I—" she gestured toward Borim— "are here in an official capacity as representatives of the dwarven people. I will personally supervise his passage. He will respect our woods."

"Very well." The elven leader gestured to another among his party, a female with flowing golden hair. Her clothing and gear didn't distinguish her from the rest of her patrol until she produced a wand—a single shaft of emerald, from the looks of it—from somewhere beneath her tunic. She touched the barrier and spoke a word in an ancient tongue. A circular opening swelled from the wand's tip.

Nick and Borim passed through, their horses in tow.

The elven leader stopped Jasmine with the tip of his sword. "What of this one?"

"She's with us as well," Ember said.

The guard looked skeptically at Jasmine's wounded hand. "Did the barrier do that?"

Zen stepped forward. "Not all of us were admitted into Alamain's presence during our last visit, but she was. Her heart is pure. Alamain trusts her and bade her specifically to return."

Still the elf hesitated.

"Would you defy the wishes of the High Priestess?" Ellessar asked.

The elf eyed him carefully, then asked to see Ember's document again. He studied the seal for a long time.

"Decide," the elven mage said. "I can't hold the opening forever."

The leader stepped aside for Jasmine to pass and returned Ember's documents.

The companions and the elven patrol camped along the border that night, within sight and earshot of the dwarven knights. Jasmine used the first hour to meditate and heal her burned palm.

"Don't fret about us," Sterling said before the company departed the next morning. "We have some Scout demons to kill. No sense letting them report back to their army."

Ellessar smiled. "I wish I could go with you."

"When you get back home," Nick added, "thank the elders for their help. We wouldn't have made it here unhindered without you."

The patrol leader beckoned to one of the elves under his command. "Escort these visitors to the capital."

A sturdy elf, muscular enough in the upper body to pass for human if it wasn't for his pointed ears and the sheen of his short platinum hair, walked his hippogriff forward and addressed Ember and

Ellessar. He placed his hand over his heart and bowed his head. "Alanel Solorren at your service."

The trip across the elven kingdom seemed exactly as Zen had remembered it from their last visit, although they had entered at a different location. That's the way it was in the elven woods. To the eyes of anyone but an experienced elven guide, every route through it looked exactly the same as every other route. Just enough mist lingered in the air to diffuse the sunlight and to prevent any non-elf from keeping their bearings reliably within a uniform forest that was dense enough to prevent a view of the horizon in any direction.

Only Alanel seemed to have a firm sense of direction. He led them, as best as Zen could determine, straight toward the elven capital, admonishing them regularly not to ride single file so they wouldn't wear a visible trail through the bed of forest grasses.

Nevertheless, the woods felt different than they had in the past: more tense, as if the entire kingdom—trees, animals, and elves—held its collective breath, waiting for the barrier to crack and the Master's armies to engulf the land. The creatures that once made sounds and fleeting appearances, or who viewed unwary travelers as prey, remained unseen and unheard, having fled or taken to their dens. Or maybe, as with the hippogriffs, the elves had enlisted them.

Four days later, bone weary and numb from the long, breakneck ride from Glintbroc, the group arrived in the magic capital of the Civilized Lands. What enchanted items might Zen come across and contrive to acquire—fairly, of course—in the elven city?

Alanel stopped at the city limit. "You know where you're going from here?"

"Yes," Jasmine said. "Thank you."

"Then I must make my report. You're free to move about the city, but don't leave it without an elven guide."

"Wouldn't think of it," Borim grumbled.

"I'll catch up with you at the high temple." Alanel trotted off toward the center of the city.

Ellessar made straight for the pearly temple of the High Priestess of Aeron. Unlike in the elven wilderness, here Zen did recognize some of the landmarks, including the spire of Glimmernook, the mages' college. The last time Zen had come here, Alamain's warders had shunned him for lack of a pure heart. That was before the companions had taken possession of the Shield of Faith—before Zen had taken the Oath of Aeron. Sure, he still craved power. But he'd been good since the incident in Dragon Tears. Maybe this time the priests would actually let him meet Alamain.

Nick staggered from his horse, his skin red and flaking everywhere. It itched—even burned—but he couldn't scratch without causing himself extreme pain. His hair, all but gone, had fallen out in clumps along the way. His nose and gums bled. Zen and Ellessar helped him to the temple doors.

The temple itself was an ostentatious display of gold, white marble with veins of emerald green, and intricately carved statuary. Ellessar dropped a handful of coins—mostly copper, as that was what they had—into the collection coffer. He displayed the symbol of his order to the acolyte at the receiving desk and asked that they might bathe.

"We must see Alamain immediately." Nick's voice was so weak he couldn't be heard from more than a few feet away.

"Bathing won't take long," Ellessar said. "And it will show proper respect for the High Priestess."

"But—" Nick hadn't the strength to argue.

Ellessar returned his attention to the acolyte and waited.

"Yes, brother." The acolyte rose and stepped out from behind the marble desk. "You and your guests are welcome."

"We request boarding for ourselves and our horses for the night," Ellessar added.

"Of course." The acolyte bowed.

"And an audience with the High Priestess..."

The boy's eyes widened.

"...At her earliest convenience," Ellessar continued. "Inform her that it's a matter of utmost, indeed grave, importance."

"Wh— who shall I say is calling?"

"Brother Ellessar, of the Order of the Shining Star."

The boy seemed only then to recognize the Shield. He pointed. "Is that—"

"The Shield of Faith, son," Borim rumbled. "Now get movin'."

"Wait." Jasmine took a step forward, finally crossing the threshold from the bright sunlight outside. The large, gold-plated door clicked closed behind her. She lowered the cowl she'd used to conceal her features for the duration of their journey from Glintbroc. "Tell her Jasmine, the demon-kin, is with him."

Color drained from the poor boy's face. He appeared to be frozen where he stood, as though Zen had woven some enchantment on him. "D— d— d—"

Unperturbed, Jasmine continued, "And Nicklan Mirrin. She'll know the name."

The boy stammered for many long moments before his gaze returned, speechless, to Ellessar.

"It's okay, son." Ellessar made a run-along gesture with his hands. "Just tell her. And don't forget the other things I requested."

"Yes, sir... I mean, brother. I—" He ran off into the shining halls of the temple.

"That went rather well," Ember commented.

Borim snickered. Before he could stifle it, a priest showed up. A second acolyte trotted past them and out the front door with a bucket, sponge, and curry comb to tend to the horses.

The priest offered the elven greeting to Ellessar. "Welcome to the high temple, brother. This way to the bathhouse."

Ellessar fell into step behind him. "We appreciate the hospitality, especially in times of such great peril. By the blessing of Aeron, we won't be here long."

Irlyren leaned against the wall of the apothecary as she had done every day for the past three months. Business had slowed substantially in her line of work, with most of the able-bodied males gone to defend the border. Those who remained were the dignitaries, who had their own supply of concubines, and the infirm, who knew better than to seek her services until they became well. That left the disabled, the young, and the females—elven or otherwise—who enjoyed their own gender. There weren't enough of these to support the trade.

Fortunately, Irlyren had no need to look for work. Day after day, she refused every potential customer who approached. Gwyndarren Lortannon was taking care of her. He paid her well for the simple service of watching the Temple of Aeron during the day. At night, he gave her the carnal stimulation to which her body had become accustomed.

Today that would all come to an end. Zenobrian Zersaash, the mage for whom Gwyndarren was paying her to keep watch, had returned.

As soon as Zen and his companions disappeared through the temple doors, Irlyren slipped into an alleyway. She snaked her way through the commercial district and into the wooded outskirts of the city, to a small, unassuming cottage.

Gwyndarren answered the door. "Irlyren? I didn't expect you until nightfall."

"He's here."

After a stunned moment, a broad smile spread across Gwyndarren's face. He placed a tender palm on Irlyren's cheek. "Fear not, my darling. You've done me a great service. Though I must leave soon, you may stay here until I return. You'll not want for coin."

"It's not the coin I care about."

"You're as beautiful an elf as I ever saw. You'll find clients enough to keep you entertained. Return now to the temple. Zen will be in a hurry. If he leaves before nightfall, follow him and tell me where he goes."

CHAPTER 21

Nick had barely stepped out of his bath when the priest returned, breathless. "Alamain will see you immediately."

"We'll be right there." Nick wrapped a towel about his withered body.

"I've sent for the ladies in your party, as well," the priest said.

"This is unprecedented," Ellessar remarked a few minutes later, once the party had regrouped and were following the priest to Alamain's audience chamber. "To see the High Priestess on such short notice—"

"She was expecting our return," Nick said. "And she has as much at stake as anyone in opposing the Prophecy. I can't think of anything she should find more important or more urgent."

Together they filed into the antechamber, where the priest lined them up along one wall.

"We must observe silence for a few moments." He gripped a

rose-colored amulet in his hand and recited a prayer before each companion. The priest examined them as though he could see straight into their hearts, which he probably could.

Finally, he announced them ready to enter the presence of the High Priestess.

"All of us?" Zen sounded surprised.

"Unless you desire otherwise. You'll need to leave your weapons and other belongings here."

Borim shook his head and backed away.

"You have to go in," Nick told him. "None of us can face the Master until we've received her blessing."

Borim's eyes widened. He stuffed enough maple chews into his mouth to mortar a battlement. His cheeks bulged as he tried to work the wad of candy, which would likely take him at least thirty minutes to do. It was just as well. If they were lucky, the audience would end before he could say anything inappropriate.

They had left most of their gear in their bedchambers, except for the talisman sword. After Nick tried unsuccessfully to raise it, Ellessar took it from him and held it out, sheathed, for the priest's inspection. "We brought this in hopes that Alamain would grant the blessing of Aeron upon it."

"The High Priestess specifically asked us to return with it," Nick added, "for this very purpose."

The priest bowed his head in acknowledgment. "In that case, I will carry the sword on your behalf." He took the talisman gently, grunted at its unexpected weight, and proceeded into the audience chamber.

He ushered them into the room. Religious symbols—stylized stars and rays representing the light and purity of Aeron—decorated the walls of the small, ornate audience chamber, the shapes carved into the polished stone and inlaid with silver. A crystal chandelier that hung from the arched ceiling held some fifty burning candles made from pure-white wax. Silver candelabra framed a gilded throne that sat on a white marble dais.

Alamain sat, stately and handsome, on the throne of her office, dressed in a pale-pink gown, a polished silver staff leaning beside her. She was old, even for an elf, her white hair thinner and her face more haggard than when Nick had seen her last. A lot had happened since then. Her lavender eyes fixed on Nick as the companions entered.

Quickly, Ellessar introduced the entire party.

Alamain rose. She padded forward a few steps and stood before Nick. "Your road has been difficult." Her voice, no more that a whisper, held no hint of a question. "It will get more difficult still." She swept the party with her gaze. "Some of you I know. Others are new to my acquaintance. Nevertheless, I thank you all for your service to our cause."

"We came—"

Alamain silenced Ellessar with a gesture. "I know why you're here. Let me see this weapon you've had forged."

The priest cradled the sword in his arms like a baby. He handed it reverently to the High Priestess.

Alamain took the talisman and unsheathed it as though it weighed nothing in her withered hands. She prayed over it for several minutes, stroking it with frail-looking fingers.

The High Priestess seemed to drift on air beneath her flowing gown to a basin of holy water. There she bathed the sword. Eyes closed and chanting in her lilting elven tongue, she raised it up as an offering to Aeron.

When Alamain finished, she wrapped it in white silk and handed it back, along with its sheath, to the priest. Then she turned to Nick. "You plan to use this to battle the Master." Again, it wasn't a question.

"Yes."

"Then I must bless all of you as well."

Borim's eyes widened further, but he said nothing, still working on his mouthful of chews.

Alamain dipped a small ivory bowl into the holy water and glided to Nick. "When we're done here, we'll see what Aeron can do for your body. His champion must be well for the battle."

Nick bowed. "I would be grateful."

Alamain spoke a prayer, again in the elven tongue. She dipped her fingers into the bowl and wet his forehead. As she moved on to Ellessar, the accompanying priest stepped up and laid a pendant around Nick's neck, a platinum chain with a clear, pink, tear-shaped crystal. Together Alamain and the priest repeated the ceremony for each of the companions, concluding with Borim, who stopped working his wad of candy and seemed to hold his breath until she stepped away.

"These pendants are wards against the whims of the High Priest of Vexetan. The Prophecy says that none in his presence can resist his will. If these wards are strong enough, and if *you* are strong enough, they'll protect you from this power. If not, then all is indeed lost."

"Thank you, High Priestess," Ellessar said. "We do not deserve such gifts."

"Perhaps," she acknowledged. "Only Aeron may judge our worth. Nevertheless, you will need them. How else may I aid your cause?"

Jasmine stepped forward and clasped her hands behind her, as if she was addressing one of her superiors at the monastery. "We have traveled the length and breadth of the Civilized Lands, from Palidor to Trondor, from North Reach to South Bend. We've crossed the Great Divide into the Wild Lands and journeyed to the fiery heart of Gildstone. Yet we have heard no word of the whereabouts of the Master. We assume he leads his army of demons, but we do not know. If you have a way, we would like to confirm this before we rush headlong into his host of evil."

Alamain's shoulders dropped slightly. She pursed her lips. "Vexetan conceals his champion. Not even Aeron has been able to penetrate his veil of deception. I have sent my agents to scour the Lands for information. They've uncovered many of his agents, but not the Master himself. He hides from mortals, and Vexetan hides him from the gods."

"Then you may know some of the Chosen," Nick said. "We've only discovered half of them." He listed Balor Culhaven, Pandalo Gundahar, Dalen Frost, Whisper, Vinsous Drakemoor, and the ogre Groot. "Whisper and Drakemoor are dead. We have also seen a dragon with a rider we suspect is a Chosen."

Alamain nodded, pensive. "I know of a few more. First, the dragon rider is a Chosen, as is the dragon—fear that one—and the leaders of the Master's three armies. You've named King Culhaven of Trondor and his general. The goblin-kin army that ravages Palidor, even as we speak, is led by the ogre you named."

Nick's heart sank at the news that Palidor, too, was overrun. No place in all the Civilized Lands remained safe, except for Lorentil, and that for only as long as they could maintain their magical barrier.

"And the demons?" Ellessar asked. "Who leads them?"

"A demon lord named Ri-T'rannoc."

Ellessar blanched and staggered back.

"You know him?" Zen asked.

"I know *of* him, though even my order believed him only a legend. I'd rather face the dragon."

"We likely will," Zen observed. "Isn't that why we carry the Shield?"

"He also has a Hunter demon," Alamain said.

Ellessar nodded, as though he had suspected as much.

Alamain continued, "That accounts for all but two. Those you will likely find at the Master's side."

"If we can find the Master at all," Zen said.

Ellessar straightened. "If we're meant to face him, Aeron will deliver us to him."

"You are, and he will," Alamain assured them, "if we're to believe the Prophecy." She paused. "Anything else?"

"What of the war?" Ember asked. "What have you learned of the deployment and strength of the enemy?"

"For that, I'll refer you to my knight general."

"I'll send for him." The priest opened the door to the antechamber and spoke quietly to an acolyte, who hurried down the hall.

Alamain returned to Nick. "Now let's see what we can do for you." With a final nod to the others, she led him through a gilded door at the back of the room.

Ellessar took the sword from the priest as soon as they left Alamain's audience chamber. He presented it to the others. "Behold the Sword of Alamain."

Borim swallowed the last of his maple chews with an audible gulp. "Is that what we're callin' it now?"

Zen spoke a few words in old elfish. "It radiates magic. Did she make it any lighter?"

Ellessar handed it to him. "Heavy as ever."

"In that case," Jasmine said, "I hope she can do something for Nick."

"If it's Aeron's will to help him, he'll do so in this place." Though only Nick had the strength to wield the Sword properly, Ellessar was more than willing to step in, if necessary, even if he had to wield the talisman in an unfamiliar two-handed style. He could begin working with it in the practice yard as early as the next morning. "Right now, we have a bigger problem. We still have to find the Master, or we've no place to take the Sword."

"I assume we'll find him at the head of his armies," Jasmine said. "But he has three, and each has its general. To which shall we go?"

Ellessar took back the Sword. "If he's with one of his armies—and that's a big if—then it will most likely be the demons. Demons are strong-willed and prone to chaos. It'll take the hand of Vexetan to unite them."

"There are at least two demon forces." Alamain's knight general strode into the small antechamber. "Possibly three."

The companions turned.

The knight, resplendent in his dress uniform, sans armor, placed his right hand over his heart and bowed his head toward Ellessar. "Lord Roslin Anglisi at your service."

Ellessar returned the elven gesture and briefly introduced his party. "Two demon armies?"

"At least. The distance from the Great Sand to the elven kingdom is at its minimum in Meuribar, just north of the Great Sand."

"I know the place," Zen said. "Nick's hometown of Cedar Falls is near there."

"If he has any family there," Lord Roslin continued, "I hope they've cleared out. The Master's Siege demons have massed there, with a hoard of their lessers. Even now they try to weaken our barrier."

"An impressive piece of magic, that barrier," Zen said. "I didn't know the elves could do such a thing."

"We can't. As soon as the Portal of the Damned opened, the fairies returned from the Mist Isles and erected it. It'll last only as long as they can maintain it. Nobody knows how long that will be. It's an enormous drain on their power."

"I can imagine," Zen said.

"Come." The knight general gestured toward the door. "Let us not tie up the High Priestess's antechamber."

"I thought the demons were heading toward Meuribar," Ellessar said. "The humans and dwarves are preparing to meet them there."

"Many are. That's the second force. There may be a third in Brinheim."

"Then where are we supposed to look for the Master?" Borim asked.

None of them had started for the door, so the knight led them out.

They were halfway to their rooms before any of them spoke again.

"I'll stop by the dwarven embassy," Ember said finally. "Maybe they have news."

"If not," Ellessar said. "I suggest we go to the Portal of the

Damned. If we close that down, the Master will come to us."

"How do we get to it through an army of demons?" Borim asked.

Jasmine gestured to Zen. "Translocate?"

Zen shook his head. "I've never been there. I can only go to a place I've seen. Even then, we'd have to be within a few hours' ride."

They fell silent as Alamain's knight rounded the corner into a large sitting room with a cozy fire burning in the hearth. The six of them were the only ones present.

Jasmine strode to the center of the room and spun to face the others. "Meuribar."

Zen straightened. "What about it?"

"You've been there. We can work our way toward the city—from the west, if necessary. We'll get as close as we can, and then translocate to somewhere inside the walls." Jasmine counted off her friend's concerns on her limited number of digits. "We can get information there. They're at the forefront of the battle. If the Master is there, someone will know. Borim, you can bust some heads with the rest of the dwarves. And it's near the Great Sand. If we decide to go to the Portal, we'll be most of the way there."

"That's a dangerous place to be if we don't find him," Zen noted. "Then we'll be back where we started. Besides, I don't know that I can translocate anyone but myself. I think I can, but I've never actually tried it. Perhaps Ember…"

"I can take two at a time," the elf girl said, "but my distance is limited. You can travel much farther than I can."

Jasmine faced Zen squarely. "If we can find a safe place to hole up for the transfer, you'll have time to make several trips. So, unless one of you has a better idea…"

Nobody did.

CHAPTER 22

Alamain spent the night on her knees, praying over Nick while he slept. She determined right away that she couldn't heal the man's illness. Aeron revealed it to be an otherworldly affliction; not from another plane of existence, which Alamain probably could have dealt with, but from another physical world—whatever that meant—and therefore beyond Alamain's purview.

That didn't mean she could do nothing for him, however. There was one thing she could *always* do, and it was the most important thing anyone could do in times of trouble. She could give the problem to Aeron and trust him with it. So she prayed that Aeron himself would provide both healing for Nick and a way for his party to locate the Master of Mortaan's Prophecy.

A great peace settled into her, and she rose painfully to her feet. She'd done what she could. Spending more time at Nick's side would avail her nothing. Besides, she trusted Aeron enough to believe he would find a way.

Zenobrian Zersaash.

Zen startled awake. Months had passed since he'd heard that voice in his head, but he couldn't mistake it.

This is Gwyndarren Lortannon. I've been waiting for your return, and I had begun to fear you'd met your demise in the Wild Lands. Meet me in the courtyard in front of Glimmernook in an hour. I have good news that will benefit both of us.

As Zen rolled out of bed and pulled on his robes, his mouth twisted into a conniving grin. He'd hoped to hear from the elf once he returned to Lorentil. Zen had seen enough evidence of Gwyndarren's involvement with the Black Hand, and with King Balor Culhaven of Trondor, to convince him that the elf was working on the side of the Master, either directly or indirectly. But Gwyndarren contacted him only when he wanted something, and he always offered valuable magic in return. Zen inventoried his supplies and grabbed his staff.

Gwyndarren would have something of power, and he would have it with him. Tonight, Zen would reveal nothing to the elf. To do so would violate his Oath to Aeron. Nevertheless, one way or another, he would acquire whatever Gwyndarren was offering. The only problem was that the elf had substantial resources. That was the only explanation for the enchanted objects he'd been able to offer. But Zen had resources too. And his own abilities had increased greatly since he'd last seen Gwyndarren.

Focusing his mind on the courtyard just beyond the temple wall, Zen opened a portal and stepped through. He could have gone directly to the square outside Glimmernook—he remembered the location well enough—but Gwyndarren or his spies might already be there, and Zen didn't want to reveal his translocation ability to the elf if he could help it.

Zen morphed into the form of a white house cat. Gwyndarren probably expected him to arrive early to check the place out—only a fool wouldn't—but he wouldn't expect Zen to show up in the guise of a small animal.

Two elven guards patrolled the square. Drunks and a few ladies of the night loitered there as well, despite the early morning hour. The taverns remained open, allowing citizens to drown the specter of war in a bottle of elven brandy. Zen had hoped Gwyndarren would pick a more private location for their meeting, but the elf was too cautious for that. Zen would have to "negotiate" carefully.

Finding nothing threatening, Zen snuck into the shadow of a darkened porch. He returned to his natural form and waited.

Gwyndarren arrived at the appointed time, apparently alone. Zen almost didn't recognize the elf, with his long dark hair concealed beneath the hood of his black cloak. He carried nothing larger than a pouch, but that meant little. Objects of power were often designed to be concealed.

The elf turned when Zen strode out to meet him. He kept his hands in the pockets of his cloak. "It's good to find you well, my friend."

Zen inclined his head politely but said nothing. Gwyndarren was no friend. The elf must have told the Black Hand of the companions' destination in the Wild Lands. The bandits couldn't have found them otherwise.

"I have good news."

Zen grunted. "So you said. Let's have it."

"When we first met, you said you wanted power and that you wanted to survive the Prophecy. My designs have been the same. Now we can have both."

Zen narrowed his eyes. "You think I couldn't before?"

"That all depends on whose side you're on. Your friends oppose the Prophecy. But we both know it will ultimately come to pass.

Mortaan has never been wrong before. Why should we expect him to be this time?"

There was that. It was a fact Zen had deliberately ignored for months.

"The problem is," Gwyndarren continued, "if you fight on the side of the Master, you end up on the side of the Master."

"So..." Zen winced inwardly, waiting for Aeron to strike him down, but he was willing to hear the elf out before he decided whether to keep the Oath of Aeron or abandon the Shield of Faith.

"When the Master rules the Civilized Lands, he'll plunge them into darkness," Gwyndarren said. "Unless you're among his inner circle, you'll live in that darkness. There *is* no winning side."

"Unless I'm among his inner circle, and without a Medallion of Vexetan chained around my neck."

"Right. That's the good news. You can be. We both can." Gwyndarren pulled his hand from his robes, dangling a Medallion of Vexetan by a slender gold chain.

"I'll not become a slave of the Master."

"Neither will I." Gwyndarren parted his robes to reveal a bare neck and chest. "I'll *never* wear one of these Medallions."

"Then how did you get it?"

"I stole it from the palace in Trondor. It belonged to Vinsous Drakemoor, the assassin your friends killed in the king's library." He leaned closer. "Though I don't wear it, I can speak with the Master through it."

"Impressive."

"Zen—" Gwyndarren lowered his already-quiet voice— "you've already betrayed your friends three times: once when you led them away from the Black Hand hideout in Forlorn Valley, once when you chose not to oppose Drakemoor the day you found the Codex, and once when you revealed to me the purpose of your errand in the Wild Lands. You've passed the Master's tests. Now we need only pay a fee of admission, and we're in, you and me. We'll stand at the Master's side when the Prophecy goes down, and he'll reward our loyalty with riches for me and power for you."

"And he'll force a Medallion upon each of us."

"He can't. They must be donned voluntarily or they're powerless."

That was a rumor Zen wouldn't have to test, not with Alamain's pendant around his neck, an assurance that might give him the courage to take the next step. "What's the Master's price?"

"The weapon you brought back for Alamain's blessing."

"The talisman sword." It would be easy enough to get. Zen had seen it in Ellessar's sleeping chamber just a few hours before, and he could visualize the room well enough to get in without opening the door.

"We deliver the sword," Gwyndarren finished, "and we're in."

Nick woke after a full night's sleep in a comfortable bed, feeling more rested than he had in a week. A few minutes later, a soft knock sounded from the door. He cleared his throat and tried to speak. "Come in," he croaked, sounding like something that had crawled out of the Wild Lands bog.

Alamain padded into the room. A fresh white dress flowed around her. "How do you feel?"

Nick examined the welts and flaking skin on his arms, which seemed unchanged from the night before. "I'm not as tired." That was the extent of the improvement. His skin still burned and his stomach tumbled when he pondered the idea of breakfast.

Alamain gestured at his enflamed skin. "I cannot heal this ailment."

"An ailment Aeron can't heal?" Nick asked.

"I didn't say that. He has not granted *me* the means to heal you. But if you're meant to face the Master, Aeron will provide a way."

The priest who'd assisted them in the antechamber the night

before stepped into the room. "Brother Ellessar has requested your presence. The Sword has been stolen."

Stolen. The word barely registered. Was there any safer place for the Sword than in the high temple of Aeron? How could it have been stolen?

Nick levered himself out of bed, still wearing the silk nightshirt he'd put on the previous evening. "I'll join you in a few minutes."

As soon as Alamain and the priest left the room, Nick eased on his tunic and britches, which had been cleaned and lain out for him. He seemed to have lost more weight overnight. His clothes draped on him. His boots were a size too big. Yet it required a monumental effort just to pull them on.

With his strength gone, desperation alone drove him as he snaked his way through the opulent passages back to Alamain's audience chamber.

Ember paced the room like a caged wolf, clenching and unclenching her fists, muttering a string of phrases that Nick didn't recognize. The words were too course to be elven. Dwarven profanity, most likely.

Jasmine stood calm and determined. A lifetime of training, her demon heritage, or the events of the past months in fighting the Prophecy seemed to have leached from her the capacity for panic.

Borim remained near the door as if he was ready to bolt from the chamber, though this time he hadn't stuffed his mouth with sweets.

Alamain's knight general, full dress armor matching that which Lord Kelton had worn at Roybal Keep, stood in the corner. His insignia of rank adorned the corner of his breastplate.

Among Nick's companions, Ellessar looked the worst. His face was tight with suppressed rage or self-loathing. He must have been the one charged with safeguarding the Sword in Nick's absence and therefore held himself responsible for the theft, as though he had failed Aeron. Only his respect for the High Priestess and the god they served seemed to keep him from ranting.

To Nick, the situation seemed much simpler than the demon

hunter would ever make it out to be. Ellessar hadn't failed; the Master had succeeded. No blame could be placed on anyone in this chamber. There was one, however, who might be culpable. "Where's Zen?"

"Gone." Ellessar spat the word through taut lips and clenched teeth.

"Easy, brother." Alamain made a placating gesture with her hands, palms down. "We mustn't jump to conclusions. At the moment, he's simply not here. We know nothing more."

Ellessar met her gaze, his expression unchanged. "I've been to his chamber. All of his things are gone. Packed up neat and tidy."

"Maybe he went after the thief," Nick said, "and didn't have time to wake us."

"He had time to make his bed."

Nick pursed his lips.

Ellessar continued, "This is my punishment for failing to be more diligent."

"You mustn't blame yourself," Alamain said. "You're not responsible for the actions of another."

The High Priestess was right. They'd all done their utmost to oppose the Master. Nevertheless, he'd been a step ahead of them at every turn, from the moment Whisper and the Black Hand had burned Nick's home to the ground in search of Grandpa Gaddy's journal, to Rancid's diversion into the hills of Palidor, which had cost the party weeks in their search for the Codex—weeks that, if saved, might have gotten the companions here with the Sword before the demons were unleashed into the Civilized Lands.

The Master had manipulated Nick into killing the king of Trondor in order to place a Chosen on the throne—a Chosen who now ruled by fear the peaceful neighboring kingdom of Faldor. The Master had even planted one of the Chosen within the companions' party. That spy, Vinsous Drakemoor, had taken the lives of two of Nick's friends.

Even after they had escaped from the palace dungeons, the Master remained a step ahead, with his dragon, his Black Hand, and his Assassin demons pursuing them deep into the heart of the Wild Lands.

HOST OF EVIL

The theft of the Sword was just another link in a long chain of subterfuge and deception, infiltration and betrayal.

"We have to find him," Nick stated, though he himself was in no shape to travel. "We need that sword."

Alamain turned to the knight. "Bring Alanel Solorren." Nick recognized the name as that of the elf who'd guided them through the forest to the city of Lorentil.

The knight nodded curtly and strode out the door.

Alamain continued. "Alanel will be at your disposal until you recover the Sword." She turned to Ellessar. "You searched Zen's room?"

Ellessar's nod looked like nothing more than a spasm of his neck muscles.

"Search it again. He must have left something of himself behind: a strand of hair, lint from his robe, a single coin. If so, I might be able to locate him."

Without a word or gesture, Ellessar left to do her bidding.

"He can resist such attempts," Jasmine cautioned.

"A lot of good it did us against the Assassin demons," Nick said.

"Unless Vexetan himself conceals Zen's movements, I will find him," Alamain assured them. "He can't hide from the sight of Aeron by his own power or by mortal-made enchantments. But I must have something of his to make the attempt."

"In hindsight," Nick mused, "Zen's whole non-detection routine might have been a ruse, a guise to conceal whatever he was really weaving day after day."

Borim, still standing just inside the door, muttered something under his breath.

"What was that?" Jasmine asked him.

"Don't make no sense." He glanced from one silent face to another. "The only reason the Master would want the Sword is to keep us from using it against him. It would have served his purpose just as well if Zen had stolen the ore before we had it forged into a weapon. He had plenty of chances. Why would he wait until we got it all the way here and had it blessed before stealin' it?"

"Good question," Jasmine said.

Ellessar returned with a strand of hair pinched between his thumb and forefinger. "Zen must have realized we might try to scry. This hair is the only one I could find in his chamber, and I'm not even sure it's his."

Alamain took the strand and examined it. "The length is about right, and the color is similar. Shall we give it a try?"

They gathered around the basin of holy water in which Alamain had blessed the Sword the previous day. She placed the hair in the middle, where it floated on the surface, and then bowed her head to pray in her flowery elven tongue. Gradually, the hair dissolved into a myriad of colors and diffused throughout the water. An image formed in the basin, a diorama of green that looked real save for its size. The companions viewed the scene from above. In the image, two horsemen drove their mounts hard, as straight as the trees would allow, through the elven woods.

Both riders were cloaked, their faces hidden. The horses were unfamiliar. Nevertheless, Zen was unmistakable. The crystal-tipped staff protruding from a saddle-mounted holder gave away his identity as clearly as anything else could. He was centered in the image. The hair had indeed been his.

Though Zen wasn't large, the rider with him had a slightly smaller build. He was cloaked in black as befitted a servant of the Master.

The Sword, if either of them had it, remained hidden.

In the image, the haze in the sky left everything in shadow. Nick couldn't determine their direction of travel. "Do we still have the Seeking Stone?"

Jasmine produced it from Nick's backpack, which she'd leaned against the wall beside her bundle. The Stone, smooth, white, and about the size and shape of a goose's egg, glowed brightly—revealing that Zen hadn't gotten far.

Alamain looked up from the basin to determine the orientation of the image relative to the audience chamber and therefore to the high temple itself. "They're headed southeast."

"Toward where we entered the elven lands." Ellessar spun on his heels. "If he gets to the border, he'll have the landmarks he needs to translocate away. We'll lose the trail."

CHAPTER 23

Zen and Gwyndarren galloped through the thick elven forest as fast as their horses could navigate the trees. The elf had selected an excellent pair, but even the best of mounts would tire. They'd have to slow down soon.

The thought made Zen's heart shudder. He reached under his travelling cloak where he'd strapped the Sword and grabbed its hilt as though he intended to use it. Warmth emanated from the talisman. His old companions, his friends, would do everything within their power, and that of the church, to recover it. Zen's only hope was that they hadn't discovered the theft until morning.

If so, maybe he and Gwyndarren had put enough distance between themselves and their pursuers to reach the elven border.

With a grunt, Gwyndarren flew backward from his horse, as though he'd run into a low branch stretched across their trail, though there was no visible obstruction. Zen yanked the reins back, pulled his horse around, and backtracked to where Gwyndarren had fallen. He snatched the staff from its holder and scanned the trees for threats.

A low, eerie chanting drowned out the usual sounds of the woods, the noise disturbing—distracting. Dread settled into Zen's gut.

With a sinister hiss, a large reptilian mount crashed through the trees and barreled toward him. Black-tipped spikes, ranging in size from a dwarf's thumb to a signal horn, covered the creature's neck, shoulders, and the sides of its head. It ran on two powerful hind legs, balanced by a long, stout, spiked tail. Short forelegs dangled ineffectually in front of its chest. An elf with a huge halberd, pointed haft lowered like a lance, rode a customized saddle nestled among the creature's many spikes.

Zen spoke a word to his staff. A wall of ice appeared and began to thicken between himself and the charging mount, but he was too late. The spiked reptile crashed through the barrier, and a stream of spittle shot from his mouth. The spray burned like alchemical fire across Zen's arm and chest, searing his skin. His horse reared and nearly trampled Gwyndarren, who struggled, dazed, to his feet.

Unable to hold both his staff and his saddle, Zen chose the former. He slipped from his horse and landed on the ground beside Gwyndarren. The elf drew his sword and the Medallion of Vexetan he carried in a pouch on his belt. He held out the Medallion, dangling from its chain, in a white-fisted grip as far in front of him as the length of his arm would allow, as though he feared it might explode but couldn't bring himself to drop it.

He probably couldn't drop it, Zen mused for a moment. Evil things were that way: always corrupting, never letting go. Gwyndarren held his sword beside him, as if he didn't think he'd need it, or feared to raise it.

Another elf, who sat astride a second spiked reptile mount, emerged from a thicket, chanting the foul cadence that suffused the area.

"You mistake us!" Gwyndarren yelled. "We're not your enemy."

Zen held his staff ready, but stayed its power and awaited the riders' response.

The lead elf's eyes shot open wide. "Forgive us, Chosen One. We thought you were messengers, bringing news or orders to the elven army." He motioned to his partner, who silenced his chant. Nevertheless, the foul chill from the elf's prayers continued to unsettle Zen.

"I'm not a Chosen," Gwyndarren replied. "But I serve the same Master as you. We're on an errand for the dark one." He approached the lead rider and the two spoke in low tones for several minutes.

Zen kept his staff ready, in case Gwyndarren had some deception planned. Though the elf had always treated Zen fairly, Zen didn't count treachery beyond him.

Finally the mounted elves rode into the woods as Gwyndarren limped to Zen's side.

"Elves who serve Vexetan?" Zen asked.

"Not just serve. Worship. They represent a small minority of my race. Elven society tolerated them until the day the Portal opened and demons began pouring into the Civilized Lands. On that day, they wisely went into hiding. They seem to be the only ones who can domesticate those nasty thorn lizards as mounts."

The riders returned, herding before them Zen's and Gwyndarren's horses, who were wide-eyed with fear in the face of the spiked reptiles.

Zen picked at the holes etched through his travelling cloak and robe. He frowned at the burns on his skin.

"They're going to wait here," Gwyndarren said, "and intercept anyone who pursues us."

Nick waited, his agitation growing. How could he have been stupid enough to trust Zen despite Rancid's repeated warnings about the mage?

It took Ellessar and Alanel more than an hour to locate the trail left by Zen and his partner on the outskirts of the elven capital. Zen and his companion, whether he was one of the Master's Chosen or just an elven guide Zen had hired to take him as far as the border, had broken into a full run just half a mile beyond the city limit, leaving a trail of divots in the native grass that even an apprentice tracker could follow.

"How do we know he's got the Sword?" Borim bellowed as they raced through the trees. His voice carried over the hoofbeats. "Zen can turn into a bird. He wouldn't leave a trail we can follow. We're chasin' decoys."

"It doesn't matter." Nick couldn't make his weak voice heard, so he shrugged. They had no other leads to follow. It might be that Zen's accomplice couldn't morph, and Zen couldn't translocate without a landmark in the elven woods. If Zen was a decoy, and the Sword remained in Lorentil or was being taken in another direction, the Seeking Stone would reveal that after nightfall.

As they rode, Ellessar and Alanel leapfrogged ahead. At the speed they traveled, the two could easily be thrown off by a false trail if their prey thought to create one, but Zen's straightforward path suggested a single-minded objective: get to the elven border, find a landmark, and translocate away.

It made sense. With a head start of several hours, and only a few days' hard ride to the border, the companions had little hope of closing the gap in time. Zen had no need for subterfuge.

Nick rode at the rear of the party with Jasmine. He welcomed the gold and green of the elven forest after the mud and muted grays of the Wild Lands bog and the rocky crags and stone tunnels of the dwarves. The change was a salve that seemed to heal more than Nick's soul.

"Alamain may have done something for me, despite her claims to the contrary," he said when Alanel and Ellessar slowed the party to study the trail.

Jasmine brought her horse to a walk behind Ember, who had closed the gap between her and the trackers. "How so?"

"I feel better today," Nick said.

"Getting your strength back?"

"Not really, but I feel rested despite the short sleep we all got last night."

Something slammed into Ember from the side. She let out a strangled cry and nearly lost her seat. She clung to the saddle and gasped for breath. Her horse sidestepped to keep her atop it.

Ellessar and Alanel spun their mounts in the direction the attack seemed to have come from.

A low chanting started somewhere in the woods. The sound carried a visceral undercurrent that resonated in the pit of Nick's stomach like rotten veal. He scanned the woods.

"There!" Ellessar pointed his sword toward a thicket of trees to their left.

A foul hiss split the air, along with the sound of heavy footsteps. An elf mounted on a spiked, bipedal reptile charged Ember. He thrust his hand out, and she tumbled off the far side of her horse.

The animal shot a stream of blood-red spittle over the back of Ember's horse and down onto her. Smoke rose from the saddle where the saliva had hit it. The horse whinnied and reared, seeking escape. Bloody, Ember spoke an arcane word and faded into invisibility.

Another stream of red spittle shot from the trees ahead, falling just short of Ellessar and Alanel.

Their guide whipped his bow from his saddle and launched an arrow into the trees.

Borim dropped from his horse with a thud. He drew his mace and ran toward the attacker in the trees, an elf dressed in a forest cloak riding a second spiked reptile. A discordant chant spewed from the elf's mouth.

Nick struggled down from his horse as well. His long stride carried him passed Borim to reach the enemy first. He swung his great sword at the animal. The blade drew blood, but the bony horns that covered its body prevented a clean hit.

Borim charged the beast. "ShatterBrand!" The spikes on his mace bit into the reptile's side.

Blood welled up and soaked the animal's spikes. The reptile whipped its head and raked Borim with the spikes on its neck. The dwarf reeled back with a howl of pain.

One of Alanel's arrows slammed into the rider's chest and threw him from his saddle to lie still on the ground. Nick waited a moment to see if the animal would run off without its rider. It didn't.

Borim whipped his spiked shield from a hook on his pack. He braced it in front of him with both arms and charged the animal like a battering ram. The reptile hissed as Borim's momentum shoved it back into the brush. The dwarf's shield remained stuck on several of its spikes. It shook itself like a dog. Borim's feet left the ground and his rotten teeth rattled like a baby's shaker, but he refused to let go.

Then the mount whipped its spiked tail around and struck Borim's armored back. Both the dwarf and his shield fell away.

Nick screamed as he charged the mount. He battered it again and again, cleaving off the ends of spikes and chucks of flesh, but the beast held its ground as fatigue overtook Nick's weakened body and forced him to stop.

Jasmine charged the elven rider nearest Ember, desperate to draw his attention before his mount could drive Ember's own horse to trample her. She punched the mount on the side of the head. Most creatures were vulnerable there. A hiss erupted from its mouth. The beast swept its head toward the blow, and dagger-sharp spikes flayed the skin on Jasmine's forearm.

The rider wore chainmail draped with animal fur, a sigil of Vexetan burned into the hide like a brand on cattle. A shield on his left arm protected his side. A steel helmet covered his head and face. He looked indestructible. Jasmine stepped back. She drew her sais and dropped into a fighting stance between him and Ember's horse.

Ellessar came at the elf from the side opposite Jasmine. The rider moved as though his armor weighed nothing. His shield intercepted an onslaught of Alanel's arrows. In just seconds, three or four stuck through it, but none made it to the rider.

Together Jasmine, Alanel, and Ellessar should have found an opening. The rider wielded his halberd in one hand, slapping Ellessar's sword away, then jabbing the pointed haft at Jasmine. All the while, the spikes, teeth, and tail of the mount took their toll on her and Ellessar's flesh.

"Go help your friends," the rider told Jasmine. He thrust his chin toward Borim and Nick across the way.

For a moment, it seemed like the best tactic Jasmine had ever heard and she turned to obey. The pendant around her neck throbbed once with warmth and the enchantment behind the suggestion evaporated. Borim and Nick clearly didn't need her help. She spun back to the rider.

"The power of Vexetan won't sustain you this day," Ellessar said. There was no other explanation for the wicked elf's speed.

Ellessar was right. Jasmine dropped her *sais* and leapt at the rider, suffering a rake of spikes across her legs. She locked his helmeted head in the vise of her grip as her body slammed into his. She yanked him from his saddle, and they tumbled to the ground together.

Ember appeared and unleashed a stream of searing fire that burned into the reptile until it fled, smoking, into the woods.

The armored elf struggled, helpless, in Jasmine's grasp until she pried off his helmet and clasped his head between her talons. Before she could snap his neck, he disappeared. Jasmine collapsed to the ground, the elf's body no longer beneath her. She sprang to her feet and sought him out.

Host of Evil

Nick leaned wearily on his sword. Borim faced off against a reptile mount, his spiked shield raised between them with a caution that seemed uncharacteristic of the dwarf. Alanel fired a rapid volley into the beast. After the third or fourth arrow—he fired so quickly Jasmine couldn't keep count—the mount stumbled, fell, and then lay still, heaving its final ragged breaths.

The missing elf stood beyond it.

Jasmine pointed. "There!"

The heads of her companions turned in unison. First to her, then to the enemy. The elf scooped up his fallen friend and vanished again.

CHAPTER 24

Half a dozen elven soldiers mounted on hippogriffs flew overhead, just above the treetops.

"Headed for the border," Zen observed.

"Surprised?" Gwyndarren asked.

Once the hippogriffs passed from sight, Zen eased his mare out of the thicket and turned her south. "No. They'll do whatever it takes to get the Sword back. Alerting the border patrols is the least I expected."

"Any thoughts about how to get out of the kingdom?"

Zen pondered the question for a moment and then smiled. "Maybe."

When they got to the border, though, the patrols proved thicker than Zen had hoped, some of them on horseback, others riding hippogriffs. More of them looked into the elven lands than those who watched for demons approaching from outside the barrier.

And for the first time since Zen left the elven capital, he recognized some of the landmarks. They were near the place he'd entered the elven lands with Nick, Jasmine, Rancid, and even that oaf Beltrann, when they first sought the help of the elven High Priestess. According to the report given them by Alamain's knight general, the demon offensive against the elven border wasn't far to the east. Zen wrapped his hand around his staff, ready to translocate.

"You know where we are?" Gwyndarren asked.

"A little too near the demon army, if you ask me."

"What did you expect? We're going to see their Master."

Of course they were, but Zen had hoped they could get to the man without riding down the throat of his army. "He'll be on the front line, right? Somewhere he can protect us from his hoards as we approach?"

"Are you kidding?" Gwyndarren's mischievous smirk looked almost genuine. "Evil men never stand where they might get shot by a stray arrow or an invoked lightning bolt."

"Wonderful." Zen slowed his horse to a walk and dismounted. The patrols began just up ahead. He probably had enough strength to translocate them both, though probably not the horses, out of the kingdom if the barrier would permit it, which seemed unlikely. If the barrier allowed translocation, Assassin demons would pass right through it. The last thing he wanted was to materialize, dazed and drained, in front of an elven border patrol.

Zen dismounted and took a spare robe, identical to the shimmering one he wore, from his pack. He put it on, draped the one damaged in the thorn-lizard attack across his horse's back, and told Gwyndarren his plan.

Minutes later, Gwyndarren approached the barrier, riding his own horse and towing two spare mounts behind him. He hailed a horse-mounted patrol.

"What's your purpose?" the leader asked.

"Quickly," Gwyndarren said. "I found these horses tied in a thicket not half a mile back." He tossed Zen's old cloak to the elf. "This was with them."

The patrol leader held it up in the light, where it seemed to flow like water in his hands. "Blessed Alamain. It's his. This belongs to the ice mage."

"It does seem to fit the description," Gwyndarren admitted.

The sentry placed his hand on one of the spare horses, and the other skittered as far away as its lead would allow. Both appeared slick with sweat. "This horse is still hot. Did you run them?"

"Of course. I came as quickly as I could for fear the thieves had left their horses and the recognizable cloak to slip across the border. But the horses were hot when I found them, not ten minutes ago."

"Then the thieves can't have gone far. Any trail?"

Gwyndarren shrugged. "I'm a courier, not a tracker. Speaking of which, I must get to the battle front."

"First show us where you found the horses."

"I can't. My message is from Alamain, and very urgent." He gave the patrol leader directions to a recognizable rocky outcrop they'd passed a few minutes before.

"I know the place."

"The thicket where I found the horses is but a hundred yards east of there."

The leader motioned his troops to follow and galloped into the woods.

As soon as they'd gone, Gwyndarren and his horses—Zen among them—stepped through the barrier into Faldor.

Nick stood guard while Ellessar and Jasmine each administered their own form of healing to the wounded, and Alanel rounded up the horses. Within an hour, they continued on their way, an estimated nine hours behind their prey. They pressed hard. The pace and long hours should have weakened Nick, but his endurance seemed to be returning. He felt tired, fatigued even, but not completely spent.

The following day, as they approached the elven border, Ellessar slowed. The trail wound through a grove of trees, finally ending in the rocky hills that marked the borderlands. "They're growing cautious."

"I would, too," Nick said. "The patrols must have been searching for them by the time they came through here."

"If Zen recognizes where he is, we'll lose him," Nick said.

"You know this place?" Borim asked.

Nick scanned the area and nodded. "Zen's been here before."

"Great," Borim grumbled. "That's just great."

Alanel and Ellessar moved from one tree, bush, and rock to another, pointing out the prints left by Zen, his guide, and the horses, wherever they could find them. In particular, Ellessar noted a pair of parallel gouges in one of the horseshoes, which confirmed that the tracks had been made by the pair they were pursuing. As they drew closer to the border, elven patrols, mounted on hippogriffs and horses alike, wandered past every few minutes.

"Zen recognized the area," Ellessar said after an hour of hard tracking over rocky ground. "His trail ends here."

Nick's heart sank. "I knew it. We'll never catch him now."

"Not necessarily." Alanel walked his horse forward to a place where the rocks were sparser. "The tracks of Zen's guide and their horses head toward the border, not back into Lorentil."

Ellessar stooped to examine them. "I count three horses now."

"Isn't that interesting?" Jasmine said.

"You there!" An elf at the front of a border patrol rode toward them on horseback. "State your purpose!"

Alanel, Ember, and Ellessar gave the elven greeting with their right hands over their hearts. Ember produced her diplomatic papers and Ellessar presented the insignia of his brotherhood.

"We're in pursuit of thieves who stole a talisman from the high temple," Nick said.

"The ice mage?" The patrol leader pulled one of Zen's robes from his saddlebag. "A rider who came through here this morning said he found this with a pair of horses in a thicket over there." He pointed toward the jumble of tracks Ellessar and Alanel had analyzed.

Nick took the robe and inspected it. "It's definitely Zen's. Which way did the rider go?"

The patrol leader pointed toward the barrier, maybe a quarter mile ahead.

"How long ago?"

"Six or seven hours."

"Not so long as we thought," Alanel commented.

"Long enough," Ellessar said sourly.

"Was one of the horses white?" Nick asked. "I mean strikingly white, like snow?"

The elf thought for a moment. "Yes, now that you mention it."

Nick gave a knowing look to Jasmine and Borim, who had hung back from the conversation. Jasmine had pulled her hood up and tucked her hands into her sleeves.

"That horse *was* the ice mage," Nick told the patrol leader. "We have to go."

The elf stepped aside and motioned his patrol to let them pass.

"These three—" Alanel gestured to Nick, Borim, and Jasmine— "will need someone to open a gap in the barrier."

"Fine." The elf led his patrol to the border, where one of his elves produced an emerald wand and let them out of the kingdom.

Just outside the barrier, where a river marked the boundary between Lorentil and Faldor, Ellessar picked up the trail. "Two horses once again, the riders mounted on them."

Borim grunted. "You'd think he'd have translocated, rather than turnin' into a horse to cross the border."

"Zen said he could *probably* translocate with another person," Jasmine said, "but we've never actually seen him do it."

"He also said he's gettin' stronger," Borim muttered.

Ember glanced back at the green glow of the energy field. "Maybe he couldn't translocate through the barrier."

"Doesn't matter," Ellessar said. "Let's praise Aeron for our blessings and not waste his gift. We still have an hour of daylight."

The trail led into a vast green basin surrounded by low hills. Signs of the thieves' passage remained clear, and the border crossing had delayed them. For the first time since they had left Alamain's temple, Nick thought they might actually have a chance to catch up. Especially if they pushed into the night.

They rode hard, lit torches to see the trail after dark, and traversed the valley by midnight. Ultimately the limited endurance of the horses forced them to stop.

Beyond the hills massed the demons.

An hour into Ellessar's watch, a steady, hypnotic hum reached out to him from somewhere in the night's moonlit gloom. The hum dulled the elf's mind and weighed down his eyelids. Then a huge insect—no, a demon—like a giant mosquito but twice the size of a hippogriff, with a bulbous abdomen, flew into the light.

"Aeron!" Ellessar cried. The sound of his god's name on his lips lifted the sleep from his mind. "Wake up!" he yelled to his companions, praying that the hum hadn't dropped their minds into a slumber beyond waking.

He launched a pair of arrows, but the demon's hide deflected the missiles. Finally, he rushed at it, kicking Borim's sleeping body along the way. "Wake up!"

The dwarf responded with a deep, rumbling snore, nearly lost in the buzz of the demon's wings.

Ellessar thrust his palms toward it. "Be bound by the might of Aeron."

Glowing golden chains sprang into being and wrapped the demon, binding its wings to its body. Like a boulder shoved from the top of a cliff, it plummeted to the ground, the buzz replaced by a high-pitched squeal.

Ellessar marched up and chopped at it with his sword, but the creature's skin proved too thick and leathery for him to penetrate. All the while, the demon raged against the chains.

Jasmine and Ember arrived together beside him.

"Stay your hand," he told Jasmine. "Not even my sword can pierce it."

Ember took a pinch of powder from her belt and produced a spark from the weave. She thrust her hands toward the demon and fire burned into it. The demon's squeals grew more frantic, its struggles more violent. A foul-smelling smoke rose from it as the fire burned through its hide.

"That's it," Ellessar said. "It's working."

Ember added more catalyst from the pouch at her belt as the flames seared the demon. Long moments passed. Still the demon struggled.

Its binding chains broke. With a screech of triumph, it tumbled to its feet and sprang at Ember.

With no further need to maintain the golden chains, Ellessar switched to the brilliant light he'd used to vanquish one of the Assassin demons in the Wild Lands.

The light burned the rest of the way through the demon's abdomen, boiling its green blood. Ember twisted out of its way as it landed in a stinking, burning heap beside her snoring brother.

In the morning, Nick felt better than he had in weeks. His strength was returning, and his raw skin began to flake away, revealing healthy flesh beneath.

The group ate a cold breakfast and set out early. It didn't take them long to find Zen's campsite.

Ellessar inspected the trail. "They slept the night. We're only a few hours behind."

Newfound hope surged through Nick. "Excellent."

"There is bad news," Ellessar said when he reached the far edge of the camp. "He knows we're catching up. They took off this morning at a dead run."

"I should have known." Jasmine sighed. "We'll have to watch the sky for birds of ice."

"And the path ahead for demons," Ellessar added. "They're besieging the elven border to the east and the capital of Meuribar in the south. Zen and his cohort are racing toward the crotch of the V formed by the two armies."

CHAPTER 25

Midday the next day, it rained, and Zen's trail dissolved into the brush and grasses of the Faldor plains.

"Can you track him through this?" Jasmine asked Ellessar.

"Oh, I can track him. But it'll take time we don't have."

"Then our choice is made." Nick thrust his chin toward a distant mountain peak. "The trail hasn't wavered since we left Lorentil. We ride straight ahead until nightfall and pick up the trail in the morning."

"If we lose it, we'll never find it again," Ellessar said.

"We have to catch him before he reaches the demon army, which by now will stretch across the plains ahead from the Great Sand to the city of Meuribar. Otherwise we'll lose all hope of recovering the Sword. The only way to do that is to forget the trail and ride recklessly forward."

"Reckless is right," Borim grumbled. "We've been reckless since Ellessar lost the darned thing."

"That's enough," Ember said. "The ride has put us all in a foul temper and the rain's not helping, but Nick's right. We must catch Zen before he reaches the demon armies."

Without waiting for consensus, Nick spurred his horse into a gallop.

Together they rode through the thickening rain until nightfall, where they reached the river that marked the Faldor-Meuribar border. They crossed and set up camp for the night. At full dark, Nick and Jasmine checked the Seeking Stone. It glowed brightly. They were still heading in the right general direction.

Ellessar completed his morning prayers at dawn. "There's an army of demons a day's ride to the south, and also to the east. Our course draws us nearer to both."

Alanel rode in from scouting ahead. "I found Zen's trail. Assuming he and his partner stopped for the night, they're about six hours ahead."

"Are you sure it's his?" Nick asked.

"The telltale pair of parallel gouges on one of the horseshoes shows up clearly in the mud left by last's night's rain."

"I don't understand why we have a trail to follow at all." Jasmine gestured to the peak ahead. "I recognize that mountain. The Order of the Sage monastery lies at the base of it. Traveler's Roost sits on a low ridge beyond. Zen knows this area. He should have translocated ahead by now."

"He could be using the Sword to bait us into a trap," Alanel said.

"And we're running headlong into it." Borim pulled his mount to a low stump and clambered onto the horse's back.

"There's no help for it," Nick said. "We need the Sword. And the

Seeking Stone continues to confirm that those we pursue have it. If there's an ambush ahead, it won't be the first time."

So they continued. At noon they paused long enough to re-acquire the trail, then only a few hours old. When they stopped again late in the afternoon, the trail had disappeared. Alanel and Ellessar found nothing after half an hour of searching.

"He must have turned," Alanel said. "We'll have to backtrack."

Nick shook his head. "We don't have time. For days, the trail has headed straight for Traveler's Roost. For all we know, he finally got close enough to translocate there. I say we check it out."

"There are demons beyond that ridge," Ellessar said. "If not atop it. We must be very careful."

"We're getting too close to the demons to camp safely," Ember said after Nick had selected a site for the night. With a stick, she drew a circle three paces across, then placed a sphere of polished glass about the size of an apricot on a small wooden stand in the middle of the circle. She touched the glass with her palm and spoke an elven command word. Something like a spark ignited inside, and it glowed dimly. "Stay within the circle and you'll remain unseen."

Borim's jaw dropped. "Where did you get that?"

"Just something I picked up in Lorentil during my years in the diplomatic service." She hesitated. "A gift, actually, from a suitor I had for a time."

Borim's eyes flared. "You had a—"

"Come," she said. "Just enter the circle."

With a huff, Borim stepped in. He examined his limbs and beard. I don't look no different."

"The enchantment doesn't work on individuals. It just fools anyone who tries to see in."

"The horses are still visible," Nick said.

Ember shrugged. "They'll have to stay outside. I can't change the size of the bubble."

"We'll remove the saddles and gear and leave the horses untied," Ellessar said. "Spirit won't wander off and the others will stay with her. A few stray horses won't draw as much attention as an encampment of people so near the demon army."

"Speaking of the army…" Alanel settled himself on the ground next to his backpack and unwrapped several portions of hardtack. He took one biscuit and passed the rest of it around. "Tell us, demon hunter, what's out there?"

Ellessar sat down near the small cooking fire Jasmine had lit. He stared into the flames. "Every kind of demon Vexetan designed, he did so for a specific purpose."

"Like the Assassins," Nick said.

"Yes. And the Hunter whose severed leg was found near South Bend, and the Devourer that sought out Zen's residual energy in the Wild Lands. Vexetan created a series of demons to make up his army as well."

Every eye locked onto Ellessar. Every ear tuned toward him. The camp grew still and silent.

"The army will consist of three primary types: Warriors, Archers, and Scouts. If we get near Meuribar, we'll probably find Siege demons as well."

"You've described the Scouts," Jasmine said. "Tell us about the others."

"Warriors are tall, eight to ten feet, with the body of a man and a head like that of a bull. Very strong. They're deadly, but not as deadly as Archers, who wield two bows at a time with their four arms. Quick and accurate."

"What about the Siege demons?" Borim asked.

"They're rare. My order knows very little about them, but I can say this: they're huge."

"Where will the Master be?" Nick asked. "Which of his three

armies will he attend?"

"It must take a great force to unite the demons. They've spent millennia battling among themselves for supremacy in the Abyss. Without the will of a strong leader, the army will lose coherence. It'll fall into anarchy. They'll fight each other."

"Then he'll be with one of the demon armies," Alanel concluded.

"Maybe." Ellessar pursed his lips and thought for a moment. "His general, Ri-T'rannoc, is such a force. If he wears a Medallion, the Master need not be present to control the army. Evil is, by definition, cowardly. I won't be surprised if the Master is pulling the puppet strings of his Chosen from a safe hole somewhere."

"Then we have no hope of finding him," Nick said, "even if we do recover the Sword."

Ellessar met his gaze squarely. "Have faith, young Nick. Aeron isn't done yet."

Zen considered his guide. Gwyndarren still hadn't shared with him their destination, which the elf presumably learned from the Master himself via communication through the Medallion.

Information, as always, was Gwyndarren's currency.

Keeping the Master's location to himself was Gwyndarren's way of ensuring that Zen included him in the exchange. Unless, of course, Zen stole the Medallion and spoke directly to the Master.

The more Zen considered the risks, though, the more he couldn't bring himself to touch the Medallion. He sought power, not subjugation. That didn't mean he had to share his own plans with Gwyndarren.

Quietly, Zen muttered an incantation and took the form of an ice owl. He left the sleeping elf. With the Medallion, Gwyndarren should be safe enough from demon patrols. There were no men about, nor members of any of the other civilized races—they seemed to have all sought refuge in the city of Meuribar or fled the kingdom entirely. If some animal killed Gwyndarren in his sleep, so be it. Zen would do what he must with the Medallion to finish this dangerous errand.

Either way, if Nick and the others caught up, it would ruin everything. With this in mind, Zen banked northward and scanned the terrain in search of their pursuers, as he had done each night since they'd left the elven capital. He found them closer than he'd expected, not more than four hours behind. But he saw only the horses, whom he'd not have recognized save for Spirit.

Zen soared high in a wide circle, searching for some sign of a campsite. Finding none before his weaving threatened to unravel, he veered back toward Gwyndarren. He considered landing for long enough to weave a magic detection enchantment, to see if his friends might have hidden nearby, but he needed to conserve his energies or take longer rests at night. He wasn't sleeping well as it was, with cold sweats and a blanket that seemed scratchier than it had been. With his old companions drawing nearer, he couldn't afford longer nights. He returned to Gwyndarren, unsatisfied.

hoofbeats sounded in the early hours before dawn. Two or maybe three riders, somewhere to the east, drawing closer.

Borim shook Jasmine awake. Nick, Ember, and Ellessar needed their rest. He would wake Alanel if necessary. "Shhhhh," Borim whispered, to the extent that a dwarf can whisper. "Horses."

"I hear them," Jasmine said softly.

They crouched at the edge of the circle, unseen if Ember's enchantment worked against demon eyes. After a time, the sound of hooves faded to the west.

In the morning, nearby tracks revealed that a pair of Scout demons had run by, a quarter mile to the south.

"Could they have seen the horses?" Nick asked.

Ellessar shook his head. "They would've slowed. We're safe."

Borim grunted. "For now."

Gwyndarren announced that he and Zen needed to change direction and head east.

Zen stopped scratching at his wrist, where the sleeve of his robe had begun to irritate him. "You sure?"

Gwyndarren dangled the Medallion from his index finger. "I'm sure."

Zen frowned. "I assumed we were going to Traveler's Roost."

"No. We'll pass north of the village, into the valley beyond."

Zen motioned for Gwyndarren to lead the way.

That afternoon they topped the ring of hills that had shielded them from the broad basin that cradled the little town of Cedar Falls, Zen's home for many years before this business with the Prophecy had come uncorked. They approached the ridge carefully and gazed down through a screen of brush and trees.

The entire basin was a black sea of demons. Tens of thousands of them. The jade glow of the elven barrier pulsed along the horizon with an energy visible even in the blaze of the afternoon sun.

The pit of Zen's stomach perched on the edge of a chasm, ready to fall—along with his courage—at the thought of proceeding. He forced calm into his voice. "The Master is in there?"

"No." Gwyndarren's eyes seemed to harbor hesitation as well. "Beyond."

"In Palidor?"

Gwyndarren said nothing for a long moment, and then finally, "Brinheim." That was a bit of information, at least, but carefully metered to ensure that Zen couldn't get to the meeting on his own.

"Then let's go the other way around, to the west of the Great Sand, where there are fewer demons."

Gwyndarren gripped the pouch in which he kept the Medallion. Veins bulged in his forearm at the tightness of his grip. "We have nothing to fear from demons."

"You don't sound sure."

Gwyndarren's head snapped up. He met Zen's gaze.

Zen gestured to the black mass that filled the basin before them. "You think every demon down there is going to let you present that Medallion? You think they'll all honor it? Some may covet it for their own."

Gwyndarren stared silently into the valley.

"How much longer will it take to go around? A few days, at the most?"

The elf nodded, distracted. "There's a demon army this size to the south, as well. We'll have to go clear around the city of Meuribar, but perhaps you're right. It'll be safer. But we must arrive before the Master's armies prevail, or the Sword will be worth nothing to him."

"Agreed."

Gwyndarren turned his horse around to descend the hill.

Zen extended his staff across the elf's path, then pointed its crystal tip toward the valley into which they'd be returning. Amid the scrub grasses and dry-climate brush, a handful of riders raced headlong toward Traveler's Roost. "Our pursuers. We'll have to cross at night, or we'll be seen. Besides, I have to rest. We may have need of the weave before this day is over, and it's been some time since I fully replenished my strength." In fact, Zen hadn't felt rested in days.

The companions approached Traveler's Roost cautiously, aware that their race across the plains would have been obvious to anyone watching from the ridge on which the little village sat. Jasmine could smell the acrid stench of demons wafting on the wind.

"Blessed Aeron," Ellessar said. "There must be thousands of them up there."

Just then, three flying creatures that looked like gargoyles launched themselves from the roof of the two-story inn that gave the little town its name. The creatures swooped down the hillside toward the companions.

Ellessar pulled Spirit up short. "Sentry demons."

"Guess they know we're here," Borim said.

"Can we take them?" Nick asked Ellessar.

"Doesn't matter. If they've seen us, they've told others."

"To the monastery!" Nick wheeled his horse around and spurred it into a gallop. The Order of the Sage was at least three hours away at a full gallop, but it and the tunnel through the mountain offered refuge from whatever might pour from the streets of Traveler's Roost and the valley beyond—if they could outrun the Sentries.

A wave of dust rose from the ridge as demons from the village raced in pursuit.

CHAPTER 26

After two hours of galloping across the plains of Meuribar, Nick and the others began a climb into the foothills that surrounded the solitary mountain peak. The horses struggled up the first hill, sweat-soaked and exhausted. Even flying, the Sentry demons had remained a mile or more behind, but that changed quickly as the steep and winding trail slowed the horses. Within minutes, it became clear that the Sentries would catch up long before the companions reached the monastery walls.

The pursuers on the ground had split up, one group falling behind while the other kept pace.

"We're not going to make it," Nick yelled over the thundering hooves and heaving breaths of the horses.

"Keep riding!" Ellessar, in the back of the party, swung his bow from his shoulder and fitted the string as he rode. "Let's draw the Sentries as far ahead as we can!"

Nick spurred his horse on. If Ellessar could dispatch the Sentries, they might lose the rest of their pursuers in the hills. Before they reached the monastery, two Sentries caught up and swooped at Ellessar.

"Form up! Concentrate fire!" Without slowing, the elf twisted in his saddle and loosed an arrow into the nearest Sentry. Up close, their resemblance to gargoyles was so obvious, it seemed they must have inspired the stone decorations typical in old human architecture. A hiss erupted from the demon as it swooped toward Spirit.

Nick swung his horse around and dismounted. He slid his great sword from its sheath with a satisfying ring.

The Sentry raked its claws across Ellessar's back and shoulders. He shoved it away and slid from his horse. Spirit reared as the second demon's claws sank into her rump. Two blazing columns of fire streaked from Ember's hands into the Sentry. It screeched and dug in its claws deeper. Spirit's back legs faltered, but she held her ground beside her master. She bucked in an unsuccessful attempt to jar the demon loose.

Nick rushed to the horse's side. The first demon circled back and slammed into him. Teeth and claws tore at his armor. It knocked him into Spirit, and he caught himself on the horse's saddle.

He shoved the Sentry away, making room for him to swing at the demon on Spirit's back. All of his frustration over his illness, the loss of the Sword, and the lack of time they had left to do anything about the Prophecy welled up in him, finding an outlet at last against the stonelike hide of the demon. His stroke nearly split the Sentry in half.

The demon behind Nick scrambled to its feet. Screeching, it lunged at him. Nick hadn't yet regained his full strength, and the weight of his sword slowed his movements. He turned too late.

The Sentry twitched as one of Alanel's arrows drove into its flesh. The demon's teeth missed their mark, snapping at the air before Nick's face.

Another arrow sank into the Sentry. The demon tumbled once

and came to its feet. It hissed at Alanel and leapt into the air. Bleeding green blood, it rose to join another of its kin, who circled overhead, just out of bow range.

Ellessar stepped into Spirit's stirrup and pulled himself into the saddle. The rents in Spirit's rump appeared serious but not life-threatening. "You all right?"

Deep scratches marred Nick's breastplate. A puncture in his side bled where one of the demon's claws had found the soft seam in his armor. "Well enough."

Behind them, three pursuing Scout demons raced along a section of trail visible through the trees, about half a mile back.

Nick mounted his horse. "Let's ride!"

The Sentries hung overhead until the Scouts caught up. By then the exhausted horses were laboring to reach the safety of the monastery, just over one last rise. Finally, Ellessar gained the fertile plateau at the rear of Nick's party.

Three Scouts rounded the last bend. The demons cleared the trees and barreled into the open. Each looked vaguely like an eight-hooved centaur. Armored plates covered the chest, sides, and shoulders of both the human-like torso and the equine body, as well as a head—which resembled a man's only in that it had two eyes, which were set in the middle of an otherwise-featureless face.

On the back of each Scout rode an Archer demon that looked, more than anything else, like a four-armed orc, its features more goblinoid than human. Their flesh was a deep, almost translucent purple, like a day-old bruise. Each Archer seemed larger than a man—maybe seven feet tall. All three had bows nocked and ready in each pair of arms, one in its right set of hands and the other in its left.

Ahead, the Order of the Sage monastery sat silent and empty, its brown walls camouflaged against the rise of the cliff, its battlements deserted. Where were the monks? Surely in such dire times, they would keep a watch on the wall.

Unless they were already dead.

The structure showed no signs of battle—no crumbling walls, no scorch marks, no arrows embedded in the clay. The heavy front gate remained intact, closed, and likely bolted shut. Impassable.

The Archer demons loosed their first volley. Half a dozen arrows whistled past. One lodged in the back of Ellessar's shoulder. His left arm went numb around Spirit's reins. Another volley followed.

As Ellessar nocked an arrow and turned in his saddle, an incoming arrow struck his thigh. A third sank into Spirit's flank. The horse stumbled for a step, then continued to run on three legs.

Ellessar couldn't accept Aeron's gift of healing until he pulled the arrows from his body—the wounds would simply heal around them—so he prayed for strength instead. The numbness in his arm subsided enough for him to launch his arrow, which bounced off the carapace of the lead Scout.

In front of Ellessar, Ember pulled her horse alongside Jasmine's. She reached out and touched her shoulder. In an instant, the two vanished from their horses.

An arrow struck Nick in the back and shattered against his plate armor. Spirit slowed, and the rain of arrows continued.

Before them, the imposing walls of the monastery stared blankly, offering no refuge.

Jasmine appeared in the deserted courtyard of the Order of the Sage monastery with Ember by her side. Despite her years of training, her senses adjusted slowly from the movement of a galloping horse to a sudden lack of motion, and to the utter, incongruous abandonment of the monastery. The chicken coops, hog pens, and rabbit hutches all sat silent and empty, the vegetable gardens untended, the practice dummies mute and alone. Surely her brethren wouldn't have left their home without a fight.

During that moment of eternity, Ember sprinted for the main gate. She heaved at the pair of timbers that braced the doors, unable to lift them by herself. Jasmine rushed to her side. She flipped a concealed mechanism, and the timbers swung out of the way. With a heave, the women shoved the gates open. Alanel thundered through, with Nick and Borim behind him. Jasmine and Ember backed toward the middle of the courtyard as the first Sentry soared over the wall.

Three of Alanel's arrows whistled over Jasmine's head into the demon, and it plunged, lifeless, to the dirt. The other Sentry came over. The lead Archer demon, mounted on his Scout, barreled through the open gate. Alanel struck the Archer in the arm and one of the demon's bows tumbled to the ground. The Sentry swooped toward the elf.

Borim turned about in his saddle. "Where to, Jasmine?"

"To the right. Across from the well."

Ellessar came through the gateway, hunched in the saddle atop his limping horse. Two more Scouts followed with their Archer riders. One charged Jasmine and Ember. The other followed Ellessar toward Borim.

Jasmine spun a leaping heel kick into the side of the charging Scout's carapace-covered head, a blow that would have felled an ogre.

The demon, huffing from the strain of its pursuit, shook off the kick and glared at her. It slipped a giant spiked ball, the size of one of Sister Rosemary's stew pots, on a ten-foot chain from a hook at the base of its humanlike torso. If Jasmine's best spinning kick hadn't hurt the demon, nothing her hands could do would either.

Borim leapt off his horse, his backside tingling from too many hours—no, too many days—in the saddle. Four doors stood in the shabby clay wall across from the well. He hobbled on numb legs toward the closest, a set of wooden double doors. Leaving his mount behind, he hefted ShatterBrand in both hands, ready to go through the doors even if he found them locked.

He didn't. They opened into a vacant room with a small forge in one corner. Hooks and lonely racks more fit for weapons than for tools hung empty along the walls. A small door opened in the back wall.

He turned. "Hey, Jas—"

Two demon arrows thumped into his chest, and he staggered back. The Archer demon before him loaded another volley and loosed them. As Borim brought his shield around, a third arrow slammed into him. The Archer's mount charged, preceded by the tip of a wicked-looking, barbed lance.

Borim's shield knocked the lance's point aside, but the force of the blow threw him to the ground.

Above him, the Archer drew back two more arrows in its twin bows. The Scout raised its lance to strike. It seemed fitting that Borim would die where he grew up, in an armory.

CHAPTER 27

Alanel got one arrow into the advancing Sentry before it landed on the back of his horse and embedded its claws into the animal. Then it was all Alanel could do to keep his mount beneath him, let alone fend off the teeth of the demon.

Nick caught up at that moment. A single stroke of his great sword split the Sentry's head.

Alanel turned then to the first Archer and Scout that had entered the monastery. The Scout had drawn a bow against Ellessar. The Archer had dismounted and was advancing on Nick, who climbed off his own horse.

"Come on, you bastard kin of a demon god!" Borim bellowed from within the building. "Make it quick!"

Alanel drew the special arrow he'd been saving for a demon Chosen, blessed by Alamain with the power of Aeron to slay the dark dwellers of the Abyss. He banished the panicked movements of his horse beyond a wall of concentration and took aim through the open door of the forge. Time slowed. His bow seemed to hover, independent of all else, as he released the string.

The arrow struck the demon Scout that stood over Borim. The Scout withered instantly into a dry husk and collapsed. The Archer demon that rode it tumbled to the armory floor.

"Behind you!" Alanel yelled to Nick as he reached once more for the reins of his own horse.

Borim groaned, rolled over, and pushed himself to his feet. From the courtyard, Ellessar pumped three arrows into the Archer that had tumbled from the dead Scout. The Archer slumped to the floor and didn't move again.

Ellessar pulled the arrow from his leg. As he reached for the one in his shoulder, an arrow from a Scout demon struck him in his side. He stiffened and toppled from his horse.

"Ellessar's down!" Borim leaned against the doorframe and pulled the arrows from his own chest. His stout dwarven armor had kept them from penetrating to a lethal depth.

The demon hunter was still alive, choking and gurgling, so Borim ventured into the courtyard and dragged the elf by the collar of his demon-skin coat into the relative safety of the forge.

Ember laid her hand on Jasmine's back and spoke a word. Jasmine's skin took on a carapace-like hardness, as it had done during the battle with the sphinxes in Gildstone.

"Thank you," Jasmine said as the Archer demon dismounted, and Ember backed away.

Jasmine circled to put the Archer between herself and the Scout, forcing the demons to face her one at a time. As she did, the Archer launched a pair of arrows.

Jasmine batted one aside. The other hit her carapace and bounced away. She launched a flying kick at the Archer before it could reload. Her foot slammed into the demon's face, and the blow stunned it enough that it dropped both its weapons. Then she swept the Archer's feet from beneath it.

As the Scout came around, Ember released a gout of flame from each hand. The demon reeled in the heat.

In an instant, the Archer regained its feet. It launched itself at Jasmine, raking with four handfuls of claws as long as Jasmine's talons and twice as sharp.

Deftly, she fended them off and landed blows of her own. She had trained for this kind of fighting, and she feared not the unarmed demon. "Hold the courtyard!" This monastery was her home. She would not relinquish it to the Master's armies.

Another wave of flames poured into the Scout, who turned its attention and its giant morning star toward Ember.

The Archer came at Jasmine, all power and rage, far from helpless without its favored weapons. With Ember's enchantment upon Jasmine's skin, the demon did little or no damage. Likewise, the Archer seemed to absorb her punches.

Jasmine landed a double kick high on the Archer's chest. Grunting as the blow forced the breath from its lungs, the demon staggered backwards. No more than a third of the demon's weight, Jasmine was thrown back by the force of her own kick. With the momentum, she completed a back flip and rolled into a backward summersault to gain distance between her and the Archer. She returned to her feet with both *sais* in her hands.

Nick faced his own advancing Archer. Only one of its bows remained in its hands. The second lay on the ground. Before the demon could recover the weapon, Nick rushed it and splintered its other bow with his sword.

Swing by swing, Nick's great sword grew heavy. The Archer ducked the blade. Its claws ripped at Nick's armor and scored a rent along his exposed arm. The demon had too many claws to deflect, so Nick ignored them. He swung his sword and, with an effort that felt monumental, severed its head.

※

Alanel turned his bow against the Scout that had felled Ellessar. His horse had nowhere to go. It pranced in small, erratic circles near the corner of the courtyard, its movements making Alanel a more difficult target as the Scout launched arrow after arrow at him.

His aim frustrated by the horse's movements, Alanel returned fire. He scored two hits on the Scout and one on the Archer facing Jasmine before his supply of arrows ran out. He vaulted from his horse and scavenged an arrow from the ground.

The Archer took that moment to back away from Jasmine. It leapt onto the Scout facing Alanel, and the two fled through the open front gate at a full gallop, likely going to report that the party they'd pursued from the plains below was actually Nick Mirrin and the fugitives from Trondor—fugitives, in fact, from the Chosen and therefore from the Master himself.

"They're getting away," Alanel yelled to anyone who might be able to stop them.

※

Borim pulled the arrows from Ellessar's body. He stood over the elf with a wad of cloth strips in one hand and a sack of honey drops in the other, wondering which he should administer first. Only then would he consider *how* to administer whichever he chose.

At that moment, Ellessar stirred and opened his eyes. Borim froze. The elf muttered a prayer, the reverence in his voice thicker than the honey used to make Borim's candy.

In the yard, Ember had become separated from all her protectors. A charred Scout demon rushed at her as the fire from her hands sputtered and died out. Borim had seen that look in his sister's eyes before. She'd spent her supply of catalyst. Her magic was gone.

He snatched his mace from the ground and charged the Scout with a battle cry he hoped would draw the demon's attention. "ShatterBrand!"

Ellessar came unsteadily to his feet and cried out a second prayer, this time loudly. A blinding beam of light shot past Borim's head.

Borim threw a glance over his shoulder at the demon hunter. "By the molten stone of Brewster's forge, watch where you're pointin' that thing." The beam bore into the Scout and drove it to the ground in a smoking heap.

"The light of Aeron will harm only demons," Ellessar said calmly.

"Then blessed be that god of yours. Maybe one day even I'll start believin'."

Ellessar stepped in front of Jasmine and sent a blinding ray of light into the fleeing Scout, who tumbled to the ground. The Archer rolled from the back of the mount. It twisted to its feet and kept running.

"It's out of my range," Ellessar said, "and with Spirit lame, I can't catch it."

Jasmine winked at Ellessar. "I can." She sprinted after the demon.

"Careful," Ellessar hollered after her.

A hundred yards from the gate, Jasmine launched herself at the Archer. As she came down on its back, she wrapped her arms over its top set of shoulders and plunged both *sais* into its chest. Its momentum carried it forward a few more steps before it toppled, face-first, and skidded to a stop.

Jasmine rolled off it and somersaulted to her feet, crouched in a defensive stance. The Archer lay completely still.

She walked back to it. The points of both *sais* protruded from its back, having been shoved all the way into its body by the force of its impact with the ground. Jasmine rolled the demon onto its back. She had to brace her foot on its chest and use both hands to pull each of her bloody weapons free.

An instant later, hoofbeats drew her attention to a stretch of trail about a half mile down the hill as the crow flies. A dozen Scout demons galloped past, each with a Warrior astride its back.

CHAPTER 28

Jasmine raced back into the courtyard. "Scouts and Warriors. A mile or two down the trail. Coming this way."

"We're spent," Nick said.

"I know a place." Jasmine scanned the courtyard. "Round up the practice dummies." Four lay scattered about the battlefield. "Tie them to the horses. Quickly!"

Within minutes they had the horses, all save Spirit, tied in a line with the dummies strapped atop them. Jasmine led them from the courtyard through a smaller side door. With a swat on their rumps, she sent them down the hill into the woods.

In the meantime, the others collected as many arrows from the ground as possible.

The group coaxed Spirit through the monastery's kitchen, down a set of stairs to the cellars, and into the hidden passage under the mountain—the same tunnel that had saved Nick, Zen, Jasmine, and others from Whisper and the Black Hand so many months before.

Huddled there in the darkness, Ellessar administered a few hasty prayers of healing. Ember took out the enchanted glass sphere she'd received from her former suitor—the only magic she had that didn't depend on her own exertions or her powdered catalyst—and erected a dome of invisibility over them all.

Nick didn't wait until morning. They couldn't spare the time, and the darkness of the night would help conceal their escape. So at about midnight, as well as Nick could guess without the benefit the moon or stars, he woke the others.

He checked the Seeking Stone. It still glowed brightly, but not so much as it had the night before. "We've lost ground. If Zen continued south, he's probably run into the demon army by now."

"Then we go to Meuribar," Ellessar said.

"That was the plan before you lost the Sword," Borim grumbled.

"Shut up, brother." Ember placed an affectionate hand on Borim's shoulder. "We'll go where they decide."

Everyone looked at Nick.

He kept the Stone out to provide at least some light in the rough-hewn tunnel. "Yes, Meuribar. For information."

Ember refilled her pouch of catalyst, mixing the powders from the three separate metal flasks she kept in her pack.

Ellessar laid healing hands upon those who still suffered serious wounds, including himself, and then knelt down to commune with Aeron. "Demons all around, but none nearer than Travelers' Roost."

"Our decoys must have worked," Nick said.

"Then for now, at least, the monastery is secure, though I can't help wondering what happened to the monks." Jasmine stood. "This way." She took the Seeking Stone and led them down the tunnel.

As they walked, Ellessar handed an arrow to Alanel, who recognized it as his own. "I pulled this from the desiccated husk of the Scout demon you killed with it. It's quite an arrow. Lightweight for one with a metal shaft. Enchanted to slay demons, I'm guessing."

"Yes. Thanks for recovering it. It's quite irreplaceable."

"Tell me about it."

Alanel examined the arrow for damage before returning it to his quiver. "It was forged by the dwarves using an earth magic they call aluminium, enchanted by the mages of Glimmernook, and then blessed by Alamain herself."

"It'll kill any demon in a single shot?"

"So I'm told. One was issued to the leader of each border patrol. Alamain gave me this one just before we left the temple."

Eventually, Jasmine came to a stop near the end of the passage. "Everybody ready?" She gave each of them a glance. "All right then." She returned the Seeking Stone to Nick and waited until he had stowed it in his backpack. Stepping around the last bend, she scanned the countryside below. "Quietly now."

With no horses save Spirit, the going proved slow and arduous. Ember continued to hide their camp behind her globe of invisibility each night. The Sword of Alamain moved farther and farther away. Other than that, their trek remained uneventful until the morning Meuribar's capital came into view.

Nick led them to a spot a few hundred feet above the plateau with sufficient rocks and foliage for them to view the city without fear of being seen.

Demon hoards blackened the landscape from a hundred yards outside the city walls to maybe half a mile in all directions. The sea of creatures extended beyond the horizon to the east.

"They're not attacking," Ellessar noted.

"That's curious. Are they cowards, these demons of yours?"

"Borim!"

"Sorry, sis. I meant to say, 'How do we get past 'em?'"

"I..." Ember hesitated. "I might be able to do it."

Nick studied her exquisite face. "Might?"

"It's a long way to translocate. I've never gone more than a hundred yards or so."

Borim grunted. "The city wall's a lot farther off than that."

"With invisibility, we might be able to slip in close enough."

"No," Ellessar said. "With the dwarf stomping around like he does, the demons will hear us coming."

"Not if we put him on Spirit," Nick said.

"I'll not—" Ellessar began.

Jasmine put her hand on the elf's arm. "Set your pride aside and seek Aeron's guidance."

Ellessar pursed his lips for a long moment. "Very well, but we'll have to tie his equipment down so it won't rattle. Why you dwarves insist on making everything out of metal..."

"I'll need to make a charm for Alanel," Ember said. "And another for Spirit."

Ellessar stepped between her and the horse. "A charm?"

"A physical object to help focus my mental and magical energies. Otherwise I won't be able to make her invisible." She looked at Spirit with her lower lip between her teeth. "I'll need a lock from her mane, maybe twenty hairs as long as my palm."

"And you need this to make her invisible?"

"Yes." Ember pulled a necklace of charms from beneath her blouse and displayed them. "I have one for each of you, except Spirit and Alanel."

Ellessar frowned. "What else can you do with these charms?"

Ember gestured at Jasmine. "I can give you magical armor."

"And translocate us into the city," Nick added.

Ember nodded. "Two at a time, if I go with you, and if we can get close enough."

"What else?" Elessar asked.

"I can swap your location with someone else that I have a charm for. They're quite limited. I can't do anything with them that will harm you."

Ellessar pursed his lips for a long moment. Without a word, he cut the hairs from Spirit's mane and handed them to the young elf.

Ember carefully laid them out on a rock and spread her necklace across them. She folded them over the chain and tied them with a piece of slender string.

Ember held the necklace up by its ends and examined her work critically. "It's not very durable, but it should last long enough to get us into the city."

Alanel stepped up. "What do you need from me?"

"Something that represents you, in my mind at least. Something uniquely you." Ember surveyed the elf. He had a sword, but she'd never seen him use it. "How about an arrowhead from one of your arrows?"

"Easily done." He whipped an arrow from his quiver and handed it to her.

She took it. The steel head was fastened to the wooden shaft with a piece of animal tendon, which had been wet when it was tied and then allowed to shrink as it dried. "Perfect." She cut the tendon with her knife and carefully unwound it. After running the arrowhead over a rock a few times to dull its edges, she used the same piece of tendon to tie it to her necklace. "I'm ready."

By that time, the others had gotten Borim settled on Spirit's back with all his gear strapped down or wrapped in bedding.

Ember laid a hand on each of them and whispered a few words in her lilting tongue. One by one, the companions vanished from sight.

"Follow my footprints," she said. "Here we go."

For the better part of the morning, the group threaded their way through the outskirts of the demon army until Scouts and Sentries surrounded them and a solid wall of Warriors and Archers barred their way. Ember stopped, her footprints ceasing to appear, and they all followed suit.

"This should be close enough," she whispered. "Jasmine, you see the ash tree next to that boulder, about thirty feet to our right as we face the city?"

"Yes."

"I can take two at a time. First, Borim and Spirit."

"Spirit—"

"Shhh." Ember's voice was nearly inaudible. "If he dismounts here, he'll make too much noise." When Ellessar made no further objection, Ember continued. "The rest of you wait by that tree until I return."

Nick walked to the ash and stood—with the others, he hoped—for interminable minutes. Finally he felt a touch on his back.

Ember's labored breath blew in his ear, hot and heavy. "Ready?" She didn't wait for an answer.

The landscape blinked into darkness and returned. Nick gasped. They stood in the no-man's land between the demon army and the city wall. He'd never felt so naked and exposed. How quickly he would die if the demons knew he was there. And they'd all be dead in an instant if the archers defending the city wall saw them and decided they were hostile.

After another flash of black, he stood within the city walls and Ember dropped the invisibility enchantment. The whole party was there. They breathed a sigh and fell in around him and their raspberry-haired beauty.

Then Ember collapsed.

Ellessar examined her. "She's not wounded, but the burden of our entry has drained her. We need to find a place for her to rest for the remainder of the day."

Borim removed his cap and knelt by her side. "I'll stay with her."

Host of Evil

A handful of dwarven soldiers rushed toward them from an alley, headed by a sergeant at arms. "By the blazes of Brimstone, how did you get here?"

"Magic," Borim said. "And not our kind neither. But real just the same."

The sergeant looked skeptical.

"This elf needs a place to rest," Jasmine said. "Is there someplace nearby?"

The dwarf took one look at Jasmine's features and drew his short sword. Ellessar stepped between them, brandishing the emblem of his order.

The dwarf gasped. "The Order of the Shining Star."

"This woman may look unusual to your eye, but she's done at least as much for our cause as anyone else has. Where may the elf girl rest?"

The dwarf took another long look at Jasmine, and again at Ellessar's emblem. He swallowed hard and nodded curtly. "The Prancing Pony. Half a block down." He gestured with his stubby sword. "Might be full, though. Can't say for sure."

"Good enough," Nick said. "For now, we just need to get her indoors."

"The rest of you," the dwarf said, "quit dawdlin' and make yourselves useful." He started to storm off to the city's east gate.

"Wait," Ellessar called. "Are there any survivors from my brotherhood?"

"Yes. And we owe you many lives. This way."

"What about the Order of the Sage?" Jasmine asked. "Are they here?"

"Stationed at the east gate." The dwarf pointed. "They're our first line of defense should the walls be breached."

"Hold on," Nick said. "We can't all go running off to our various orders. We still have the Sword to find and the Master to face. Get what news you can and meet back at The Pony at dusk. Alanel, keep Ember safe. Borim, find out if Captain IronForge made it back here. I'll ask around on the off chance that Zen and his guide came through this way."

Ellessar spotted Lord Peldair, champion of the queen of Brinheim, on the battlement near the city's eastern gate. The man stood out in his vestments of rich blue fabric draped over his full plate armor, with the emblem of their order embroidered in gold. He wielded Demonbane, the sword forged by an angel of Aeron in the fires of the Abyss.

Ellessar climbed the stone steps to the battlement and marched up to the man. Dwarves and humans stood side by side, measuring the silent demon army below. The only sound came from the dwarves who worked tirelessly to repair damaged sections of the wall. All around them, rubble from previous attacks, the remnants of burned-out wooden structures, and the pitch-scorched walls of stone buildings bore mute witness to the brutality of the initial demon onslaught.

"What are they waiting for?" Ellessar asked. "Surely there are enough to overrun the city."

Peldair glanced at him, his eyes settling on the holy emblem hanging from a chain around Ellessar's neck. "You underestimate our resilience, brother. That army has pounded these walls for two weeks, and to no avail. Even *their* destructive potential can't outmatch the industry of dwarven stonesmiths and the courage of men."

"Then their delay can mean only one thing. They expect help to arrive."

"I fear that's true." Peldair twirled the Demonbane sword absently, as though he took the blade for granted. But it reminded Ellessar of another enchanted sword, one he himself had failed to safeguard. "Until we know what form that help will take, we can do naught but remain vigilant."

Along the battlement, each member of their order wore his ceremonial tunic with its shining golden star. Ellessar had one like it tucked in the bottom of his pack. He would have donned it if Aeron had bidden him to stay and fight with his order. "The brotherhood is well represented."

"Surprised?"

"Frankly, with the time you bought the civilized races and the number of demons against you, I expected to learn of greater decimation within our ranks."

"The flow from the Portal began as a trickle, and many of our brothers have indeed passed into the hands of Aeron."

"I wish I could have been a part of it."

Peldair eyed him critically. "You are now."

All the rooms at the Prancing Pony were full, but the innkeeper was gracious enough to let Nick and Alanel lay Ember's blanket on the floor in his family's private room for a single night. He refused Nick's coin. "We make what sacrifices we must in times like these."

As soon as Ember was settled, with Alanel by her side, Nick led the innkeeper back to the front desk. On the way, they passed the doorway to a taproom filled with women and children, their conversations muted, the mood black and miserable. "We're looking for somebody who might have come through here in the past day or two."

The innkeeper stepped behind the counter. "Nobody just comes through here. If they're here, they're trapped. If not, there's no way in."

"*We're* just passing through."

"So you said. Truth is, that's why I offered up my own room. If it's true, your errand must be important."

"It is. We're looking for a particular elf-kin, one you may have heard of. His name is Zen, but most know him as 'the ice mage.' He carries a crystal-tipped staff and wears a jeweled silver headband and a shimmering blue-gray robe. He can translocate over significant distances, so he can get in and out of the city without any problems."

The innkeeper sucked in a quick breath. He leaned in with both palms braced on the tile-topped counter. "*He* was the ice mage?"

"You've seen him, then."

"He came in here two nights hence. Woke me in the middle of the night to ask for a room. I was full, so I sent him on his way."

"Did he have a sword with him?"

"Yeah. Odd thing for a mage. Carried the scabbard in his hand with his staff. Your friend didn't look well, though. Had red splotches on his skin. Much like yours, though his hadn't begun to heal."

"He was ill?"

"I'll say." The innkeeper gestured at Nick's skin. "Is it contagious?"

"No. Zen stole something from me. The item must be causing the illness. I began to heal after he took it."

"Maybe it's better to let him keep it."

"I can't. Unfortunately I need it to complete my own mission against those hordes out there." Nick waved his hand toward the door and the eastern city wall beyond it. "Did he say anything about where he was headed?"

The innkeeper massaged his chin and stared at the ceiling. "Hmmmm."

Nick tossed a single silver coin onto the counter to jog the man's memory, one of several the high temple had provided to fund their pursuit of the Sword.

"Sorry." The innkeeper slid the coin back to Nick. "Old habits, you know. The mage asked if the road was open to Brinheim. Don't know if he meant the kingdom or the capital city." He paused. "Can't see why he'd stop here when he'd be better off steering clear."

"He probably needed supplies. And he hasn't got much cause to fear the demons. Keep the coin. You've been a tremendous help."

The next morning, Nick woke to the roar of a thousand cries from the battlement.

"Quickly." Ellessar snatched up his armor and belt.

Jasmine got to her feet instantly and checked on Ember, who had also woken to the cry. Alanel and Nick scrambled into their armor. Borim tugged his knit cap down past his ears, muttered something unintelligible, and drew the covers over his head.

More shouts drifted into the room, along with blood-chilling screams from wounded people. An arrow skipped into the courtyard, just outside the window.

"Come on." Ember nudged Borim with her foot. "Let's go bust some heads."

The dwarf mumbled something that might have been, "Heads?" He rolled to his feet and palmed his mace in one fluid movement. Though he'd been the last to awaken, he'd slept in his armor and was the first one out the door.

The others followed. Demons surrounded the city, but all the cries came from the direction of the eastern gates. Either the demons had tired of waiting, or their help had arrived.

Chapter 29

Nick stopped before entering the wide plaza between the eastern gate and the alley through which he and his friends were approaching the chaos. A rain of arrows came over the walls and struck the unfortunate and the unprepared alike. "Ready?" he asked Ellessar.

The demon hunter hefted the Shield of Faith above his head and stepped close to Nick.

Jasmine scanned the courtyard. "Where's Borim? He was ahead of us."

"Who knows?" Ember gestured toward the mayhem. "Out there somewhere." She put one hand on Jasmine and the other on Alanel. "See you on the wall." In a blink, all three were gone.

Together Nick and Ellessar bolted across the plaza under the protection of the Shield. Any arrows that came near seemed drawn to it, where they shattered and fell harmlessly away.

They bounded up the stairs two at a time until they gained the battlement.

Beyond the wall stood the sea of demons, still pouring in from the direction of the Great Sand, an army comprised mostly of Warriors and Archers. Sentries flew overhead, low enough for those on the ground to make them out, but too high to reach with arrows. Scouts roamed the perimeter of the ring that encircled the city.

"Blessed Aeron," Ellessar breathed. "That's what they were waiting for." He pointed to a trio of huge fur-covered demons with long arms like a gorilla's and ram-like heads. "Siege demons, probably called away from the attack on the elves' energy barrier."

The giants waded forward through the demon ranks, a good distance out but closing with inevitable finality. They stood half again as tall as the city wall and cast Warrior and Archer demons carelessly aside as they advanced.

"I'm glad we're here to help," Nick said.

"Get those ballistae loaded," yelled a rough-looking man with graying hair to the men in the courtyard behind him, whose efforts were hampered by the rain of arrows launched by twos from the ranks of Archer demons.

"That's Lord Peldair, the head of my order." Ellessar crouched below the battlement and ran to him.

Nick followed. Jasmine and the others stood several yards beyond, assessing their new enemies.

Warrior demons pressed forward, heedless of the arrows, crossbow bolts, and cauldrons of simmering oil that had already decimated small clots of demons among their ranks. Mages, dressed as ordinary soldiers, launched fireballs into the pockets of demons that reached the base of the wall, and lightning bolts into individuals that gained the lip of the battlement.

The lead Siege demon picked up a rock at least the size of a wagon and lifted it above its head. It lumbered forward with the burden until it was fifty yards from the wall.

Then it threw the boulder.

The wall lurched inward, weakened but standing, where the rock hit. The whole battlement shook. Bits and chucks of stone and crumbled mortar littered the plaza below. Dwarven stonesmiths rushed forward to make repairs before a second rock hit the weakened spot and brought the whole wall down.

Shouts and screams formed a constant din. Arrows rained into the courtyard. Men cranked the rope to get the bolt locked into place on the ballistae.

When the Siege demon reached the wall, it picked up its boulder again and hurled it over the battlement. It smashed one of the two ballistae, along with half its crew, and tumbled through the storefront behind it. The boulder nearly filled the whole of the poor merchant's shop.

The Siege demon scanned the courtyard and battlement, ignoring the arrows from the defenders, which seemed unable to penetrate its thick coat of wiry fur.

The crew of the remaining ballista cranked the wheel to aim at the monstrous demon, who swept away, in a single stroke, scores of the men and dwarves who'd rallied on the battlement to fight it.

It pulled stone blocks from the damaged wall and hurled them one way or the other along the battlement, each taking out a swath of defenders before dropping into the courtyard.

When the ballista fired its huge, arrow-like projectile, the demon blocked it with its hand, and the five-foot bolt skewered its massive palm.

Jasmine sprinted toward the demon.

The demon plucked the bolt from its hand and tossed it at Jasmine, who ducked aside and continued her charge. The Siege demon pointed toward the remaining ballista. Archer demons below corrected their aim accordingly and rained arrows down upon the machine. The entire crew perished just as they finished loading the next ballista bolt.

Jasmine leapt onto the demon's shoulder and scrambled around to the small of its back, gripping its rough black fur. It tried to reach her for long moments. Unable to do so, the demon returned its attention to dismantling the wall.

Nick held out his hand to Ellessar. "Shield!"

The demon hunter hesitated.

"Now!"

Reluctantly, Ellessar relinquished the Shield of Faith to Nick, who leapt from the wall and crashed to the plaza below. A sharp pain stabbed through his right ankle as it twisted beneath him. Ignoring the pain, he raised the Shield above him and launched himself toward the ballista. Another wave of arrows came over the wall and shattered against the Shield. Nick limped to the rear of the ballista, clambered onto it, and peered through the aiming sights.

Jasmine climbed to the top of the demon's head and clawed at both of its eyes with her talons. The demon jerked erect with a roar and reached for her.

Nick turned the cranks to adjust the ballista's aim slightly to the left, then cut the restraining rope with his sword.

The bolt plunged into the Siege demon's chest.

After wavering for a moment, the demon collapsed into the damaged wall, reducing it to a rubble heap strewn across the plaza.

Warrior and Archer demons scrambled over the fallen blocks and into the city.

Ellessar's brothers dove into the demon ranks with Lord Peldair at their head. His Demonbane sword killed any demon it touched. Jasmine somersaulted to her feet, *sais* in her hands, and joined the brothers and sisters of her order in a charge to halt the Warriors as they scrambled over the rubble. Mages in the plaza threw up barriers of energy and stone to bottleneck those that gained the courtyard. Dwarves barreled in as well, combatants and stonesmiths alike.

The clear call, "ShatterBrand!" rang out amid the rumble of the dwarven charge.

Arrows continued to sail over the wall into the courtyard. The two remaining Siege demons lumbered forward, one carrying a boulder the size of a small cottage. Still a quarter mile from the city wall, the demon labored under its heavy load, its advance relentless.

Beside Ellessar, Alanel held his enchanted arrow, tapping it with a nervous finger.

Ellessar pointed. "Can you hit that demon from here?"

"Yes."

"Then why do you hesitate?"

"I've only got one demon-slayer arrow. If I launch it into that sea, I'll never get it back. I fear we may need it later."

"If that demon gets within throwing range of the wall, we'll lose this whole city. There won't be a 'later.'"

After a few seconds, Alanel pursed his lips and nodded. He nocked the arrow, drew back, held it for a moment, and released.

Ellessar lost sight of the arrow in the glare of the morning sun, still low at the demon army's back. But then the Siege demon's face contorted with rage or pain—the demon itself probably couldn't distinguish between the two. The huge boulder tumbled from its hands, crushing a dozen or more Archers and Warriors beneath it. The Siege demon's body shriveled to a mummified husk and lay, inert, on the battlefield.

The last Siege demon had advanced much closer. Unburdened by any boulders or other discernible weapons, it headed straight for the breach that its kin had already made. The loose blocks from the wall itself would provide plenty of missiles for it to throw, and doing so would scatter the materials the dwarves needed to repair the breach.

Ellessar grabbed Ember's arm and pointed to the monstrous demon. "Can you take me to the shoulder of that thing?"

Ember swallowed hard. "In a minute."

"We haven't got a minute."

"I must prepare."

She spoke an elfish phrase, and a dim blue glow flashed around her. She touched Ellessar and repeated the incantation. His skin hardened to a tough leather hide, similar in color and texture to that of his demon-skin coat, which he'd left at the Prancing Pony in his haste.

He flexed his arms and found himself unhindered by the enchantment. "Quickly!"

Ember faded into invisibility. Her hand touched him. "Ready?"

Ellessar drew one of his bone-handled swords. "Go."

In an instant, the battlement disappeared. The ground—no, the demon—rocked beneath his feet. Ember cried out. Her hand left Ellessar's back as she fell.

Ellessar grabbed a fistful of demon fur in one hand and snatched for Ember's unseen arm with the other. His sword was lost in the mass of Warriors and Archers that milled beneath them.

Ember seized his wrist, and both clung for their lives.

"Grab its fur," Ellessar yelled over the snarls and gleeful hisses of the demons around them.

The stench of the throng was unbelievable, something between smoke and decay. It didn't just assault Ellessar's sense of smell; it actually burned the inside of his nose. Warriors yelled and pointed up at Ellessar. Archers loaded their bows. He had but seconds to do whatever damage he could.

"Got it." Ember released his arm.

The Siege demon swatted at him, as though he was merely a blood fly on its neck.

Counting on his handful of the demon's fur to support him, Ellessar swung around to the center of its back, where he couldn't be easily reached. He drew his remaining bone-handled sword and whispered a two-word prayer to Aeron: "Strengthen me." He jammed the sword to the hilt in the demon's neck where the main blood supply would flow in a human or elf.

Gouts of green blood surged out, threatening Ellessar's grip on the sword.

Arrows from below pelted his back. He felt the impacts against his skin, painful but not penetrating, and silently thanked Ember for taking those few moments to provide the enchantment.

The demon stumbled.

"Done!" he yelled to Ember.

She grabbed his ankle. An instant later, the two reappeared in a heap on the city wall.

Ellessar sorted himself out from the tangled limbs of several city defenders whom he and Ember had bowled over upon their return. His sword and arm were drenched in demon blood, but he himself was unhurt. Ember became visible beside him, shaken but smiling.

The third and final Siege demon stumbled forward a dozen more steps. Arrows from the defenders on the wall rained onto it, piercing the creature. It dropped to its knees. Green blood, still flowing freely onto the ground, soaked one of its sides from the neck down. Finally, the demon fell forward and lay still, not thirty feet from the broken section of the wall.

Using the Shield of Faith to protect him from demon arrows, Nick limped back to the cover of the wall and up the stairs to the battlement in time to watch the last Siege demon fall. As soon as it did, he called out to Ellessar, Ember, and Alanel.

Below, Jasmine must have heard him yelling. She disengaged from the defense of the breach. The fighters around her, hearts boosted by the cheer above them, began to repel the clot of Warrior demons bogged down there.

Nick signaled for her to join them on the wall.

Breathless but apparently uninjured, she bounded up the stairs. "What is it?"

"We have to go." Nick scanned the plaza. "Where's Borim?"

"Here!" the dwarf called.

Sterling IronForge and twelve of his knights followed Borim up.

"We can't leave now," Ellessar said. "We have to fight the demons back, at least until the breach is sealed."

"I agree," Jasmine said.

Nick made a sweeping gesture toward the throng. "We can't afford to get caught up in this. We've stopped the Siege demons. They were the immediate threat. Now the rest will either overtake the city or not. At this point, the six of us will make little difference one way or the other." Nick turned to Ellessar. "I know which direction Zen has gone, but he has a two-day head start. We can't lose sight of that sword." He surveyed the battle beneath them. "If we don't kill the Master, none of this will make any difference."

"Okay." Jasmine wiped the green blood from her *sais* and tucked them into her belt. "But we can't go out the way we came in. We can't afford for Ember to collapse like she did last time, not out there with the demon hoards."

Ember nodded. "I've spent a lot of my energy already, and the day's still young."

"*We'll* get you through." Sterling puffed out his gut. "This breach is the perfect diversion. But we'll need horses."

Nick took the dwarf's hand. "Good to see you."

"We wouldn't miss this. We tracked down those demon Scouts and finished them." Sterling's gaze grew briefly distant and sad. "Costly battle, that one." He seemed to shake it off. "Then we came here to aid the defense of the city. But you, my boy, are our charge."

"We have to grab our supplies—" Nick said.

"And Spirit," Ellessar added.

"Secure some horses," Nick told Sterling, "and meet us at the south gate."

Nick and his friends skirted the edge of the wall to avoid the rain of arrows until they'd gone far enough to move about safely.

"You're limping," Jasmine noticed.

"Sprained ankle. I'll live."

She nodded. "I'll wrap it for you when we get to the Prancing

Pony. Won't take a minute."

They continued the rest of the way in relative silence. The shouts and screams of battle faded as they ducked into the inn to collect their gear.

When they reached the southern gate, Nick climbed the battlement. Sterling had been right. The Archers and Warriors weren't nearly half as thick here as they'd been all the way around the city the previous day.

"Question is," Nick asked, "how do we get through them?"

Jasmine climbed the ladder and came up beside him. "I have an idea."

CHAPTER 30

Nick helped his friends tie a saddled horse on a tether to each of the dwarven knights' mounts, as though they were spares. He, Ellessar, Jasmine, Borim, and Alanel each mounted one of the tethered horses. Then Ember walked down the line and turned the five of them invisible, along with the belongings they carried on them.

"You may be tempted to fight," Jasmine told her friends. "Don't. If the demons realize we're riding the spare horses, they'll pursue us to our end."

Borim grumbled a dwarven oath that even Nick recognized as profanity, but he made no overt objection.

Ember mounted her own horse and faded to invisibility. Seven of the spares remained riderless. "Ready," Ember said quietly.

Sterling motioned for the head of the watch, a lieutenant in the Meuribar city guard, to raise the gate. The lieutenant nodded once to each of the two squads of reserve soldiers stationed in the southern plaza in case of a secondary attack. The soldiers tensed, weapons in hand, ready for the worst. The lieutenant then looked to a handful of mounted runners prepared to raise the alarm, should the need arise. Finally, he consulted a sergeant stationed on the battlement, who confirmed with a nod that the demons remained out of arrow range. Only then did the lieutenant signal the gate crew to raise the locking bar and portcullis.

The demons had been milling in a loose band, thirty or forty demons deep, just beyond bowshot from the battlement. As soon as the gate swung open, they drew their weapons. The roar from their ranks was part cheer, part cackle, and part growl.

When the dwarves charged into battle, it looked for all the world as though they'd simply brought spare mounts to speed their way on whatever urgent errand they were undertaking.

Sterling's knights had clearly fought from horseback—or at least from pony or mule—before, but Nick had never seen anything like their tactics. As they charged into the demons' front line, they used their horses like battering rams and their armored formation like a plow. They whipped their weapons over their heads, swung at anything that came within reach, and stopped for nothing, least of all their own fallen knights.

The "spare" horses remained sheltered within the V of their wedge formation.

The dwarves quickly drove a path through the thinned demon line. Eight of the knights made it through and the demons closed ranks behind them. As soon as they passed the last line of demons, they pressed their horses into an outright run.

A pursuit party, scores of Warriors and Archers mounted on Scouts, formed up behind them. The pursuit lasted for nearly an hour before it became clear that the Scout demons would eventually outpace the horses.

Once the Archers came within bowshot, all of the knights cut the tethers to their spare mounts and, as one, wheeled around to fight.

Only then did Nick realize that the dwarves never meant to escape with them, or to return to the city of Meuribar...but to serve as decoys. And to die. He wheeled his horse around.

Spirit came up alongside him. Ellessar, still invisible, grabbed the reins of Nick's horse and held it fast. "It kills me to not turn and slay as many of those demons as I can before they take me down, but if we go back, our quest is over and the Master has won."

Nick's reply dripped with self-disgust. "Too many people have died for the sake of my quest."

"*Our* quest. And if we're unsuccessful, all among the goodly races will die or become enslaved."

The pursuing demons slammed into the dwarven knights with a crash and immediately surrounded them. None bothered to chase down the spare horses. Within seconds the dwarves began to fall.

"You see," Ellessar said. "They're already lost." He gave Spirit enough slack in her reins to graze, so she would behave like the stray she was supposed to be. The other horses, whether ridden or actual spares, milled around as well.

When the slaughter ended, a couple of Scout demons watched the distant horses for a few minutes. Apparently convinced there weren't additional enemies among the strays, the demons returned to the besieged city.

"Come," Ellessar said once the demons were out of sight. "We have a thief to catch and a sword to recover. We mustn't let the dwarves' deaths be in vain."

Nick and his friends pressed hard until they reached South Bend—with very little interference from the demon hoards, who seemed to have concentrated their forces around the city of Meuribar and against the elven boarder. Ember continued to conceal their camp at night, while allowing the horses to graze and trusting

Spirit's loyalty to keep them all from wandering off.

Nick inquired about Zen in South Bend and Loran. The elf-kin had gone into both cities, the latter within the preceding twenty-four hours. Even with the spare horses Nick retained from their escape from besieged Meuribar, he hadn't expected to gain that much time.

"He's slowing down," Alanel observed. "Maybe he figures he's lost us."

"A reasonable assumption," Jasmine said. "If he's been checking the trail behind him during the night, he won't have seen us since before the monastery."

Nick scanned the sky for snow-colored birds. "Let's keep it that way. We might catch him within the next few days."

The kingdom of Brinheim was oddly quiescent. Even though it bordered the Great Sand, where the Portal of the Damned was located, it remained untouched by the war.

Brinheim's fertile plains stretched from Loran across the northern hill country, all the way south to the Great Divide. The temperate climate made Brinheim the greenest kingdom by half in all the human lands, its lush lowlands rivaled only by the Sunburst Plain in Gildstone. Its beauty lifted Nick's spirits as time healed his skin, his illness all but gone except for the scars—which would likely remain for the rest of his days.

"I wonder," Alanel said.

"What?" Nick asked after a moment.

"Do the demons leave this place alone because their Master resides here, to preserve his home?"

Ellessar scanned the countryside ahead. "I wonder, indeed."

The party stopped at the capital city long enough to question the guards at the city gates. Zen had left the city, heading south, alone and on foot, in the wee hours of that very morning. There were no large settlements south of the capital, though numerous villages and homesteads dotted the area, serviced by marginally maintained dirt roads rutted with wagon tracks.

"He's headed for the Great Divide," Nick guessed.

Ellessar gazed at the mountain range, still gray in the distance. "If he goes into the Wild Lands, we'll lose him. He can fly over the mountain or translocate to the other side. But unless there's a pass we don't know about, we'll have to circle around through Roybal Keep."

"Then let's catch him before he gets there," Nick said.

An hour later, they came across a campsite directly south of the capital. Alanel pointed out a hoofprint with the distinctive pair of parallel gouges that marked the left-front foot of either Zen's horse or that of his elven guide. "These tracks aren't more than a few hours old."

His hope renewed, Nick urged his friends to the greatest speed they could manage without losing the trail. Hour by hour, the gap between pursuer and prey closed.

The next day, Ellessar and Alanel agreed that they must be no more than an hour behind when Zen's trail veered off the rutted track and climbed up into the foothills of the Great Divide, the southern boundary of Brinheim. There they found two horses tethered to a tree at the point where the hill became too steep for the mounts to climb.

Ellessar checked the left-front hoof of each horse for the telltale gouges. "These are theirs." The horses were still saddled. Ellessar placed his hand on the chest of one. "They're cool. They've been here for more than a few minutes."

Nick tethered his horses to a nearby tree. The others followed suit, except for Ellessar, who looped Spirit's reins around her saddle horn, trusting her to stay put.

"Careful," Borim warned as they climbed the slope. "The mage may yet be watchin'. I, for one, don't care to get caught in one of his weavings."

"Neither do I," Ellessar agreed.

The group spread out so they wouldn't all fall victim to a single ice ball or hailstorm wrought by Zen's staff. Single file, with Alanel in front, picking out their prey's soft boot prints, they followed the trail through a cleft and into a dark tunnel that cut deep into the mountain.

"Wait." Nick drew his great sword and moved up to take the lead. No side passages branched off the main tunnel. Unless Zen translocated, which he could only do if he was familiar with his destination, the trail would be impossible to lose there. Ellessar fell in behind Nick, then Jasmine, followed by Borim and Ember. Alanel brought up the rear.

The tunnel extended for nearly a mile before opening at one end of a huge, hourglass-shaped audience chamber lit by evenly spaced torches mounted on the walls and on the few natural pillars.

At the far end of the hall stood six men—no, Nick corrected himself, three men, a woman, an elf...and Zen. Nick recognized Dalen Frost, still wearing the uniform of Trondor's Home Guard. Another man and the woman wore mage's robes. The elf, dressed in a black traveling cloak that shadowed much of his face, looked like Zen's guide, the one they'd seen riding with him during his escape from Lorentil.

Centered at the rear of the formation stood the Master of Air and Darkness. Even in the flickering torchlight, Nick couldn't mistake him. The emblem of Vexetan glowed a ghastly yellow from a band woven of taupe cords—human sinew, according to the Prophecy—that adorned his head. A lock of white hair stood out in his black mane. He was an image straight out of the pages of Mortaan's Final Prophecy.

The Sword of Alamain was nowhere in sight.

Nick stopped just inside the entrance and scanned the cavern. A pair of twenty-foot-tall onyx statues of a slender, faceless, hairless being, vaguely humanoid in shape with long arms and clawed fingers, flanked the narrow waist of the chamber. Beyond the statues, the contours of the chamber blocked the sides of the audience hall from view. There could be an army of orcs—or worse—hidden there. Similarly, to Nick's immediate right and left, dark shadows shrouded the corners, concealing anything that might lurk there.

The place remained still and silent until the Master spoke. "Come in, my new friends. Join me, and join my cause."

The pink, tear-shaped charm Alamain had given Nick grew hot against his chest, but it wasn't enough. He resisted the Master's words to the core of his being. He planted his feet on the floor and resolved to stand firm on the cavern threshold. Yet his feet carried him into the audience chamber.

All of his friends followed.

When Zen had entered the Dark One's audience chamber, his heart had soared just to be in the awesome presence of the Master. Whatever the Master's views or beliefs, whatever god he worshipped, whatever his cause or means, he knew best, and Zen must support his every action, even desire, no matter the cost. Such was his power and his aura of confidence.

The Master beckoned. "Come in, Gwyndarren Lortannon."

Gwyndarren led the way into the chamber. Beside the Master stood a pair of his Chosen, an old man and a handsome woman, both in mage's robes, each with a prominently displayed Medallion of Vexetan. Behind them crouched stone gargoyles atop black marble pillars lined with veins of green.

A gargantuan monster, a demon by the looks of it, slunk from the shadows. Neither crab-like nor spider-like in appearance but some mix of both, it stood fifteen feet tall. It had a sleek abdomen like that of a praying mantis, a broad head, an ink-black carapace, and eight legs—no, seven. One foreleg had been severed at the first joint. A giant pincer clicked menacingly at the end of its remaining foreleg.

This must be the demon they'd heard about at Roybal Keep months before, the demon that had killed Nick's uncle and devastated his caravan, strewing dwarven-made weapons for a mile or more along the road west of South Bend.

Pandalo Gundahar, general of the Trondorian army, and Dalen Frost, captain of Trondor's Home Guard, were there as well, armed and armored, ready for battle. Pandalo wore a cloak of shifting colors, similar to the one Sierra had worn. His form seemed to fade in and out of view against the cave wall behind him as he moved. Only his head was clearly visible. The fact that these two weren't with their king could only mean that Balor had completed his conquest of Faldor.

Come in, Zenobrian Zersaash," the Master commanded. "Bring me the Sword of Alamain."

Zen did as he was told. He could do nothing else. All the while, his mind screamed, *No! No! This is not how it's supposed to be!* The pendant Alamain had blessed for him burned against his chest, against his very heart. It was supposed to prevent the Master's charm from enslaving him, but it wasn't strong enough. Zen tried to resist, though he could no longer remember why it was important for him to do so. All the while, his hands and feet obeyed the Master.

He passed a pair of twenty-foot-tall statues, one on either side of the hall, presumably idols of Vexetan—though Zen had never seen an image of the Dark God—black as obsidian, shiny, reflecting the torchlight. Faceless, with long, clawed fingers.

A fierce grin tried, and failed, to cross Zen's face as the Master reeled away from the Sword in Zen's outstretched hands.

"Give it to Addicus." The Master motioned to the old mage, who stood just beside him. "Quickly!"

Physically, Zen's strength was failing him. He could feel the same fatigue and weakness he'd experienced when he bore the stone from the behemoth's lake. This time, though, it had become much worse. His skin was red and peeling, as Nick's had been.

He'd recovered when Nick began carrying the rock, but it had started again as soon as Zen had stolen the Sword of Alamain. Something about the metal in the blade sickened its wielder. Imagine, Zen thought, what it could do to one who was actually cut by the thing.

Yet Zen's affliction seemed to be physical only. His mind remained as sharp as ever, or at least it had until he'd entered this chamber. Now, apparently, Zen's body and mind belonged to the Master. Zen handed the Sword of Alamain to the old mage.

This was all wrong. The Sword wasn't supposed to be a gift for the Master—or even the payment for admission into his sacred inner circle, as Gwyndarren had arranged. It was Zen's only bargaining chip. Once the Master had it, Zen would have nothing except a mind in thrall to the Master.

"Lock the Sword up until you can find a way to destroy it," the Master told Addicus.

The old mage hurried down a tunnel in the back of the audience hall. Zen followed—the Master's commands permitted that much—and his heart returned to him as soon as he left the Master's presence. He cursed Alamain for the inefficacy of her priestly charm and considered what weaving he might launch at Addicus.

Zen could take the Sword back. He was sure of that. The doddering old man would never see what hit him. But that wouldn't serve Zen's purpose. He'd come here to gain the Master's trust. However the final showdown developed, Zen required the Master's trust.

He followed Addicus into a workshop filled with an assortment of furnishings. Crystals, candles, and rare substances cluttered the shelves. Live coals burned beneath a brazier that dominated the center of the room. A single scrap of the burnt journal that had belonged to Nick, and Nick's grandfather before him, lay on the desk next to the brazier.

Addicus opened a hidden panel in the back wall, where a closet contained a multitude of artifacts. As soon as the opportunity arose, Zen promised himself, he would return for as many of these as he could carry.

Addicus placed the Sword beside the original Codex of Moran, which Zen and his companions had found in King Gremauld's library. Jasmine's copy from the Order of the Sage lay beneath the original. Then Addicus backed out and closed the door. He made a point of sealing the entrance with an enchantment of warding.

Zen probed the mage's weaving, gently testing its strength. He could break through it, should the need arise, but to do so would likely alert the Master. He had better ways to get inside.

A gong sounded from some ethereal source, neither within Addicus's workshop nor beyond it.

"Quickly," the old man said. "We haven't much time."

"Time for what?" Zen asked, but Addicus had already disappeared through the door, down the corridor toward the audience hall. With a brief glance at the closet, Zen hurried after him.

Once they arrived, the Master and both of his mages spoke a flurry of divine and magical enchantments over themselves, each other, and the soldiers. Pandalo pulled up the hood of his cloak and disappeared into the background. The demon retreated into one of the shadowed corners.

"Come in, my new friends," the Master commanded Zen's former companions as they emerged from the entrance tunnel. "Join me, and join my cause."

Zen was too late. Everything was happening too fast. He was supposed to have some warning. His only hope came from the burning pendant that only then, finally, seemed to shield his heart from the will of the Master.

CHAPTER 31

"Come in, my new friends. Join me, and join my cause."

The insistence in the Master's voice burned away Nick's brief thoughts of defiance. How, he wondered, could he ever oppose so noble a man or mission. He strode into the audience hall. Around him, his friends advanced as well. As one, they sheathed their weapons and walked forward.

The pulsing pendant hanging beneath Nick's armor burned his skin. The pain tugged at his concentration.

Here, in this place, Nick and his friends would become enthralled or die. The Prophecy was vague about that particular detail. It said only that they would fail because they lacked a weapon that wasn't forged of this world. And the Prophecy was right. Because Zen had stolen the Sword and led them here, Mortaan would prove once and for all that he was never wrong. Here and now, the Prophecy would come to pass. Today the Age of Darkness would begin.

Nick, Jasmine, Ellessar, Ember, Borim, and Alanel stopped in a loose knot, just before they passed the pair of gargantuan statues that guarded the waist of the hourglass-shaped chamber. Because Alamain's pendant charms had proven to be insufficient against the power of Vexetan, Nick and his companions would be denied even the dignity of a fighting death.

Nick studied the people on the dais. The female mage on the Master's left was the dragon rider who had hunted the companions through Faldor on their flight from Trondor to Roybal Keep. Her presence suggested that the dragon was likely nearby as well. The woman fixed her attention exclusively on Jasmine. The old mage on the Master's right was a man Nick and his friends hadn't yet encountered. Dalen Frost and Zen's guide stood with their hands poised above their swords, their eyes fixed on the helpless knot of victims Nick and his friends had become.

Four Chosen, Nick counted, including the demon clicking its crab-clawed legs against the floor in agitation, half hidden in the shadows to Nick's left. Five, if the elven guide wore a Medallion beneath his travelling cloak.

Zen gestured in the air. A portal opened before him and he vanished into it.

The Master scanned the chamber, peering systematically from shadow to shadow, pillar to pillar. "Kill anyone who attacks me or any of my Chosen." The command, addressed to everyone in the chamber, immediately separated the combatants into two sides: those enthralled by the Master against anyone who wasn't.

Nick glanced about his friends nervously. If any resisted the charm and attacked one of the Chosen, the Master's enchantment would compel Nick to at least try to kill them.

Host of Evil

Zen stepped out of his icy translocation portal into Addicus's secret closet, wove an enchantment to allow his sight to pierce the darkness, and snatched up the Sword of Alamain. He returned to the audience hall an instant later, but not at the dais. Instead, he emerged behind a pillar near Nick. Zen tossed the Sword at his friend's feet and hoped that Nick's pendant had overcome the Master's charms. If it hadn't, Nick would be forced to give the Sword back to the Master.

From nowhere, a sword—no, *the* Sword—clattered to the stone floor at Nick's feet.

Zen crouched nearby with a pillar between himself and the dais. "I led you to the Master. Let's see if we can spoil Mortaan's perfect record." The mage's skin was red, raw, and blistered from his having possessed the talisman for the past couple of weeks.

During that time, Nick had healed. Physically, he felt like his old self again. He understood the cost of bearing the otherworldly weapon. Nevertheless, he scooped up the Sword. It felt lighter than he remembered it, or more of his strength had returned than he'd realized. He scanned the room for threats to his Master and the Chosen. Certainly, Zen's words threatened, but the Master's instruction compelled Nick to kill only those who actually attacked. His friends peered, sidelong and wary, at one another. Surely they weren't among those who would threaten the Master. If they were, Nick would do what he must.

"No!"

Nick's attention snapped back to the dais. The Master glared at him, red-faced with anger. What had Nick done but pick up the greatest weapon ever forged so that he could use it to do the Master's bidding? Yet the Master seemed to take it as some sort of affront. With a sweeping gesture that took in the whole of the cavern, the High

Priest of Vexetan unleashed his minions. The Chosen would quickly separate his friends from anyone in the chamber who would prove disloyal.

Beside Nick, Ellessar flung the Shield of Faith from his arm as though it had burned him, a sure sign that he too had come to his senses—that he now backed the Master.

The spider-crab demon charged from the shadows. A Medallion of Vexetan hung from its neck. Alanel drew his sword and advanced to intercept it. It swiveled its head toward the elf, its eyes glowing red. An instant later, Alanel's entire body stiffened and turned to stone. Then the demon charged toward Jasmine, the farthest of Nick's friends from its position.

The attack made no sense. The demon would have to run past the entire line of potential enemies just to get to her. Maybe it understood something Nick didn't. Maybe with Alanel's death, Jasmine remained the only enemy of the Master among them.

That proved untrue. There was another, placed at the left hand of the Master. "No-o-o-o-o-o-o!" The white-robed dragon rider leapt from the stage, gesticulating in the air, a mask of impotent horror etched into her mature features.

An Assassin demon appeared from the ether and blocked the path of the charging crab-demon. It raked its long claws across an outstretched pincer. Dalen, Borim, and Zen's guide raced to oppose the Assassin, for it had attacked a Chosen.

Nick stood rooted. He focused on the pain emanating from Alamain's pendant, determined not to move until he broke free of the Master's will.

The Master turned his hatred upon the woman. A ring on her finger blazed a furious red and she grasped the Medallion of Vexetan that hung from her neck. The two struggled for only a moment before the ring exploded, leaving the woman's arm a charred and ragged stump. The blast threw her to the ground, the Medallion of Vexetan smoking as it lay on her blackened chest.

Zen's elven guide drew a long sword and advanced toward the

melee, while the Master ducked into a dark tunnel behind him. The gray-haired mage remained on the dais, weaving.

No longer stifled by the direct presence of the Master, Alamain's pendant blazed like the sun liberated from the clouds. It burned away the haze that had blinded Nick's heart, and for the first time since he'd entered the audience hall, he saw the enemy for who they truly were: a threat not only to himself and his friends, but to all in the Civilized Lands.

The Master returned a moment later with a scepter, a black shaft with a ruby-red sphere at one end—familiar from Grandpa Gaddy's journal—in his hand. As he raised it, the ruby tip began to glow.

Giving Nick the Sword while he might be in thrall to the Master was the greatest risk Zen had taken in this ever-more-perilous quest against the Prophecy. Nick could simply turn the Sword against Zen. Or the Master himself might strike Zen down.

Neither of these things happened. Zen's doom came from an entirely different quarter. Pandalo Gundahar separated himself from the rugged, shadowed wall of the cavern. He spoke a simple command word, and his sword ignited with flame. With another word, a small fireball blazed from the tip of his blade.

Zen had only enough time to pull his cloak over his head before the blaze hit him and exploded. Flames ignited Zen's cloak and the blast threw him back against the pillar. He twisted out of the burning garment and wove a layer of frost to douse the remaining flames that scorched his skin and singed his hair.

Pandalo raised his flaming sword and charged. Zen scrambled to his knees and flung up a weaving that should have turned the man's brain into a frozen chunk of meat. Pandalo didn't react. He was probably protected by either his Medallion or some other magic of the Master and his mages.

Zen staggered back, reeling against hope to stay out of the arc of Pandalo's flaming sword. Pain made his movements jerky. Pandalo's first swing whistled past Zen's face. The sword tip nicked his cheek before it knocked a fistful of rock from the pillar. Zen blocked Pandalo's second strike with his staff. The force of the blow threw Zen to the ground once more. Rock and dust ground into Zen's raw, blistered skin as he rolled with the fall.

He couldn't get ahead of Pandalo's strikes, regain the initiative, or even weave a defensive enchantment. He managed only to get to his hands and knees before Pandalo loomed over him. The general glared into his pleading eyes and swung his sword to split Zen's skull.

Borim charged past the Assassin demon, straight at the elf who had been Zen's guide, ShatterBrand poised to "negotiate."

As soon as the Master left the dais, however, the elf blinked twice and then gazed around the cavern as if seeing it for the first time. He dropped his sword and threw out his hands before him. "Wait! I'm on your side."

Borim slid to a stop. He didn't for a second believe the elf's words, but he wasn't willing to bust the head of an unarmed opponent—even an elf. Muttering a curse, he spun toward the crab-demon.

The elf snatched up his sword and slipped into a side passage.

Fire from the crab-demon's mouth engulfed the Assassin demon. Ignoring the blaze, it clamped a giant set of mandibles about the Assassin's head and grabbed its torso with two of its three remaining pincers. The crab-demon ripped the Assassin in two, littering the floor with its remains.

Stone-faced, Ellessar stood before the monstrous demon, ready to face it alone with his one remaining prayer-etched sword. "Good Aeron, help us."

Dalen shot an arrow into Ellessar's shoulder from across the cavern. The demon hunter's sword fell to the ground, and the crab-demon plowed him over in its single-minded charge at Jasmine. The demon spit a stream of liquid at the monk. Jasmine twisted aside and dodged the bulk of it. A few drops that landed on her skin hissed and smoked. She darted behind a pillar as she drew her sais.

"ShatterBrand!" Borim barreled in behind the monster in a vain effort to distract it.

Finally recognizing the Chosen as his enemies, Nick sprang forward with the Sword of Alamain and deflected Pandalo Gundahar's strike at Zen's head. Nick stepped between the two of them, and Zen vanished through one of his extra-dimensional portals.

Invigorated by the return of his strength and the recovery of the Sword, Nick lunged at Pandalo. A furious ring of metal filled the chamber as they came together in a clash of swords. The heat from Pandalo's flaming blade singed Nick's skin and soaked his body with sweat, until a welcome wave of cold rolled past them. One of Zen's balls of ice and slush emerged from the corridor through which they'd all entered. The ball raced across the audience hall and burst on the dais with an explosion of dagger-sharp ice splinters and freezing air.

From nowhere, Ember appeared behind Nick and locked her grip onto his shoulders. "The Master is down." In one black flash, she translocated Nick and herself onto the dais, leaving Jasmine and Borim to face Pandalo and the crab-demon alone. The two weren't nearly a match for the pair of Chosen, but Ember was right. The Master was their priority.

Rock and debris scattered by Zen's ice ball shifted under Nick's feet. Ember went down in the rubble beside him.

The creature that lay at Nick's feet, however, was anything but human. Dressed in only a light shift that resembled a simple cloth sack, it had the horns, legs, and feet of a goat, and a face featureless save for a pair of sunken, colorless eyes and a slit for a mouth. Of all the trappings that had adorned it before the ice ball had exploded, only the scepter remained, lying on the ground beside it. The crown of human sinew was gone. Like the other Chosen, it bore a Medallion of Vexetan around its neck. The ice-flayed skin dangling in ribbons from the half-frozen body made it clear that the thing was dead.

This doppelganger wasn't the Master of Mortaan's Prophecy, but some sort of body double. No wonder Nick had regained control of his mind. The real Master had fled the battle as soon as he'd lost control of the Sword of Alamain and his dragon rider.

The old mage who'd been on the dais a moment before was nowhere in sight.

Jasmine kicked the crab-demon's carapace and cracked it. She avoided meeting its gaze and stayed out of the way of its fiery breath and corrosive spittle. Even as she scrambled around the pillar to stay out of reach of the demon's huge mandibles, the crack in its carapace began to heal.

"ShatterBrand!" Borim's mace smashed into the demon's abdomen with a loud crunch, and the creature released a wail of anguish.

Pandalo Gundahar, his sword afire, closed on Borim and pressed the dwarf hard.

The demon's attention, however, never left Jasmine. Its giant claw swept around the pillar and crushed her forearm. She reeled backwards. Her thoughts turned inward, willing the healing energies of her body to tend to the fracture.

Another stream of liquid shot from the demon's mouth.

CHAPTER 32

Borim's mace struck Pandalo. One of the spikes penetrated the breastplate and sank into the man's chest. Pandalo stumbled backward for a moment, and then he came at Borim with renewed vengeance. The dwarf was no match for the general, wounded though the man was. Borim hid behind his shield and mace as Pandalo's rain of blows pounded him further and further off balance. "Sis, help!"

Nick scanned the chamber for nearby enemies. Dalen Frost stood a dozen yards in front of the dais. Ellessar had crawled behind a stone pillar and Dalen had pinned him down with a volley of arrows. Dalen was facing away from Nick. He didn't even seem to know that enemies had gained the dais behind him. Without warning, Nick charged the man and ran him through from the back with the Sword of Alamain. His weight drove Dalen to the ground, where the man gurgled briefly, let out a wet sigh, and then breathed no more.

When Borim called for help, Nick glanced up and saw the dwarf's peril in the eerie light of Pandalo's flaming sword. He spun on Ember. "Send me!"

Ember grabbed a pair of the charms on her necklace and spoke a word of power. In an instant, Nick and Borim switched places. The transference disoriented Nick, but Pandalo was bleeding from a puncture wound in his chest. Instead of attacking, the general stepped away. With an arc of his flaming sword, he produced a wall of fire between them.

Jasmine dodged the stream of spittle that spewed from the demon's mouth and almost got caught in the wall of flames as it rose between her and the monster she faced. She took that moment to help Ellessar to his feet. The elf was limping. She, Ellessar, and Nick stood on one side of the flaming barrier, Pandalo and the crab-demon on the other. The general would likely stay on the far side. He appeared too wounded to continue. The demon, on the other hand, had set upon Jasmine with a senseless, personal rage. Flames wouldn't stop it.

Nick moved to stand beside her and the demon hunter.

One of Jasmine's arms hung crooked at her side. She gripped a *sai* in her other fist. "Don't look at its eyes."

Pandalo backed away from the flames. His chest heaved. Blood filled his lungs, drowning him. If he could finish this fight, his Master would heal him. But if he fled before that, he'd receive punishment through the Medallion instead.

A hippogriff made of ice trotted into the audience hall from the main entrance tunnel. It surveyed the room, then advanced toward Pandalo.

If not for the pain in his chest, Pandalo would have laughed out loud. The mage was as wounded as Pandalo himself, and he thought to beat the general with ice? Pandalo swept the chamber with a second wall of fire, perpendicular to the first, sealing himself into a corner of the massive cavern. Let the hippogriff come through that.

The hippogriff took flight. Drops of melted ice sizzled in the flames as it flew over the barrier. By the time it reached Pandalo, its shape had become vague. It lacked the detail and definition it needed to remain in flight.

Pandalo shattered it with a single stroke of his flaming sword. A large piece of it landed in one of the walls of flame and erupted into a cloud of steam. As the flames reclaimed the gap, a fit of coughing wracked Pandalo's body. He spat handfuls of blood.

"Are you all right?" Jasmine asked Ellessar.

"Well enough. Let me help you." He laid a hand on her shoulder. "Mighty Aeron, lend your healing power to this friend of ours so she may continue to serve your cause."

The pain that ripped through Jasmine's broken arm was intense, almost crippling, but momentary. By the time it passed, the bones had knitted enough so they wouldn't shift inside her arm, but she dared not try to block a blow or throw a punch with that arm—at least until she could find the time to meditate and complete the healing.

The crab-demon stepped through the wall of flames, apparently oblivious to the heat that left scorch marks along its carapace. It snapped its mandibles. Jasmine ducked aside, keeping her eyes on its giant pincers, so as not to risk meeting its gaze. The claw could easily reach a dozen feet, and it was too strong for her to swat away.

In the demon's single-minded focus on Jasmine, it advanced

heedlessly past Nick and Ellessar. Nick sliced through one of its legs with the Sword of Alamain.

The demon shrieked. Without turning, it swept a giant pincer at Nick's head. When he blocked it, the Sword of Alamain cut the pincer clean off at the joint, and the carapace-covered stump smashed into his face with a crack. Nick went down in a spray of his own blood.

Jasmine leapt to the side of the demon and snapped a kick into its flank, cracking the carapace along its abdomen. It pivoted and snapped at her with its giant mandibles.

Beside her, a prayer rose from Ellessar in the old elven tongue. Searing light erupted from the extended fingers of both hands. The light burned into the demon and it spun toward him. Smoke hissed from its chest as it fought its way forward. Ellessar gave ground a little at a time, all the while keeping up the intensity of Aeron's light. Finally the demon slumped, shuddering, to the cavern floor.

As Jasmine rushed to Nick, a cold mist snuffed out Pandalo's blazing barriers. Zen, his robes and skin severely burned, stood over the body of the Trondorian general, who lay in a pool of his own blood.

A single word, spoken in the foul tongue of Vexetan by a quavering, aged voice, drifted to Ember from the shadows on one side of the dais. Dalen Frost's body twitched, shook, and then sat up. Its milky-white eyes stared blankly. The wound from Nick's sword seeped but no longer poured blood.

"Borim!" Ember pointed to the foul, animated corpse.

Her brother, who'd been walking toward her, spun to face the corpse as it rose with its sword in its hand.

"Oh, now why couldn't you just stay dead?" Borim charged the thing, swinging ShatterBrand.

The old mage who'd stood at the Master's side when Ember entered the room hobbled out of the shadows in the direction from which the voice had come. His eyes, one green and one yellow, didn't seem to be looking in quite the same direction. His hair had gone awry, his robe was tattered—shredded by countless splinters from Zen's ice ball—and he was limping, but some enchantment had protected his body from the worst of the cold and the blast that had blown him from the dais. A Medallion of Vexetan hung from his neck. He held a wand in his left hand that appeared to have been made from bone. His green eye fixed on Ember.

She stepped between the old mage and the body of the doppelganger. Ember didn't know what a wand of necromancy would do to her, a living person, but she had to keep the man from animating the doppelganger's corpse. She couldn't fight both it and him.

The old mage grunted, then pointed the bone wand at the white-robed mage who had called the Assassin in an attempt to stop the crab-demon. Her body lay motionless several yards in front of the dais.

Without waiting to see what would happen, Ember snatched a pinch of catalyst from the pouch at her belt. She conjured a small flame in her palm and launched a stream of fire at the old man. His right hand came up, holding a second wand. With a command, he swept the stream of fire aside.

The old man thrust his second wand toward her and spoke yet another foul command. A force that felt like a punch in the gut threw Ember backwards off the dais.

As Ember caught her breath, the old mage raised the doppelganger's corpse. Regaining her feet, she launched a stream of flames at the body. It caught fire but continued to lumber towards her. The fire might eventually consume the foul thing, but that would take too long. She snatched the entire pouch of catalyst from her belt. Sparing one pinch for later use, she threw the bag at the burning doppelganger and dove into the lee of her side of the two-foot-high dais.

The catalyst exploded, and a wave of fire and charred flesh washed past, above her. As soon as it subsided, she took a deep breath and stole a glance across the dais. Pieces of the doppelganger smoldered on the stage. Beyond, Borim had reduced Dalen's corpse to a twitching, oozing mass of pulp. Borim lay beyond it, sputtering and cursing. Apparently the blast had knocked him from his feet.

The old man rose with an oath from the sheltered lee on his side of the dais, within which he had taken cover.

Ember had just enough of her powdered catalyst in the pinch between her thumb and forefinger for one more stream of fire. If she launched it at the old mage from there, he would simply turn it aside with his wand of force. She ducked back down and moved her free hand to the rough granite charm that hung on the chain around her neck. In a blink, she swapped places with her brother.

The old mage had his attention fixed on Ember's hiding place, wand ready. Ember didn't rise from there, however. Borim did, still cursing. By the time the old man realized what that meant, Ember had released her fire.

The stream of flame engulfed the mage, and his robes lit as readily as Sierra's had. Screaming, the old man dropped both wands and ripped at the tattered garment. His skin was red from the heat, but not blackened and bubbling as it should have been. Some enchantment still protected him from the worst of the damage.

Ember drew her sword and charged. Just as the old mage cast his burning garment aside, she ran her sword through his heart, and he collapsed beneath her. She watched him carefully for signs of life as a pool of his blood spread beneath him. He didn't rise again.

Borim rushed to the body of the dragon rider and raised Shatter-Brand to crush her skull.

She lifted her remaining hand feebly. "Wait," she wheezed. "I can help you."

Borim would have busted her head with no regard for any deception she might speak, and in spite of her apparent intervention on Jasmine's behalf against the crab-demon—for that could have been part of her ruse. He stayed his mace because the onyx center of her Medallion was both cracked and clouded.

The scorched and tattered stump of the woman's left arm lay limp at her side. What would she do now that she was free from the Master?

ShatterBrand hovered over Borim's head.

"Please." The word came out with the effort expended by a goblin hoard sworn to overcome the battlements of Glintbroc, and the result was nearly as futile.

Borim had to stoop to hear her.

"My sight is failing. Even you are growing dark to my eyes. Where's my daughter? Does she live?"

"How in the fire's fury of Brimstone should I know?"

"The demon-kin who came in with you. I haven't seen her since she was a few days old, but there can be only one like her. She's my daughter."

CHAPTER 33

"Jasmine!" Borim called. "I think we have a problem."

Jasmine helped Nick sit up. His nose was broken, and a gash on his forehead bled freely, but his eyes seemed to focus on hers. "Are you okay?"

Nick touched his forehead and winced. His hand came away bloody. "I think so."

She helped him climb to his feet and steadied him while he took a few shaky steps. "Can you walk?"

"Yes. Go."

Jasmine released his arm. She watched him for a moment to make sure he wasn't going to fall, and then rushed to Borim.

The dwarf gestured disdainfully at the dying mage. "She says she can help us. Says she's your mother."

Jasmine squatted beside her. She examined the woman's face, searching for some memory of her, or for some resemblance between the woman's features and her own. She found neither. "What's your name?"

The woman reached for Jasmine with her good hand. "Ryanna Pruitt. Are you well?"

The abandoned keep on the mountain near the monastery was called Pruitt Keep, but that proved nothing. The name was well known.

"What do you know of my father?" Jasmine asked. All she knew herself was that he had melded her with a demon using some dark magic, but that was not common knowledge. If this woman was her mother, she would know that much.

"Ka-G'zzin is your father."

"Who?" Borim spat.

Zen, Nick, Ellessar, and Ember gathered around. Nick held his sword, and like ShatterBrand, it was ready to strike at the first sign of treachery.

"The demon," Ryanna said. "Didn't you see the way it came at you? How it came at only you?"

"What?" Borim thrust his mace toward the crab-demon, smoldering beside a nearby pillar. "That thing?"

"In my foolishness and pride, I called it from the Abyss. But it was too strong. It broke free from my will."

"She's lying," Nick said. "Anatomy alone makes such a tale impossible."

Jasmine shook her head at Ryanna. "I was created by my father in some failed attempt to combine a human and a demon."

"No. You're a child of rape. The union left wounds that pain me still. The mating would have killed me, but I know enchantments... Even now I prolong my life, though this—" she raised her scorched stump feebly— "should have killed me."

"Step back," Jasmine told the men around her. "She can't threaten us now." She waited for them to do so, and then she started to raise Ryanna's robes.

She stopped. "May I?"

Ryanna nodded weekly.

The woman's pubic area was grossly misshapen, visible even beyond the scanty undergarment she wore. Scars mottled her skin from her navel to halfway down her thighs. Jasmine resettled Ryanna's robes, covering her body once more.

"Ka-G'zzin never expected a child," Ryanna continued. "He just wanted to dominate and hurt me. When he learned of the offspring, he came after them—came after you—to purge his tainted seed. I couldn't protect your brother, who appeared much more like a demon than you do, but Ka-G'zzin didn't know I'd had twins. The only way to save you was to leave you with the monks at the monastery. Then I fled into hiding."

Jasmine wanted to say something—anything—but her chest tightened, and words wouldn't come.

Nick returned to Ryanna's side. He wiped blood from his eyes with the back of his hand. "How did you come to work for the side of darkness?"

"There's no time." The woman's voice grew stronger with her conviction. "Even now the Master flees from the sword you carry. You can catch him, but you must hurry. The dragon will come quickly to his call."

Nick leaned over her threateningly, but the woman didn't seem to notice. "Answer the question, or else we have no reason to trust you."

After a moment, the woman said, "The Master tracked me down. He needed someone who could call demons from the Abyss. He sent his seer, Addicus, to the ruins of my old keep to find a possession of mine—it didn't matter what—to burn in his crucible. By this he tracked me down."

"That doesn't explain why you agreed." The gentleness of pity filled Jasmine's voice.

"The Master can be very persuasive. Surely you felt his presence." She raised the stump again. "But I never gave myself to him completely."

Jasmine had indeed felt the power of the Master's will. Without Alamain's charm of protection, even Jasmine's deep meditation might not have saved her from total enslavement to him.

Ryanna grabbed Jasmine's robe with failing fingers. "By now the dragon is coming. You must hurry."

Jasmine looked at Nick, who shrugged and nodded. "Which way?" she asked.

"Down the hall at the back of the dais. At the bottom of the third flight of stairs is a door hidden in the rock. He'll have gone that way."

"I know the stairs," Zen said. "But I didn't see any door."

"I'll find it." Borim shouldered ShatterBrand. "Not even he can hide a stone door from a dwarf."

"Wait," Ellessar said. "None of us can face the Master without Aeron's healing, much less the Master *and* a dragon."

"We don't have time to argue," said the surly dwarf. "If you must do it, do it fast."

Ellessar laid a hand on him and spoke loudly, as if to overcome the evil that so recently dwelt in the cavern. "Aeron, hear my prayer. If it's your will that this dwarf be healed, use me. Use my body, my heart, my very soul to see it done."

"Oh by the—" Even as Borim rolled his eyes, his muscles stiffened. He gritted his teeth as his wounds began to mend.

Ellessar stopped before they healed completely, saving some of his strength to help the others.

Without complaint, Borim ran on his stubby legs toward the back of the chamber.

Jasmine touched Ellessar's arm. "Can you help my mother? She's beyond anything I can do with herbs and salves."

"No!" Ryanna's gasp was almost desperate. "Save your healing for your friends. They'll need it." She must have released whatever enchantment she'd been using to keep herself alive. Her chest fell softly as she exhaled her last breath.

Then she lay still.

Ellessar sought Jasmine's pleading eyes. "She's beyond my help now, too. I'm sorry."

Without a word, Zen stepped up next for a helping of Aeron's healing.

Ellessar gave him a hard look.

"I only did what was necessary to find the Master," Zen said. "And I made sure you never lost our trail, starting with those parallel gouges on my horse's shoe—not good for my knife, by the way. Tell me you didn't miss those."

Ellessar said nothing, waiting for more, so Zen continued. "I checked back along our trail every night to make sure you were still behind us. When I discovered that you weren't, somewhere around the monastery where Jasmine grew up, I began translocating into every town we passed. Each time, I went into several mid-range inns—dressed in my recognizable robes with my unmistakable staff and the Sword of Alamain—and let slip which direction we were going, to the extent that I'd been able to extract that information from Gwyndarren. And in case all that wasn't enough, you had the Seeking Stone."

Ellessar glared at him. They would need Zen's help against the dragon, if not against the Master, but trusting the mage was a whole other matter.

Zen huffed. "I gave Nick the Sword as soon as you got here. What more proof do you need?"

It really wasn't a matter of proof at that point, if Ellessar was to be honest with himself. He just didn't know how to get past his anger at Zen for having stolen the Sword, or past his own shame for being careless enough to let Zen take it.

"Come on!" Zen yelled.

"When this is over—" Ellessar's voice was quiet and threatening— "you will submit to a Zone of Truth." Finally, he spoke a healing prayer.

Zen caught up to Borim, weaving as he ran. He grabbed the dwarf by the shoulders and the two vanished into one of Zen's translocation portals.

Urgency pumped through Nick's veins as he recovered the Shield of Faith and stepped up to receive Ellessar's healing prayers. If the Master fled on the dragon, it would set Nick and his friends back to where they'd been in Lorentil: with the Sword of Alamain firmly in their grasp and no way to find its target. On the other hand, to face the Master without at least some healing would be nothing short of suicide.

As soon as Ellessar released him, Nick sprinted down the corridor behind the dais. The staircase was easy to find. Zen and Borim had found the secret door and left it open. Two torches bobbed in the distant gloom of the tunnel beyond. Nick snatched a torch from a nearby sconce and ran after them.

He caught up to Borim, and to Zen shortly after. Nick considered slowing his pace so Zen could keep up. His friend had become the most powerful mage Nick had ever known or heard of. Even if his enchantments couldn't harm the Master, his magic might prove invaluable against the dragon. Ultimately, however, urgency won out over prudence. If the Master was still within Nick's grasp, he meant to keep it that way. Gradually, his long strides took him out into the lead.

His speed, though, couldn't match Jasmine's. She caught up and could have quickly outdistanced him, but she didn't. Nick was the champion meant to wield both the Sword of Alamain and the Shield of Faith. Jasmine could do nothing against the Master alone. And with only her sais—now one in each hand—she probably couldn't fight the dragon either. Nevertheless, her presence buoyed his spirit.

The two rounded a corner and faced a stone staircase leading up.

They climbed for several minutes with a landing every one or two hundred steps. Despite the pain of sweat pouring into his partially healed wounds and the shortness of his breath from the exertion of the climb, Nick pushed himself forward. Finally, torchlight gave way to sunlight.

Nick and Jasmine paused only briefly to drop their torches and peer through the screen of vines that dangled in front of the tunnel opening.

The Master stood on a green hilltop a few hundred yards away, his arms raised toward the sky. Beyond him, soaring out of the evening sun, flew a giant black dragon with a belly as red as burning embers.

"You get the Master," Jasmine said. "I'll try to distract the dragon."

Nick noticed for the first time how small she really was, and how fragile she appeared with just her sais and no armor. It felt strange to doubt her abilities after all they'd endured together, but he couldn't help asking, "How do you plan to do that?"

"No idea." She shoved him through the vines into the clearing.

Nick didn't waste the momentum. The dragon was yet a mile or more away, but it was closing quickly. With luck, Nick would reach the Master first.

After Ellessar retrieved his sword and left the chamber, Ember proceeded from body to body and gathered up a total of six Medallions of Vexetan, including the clouded one from the body of Jasmine's mother. Ember didn't have enough strength left to oppose either the Master or the dragon, and she'd spent the last of her powdered catalyst to defeat the old mage and his undead abominations. If Nick and his friends failed, she must at least prevent the Master from recovering the Medallions. When this was all over, she could deliver them to the Dwarven Intelligence Guild. They would know how to safeguard them. She removed the one from the Trondorian general last.

When she turned back toward the dais, the tunnel her friends had taken was clear across the audience hall. Between her and it stood Zen's guide, the elf who had fled the battle after the doppelganger had replaced the Master. All of Ember's friends had long since left.

The elf met her in the middle of the cavern, between the two gargantuan statues. He stretched out his hand with the confidence of one who was used to getting what he wanted. "I'll be taking the Medallions."

CHAPTER 34

The Master signaled the dragon to attack.

As the giant beast veered toward him, Nick's mind froze. He'd seen the creature before, during the flight from Dragon Tears to South Bend, but then the dragon had remained high in the air. Now it was diving straight for him. The dragon's giant inhalation sucked the courage from Nick's very bones. It took him a moment to realize that his feet had stopped. He simply stared at his coming death.

Jasmine had stopped beside him. At the last moment she darted away, as if to draw the animal's flaming breath from Nick. The dragon ignored her.

It was all Nick could do to raise the Shield of Faith before the world burst into flames around him. For a moment, he knew what his mother must have felt, trapped in their burning house, just before the fire engulfed her. When the conflagration ceased, smoke clouded the air from a long, wide swath of smoldering grass. Only a small shield-shaped patch of ground at Nick's feet remained unburned.

Just at the edge of the burned region, Jasmine continued to run. She pulled the remains of her smoldering robe over her head and tossed it aside. The skin on her back was red, blistered, and bleeding where her undergarments didn't cover it. Without hesitation, she sprinted toward the Master even though she could have no hope of harming him.

The dragon banked and returned for another pass. Nick raised the Shield again, but this time the dragon withheld its breath. It sailed over, just out of sword's reach, and dove at Jasmine.

Bolstered by her courage, Nick shook off the unnatural aura of fear that the dragon imposed upon its enemies. He too, charged the Master.

If Jasmine had been any closer to the center of the flames, they probably would have consumed her. Her skin burned like it was on fire. It tightened over her muscles, hindering her movements. On her way toward the Master, she willed the healing systems of her body to tend her wounds. The pain and tightening eased only slightly.

Several feet short of the Master, she slammed into an invisible barrier. It felt like a wall of stone. Air burst from her lungs and blood from her nose. The world swirled and went dark. A moment later, she was lying on the ground, sucking air back into her chest, the dragon descending toward her.

She leapt to her feet and tumbled away as its giant talons reached for her. The claw missed her, and the dragon veered back up. Jasmine tried to rise again, but the dragon's tail slammed into her.

She flew a dozen feet. Dirt and gravel ground into her burns as she rolled.

By the time she regained her feet, the dragon had circled for another pass. This time, it came for Jasmine. *Good!* She ran with all she had, to give Nick a chance to do what they had come to do, but the dragon closed the gap quickly. With desperate hope, Jasmine sprinted for a grove of trees just down the hill. She slipped under the first boughs as the dragon inhaled.

An instant later, the forest blazed with flames she couldn't hope to outrun.

"Join me," the Master said again as Nick approached.

This time Nick didn't think about the pendant, or the pain it caused as it burned his chest. He thought about his mother and the fire that had taken her life. This was the man ultimately responsible for her death. He brushed the Master's suggestion aside and, with the Sword of Alamain in his fist, pressed his way through the barrier.

The Master began to pray in Vexetan's cursed language, a continuous chant that made Nick's skin crawl. Dread seemed to hollow out his gut, much like the song of the reptile-riding elves they'd encountered in Lorentil's forest. This, though, was much worse—more visceral and intense. It made Nick want to puke.

The Master had no visible armor. He wore only his priestly robes and a crown woven from human sinew. An emblem that matched the Medallions of Vexetan adorned the band.

As Nick drew back the Sword of Alamain, the Master's right hand whipped out and touched him through a gap between armor plates near his shoulder. A rip tore through Nick's skin, across his arm and down his chest. He gritted his teeth against the pain and dealt a blow that should have cut the Master in half.

The Master thrust out his left hand, palm open, facing outward, fingers splayed—a defensive action that the Sword should have sliced through. But an invisible shield mere inches in front of the Master's hand deflected the blow. Stroke by stroke, Nick determined the ex-

Host of Evil

tent of the shield. This was not the barrier Jasmine had hit. This was a small shield, like an invisible buckler, that moved with the Master's hand.

The Sword of Alamain was nearly as heavy as Nick's great sword. It was shorter and more nimble, but both hands were required to wield it properly. Nick backed up to put a few feet between himself and his enemy. He shook the Shield of Faith from his arm and let it drop to the ground, counting on his friends to keep the dragon occupied. It was perhaps the greatest gamble he'd ever taken.

Nick never strayed far from the Shield, however, so he'd have some chance of getting to it if the dragon circled back around. All the while, the Master continued his incessant chanting.

With a roar, Nick lunged at the Master and pressed him with a flurry of strokes that would have challenged Sierra Glenwood. The Master was quick with his shield, but eventually Nick landed a stroke that split the Master's right collarbone and cut down into his chest. The wound should have killed him outright. It would have killed anyone else.

The Master screamed and reeled back, but the wound closed as quickly as the Sword of Alamain had made it. His left hand reached for Nick, the invisible shield momentarily gone.

Nick tried to dodge, but the Master struck lower than Nick had expected. That single touch shattered a plate of armor and flayed a wide swath of skin from Nick's thigh. Blood seeped from the exposed muscle and soaked his shredded pant leg. He screamed against the blinding pain, but the muscle remained strong, and the leg still held his weight.

Rage took over. Nick struck the Master again and again. The wounds all closed, but slice after slice, he began to make headway against the Master's healing rate. In return, the Master stripped Nick's armor and skin with every touch...skin that wouldn't heal like that of the Master. Pain cut into Nick's concentration. His movements slowed and his strength faltered, finally forcing him into a defensive posture while the Master's wounds healed.

Zen climbed from the staircase into the waning twilight in time to see Jasmine disappear into a grove. The dragon soaring behind her seemed to wait until she vanished into the trees, and then it lit a whole swath of the forest with a long breath of flames. Zen could feel the heat from hundreds of yards away. Even if the flames didn't touch Jasmine directly, she wouldn't survive the temperature in the grove.

But Zen couldn't indulge any grief until the battle was over, one way or the other. From this distance, any enchantment he wove against the Master would engulf Nick as well. That wouldn't have stopped him if he thought it would get the job done, but according to the Prophecy, such a weaving would fail. Nick's sword was the only thing that might be able to kill the Master.

As for the dragon, it was much too powerful for Zen to fight alone, especially in his wounded state. An army of ice creatures wouldn't last long against its fiery breath, so he attempted something he'd never tried before. He dared to weave an enormous block of solid ice into existence, to encase the dragon in mid-flight.

Nobody seemed to be aware of his presence, so he took his time and knit the weave carefully. When he dropped it into place, however, the dragon shook it off and winged toward him. Zen struggled to hold the weave together and nearly did so, but he lost his tenuous grip on the threads and his enchantment unraveled.

Ice mage. The dragon spoke directly into Zen's mind. *You will pay for your treachery.*

Zen rebuilt the weave he'd attempted a moment before. His previous failure revealed the weaknesses in the enchantment. This time, he shored them up. When he dropped it around the dragon, the enchantment held. The dragon plummeted to the earth, encased in a solid block of ice. The block hit the ground about fifty feet from Zen and shattered with a great crash. With a roar of fury, the dragon scrambled free and wheeled on him.

Zen threw a dome of ice over himself. The dragon smashed through it with its head and clawed it apart like an eggshell, with Zen the tasty yolk inside. The full force of the dragon's terrifying aura slammed into Zen. Any semblance of coherent thought left him. He could do nothing but stagger back in horror as the dragon sucked in a breath that seemed to steal every bit of air from inside the broken dome.

CHAPTER 35

Nick couldn't afford to fight defensively. The Master's wounds healed and his hands proved too deft for Nick to avoid. Nick's own armor had been shredded. His body burned with the pain of flayed skin and ripped tissue. He felt like he was on fire.

Yet it was up to him, and only him, to save the civilized races. Nobody could break through the Master's barrier to help him. So he redoubled his effort and took the offensive once more. They would see who could take more punishment.

He struck this time at the Master's arms, severing one completely and leaving the other hanging by a thin strip of tissue. The Master prayed all the louder. His dangling arm began to heal, but the prayers cost him time.

Nick thrust the Sword of Alamain through the Master's gut. A vicious sneer stretched across the dark priest's face, but he staggered back. Even that wound began to close as Nick struck again.

Deep cuts crisscrossed the Master's body before he finally slowed enough for Nick to get a clear strike at his head. Nick's sword cleaved deeply into the Master's skull and, perhaps more importantly, cut through the sinew crown.

The Medallion from the Master's forehead dropped into the grass. The dark priest toppled backward and lay still. His last breath flowed out of him like coagulated blood squeezed from a wineskin.

The Master's presence departed. L'Nordian spun his head in time to see the human stake the Master to the ground, through the heart, with the otherworldly sword.

"This one's for Brewster AxSwipe," the human said as he did so.

For the first time since he'd met the Master in the bowels of Spitfire Mountain, L'Nordian was free.

He shook the chain from around his neck and dropped the Medallion of Vexetan onto the ground at Zen's feet. *Thank you.* He spoke not only into the minds of the ice mage and the human, but also into the minds of the dwarf and the elven priest of Aeron who had just emerged from the tunnel opening.

L'Nordian swung his head in a gesture toward the still-burning grove. *Sorry about your friend.* That's all his pride would allow him to offer. He leapt into the air and winged away to the northwest to free his brethren from Spitfire Mountain.

Zen wrapped the dragon's Medallion in cloth, unwilling to touch the thing with his bare hands, and then put it in one of his pouches. The group could take the Medallions to Alamain. Let her decide what to do with them.

Zen wove a portal through the plane of ice to Addicus's hidden closet. He used a night-vision enchantment that lit the small room in shades that varied from snowy white to charcoal gray. Books, bottles, jewelry items, robes, lockboxes, and cloth-wrapped bundles lined the shelves. Zen perused the objects he could see without touching anything. The original Codex of Mortaan sat on a shelf with Jasmine's copy from the monastery stacked beneath it. He stuffed both tomes into his backpack. He would return Jasmine's copy to the Order of the Sage on his way back to Lorentil.

Zen opened his eyes to the weave. This closet was Addicus's treasure vault, a collection of the most powerful items the old mage had acquired for the Master. Except for some of the books, every item radiated magic, but considering who had collected them, many were likely cursed.

Zen chose carefully which items to take. He left the mundane books. The lockboxes were too large to stuff into his backpack, but a few of the charms had auras that didn't appear too sinister. He stuffed several scrolls into the bottom of his pack as well—he'd look later to see what enchantments they'd been inscribed with. Next to the door hung a half-dozen wands in a rack mounted to the stone wall. Zen slipped them into a deep pocket inside his robe. The instructors at Glimmernook, the mages' college in Lorentil, could teach him how to determine their functions.

Then he stepped into Addicus's laboratory. Most of the items here were mundane: charms and focusing agents, alchemy supplies, ink and parchment of the type used to produce enchanted scrolls, and items undoubtedly awaiting later enchantment. A large marble brazier beside the desk radiated an aura of powerful divination. It was much too large and heavy to take, so he left it. Here, he pocketed only a few silver items he could sell to fund their trip home, including three drinking flasks, a dagger, a pair of goblets, and a small mortar and pestle.

With his magical energies all but spent, he decided to hike the stairs back to the hilltop where Nick had killed the Master.

Ellessar rushed to Nick's side, reaching him just as Nick collapsed beside the body of the Master. Nick's armor was shredded, his clothes torn, and his skin flayed down to the muscle on his arms, thighs, and across his chest. His blood seeped freely from the wounds. Without bothering to strip away what was left of Nick's armor, Ellessar placed his hand on Nick's shoulders and prayed for healing.

Aeron's power flowed through him. Nick tensed, and then he convulsed as a layer of new skin formed, pink and tender, across wide swaths of his body. By the time Ellessar had done what he could, Nick's deeper wounds had scabbed over. Complete healing would likely be long and painful.

Nick sat up. He flexed his arms experimentally and nodded his thanks before easing himself gingerly to his feet and recovering the Sword of Alamain.

Borim joined them, finally, huffing from the long uphill run from the Master's audience hall. He kicked the Master's body. "Is it over then?"

"Almost." Nick severed the Master's head from the rest of the corpse with the Sword of Alamain. He tried to approach the burning grove, but his new skin was still too sensitive, the pain from the heat too great.

Borim came up beside him and took the gruesome load. "I'll do it." He marched forward, gripping the severed head by a handful of hair, and heaved the thing into an area bathed in dense flames.

The grove was far too hot for anyone to enter, let alone survive. With hopeless optimism, Nick peered through the sweltering waves of heat and thick screen of smoke. Nothing moved inside.

For the first time since his mother's death, tears welled in his eyes. None of his friends had earned Nick's respect more than Jasmine had. She'd been his steadfast anchor throughout, the one certainty in this journey fraught with hidden motives, shifting loyalties, and blind treachery. She, above all the others—above even himself—deserved to survive and enjoy the world that together they had made possible...whatever that world might become.

Just then, the elf from the dais, the only person among the Master's entourage who hadn't visibly worn a Medallion, climbed out of the tunnel from the audience hall. Ellessar drew his sword and placed himself between the elf and the others.

The elf stopped several strides away. Without making any move toward his own sword, he placed his right hand over his heart and bowed his head in a nod to Ellessar.

"That's as far as you go," Ellessar said. "Your Master is dead."

"I answer to no master."

Ellessar considered him for a long moment. "Who are you?"

"My name is Gwyndarren. I'm a friend of Zen's."

"That carries no credit with me."

Gwyndarren shrugged. "Zen's errand was his own. I merely served as a guide." He scanned the battlefield, noting the Master's body and the burning grove. "Where is the ice mage?"

"You tell me. He vanished as soon as the dragon left. I figured he was with you."

Gwyndarren shook his head.

Ellessar glanced over the elf's shoulder. "Where's Ember?"

"Ember?"

"The elven female who came into the audience hall with us. She stayed behind to collect some things."

The elf shrugged again. "Haven't see her."

Ellessar placed the tip of his blade against the elf's throat. "I don't believe you."

Gwyndarren didn't flinch. "Believe whatever you like. I just want to verify for myself that the Master of Mortaan's Final Prophecy is truly dead. Then I'll be on my way."

"Show me your neck."

Carefully, Gwyndarren spread the collar of his travelling cloak to expose his bare neck. Ellessar hooked the hem of the elf's shirt with the tip of his sword and ripped the garment clear down to his belly. No Medallion. "You'll approach the Master with my sword at your throat."

"Why not? I've your sword at my throat in any case. If you intended to kill me, you'd have done so already."

"I may yet." Ellessar inclined his head toward the body. "Move slowly."

Gwyndarren eased up to within twenty feet of the Master and stopped. The crown of sinew lay on the ground where the Master's head had been. "And the dragon?"

"Gone. Shed its Medallion and left."

Gwyndarren nodded carefully. "I'm satisfied. May I go?"

Ellessar shoved the elf to the ground, away from the body.

Without a word, Gwyndarren picked himself up. He shook off his robes and walked back toward the tunnel through which they'd all come.

CHAPTER 36

Zen appeared from the entrance to the Master's sanctuary. Just outside the opening, he spoke briefly with Gwyndarren, then gestured toward the south. There was nothing in that direction but the Great Divide, and beyond that, the Wild Lands. And then Gwyndarren disappeared back into the hole from which they'd all emerged, back toward where they had left their horses.

Zen strode up to Ellessar and squared his shoulders. "I'm ready for your Zone of Truth."

Ellessar's eyes appeared sunken, his face haggard. "Tomorrow."

By refusing to invoke the Zone, Ellessar had as much as admitted that he was spent. He'd used the last of his energy to heal Nick. If Zen meant the party ill, that would have been the moment for him to act. Nick was in no shape for more fighting, and he harbored no delusions about how a conflict between Borim and Zen would end. Ember hadn't yet arrived at the hilltop.

Host of Evil

Zen spoke softly. Exhaustion filled his voice. "Everything I did was a subterfuge against Gwyndarren, to get him to lead us to the Master." He paused. "Could we have found the Master otherwise?"

"It's not the result I question," Ellessar said. "It's your means."

Zen shrugged.

"You could have trusted us," Ellessar countered. "You should have told us what you meant to do. You didn't have to steal the Sword."

"If you had guarded it properly—" Zen grinned as though he enjoyed Ellessar's discomfort— "I wouldn't have been able to steal it."

Ellessar's glare was so hard and cold that his eyes might have turned to iron. Without a word, he returned to the Master's body, doused it with lamp oil, and stood vigil while it burned.

Zen pulled up the sleeves of his robe, showing Nick his welt-covered hands and forearms. "This started soon after I left Lorentil. Alamain's blessing notwithstanding, I believe that sword of yours is cursed."

Borim grunted. "I think it's some property of that other-worldly metal. I suggest you get rid of the thing."

"Alamain will find a safe place to store it," Nick said, "in case it's ever needed again."

"Come on." Borim turned. "Let's go find my sister. She should have joined us by now."

"There." Nick pointed.

Ember lay near the middle of the Master's audience hall in a pool of blood.

Borim broke away from the group at a run. He was the first to reach her. "Awww, no!" he groaned.

The blood was Ember's own—too much of it, having poured from a sword wound that ran all the way through her chest and out her back. She was already dead. Her sword and backpack lay beside her. The latter had been ransacked.

Borim knelt beside her and cradled her head in the palms of his fat hands. For many minutes, he rocked back and forth gently, muttering over and over again, "Oh, sis. Oh, sis, I'm so sorry."

Nick and Zen stood behind him, respectfully silent. Nick had no idea how to comfort the dwarf. The only consolation that he himself could find was that Ember would be the last person to die for his quest. He didn't know what their future held—Mortaan could no longer tell them—but Nick's own part in the whole mess was finished.

Torches still burned in sconces on the walls and pillars. The crab-like demon that had killed his uncle lay dead, just a few yards to his left. Alanel, now a stone statue, stood to Nick's right. The only other body close enough for him to see clearly in the dim torchlight was that of Pandalo Gundahar. Both his camouflage cloak and his flaming sword were gone.

After several minutes, Nick stepped away from Ember and Borim to examine the Trondorian general more closely. He checked the man's neck. His Medallion of Vexetan was missing.

Nick's movement broke Borim's trance. He looked suddenly up at Zen. "This was your doin', mage."

Zen held up his hand, palm outward, to fend off the accusation. "Whoever did this, it happened while I was out there with you and the others—" he inclined his head in the general direction of the hilltop— "fighting the dragon."

"Yeah, but you came back in afterwards. Translocated or whatever ya call it. You disappeared for a time after the dragon left."

"I came back in, but not to this chamber. The Master's old mage had a workshop." Zen lowered his pack to the ground and dug out the original Codex of Mortaan and Jasmine's copy. "I went back for these." He handed them both to Nick.

Borim stood up, his jaw clenched. He ground his rotten teeth for a moment before responding. "You coulda done both."

Nick placed a hand on Borim's shoulder. "Your sister was killed with a sword. Her own is on the ground beside her. She died fighting. In a battle of blades, not magics."

"It must have been Gwyndarren," Zen said finally.

Borim's jaw set. "And you were workin' with him."

"I was *using* him. I knew he had some hidden agenda in all this, but I didn't know what it was. We needed him to find the Master."

"How did you find *him*?" Nick asked.

"I didn't. Gwyndarren found me. Somehow he knew about the Sword and had made some kind of deal with the Master in exchange for it. He approached me in Lorentil to get it for him. I agreed to do it as long as he took me with him."

"Now how do you suppose he found out about the Sword?" Borim asked.

"He's an information dealer. It's his business to learn of such things. A few people have known what we've been up to along the way. In Brimstone, Glintbroc, and Lorentil. Maybe there's a spy among the acolytes in Alamain's temple."

Borim fell silent and knelt once more at Ember's side. Nick had never seen a dwarf shed tears before, but Borim's face was wet with them.

Nick gestured at Pandalo's body. "The elf seems to have confiscated all of the Medallions and other enchanted items from the bodies." He paused. "Unless you took them."

Zen shook his head. "I went only to the mage's workshop."

Nick raised the thick tomes Zen had given him. "Is this all you took? Or is there more?"

This time Zen hesitated. Finally he drew a handful of wands from within his robes.

"What do you plan to do with those?"

"Not use them. Given where I found them, they're probably cursed." He put them back in a pocket somewhere. "I thought I'd take them to Glimmernook, the mages' college in Lorentil. See if I can trade them for a formal education in the weave."

Jasmine sought desperately for an escape from the heat and flames. At first, the tree boughs themselves provided cover—the dragon's breath had failed to penetrate the branches—but within seconds, burning debris from the treetops ignited the mattress of dry pine needles that carpeted the grove. All around her, the fire raged, offering no escape, so she looked to the ground for salvation.

She spotted an old badger's hole and dove inside it, the earth scraping her already-raw skin. The heat of the fire followed her down. As the tunnel narrowed, she used her sharp talons to widen the burrow. Finally, she had to dislocate both of her shoulders to squirm through a rocky, narrow opening. She used her legs and feet to shove herself into the deepest part of the deserted den, where the temperature remained tolerable.

There, she slowed her breathing to the steady pace of one in a deep sleep to preserve whatever oxygen reached her through the conflagration, and slipped into a deep, healing meditation.

It was nearly dawn by the time the flames passed and the grove cooled enough for her to crawl out and seek her friends. Fortunately, her boots remained intact. She picked her way around the still-smoldering logs that littered her route back to the hilltop.

Burned remains of a headless body lay where Nick had faced off with the Master. The body was too small to have been Nick's. Jasmine nodded with grim satisfaction as she turned away.

She didn't return to the Master's underground complex—dangers might still lurk there—but hiked instead down the rocky mountainside to where she and her party had left their mounts the day before.

Her friends were huddled in a tight camp around the horses at the base of the foothills.

Nick spotted her before the others did. "Jasmine!" He jumped to his feet and rushed to her. "You survived!"

Jasmine smiled. "I could say the same to you." She stepped forward to hug him, but his skin appeared to be as raw and tender as her own.

He moved toward her as well and then stopped, seeming to make the same observation. The two stared at each other until the moment became awkward. Then they both burst into laughter, releasing a year's worth of stress and hardship in seconds. Afterwards, Jasmine felt drained…and truly at peace for the first time in a year.

Finally, she scanned the camp.

Ember's body lay off to one side with Borim sitting, silent and stoic, beside her. They were too far from Gildstone to give her a proper dwarven burial, so Ember, wrapped in her own blanket secured with twine, awaited a morning burial in accordance with the elfish custom. The body of Ryanna Pruitt, the dragon rider—Jasmine's mother—lay next to Ember.

Two graves had been dug.

After the burial, and after Ellessar had left to return the Shield of Faith to the temple of Aeron in Spitfire, Nick unpacked the tomes that Zen had recovered. He handed Jasmine's copy to her and settled the original in his lap.

Unable to believe that they had averted the Prophecy, that Mortaan had actually been wrong, Nick opened the original Codex and reread the ending. Maybe some interpretation of the words actually fit the outcome. Otherwise, he feared that they had merely bought the people of the Civilized Lands some time, that the Prophecy had just not yet come to pass, that they had only delayed the inevitable—that it had all somehow been for naught.

Once he found the page, he stared at it, unable to process what he saw. Unlike the last time he'd seen it, this Prophecy had the telltale spacing anomalies that characterized every other prophecy in the original manuscript.

Early in their journey, Nick had spent many hours poring over Jasmine's copy of the Prophecy, particularly its ending, searching for some loophole of interpretation to exploit. He knew the words by heart. And for this prophecy, the original Codex had matched Jasmine's copy exactly, right down to the confusing punctuation.

He closed the Codex and examined the cover. It looked like the original they had found in the king's library in Trondor. He opened it to the first page and found the inscription scrawled, nearly illegibly, by the prophet himself: "From my mind's eye... Ageus Mortaan." This was indeed the same book.

But the Last Prophecy of Mortaan no longer matched Jasmine's copy. Jasmine's copy read:

> ...the heroes of the land of will to bring the fight to The Master, but all will fear. And they will fail. falter before the Master, who cannot be harmed by any weapon, or another, forged of this world. The armies of darkness will. crumble, those of the civilized races, bringing forth the Age of Darkness from which there Will be no Enlightenment...

After all was said and done, the original Codex now read:

> ...the heroes of the land   will   bring the fight to The Master   .   he will   falter before
> a   weapon   not forged of this world. The armies of darkness will crumble,
>   bringing forth the Age of
>   Enlightenment.

Similar changes appeared throughout the document so that the Prophecy depicted events not as they were to happen, but as they *had* happened. The passage that once read, "...the return of the dragons..." as a precondition of the Prophecy's fulfillment now read, "...the return of the dragon ..." Singular—only one dragon—which was all any of them had ever seen.

A broad grin stretched across Nick's face. The aura of deception Zen had once detected on the original Codex didn't prevent accurate copying, as they had all assumed. Rather, it deceived those who thought the Prophecies, and therefore the future, were predetermined.

The genius of Mortaan had not been his ability to see a single ordained future. It was much greater than that. His gift was to see the potential futures and write them all simultaneously into a single passage of text.

"What is it?" Zen asked him.

"See for yourself." Nick displayed the Prophecy for them all to see.

EPILOGUE

Allushen the Taleweaver took the stage at the Wicked Sailor Alehouse for the first time in a year, but he would tell a very different story than he had the last time he'd visited. Much had changed. Even the very age. The world no longer lived beneath the executioner's ax, beneath Mortaan's Last Prophecy. Instead it lived in the surprised gasp that preceded a bright and promising, though unknown, future.

Allushen arranged his incense bowls at the corners of the stage and upended into each a small pouch of herbs, a proprietary blend he mixed himself from supplies he'd purchased at the herbal shop, the apothecary, and a seller of enchanted wares. He poured an equally secret oil over the herbs and lit the concoction with a single practiced flick of his steel over flint. The resulting smoke, to which Allushen owed his fame, would not only bring his stories to his audience in a way that only his hallucinogens could, but also lift their spirits and encourage their generosity.

He started the evening with common tales of ages long past, holding the fresher elements of his repertoire for late in the night, after the taproom had filled beyond capacity with drunk, eager, and—if his heralds had done their jobs in the upscale sections of Tradestar—wealthy patrons.

At midnight he began his newest and most popular tale, one that would take him two hours to relate—the tale of a handful of extraordinary people from the length and breadth of the Civilized Lands, who had conquered all odds to bring the Age of Prophecy to a close. But this tale was not so much about the end of the Age of Prophecy as it was about the beginning of the Age of Enlightenment.

As he told it, the minds of Allushen's audience filled with the images of mighty armies, detestable goblins and their kin, bandits, powerful mages, creatures of air and ice, a fire-breathing dragon, and minions of the Dark Lord called from the very bowels of the Abyss, all arrayed against the brave efforts of a handful of heroes. Finally Allushen showed his audience the death of the Master and the departure of L'Nordian.

"With the silencing of the Medallion around its neck," Allushen recited, "the demon king, Ri-T'rannoc, threw the symbol to the ground and stormed off to reap his own brand of mayhem throughout the Civilized Lands, rather than remain a slave of any human master.

"The whole of the demon army paused, unable to believe that their general had just walked away. For most, this was the chance they'd been waiting for, the throwing off of their own yoke of servitude. At once, they turned upon one another, each vying for its place in whatever hierarchy would emerge among those of its kin that survived.

"With help from Brinheim, the king of Palidor defeated the ogre Groot and his goblin army. He then decreed that keeping goblin slaves, or slaves of any kind, was simply too dangerous and therefore unlawful.

"After the demon infighting settled into skirmishing factions scattered across the kingdoms, the dwarven, elven, and human kings alike sent warrants to Balor Culhaven to return to Trondor or face a war he couldn't possibly win, leaving him no choice but to scurry back to his own kingdom.

"The civilized races continue to rout and destroy the demon pockets that remain, while the fairies of old work tirelessly to banish the worst of them back to their otherworldly prison, its gate closed once more, and the Guardian of the Abyss dispatched to realms unknown for safe-keeping.

"As for Gwyndarren Lortannon…"

The scene shifted to the elven opportunist as he watched Zen, Nick, and Jasmine mount their horses for the long road back to Lorentil.

"Gwyndarren possessed seven of the Medallions, one that he had stolen from Balor's palace and six from the elven witch, Ember. Zen held two more, including the one from the Master's crown. If Gwyndarren couldn't barter with the ice wizard to acquire those two, he would steal them. Then if he could recover the one from the behemoth's lake in the Wild Lands and those from the Master's generals, he'd have the complete set. There's no telling what he might do…"

The End

About the Author

Kirt Hickman, author of the award-winning science-fiction thrillers *Worlds Asunder* and *Venus Rain*, has also written *Mercury Sun*, the fantasy novels *Fabler's Legend* and *Assassins' Prey*, and two children's books. He teaches self-editing classes through SouthWest Writers. He has been a mentor in the SWW mentoring program, has spoken at numerous conferences, and has contributed a monthly column entitled "Revising Fiction" to SouthWest Sage. His writer's guide, *Revising Fiction—Making Sense of the Madness*, won a New Mexico Book Award for Best How-To and was a finalist in the international IBPA Benjamin Franklin Awards.

www.ingramcontent.com/pod-product-compliance
Lightning Source LLC
LaVergne TN
LVHW041043300325
807010LV00001B/2